THE KISS

"How could Melissa have married me?" Hunter scoffed. "Would she have caught my breakfast in the Sacandaga, or slept on the ground to be with me? Would she have made even the smallest sacrifice to be my wife?"

"I don't know what she might have done. Did you two talk about marriage?"

Alanna's expression mirrored the innocent sweetness of her soul. "The only conversation I can recall is our last one, and I won't repeat what she said then."

Hunter was growing adept at using his cane to get to his feet and he did so now. "I've had enough. Stay here. I'll come back."

"But I didn't mean—" Hunter turned away, but Alanna had seen his expression and knew. Clearly he was the one who had been betrayed, not her cousin, and she felt desperately sorry she had reminded him of it.

"Hunter, please wait," she called.

Intending to tell her to leave him be, Hunter turned back, but Alanna had also gotten to her feet, and as she hurried toward him, the hem of her dress swung dangerously close to the fire. "Be careful!" he shouted, but startled by the harshness of his tone Alanna drew back, sending her hem directly into the flames.

The damp fire-kissed fabric sent up a small cloud of steam and smoke that instantly caught Alanna's attention. Fearing her gown would burn brightly as a torch, she moved back so quickly, she tripped and fell. Seeing her trapped in her still-steaming garment, Hunter rushed forward and threw himself across her feet to smother what he mistook for the first hint of flame.

Pinned to the ground, Alanna struggled to sit up and push him away, but realizing the danger to her had been slight and was over now, Hunter moved forward rather than away. His momentum again forced her back against the ground, and when he grabbed her hands, that's where she had to stay.

"Even a wood sprite can get burned. Why weren't you more careful?"

He was so close, Alanna had no time to reply before his lips found hers. . . .

PHOEBE CONN

BELOVED

ZEBRA BOOKS
KENSINGTON PUBLISHING CORP.

ZEBRA BOOKS are published by

Kensington Publishing Corp.
850 Third Avenue
New York, NY 10022

First Printing: December, 1994

Printed in the United States of America

*This book is dedicated to
Julian J. Edney, my favorite Englishman,
in grateful recognition of
his friendship and support.*

Part One

One

Had the Indian known the Barclay brothers lived in such magnificent splendor, he would not have accepted their invitation. Regrettably, now that their *bateau* had rounded the bend in the James River and the stately, three-story brick manor had come into view, it was too late to create an urgent need to be elsewhere. The Indian tried not to gape at the mansion he had mistakenly assumed would be a simple, wooden farmhouse not all that different from the long houses of the Iroquois.

The Indian prided himself on being clever, but he had certainly outsmarted himself this time. An excellent trapper, he had learned how to speak English from William Johnson. One of the few honest traders, Johnson not only paid Indians what their furs were worth, he also sold them goods at fair prices. The Indian had learned that Johnson could be trusted, and because the white man spoke the Iroquois language, the brave had become determined to learn his. Not satisfied with that accomplishment, he had worked to master reading and writing as well. It amused him to possess those skills, when there were white trappers who had to draw a crude *X* for their mark.

He found no humor in his present situation, however.

The sun's late afternoon rays reflected off the imposing home's leaded windows in blinding flashes that pained him almost as badly as his injured pride. The Barclay brothers might have been eager to hire him to scout for the Virginia Militia, but the Indian doubted the rest of their family would welcome him to a home fit for King George. Determined not to be humiliated, he steeled himself to face whatever insults he might soon hear, without suffering a loss of dignity.

A shout from the yard drew Melissa to the bedroom window. "It's Byron and Elliott!" she called excitedly to the quiet cousin who shared her room. Giving Alanna no opportunity to view the returning pair, Melissa grabbed the shy girl's hand and did not release her until they had left the house. Melissa ran on across the lawn toward the dock, but without her enthusiastic lead, Alanna's pace slowed to a hesitant walk.

Eager to greet her brothers, Melissa had already thrown herself into Byron's arms before she noticed the buckskin-clad stranger removing their gear from the *bateau*. His back was toward her, and because of his rustic garb, she dismissed him as a frontiersman of little consequence, and hurried to hug Elliott as well. "I've missed you!" she assured them both. "With you and your friends away, being home has been excruciatingly dull."

"I can't believe your Lieutenant Scott didn't come to call just because we weren't here," Byron teased.

Not above flirting with her handsome fair-haired brothers, Melissa struck a coquettish pose. "I'll admit that Ian stopped by a few times, but he's your friend as well as mine, and don't bother to deny it."

While the brothers continued to exchange playful jests with their sister, the Indian removed the last of their belongings from the boat, and squaring his broad shoulders, straightened up to his full height. Nearly six feet tall, he was Byron's equal in stature, and slightly taller than Elliott. The brothers had mentioned their sister, but had failed to comment on her remarkable beauty. One glance at the petite blonde in the pretty blue dress, was all the Indian needed to doubt that a lieutenant was her only suitor. He was curious as to what her response to him would be. Growing impatient to meet her, his attention strayed to the young woman who had accompanied her from the house.

Unlike Melissa, she was not dressed in a bright silk gown with a graceful hoop skirt. Instead, she was clad in plain home-spun fabrics in faded shades of lavender, and her skirt fell about her ankles in limp folds. Melissa's white cap was lavishly decorated with lace to provide a delightfully feminine accent to her curls, while this girl's unadorned cap appeared to have been yanked into place in a vain attempt to cover an unruly tawny mane. The Indian assumed she was Melissa's maid, but was puzzled as to why the attractive young lady would employ such an unassuming servant.

Then the unkempt girl's gaze met his and the Indian ceased to ponder the question, for she had the most exquisitely beau-tiful green eyes he had ever seen. Trained to recognize signs invisible to careless men, he could successfully track a stag through the heart of the forest, when others had given up in frustration or despair. How a man with his keen powers of observation had failed to discover at first glance that this re-served young woman was far more lovely than the Barclay's vivacious sister, mystified him. Her features were every bit as delicate and sweet as Melissa's, but her eyes held the promise of a depth of character completely lacking in Melissa's flirta-tious gaze.

Instantly deciding that he liked her, the Indian broke into a wide, charming grin. Rather than responding with the shy smile he had come to expect from white women, however, the girl's expression filled with anguish, and with a stifled cry of alarm she fled the dock and ran back toward the house.

Startled by Alanna's hasty departure, Melissa stared after her until she had disappeared from view. It wasn't until she turned back toward her brothers that she saw the Indian's face for the first time, and realized instantly what had frightened her timid cousin. Rather than lash out at him for simply being what he was, she began to berate her brothers.

"I believed you to be gentlemen, not insensitive brutes! Whatever possessed you two to bring an Indian here?" she asked. "Didn't you realize what the sight of him would do to Alanna?" As Melissa gestured in the Indian's direction, she was startled to find him studying her with a darkly insolent stare. She had never been that close to an Indian brave, and that this one was handsome was all the more disconcerting. He wore his thick, black hair tied at his nape in the style white men favored, rather than flowing free; so it was no wonder that at first glance she had mistaken him for a woodsman.

His attractive features were well-chiseled, and his smooth bronze skin unmarked by the tattoos she had seen Indians wearing in book illustrations. Her curiosity piqued, her eyes swept down his well-muscled physique, and she could not help but wonder if his sleek body were adorned with decorative patterns in places his buckskins hid from her view. Blushing at such a scandalous thought, her gaze returned to his face, and this time she smiled.

"Do you speak English?" she asked very deliberately.

"Some," the Indian replied, but neither his manner nor expression was friendly.

An impatient nod from Melissa prompted Byron to introduce the Indian. "He's asked us to call him Hunter, which is far easier to remember and pronounce than his Indian name. I'm sorry," he then apologized to the brave. "That was our cousin, Alanna, who just ran off. She's the daughter of our father's younger brother. When she was small, she and her family lived in Maine. One day her mother sent her to the neighboring farm on an errand. She returned to find the Abenaki had raided her home and killed everyone. She came here to live with us then. She's always been shy, and while it's understandable that she'd be terrified of Indians, I thought because you were with us, she'd be all right."

Melissa watched Hunter closely during her brother's explanation, but not a glimmer of sympathy showed in his dark eyes. His looks might be pleasing, but he had to still be a savage, if he were not touched by the horror Byron had described. "Alanna was only six," she added as she took a step toward him. She half-expected Hunter to back away, but he stood his ground.

"The Abenaki murdered not only Alanna's mother and father, but her two younger sisters and baby brother as well. The Indians crushed their skulls with tomahawks. How great a coward does a man have to be to kill a six-week-old babe in his crib, or little girls who are only two and three? What honor can there possibly be in such barbarism?"

"None," the Indian promptly replied. "But you must not confuse me with the Abenaki. I am Seneca."

"All Indians are not the same," Elliott interjected. "The Seneca are part of the Iroquois League of Six Nations, and allies of the British. Byron and I are convinced we can trust Hunter, or we'd not have brought him here. We expected everyone to have confidence in our judgment."

What the Indian inspired within Melissa was not trust, but a far more primitive emotion she dared not name. Fascinated by the darkly handsome stranger, she softened her objection to his presence in their home. "Yes," she agreed slowly. "Mother and Father will certainly welcome him, as will I, but you're asking too much of Alanna, and you should have considered her feelings, too."

Justly chastised, Byron and Elliott bowed their heads in shame, and Hunter seized the opportunity to remove himself from what he considered a most unfortunate situation. "I do not want to cause trouble," he stated simply. "I'll find another place to stay until I'm needed."

"No," Elliott argued. "You needn't go. I'll talk with Alanna. I can make her understand she has nothing to fear from you."

Hunter recalled Alanna's muffled shriek, and doubted anything Elliott could say would make any difference. He was not used to becoming involved in the affairs of white men, but he felt very badly about the massacre of Alanna's family. He also believed he was partly to blame for the unnecessary fright he had inadvertently caused her that afternoon.

"I want to come with you," he offered.

"No, that's not a good idea," Melissa argued.

"Why not?" Hunter challenged. "She is terrified of me, not Elliott. I'm the one she will have to learn to accept, not him."

During their conversation, Hunter had revealed, perhaps unwittingly, that he spoke far more English than he had first admitted, and Melissa wondered what else the handsome brave knew and might attempt to conceal. "Well yes, that's certainly true," she agreed hesitantly. "But if you speak to her *now,* you'll only succeed in frightening her out of her wits, and that won't be good for either of you."

"I want to try," Hunter insisted. "Take me with you," he again asked Elliott.

Because Elliott knew the Indian to be an intelligent man with a gentle nature, he agreed. "When Alanna's troubled, which is quite often, she likes to sit out by the well. Let's look for her there first."

"Wait a minute," Melissa begged. "Just in case Alanna doesn't respond as you hope, I think I should go along, too."

When Elliott looked toward him, Byron shrugged. "There's no point in all of us going after her. I'll see that everything gets taken into the house. That way at least one thing will have been accomplished before nightfall. Where are Mother and Father?"

"They had no way of knowing you'd be back today, so they went into town," Melissa explained. "They should be home soon though. Now let's go. If you two actually think you can

impress Alanna favorably, you better start now, or you won't
be finished by supper."

"Yes, ma'am," Elliott replied, but when he added a jaunty
salute, Melissa would have slapped him with the back of her
hand had he not quickly stepped beyond her reach. "Come
on," he called to Hunter. "The well's out back."

The Indian followed Elliott toward the house with a long,
fluid stride. He could feel Melissa watching him. Unlike her
fearful cousin, her eyes were as blue as a cloudless summer
sky, but Hunter did not enjoy being studied so closely. He was
merely a man, like any other in his view, but it was clear
Melissa considered him an object of curiosity, and he did not
appreciate being observed so openly.

Hoping to make her feel ashamed for staring at him, he
glanced toward her suddenly, but she responded with a sweet
smile, rather than the embarrassed blush he had expected. He
reminded himself it was Alanna who had run from him, not
this confident beauty who actually appeared to be inviting his
attention. Indian women considered him handsome, but it always surprised him when white women did, too. Flattered, he
had to force himself to recall it was not Melissa who concerned
him now, but her tormented cousin.

As they rounded the corner of the house, the variety of small
structures clustered nearby came into view. There were perhaps
a dozen buildings in all, each serving a specific need of the
prosperous tobacco plantation. The kitchen with its large chim-
ney was closest to the house, and beside it stood a circular
brick well sheltered beneath a free-standing, shingled roof. A
plank bench connected two of the posts which supported the
roof, and just as Elliott had predicted, that's where Alanna was
seated.

She had looped her arms around the post at her right, as
though she intended fighting anyone who might attempt to
drag her away. The despair of her pose brought Hunter to an

abrupt halt, and Elliott and Melissa stopped beside him. Not wishing to insult their family, the Indian was cautious in his choice of words.

"Is your cousin merely easily frightened," he whispered, although they were standing too far away for his comment to be overheard by Alanna, "or does everything confuse her?"

Immediately understanding the intent of his question, Melissa hurriedly came to Alanna's defense, but she also took the precaution of speaking in a hushed tone. "She's not crazy. Is that what you're asking?"

Hunter glanced toward the slender girl huddled by the well. He could easily imagine the horror she had found after the Abenaki raid. Her house must have been awash in blood. The gore would have been splattered across the ceiling and dripping down the walls. Although Melissa had not mentioned it, he was certain Alanna's parents would have been scalped. No child should ever be exposed to the carnage Alanna must have seen, and Hunter would never fault her if it was more than a child's mind could sanely bear.

When he looked down at Melissa, the hostility of her expression certainly did not invite him to explain, but he felt he had to make the attempt anyway. "Sometimes when people see awful things, they retreat into their minds, perhaps into whatever pleasant memories they have. They are not crazy, but too filled with grief to enjoy the company of others."

Embarrassed that the Indian could describe Alanna's desire for privacy in such lucid terms, Melissa's expression softened instantly. She had known precious little about Indians until she had met this one, but he was so enormously intriguing in both appearance and manner, that she now wished to get to know him well. "You're very kind," she assured him, "but Alanna is a capable young woman, who was tutored right along with my brothers and me. She's bright, and merely shy rather than reclusive or withdrawn. If only Elliott and Byron had had sense enough to tell her they had invited an Indian friend here for a visit *before* she saw you, I don't think there would have been any trouble."

"We've already apologized," Elliott mumbled.

"Not to Alanna," Hunter chided. "How old is she?"

"Seventeen," Melissa answered. She followed the Indian's gaze and volunteered more information before being asked. "We're only a year apart in age, and my mother used to dress us alike. Alanna would still have as lovely a wardrobe as I do, but she refuses to dress attractively. She doesn't want attention from anyone, least of all men."

"All men?" Hunter asked. "Even handsome lieutenants?"

A slow smile tugged at the corner of Hunter's lips, and Melissa was amazed to find him flirting with her. Even more astonishing was how greatly she enjoyed it. Her mother would never approve, but after all, she was shopping in Williamsburg and would never know anything about it. "Yes," she responded after licking her lips with the insouciance she had discovered made most men nearly drool with desire. "All my brothers' friends are sweet to her, but she'll exchange no more than a pleasant greeting."

"You two just stay right here," Elliott directed. "Let me talk with her alone first."

Rather than argue this time, Hunter relaxed into a more comfortable pose to ease the wait. Obviously eager to make amends for the fright she had suffered, Elliott called out to Alanna as he approached, so she would not be startled when he knelt in front of her. From where Hunter stood, he could not make out Elliott's words, but his friend's expression was almost painfully sincere.

"Elliott and Alanna are very close," Melissa whispered. "When she first came to live with us, she tagged along after him like a duckling trailing its mother. He claimed not to enjoy it, but never complained within her hearing, and I think he was more flattered than annoyed by her devotion."

While the family resemblance between Elliott and Alanna was not nearly as strong as that between Alanna and Melissa, Hunter could still see it. Their hair was the same honey-blond shade, and Alanna's profile could be interpreted as a feminine version of Elliott's. As they leaned close to talk, their gestures were identical.

"Do cousins ever marry?" Hunter asked.

Surprised by his question, Melissa needed a moment to thoughtfully consider a reply. "Yes, they do, but probably not when they've been raised as brother and sister the way Alanna and Elliott have."

She glanced up at the Indian, but quickly looked away when the intensity of his gaze struck her as being far too familiar. Apparently he spoke his mind regardless of the topic, but she did not think marriage an appropriate subject between them. She knew there were white women who had wed Indian braves, but she believed they had all been taken captive as children and raised to be more Indian than white, rather than young women from fine families with honorable traditions to uphold.

When Elliott waved for him to come forward, Hunter walked slowly to his side and, following his friend's example, he also knelt in front of Alanna. While he was certain that made him appear far less threatening than if he stood towering above her, the bright glow of panic hadn't left her eyes. Despite Elliott's undoubtedly soothing words, she was still clutching the post tightly, and Hunter believed his offer to leave had been his best idea where Alanna was concerned. He had asked to speak with her, however, and felt compelled to try.

When he began to talk, his voice was soft and low, barely above a whisper. "There are some who say that Indians and whites are too different to ever be friends, but I disagree. When it is winter, we both shiver with the cold. When there's nothing to eat, we are both gnawed by hunger. When we are happy, we both laugh, and when we lose someone we love, we both feel the pain of a broken heart."

With immense tenderness, Hunter reached out to pat Alanna's knee lightly. He then offered his hand. "Do you want to touch me? My skin is warm. If you close your eyes, you won't be able to tell which hand is Elliott's and which is mine."

Alanna had been holding her breath since the Indian's approach and, growing faint, now had to force herself to breathe deeply. She attempted to simply observe dispassionately, rather than react to his presence, but it took all of her courage to remain on the bench rather than again bolt, in spite of the fact he looked nothing like her gruesome mental image of the savages who had butchered her family. Viewed with the detachment Elliott had encouraged, she could even call him handsome.

His eyes were framed by a thick fringe of black lashes, and were so dark a brown that she could not distinguish between iris and pupil, but his gaze was sympathetic rather than menacing. His nose was straight, his well shaped lips slightly full, and his chin rounded yet firm. Despite the harmonious nature of his features, he was Indian, and that was what she could not forget.

His deep voice was accented by a language she had never heard spoken, nor did she wish to. She would sooner allow a cottonmouth moccasin to slither over her hand than touch him and, recoiling in dread, she gave her head a violent shake sending her already tilted cap further askew. Her cousins might call him a friend, but she had no wish to associate with an Indian. Rather than respond politely to his friendliness, she stubbornly refused to welcome him.

"Let's just avoid each other," she suggested and, pretending that he did not exist, she looked away.

Hunter tried to console himself with the fact that Alanna had not fallen into hysterical fits, nor had she spit on him or lashed out at him with her fists. She had not reviled him with scathing insults he would never forget, but she had dismissed him rudely, and as he rose to his feet, he was sorry he had bothered to speak with her. Obviously she could think as clearly as he, but he could do nothing about the sorry conclusion she had reached. He walked back to where Melissa stood waiting for him.

"I tried," he told her, "but it was no use. She hates Indians too much to make friends with me."

"I'm so sorry," Melissa assured him sincerely. "I hope that her fears won't prejudice you against the rest of us."

"Not if her fears do not prejudice you against me," Hunter countered smoothly. He was uncertain what game this enchanting, blue-eyed young lady was playing, but was sufficiently intrigued to follow it through to its conclusion.

Struck with embarrassment, Elliott waited until Melissa and Hunter had begun to walk away before he sat down beside Alanna. "We need Hunter," he stated emphatically. "He knows the Ohio Valley as well as we know this yard, and without skilled Indian scouts like him, we'll never succeed in keeping the French off British land. I'd trust him with my life. Can't you at least be civil to him?"

Alanna adored Elliott, and to deny him anything hurt her badly, but that pain did not even begin to compare to the agony of losing her family to a brutal band of savages. The tragic deaths of her loved ones had created an open wound in her heart that would never heal. Elliott was asking too much, and tears of regret stung her eyes because she could not please him.

"When are you going out with George Washington?" she asked.

"We'll be leaving for Alexandria to join him and Colonel Fry at the end of the week. Can't you be polite to Hunter until then? That's all we're asking. I know it's a big favor, but can't you do it for Byron and me?"

Alanna shuddered. "No. I'll eat my meals in the kitchen and stay out of his way. That's all I can do. Please don't ask more of me."

Elliott sighed unhappily and rose to his feet. He offered his hand, but Alanna shook her head and remained seated, leaving him to feel torn between his loyalty to her and the common courtesy he had expected his family to show his new friend. It was an uncomfortable sensation, and desperate to win her support, he forgot how stubborn she could be and attempted a new approach.

"The French constantly encourage their Indian allies to raid British settlements in New England, and they are surely to blame for the Abenaki attack on your parents' farm. With Hunter's help we'll finally be able to avenge such senseless killings. Can't you be grateful to Hunter for making that possible, rather than hate him for being Indian?"

"I don't hate him," Alanna denied softly. "I just don't want to be anywhere near him."

Still wishing he possessed the eloquence to make her see things as he did, Elliott finally realized that no amount of logical arguments or politely worded pleas would bridge the moat of sorrow encircling his dear cousin's heart. He leaned down to kiss her cheek, and with his shoulders bowed in a dejected slump, he followed Hunter and Melissa into the house.

Hunter was given a guest bedroom on the third floor. It had been painted with whitewash tinted with verdigris to achieve a pleasant green color. Dormer windows eased the steep slant of the ceiling and provided him with a fine view of the river, but he would have been far more comfortable quartered in the barn. Fearing the elegantly carved cherrywood furnishings would shatter beneath his weight, he sat on the floor until Elliott returned to escort him to supper. He and Byron had changed into clean blue-coated uniforms of the Virginia Militia, while Hunter had seen no point in donning another set of buckskins which would be indistinguishable from the deeply fringed pair he had worn upon his arrival.

As soon as they entered the parlor, Hunter was introduced to his friends' parents, John and Rachel Barclay. Unlike their fearful niece, they had had the benefit of a warning and had known they would be entertaining him at supper before they had to meet him face-to-face. Still somewhat nervous, their smiles were too quick, but having had no success with Alanna, Hunter made no effort to ease whatever fears about him they might hold.

A tall man, John Barclay took great pains to maintain his handsome appearance. He wore the elegantly tailored clothes and expertly styled white wig a man of his wealth would be expected to own. Deeply tanned, his weathered skin made him appear slightly older than his actual fifty-two years, but he was still fit and attractive. His wife was a dozen years his junior, as petite as her daughter, and as beautifully groomed and gowned.

At a light touch on his arm, Hunter turned to find Melissa with a British officer whom she introduced as Ian Scott. The Indian recognized the name, but when her brothers had teased her about him, Hunter had mistakenly assumed Lieutenant Scott was also a member of the Virginia Militia. Ian's fair complexion was sprinkled with freckles, and the fiery red curls which escaped the confines of his wig at his nape lent him a boyish rather than properly military appearance.

"I understand you're an expert scout," the lieutenant said.

The Englishman had a charming smile, and although his hazel eyes danced with a mischievous sparkle, Hunter doubted the good-natured young man had ever made an enemy. He was obviously sincere in his praise, but Hunter was unused to flattery and unable to accept Ian's compliment graciously. "I certainly hope so," he replied, without realizing his response might be interpreted as arrogance.

Elliott, however, assumed Hunter was joking and laughed. "Don't let him tease you, Ian," he said. "He's known as the best scout in the Ohio Valley."

Hunter was positive that boast wasn't true, but when Melissa favored him with a delighted smile, he could not bring himself to deny it. Supper was announced then, and he hoped another topic of conversation would begin when they reached the table. He and Ian were seated on either side of Melissa, her brothers took their places opposite them, and their parents occupied the ends of the elaborately set table. It wasn't until after John Barclay had intoned a lengthy prayer that Hunter realized Alanna must not have been expected to join them, for there were no empty places at the long table.

Insulted that she would not share a meal with him, he paid little attention to the conversation, unless it was directed to him. Having been away, Byron and Elliott both had a great deal to discuss, which kept Hunter's inattention from being obvious. He had eaten ham and sweet potatoes, but took note of how Rachel Barclay ate her meal in an attempt to appear to possess the same fine manners. Adept at mimicking the actions of others, he succeeded quite well in his ruse. He never drank wine, but either no one noticed—or if they did—cared enough to comment. The meal was flavorful, the company charming, but Alanna's absence made him fear he might always be viewed as an outsider in the Barclay home.

After supper, they returned to the parlor. Because the dining room chair had supported Hunter's weight without mishap, he had gained confidence in the strength of the Barclays' furniture, and took the chair Rachel offered. Rachel then played several tunes on the harpsichord, and at her brothers' urging, Melissa added three more. Both women were accomplished musicians, but Hunter's attention frequently strayed to his companions.

During Melissa's turn at the finely tuned stringed instrument, Ian Scott's expression mirrored his delight, while her parents' faces were aglow with pride. Byron and Elliott were seated in relaxed poses, and appeared to be enjoying themselves, too. Hunter tried to look as comfortable as his friends, but he preferred the lively melodies he had heard fiddlers play at Johnson's trading post. The parlor and furnishings were in soothing shades of blue, and sedated by the ladies' delicate harmonies, he soon began to yawn.

Equally tired, Elliott and Byron reminded everyone of how fatiguing their day had been, and begged to be excused. Hunter left the parlor with them, but while the brothers went upstairs to their rooms, he went outside to get a drink from the well. He had not really expected to find Alanna still seated there, but the fact she was gone struck him as another insult.

Melissa had sent him frequent smiles during dinner, and later as she had entertained them with music. Amused by her interest in him, the brave broke into a sly grin. Perhaps it did not matter that Alanna planned to avoid him, when her charming cousin obviously had no such intention. He laughed to himself as he walked back toward the house. It was a shame Alanna was so frightened of him, but far more intriguing that Melissa had not realized just how dangerous he truly was.

Two

Hunter awoke with the dawn. He had tried to sleep on the four-poster bed, but the feather mattress was too soft for his tastes, and he had abandoned it for the floor. He sat up, for a moment disoriented by the strange surroundings, but he swiftly recalled where he was. He stood, and then stretched lazily. The house was quiet, and he thought it might be several hours before Byron and Elliott awakened. He used the pitcher of water on the washstand to clean up, donned his buckskins, carefully refolded the blanket he had used, and placed it on the bed. With his moccasins cushioning his steps, he left the house with the same stealth with which he moved silently through the forest.

Possessed of a curious nature, he began to investigate the purpose of the buildings located nearby. From their number, it appeared there was work aplenty on the Barclay plantation. Byron had mentioned they employed free men rather than slaves, which was one of the reasons Hunter had mistakenly gathered the impression that they owned a farm rather than a vast plantation. The kitchen staff had yet to report, but Hunter was growing hungry and hoped whoever was responsible for cooking breakfast would soon appear.

Not wishing to be found lurking outside the kitchen like a ravenous cat, he peered into the scullery next door. A stack of pewter plates sat on the table, along with numerous serving pieces. There were more dishes in the cupboards and large cooking utensils dangled from hooks on the walls. The scullery was as neatly kept as the kitchen, and Hunter wondered if the cook would be a large man who liberally sampled each dish he prepared, or perhaps a tiny woman who was too busy cooking for the Barclays to ever stop and eat. Whoever the cook might be, it was plain they demanded cleanliness and order.

Hunter went on to the smokehouse, but a quick look at the hams and bacon hanging just inside the door satisfied his curiosity there. He recognized the dairy by the churn standing outside, and long clotheslines decorated the yard by the laundry. A fully equipped blacksmith's forge stood between the carriage house and stable. A cooper's shed where barrels were made to pack tobacco for shipping was the last building to come into view.

The Indian was impressed to find the plantation a complete miniature city, and continued to explore. Convinced the Barclays would own fine mounts, he entered the stable by the rear door and waited for his eyes to adjust to the dim interior. Before that had occurred, someone threw open the tall double doors at the opposite end of the long barn and, fearing he might not be able to explain his presence to a stranger, Hunter shrank back into the shadows and hoped they would soon leave.

When he heard a sweet, feminine voice calling out greetings to the horses, his initial thought was that it was Melissa. Relaxing slightly, he peered out of his hiding place, but silhouetted against the bright sunlight, the young woman was impossible to recognize. Fearing she might be one of the Barclays' many employees rather than his friends' sister, he dared not call out to her. Instead, he waited quietly as she made her way through the stable.

Unlike Hunter, the horses recognized their visitor's voice and stretched their necks over the doors of their stalls to nuzzle her apron pockets. For their impertinent antics, they received a gentle scolding delivered between bursts of lilting laughter. None was deprived of the expected treat, however, and each was given an apple before the young woman moved on to the next.

Framed by the glistening specks of dust dancing in the early morning light, from where Hunter stood she was surrounded by a mist of shimmering gold. It was an enchanted scene, and he held his breath when she reached his end of the barn for fear a sudden glimpse of him would frighten her away. She paused and peered into the darkness, for an instant looked right at him. Perhaps she sensed his presence, but unable to distinguish his features from the deep shadows in which he stood, she moved on.

She had been close enough for Hunter to recognize her though, and since he had not even considered the possibility that the cheerful lass might be Alanna, he was doubly shocked. Unaware that she was being observed, Alanna continued to lavish her affection on the horses, for each was an adored pet. With her tragic background, Hunter wasn't surprised that she would prefer the company of a horse to him, but that rationalization did not ease the lingering humiliation of her rebuff.

Horribly uncomfortable, Hunter darted out of the stable the instant Alanna exited from the opposite end. Unfortunately, he had no time to savor the relief of having avoided another potentially disastrous confrontation with her before a bearded man in a leather apron called out to him.

"Hey, you there!" the blacksmith shouted. "Get away from the barn. You've no business being in there. Go on back where you belong, or I'll set the dogs on you. Now go on, git!"

Hunter hadn't seen any dogs, but knowing many men kept half a dozen or more for hunting, was enough to convince him the blacksmith wasn't making idle threats. He might be an invited guest, but doubted that fact would be believed without confirmation from one of the Barclays. Besides, even if he were a guest, he supposed he ought not to have been in the barn. Undecided about what to say, he remained silent as the blacksmith approached carrying a long pair of iron tongs.

"Dogs don't scare you?" the hostile man asked in a challenging hiss.

Alanna rounded the corner of the barn in time to see the blacksmith raise his tongs in a menacing gesture, while Hunter made no move to protect himself. She had no idea what the Indian had done, but knew her cousins wouldn't want him to be mistreated in any way. Hoping to see someone else close enough to intervene, she looked around with an anxious glance, but quickly discovered that if anyone were going to come to the Indian's rescue, it would have to be her. That was the very last thing she wished to do on that day or any other, but since she had no choice, she gathered her courage and called out to the blacksmith.

"Jacob, leave him alone. He's a scout Byron and Elliott hired."

For several seconds the blacksmith seemed not to have heard Alanna's command, but then he lowered the tongs, frowned darkly, and ambled over to her. "I should have been told, Miss Alanna," he began without bothering with a polite greeting. "None of us expects to find Indians creeping around here."

"Is that what he was doing, 'creeping around'?"

Jacob shrugged. "He left the barn like he was up to no good. Maybe we ought to go check on the horses."

Having just come from the barn, Alanna was understandably shocked by Jacob's comment. Hunter hadn't moved, but was watching them closely, and came forward when she motioned for him to do so. "Jacob says you were in the barn just now. Why didn't I see you?"

"Are all of Byron and Elliott's friends treated like thieves?"

"Please just answer my question," Alanna replied in a softer tone.

Hunter nodded toward Jacob. "It's no business of his what I do."

Insulted, Jacob widened his stance, and Alanna quickly dismissed him rather than allow the two men to come to blows. Clearly disgruntled, the blacksmith started toward his forge, but before reaching it he turned back and shot Hunter a disgusted glance, deliberately taunting him to follow. Alanna gasped, thinking the Indian might do just that, but his gaze had never left her face and he had failed to note the provocative gesture. That realization was even more alarming than how quickly he had made an enemy of Jacob McBride.

"Why didn't I see you in the barn?" she repeated.

"You were the one who suggested we avoid each other," Hunter reminded her.

"So you were merely avoiding me, rather than hiding?"

"I was hiding to avoid you!"

Appalled by that flash of temper, Alanna stepped back to put more distance between them. Elliott had praised Hunter's tracking skills, but failed to mention that he had such an obnoxious personality. The Indian had been polite rather than rude the first time they had spoken together, however, and when she noticed the pulse throbbing at the base of his throat, she was stunned by the sudden awareness that despite his show of ill-tempered bravado, Jacob had frightened him.

She regarded Indians as the most fearsome creatures ever to stalk the earth, and had never even imagined they could be frightened by anyone, or anything, they encountered. That this man was as human in his responses as the other men she knew was almost beyond her comprehension, but she made a serious attempt to grasp the possibility. She looked away for a moment in hopes of seeing their confrontation from Hunter's point of view. It did not take long for her to understand why he had been so insulted.

"I'm sorry Jacob reacted to you in such a threatening manner. You're the first Indian we've ever had staying here, and he obviously assumed the worst. I'll see the others are told you're a guest."

Believing it must have hurt her pride to apologize to him, Hunter tried to be equally gracious, but all he could manage was a stilted nod.

Elliott had made a point of impressing Alanna with Hunter's importance, and she felt badly that his feelings had been hurt unnecessarily. "Would you like to take another look at the horses?"

In light of his earlier experience with her, Hunter could not help but suspect her motives, and he grew cautious. "Are there stable boys who will come after me with pitchforks?"

Alanna doubted he was teasing and tried to allay his fears. "There are two stable boys, and they do use pitchforks to clean out the stalls, but if you're with me, you'll be safe."

"You want to show me the horses yourself?"

Alanna knew he had every right to be incredulous, because she had been only slightly less hostile than Jacob when he had been introduced to her, but damn it all, he was an Indian! Her eyes started to fill with tears, and she bit her lower lip to force them away. Although she supposed she deserved his sarcastic question, it seemed very unfair.

"I won't force my company on you," she assured him. "There's a barrel of apples to the right of the main doors. Hand them out the way I did, and you'll easily make friends. I'll find the stable boys, and tell them you're welcome here. I'll make certain everyone who works for us gets that message."

Fearing he had just ruined whatever slim hope he might have had to make friends with her, Hunter tried to think of some way to let her know how much he would enjoy her company. Before he could, Melissa appeared, and the opportunity was lost. She was smiling prettily as she approached them, but her warmth did not erase his guilt at having spoken harshly with Alanna.

"Breakfast is ready, and Byron and Elliott are waiting for you. We're all going to ride into Williamsburg after we've eaten. You want to come along with us, don't you?"

"Will the townspeople stare at me?"

"Probably, but you're very handsome, so why should you mind?"

Distracted by Melissa's flattering compliment, Hunter agreed to visit Williamsburg as they walked back to the house. He didn't notice that Alanna hadn't followed them until they reached the dining room, and then what she thought of him was all too clear. She might have chosen to avoid him again, but with Melissa's charming attentions, Hunter's resulting embarrassment quickly faded.

As promised, Alanna informed the stable boys that her cousins were entertaining an Indian scout, whom they were to treat with the utmost respect. She then sent them off to tell any of the other employees who hadn't heard about Hunter's arrival the previous evening. She seldom went into Williamsburg, and knew neither her cousins nor their Indian friend would miss her that day. She busied herself helping to make bayberry candles, and whenever her thoughts strayed to the attractive brave, she quickly banished them from her mind.

After a fire destroyed Jamestown's fourth statehouse at the close of the seventeenth century, the capitol of the Virginia Colony was moved to a settlement known as Middle Plantation, and renamed Williamsburg in honor of King William III. Built on a plan devised by the presiding Royal Governor, Francis Nicholson, the city soon grew to be a model of beauty and prosperity.

The hub of a plantation economy, Williamsburg resembled

towns in agricultural areas of England more closely than did any of the large cities of New England. The main street was named for the Duke of Gloucester, and connected the Wren Building at the College of William and Mary with the new capitol building nearly a mile away. The streets running parallel to the main boulevard, Francis and Nicholson, paid tribute to the city's designer.

Charming frame houses were built on half-acre lots and required to have fences to keep stray animals out of the home-owners' gardens. All manner of shops dispensed the latest in goods and fashion, while Market Square was the site of auctions and fairs. Taverns were popular places for those with leisure hours to enjoy. Bruton Parish Church provided for the spiritual needs of the city's faithful.

Hunter entered the outskirts of the picturesque town not really knowing what to expect, but determined not to stray far from the Barclays. While he did not relish the prospect, he did not really mind being stared at by curious strangers. It was being treated like a stray dog—as Jacob had regarded him that morning—that he could not abide. Without warning, the memory of that unfortunate incident intruded upon his thoughts and his expression darkened.

Melissa loved to ride, and she was delighted to find Hunter was an expert horseman. When her two brothers urged their bay geldings out in front to narrow their procession, she was quick to start a conversation with the Indian. "I know you're at home in the woods, but have you seen many of our towns?" she inquired.

"A few."

"Are they anything like Indian villages?"

Hunter shook his head. "The Iroquois build houses of wood and surround them with stockades. They are like your forts, with corn and squash fields outside the gates, not open like this city."

"You grew up inside a fort?"

Melissa's question made Hunter smile. "No, we're not confined to the space we have chosen to defend from our enemies. I was free to hunt, to explore, to learn whatever I could."

Both of her brothers were graduates of the College of William and Mary, but she had had ample opportunity to observe how they treated Hunter as an equal. "You didn't go to school?"

"My father taught me everything I needed to know to be a Seneca warrior. Whatever I have needed to learn to deal with white men, I have taught myself."

He was obviously proud of that accomplishment. In sharp contrast to the bronze of his skin, his teeth were very white, creating one of the most charming grins Melissa had ever seen. She was unsure just how much the appealing brave did know, but he possessed a confident manner she could not help but admire. She was pleased to have him for an escort. It would surely be the talk of the town by evening, and she hoped the tale would prompt another visit from Ian Scott. She was fond of the English officer, as he was far more entertaining than any of the young men she had known since childhood.

Upon entering Williamsburg, the Barclay brothers continued to lead the way down Gloucester Street. It was now mid-morning, and they waved and called out greetings to acquaintances passing by on the street. Their first stop was to inquire if there had been any change in the militia's plans, and to introduce Hunter to the others who would be traveling with them to join Lt. Col. George Washington's expedition into the Ohio Valley. An advance party of forty frontiersmen had already been sent out to begin construction of a fort at the junction of the Monongahela and Allegheny rivers, and Byron and Elliott were anxious to join them.

Hunter understood how vital a part the new fort would play in securing the Ohio Valley for the British, but while his young friends appeared eager to help build it, he did not think they appreciated how violent the French opposition would surely be. Building a fort was merely the preliminary goal, in his view, defending it would be a far greater challenge. Because he had not been hired to be an officer and plan strategy, he offered no opinions on the subject, but he was convinced his grasp of the situation was far more realistic than the Barclays'.

Their primary reason for the visit to Williamsburg complete, the Barclays began to attend to more personal business. Byron needed to stop at the boot-makers, and with Melissa's urging, Hunter accompanied them inside. The sharp smell of newly tanned leather reminded him of home, but he stayed well out of the way until Byron paid for the new pair of boots he had ordered.

"You'll not need new boots where we're going," Hunter then advised.

"I know better than to wear new boots in the wilderness," Byron assured him, "but these will be waiting for me when I get home."

Hunter was tempted, but did not tease the young man about his probability of returning home. The boot-maker had been too busy to notice him until that exchange. Clearly astonished to look up and find an Indian in his shop, his mouth fell agape, and Hunter winked at him before going out the door. He suspected the man would be talking about him all week, but he did not care.

Melissa wanted to stop at the basket shop next, and Hunter remained outside with her brothers while she went inside. She soon returned with an attractive basket she tied behind her saddle. She needed perfume, then fancy lace handkerchieves and ribbons, and before long Hunter had lost track of how many shops she had stopped to visit.

Elliott feared Hunter was growing bored. "Do Indian women enjoy going into town as much as Melissa?" he asked.

"No, there's no need. They make the clothes and moccasins they wear and most of the implements they use themselves." He thought about the sheltered lives of Seneca maidens, and pained by how little they knew of the world outside their tribe, he rephrased his reply. "Few ever visit more than a trading post, but I think they would like coming to a place like this just to see it."

Their last stop was at a fabric shop which sold expensive imported silks and satins, but after perusing their latest shipment for half an hour, Melissa left without making a purchase. By then her brothers were ready to visit the Raleigh Tavern, where they were certain to find several of their friends. Melissa often attended elegant private parties there in the Daphne Room, but she had absolutely no desire to enter the tavern proper. Her brothers had already dismounted, but Hunter still sat astride his horse, and she quickly offered him an alternative.

"Would you rather come home with me now rather than stay here with them? I noticed you didn't touch your wine last night. If you don't drink, you might feel rather out of place in a tavern."

Hunter felt out of place whenever he left the forest, but he had learned simply to ignore that uncomfortable feeling and go wherever he chose, because it enabled him to learn far more than if he remained solely in the company of his own kind. In this case, however, Melissa was correct: he had no desire to drink or watch other men get drunk.

"If you want to go home, I will ride with you," he offered.

Byron and Elliott exchanged a worried glance in which it was obvious they doubted the wisdom of allowing Melissa to return home with such an unusual escort. They might have refused to allow it, but lured by the greetings of their friends, they were in a hurry to enter the tavern, and Byron dismissed his sister with a brief bit of advice. "Go straight home, and if anyone bothers you, tell them Hunter is a scout for the militia."

"I don't need a woman to speak for me," Hunter insisted, despite the fact that he had been very glad to have Alanna call off Jacob before he had been forced to remove the tongs from the blacksmith's hand and crush his skull with them. "I will see that she gets home safely."

"We know that you will," Elliott called back over his shoulder, then followed Byron into the popular tavern.

Hunter looked up and down Gloucester Street, and confident he had seen the most interesting part of Williamsburg, he turned his horse toward the road they had taken into town. Melissa brought her mare up beside him, and while Hunter saw more than one disapproving frown as they rode along, he was pleased to have the charming young lady all to himself.

"Is Lieutenant Scott your sweetheart?" he asked.

Melissa could not help but blush as she offered a thoughtful reply. "No, not really. I know that he likes me, but we're merely friends, not sweethearts. That word implies far more."

Intrigued by her uncharacteristically demure response, Hunter pursued the matter. "More what?"

Melissa licked her lips before attempting to explain. She had made the tantalizing gesture so often, she was unaware she had just done it again. "A romantic element," she speculated softly. "Sweethearts are in love."

"And friends are not?"

"No, if friends are in love, then they're sweethearts," Melissa broke into teasing giggles, as she glanced toward the handsome brave. "I can't imagine sweethearts not being friends first, but there are several men I consider good friends, and none is a sweetheart."

"Do you consider me a friend?"

"We've only just met, but yes, I think we're becoming friends. My brothers like and trust you, and they always choose their friends wisely."

"We're not talking about Byron and Elliott," Hunter pointed out with a sly smile. "We're talking about you and me."

When presented with the opportunity, Melissa had swiftly arranged to ride home with him, but she had not expected him to ask such embarrassing questions. She was accustomed to men like Ian Scott, who were gentlemanly in all their words and actions. But Hunter was an Indian, and she really had no idea what to expect from him. A confident young woman, she attempted to bluff her way out of her present predicament.

"I can make up my own mind," she responded flippantly. "But what about you, do you have an Indian sweetheart?"

Hunter paused as though he had to give considerable thought to her question. Finally he glanced toward her. "No."

"Why not? You're very nice-looking. Aren't Indian girls equally attractive?"

"Yes, many are very beautiful, but I'm seldom home, and sweethearts need a great deal of attention, or they become unhappy and begin to look for someone else to love."

Surprised that he understood how greatly women appreciated a man's attentive company, Melissa relaxed slightly. "Did you lose a sweetheart to another brave?"

Hunter eyed the charming girl with a suggestive glance. "Only one, and I don't miss her."

Melissa had always felt her ability to flirt was as natural a gift as her beauty, but she had never before met a man who could answer her teasing questions in a more provocation fashion than she had asked them. Hunter did it with such masterful ease, she could not help but wonder what it would be like to take flirting another step and kiss him. Such a prospect shocked her for only a few seconds, and then she realized Hunter would soon be leaving with her brothers and probably not return for several months, if ever.

What difference would it make if she kissed him a time or two? No one would ever know, and it would be such a delicious secret. She smiled, and spoke with well-practiced innocence. "I can't believe that she doesn't miss you."

Hunter stared straight at Melissa. "Will you miss me?"

His dark eyes promised that she most definitely would, and lost in his seductive gaze, Melissa forgot everything she had been carefully taught to remember. Rather than an Indian brave, she saw only a dashing young man who excited her senses as no proper gentleman, colonial or English, had ever done. Without a conscious thought, she drew her mare to a halt.

Hunter did not need any further urging to also stop his mount. He reached out to cup Melissa's chin in his palm, then leaned over and kissed her. Her lips were very soft, her taste sweet, and one kiss was not nearly enough. They exchanged half a dozen before she drew away.

Suddenly recalling that they were in the middle of a public road, Melissa gasped sharply and turned to look for a more private spot. A convenient stand of cottonwood trees beckoned invitingly, and she knew without having to ask that Hunter would follow her when she urged her mare toward them. The grass was thick here, the shade deep, and when Hunter grasped her around the waist to pull her from her saddle, she went into his arms more than willingly.

Another six kisses and Melissa and Hunter lay in the grass in a tangled embrace. She felt the Indian's hands moving over her, gently tracing the contours of her lush figure as no white man had ever dared attempt. When his fingertips circled her breast, she knew she ought to be outraged by his touch, but it was far too thrilling to inspire even a murmur of complaint. She raised her arms to encircle his neck, and when she loosened the leather thong with which he tied his hair, his gleaming black mane spilled over them like ebony rain. Warmed by the sun, it formed an erotic curtain that shut out the light and instantly plunged them into the dark world of dreams.

Melissa had never been kissed with such devouring grace,

and each time Hunter's tongue caressed hers, she felt more a part of him. She slid her hands along his broad shoulders and down his spine to caress his muscular back. She wondered again if his dark skin was decorated with tattoos. In a silent response to her unspoken question, he pulled his shirt off over his head, and she saw that his golden brown skin was unmarked by any design or flaw. As his lips again found hers, she tasted the answer to all her questions in his kiss, and ceased to think at all.

Hunter had had no intention of stopping with kisses, when Melissa's response was so passionate. He wanted so much more, but the sound of approaching riders jarred them both from their romantic reverie. Hunter placed a fingertip on Melissa's kiss-swollen lips to keep her still, before glancing over his shoulder toward the road. When he saw Byron and Elliott riding by, he could scarcely believe his eyes. He waited until they had passed, then leapt to his feet and pulled Melissa to hers.

"That was your brothers. Is there a way we can still beat them home?"

Melissa had expected Byron and Elliott to remain at the Raleigh Tavern all afternoon, and unable to believe Hunter had seen them, she edged past him to take a look for herself. She recognized her brothers only too well, however, and appalled by how close they had come to discovering her with Hunter, she hurriedly pulled her clothes back into place.

"There's a narrow trail through the fields. If we hurry, we can still be home first."

Hunter slipped on his shirt and retied his hair, as he started toward his mount. "You lead the way, I'll follow."

Melissa had not expected a few stolen kisses to get so wildly out of hand, and she was shaking so badly she needed his help to get into her saddle. She dared not imagine what her brothers would have done had they found her with Hunter, and the terror of that possibility inspired such a wild ride that they arrived home in plenty of time. She rode straight into the barn, slid off her mare's back, removed the purchases she had stored behind her saddle, and handed her reins to one of the stable boys. Hunter drew his mount to a halt at the stable doors, uncinched his saddle, yanked it off, and grabbing up a brush, began to curry his horse's glistening coat with long, savage strokes.

Melissa dared not waste a minute, and rushed by Hunter with no more than a hint of a wave. She gulped in air as she walked toward the kitchen, and by the time she reached it, she could draw breath enough to speak to Alanna, who had just finished making candles. The spicy scent of bayberry filled the air, and drawn to the sweet coziness of the kitchen, Melissa tarried by the door.

"I brought you some ribbon," she announced.

Polly McBride, and two of her daughters, Catherine and Rosemary, worked in the kitchen. She noted Melissa's presence only because it made a difference in how much food they would need to send to the house for the midday meal. "Thought you and your brothers were staying in town, Miss Melissa."

"We came home earlier than expected," Melissa managed to explain.

Alanna assumed the color in her cousin's cheeks was due to exposure to the sun and would have given it no further thought, had she not noticed a sprig of grass caught in one of the ribbons adorning Melissa's cap. She stepped close, and after removing it, sent Melissa a questioning glance. When Melissa's face flooded with an incriminating blush, Alanna was puzzled as to the cause, but before she could comment, she saw Hunter approaching.

He paused several steps away from the kitchen door. "If

they're looking for me, tell Byron and Elliott I'll be down at the dock."

Alanna expected Melissa to respond, and when her cousin only nodded shyly before quickly looking away, she grew even more suspicious. She stepped outside to watch Hunter walk away. There had been something in his manner just now that she hadn't seen earlier that day. It certainly hadn't been diffidence, but could it possibly have been guilt? she wondered.

Alanna twirled the curious sprig of grass between her fingers, and when she noticed the horror with which her cousin was regarding her gesture, she grew faint. She reached out for the kitchen door to steady herself and prayed that her suspicions could not possibly be true. Melissa was a flirt, but surely she could not have been with Hunter.

"Just where are Byron and Elliott?" Alanna finally had the presence of mind to ask.

"We came home by ourselves, but I'm sure they'll be here soon."

"You were alone with Hunter?" Alanna whispered accusingly.

Finally seizing the initiative, Melissa reached out to yank the sprig of grass from Alanna's hand and quickly tossed it aside. "So what if I was? It's a lovely day, and we had a pleasant ride. Now come on, let's go up to the house and get ready to eat."

Even knowing that Hunter was down at the dock rather than waiting in the house, Alanna had never felt less like eating, and she remained right where she was.

Three

A perceptive person, Polly McBride noted Alanna's reluctance to follow Melissa and easily guessed why. A tall, buxom woman, who handled all her chores at a careful, deliberate pace, in both appearance and manner she was completely at odds with Hunter's mental image of a female cook. She had been with the Barclays twenty years, and was a warm and sympathetic friend to them all.

"It ain't right having an Indian here," she mumbled loudly enough for the pensive young woman to overhear.

"He's a talented scout," Alanna responded.

"His talents don't matter," Polly argued. "He ought not to have been invited here. It was Indians who left you an orphan."

Alanna argued without enthusiasm. "It wasn't his tribe."

"Indians is Indians, Miss Alanna," the cook swore.

And Melissa was Melissa, Alanna thought to herself, which was an even more terrifying thought. If Melissa had foolishly encouraged Hunter's attentions, she was toying with his emotions when she could not possibly accurately predict his reaction. Her cousin was not merely being incredibly stupid, she was creating a situation which could easily have disastrous consequences for them all.

Byron and Elliott's arrival brought an end to Alanna's preoccupied mood. She returned their waves, and they drew to a halt just outside the kitchen door. "Did Melissa and Hunter get home all right?" Elliott called out.

Alanna was uncertain just how such an ambiguous question ought to be answered, but after a moment's hesitation offered a response that supplied the truth, if perhaps not all of it. "Yes, they're here. Hunter said he'd be down at the dock, if you need him."

Elliott turned to his older brother. "You see, there was no reason to leave the Raleigh so soon. I told you they'd be fine."

A surly frown was Byron's only reply, and when he rode on toward the barn, Elliott urged his mount to follow. Alanna knew they trusted her, and while she had not lied to them, she had certainly hidden her feelings. She was deeply distressed not only by her suspicions, but also by her inability to confide in the two young men. Not wanting company, she wandered around to the flower garden on the west side of the house, rather than her usual spot by the well. She waited on a bench there until she was certain the midday meal had been eaten, and Melissa would have gone upstairs to their room to rest.

Hoping to make Melissa see the danger in continuing a flirtation with Hunter, Alanna then slipped in the backdoor and hurried up to their room. She had minimal experience with young men compared to Melissa, but what she did know made it impossible for her to keep still. "So that I won't misunderstand," she began tactfully, "would you please tell me what happened between you and Hunter this morning?"

Melissa had been sorting through her handkerchieves before adding her latest purchases to her collection. Interpreting Alanna's genuine concern as nothing more than blatant prying, she paused to control her temper before looking up. "You have a wonderfully creative imagination, but it's led you astray this time," she countered with sweetly laced sarcasm. "Hunter and I are no more than friends."

"Do you roll around in the grass with all your friends?"

Shocked by the accuracy of her cousin's accusation, Melissa instantly grew indignant. "We did no such thing," she denied sharply. "How could you even suggest that I would stoop to cavorting with an Indian brave in such a shameful fashion?"

Alanna merely shrugged. "Tell me what you did do then."

"I already have. We rode home together. There's nothing more to tell. If I picked up a blade of grass on the way, it was undoubtedly blowing in the wind."

"There's no breeze today."

Totally losing patience with her inquisitive cousin, Melissa plunked her new handkerchieves atop the others and angrily shoved the dresser drawer closed. "Let's not fight over an Indian who'll swiftly be gone," she bargained. "Why don't I ask Ian to bring one of his friends with him the next time he comes to dinner? I'm sure they're all as nice as he is and I'd like for you to have a beau, too."

Melissa's abrupt change of subject wasn't lost on Alanna, but she could readily see by the defiant tilt of her cousin's chin that she was not going to reveal anything of any importance that afternoon. She prayed that Melissa was right, and that Hunter would be gone before anything dangerously improper occurred between them. It was plain the warning she had meant to deliver would fall on deaf ears, and reluctantly, she ceased to try.

"Ian's friends are undoubtedly nice," she agreed, "but I'm not interested in meeting them."

"Do you plan to spend your entire life alone?"

"I'm not alone here," Alanna pointed out.

"No, of course not." Melissa dismissed her objection with a nervous wave. "You're not alone in the strictest sense of the word, but you most certainly are in every way that matters. Don't you wish to marry and have children?"

Alanna could not even look at a small child without feeling a sickening sense of dread. All she had to do was close her eyes to instantly view the bloodly scene where her baby brother and sisters had died. The cursed image had been burned into her memory for all time.

"No, I don't think I'll ever marry. I'm content here, and your parents have told me innumerable times that I need never leave."

"Well, of course not," Melissa cried. "They'd never make you go, but don't you want to live your own life?"

"I already do."

Melissa was delighted by how easily she had distracted Alanna from her appalling innuendos, but failed to recognize that her inquiries were equally unsettling to her cousin. "Here are the new ribbons. I bought pink and yellow for me, and lavender and blue for you."

Alanna reached out to take the satin streamers. "Thank you. It was kind of you to think of me."

"Nonsense. You should have come into town with us."

"Perhaps next time."

"Yes, do." Grateful to have extricated herself from an embarrassing confrontation, Melissa breathed a sigh of relief as she turned away. Alanna's fear of Indians was certainly understandable, but she did not share it. In her view, Hunter was a fascinating man, and she immediately began to plot another opportunity for them to be alone together.

Hunter spent the afternoon with Elliott preparing for the upcoming trip, but thoughts of Melissa's supple grace were never far from his mind. From what he could tell, the Barclays lived a good life on their plantation, and without too much difficulty he could picture himself becoming part of it between forays into the wilderness. John Barclay was one of the organizers of the Ohio Company, the group sponsoring the exploration of the Ohio Valley. Hunter thought he might be able to exploit that tie as a reason for frequent visits, without any mention of the man's beautiful daughter.

Then again, he had not seen enough of his friends' father to know whether or not John Barclay would be easy to fool. Hoping to remedy that situation, he began to ask discreet questions. "Don't most of the plantations have slaves?"

"Yes, they do."

"Then why haven't I seen any here?"

Elliott frowned slightly as he struggled to provide a coherent answer. "Our grandfather owned quite a few," he admitted, "but when he died, Father set them all free. That's a decision he's never discussed with us, but whenever he's questioned about it, I've heard him mention that in the beginning the plantation was worked by indentured servants from England. He claims to prefer to surround himself with the same hardworking class of men. We no longer have bondsmen, but we pay good wages, and have loyal workers as a result."

Hunter sincerely believed he could be described as hardworking, and made a mental note to see that his value to the militia was mentioned frequently in whatever letters Byron and Elliott sent home. Because they were already convinced of his ability as a scout, he thought he could inspire them to praise his talents in their letters. He would never be one of John Barclay's men, however, because his first loyalty would always be to the Seneca.

"Do you consider Jacob loyal?" the Indian inquired.

"Our blacksmith? Yes, he's been with us for years and years. His wife is our cook and their daughters help her in the kitchen. Their son works with the cooper. We have several whole families working for us. The cooper's wife is the laundress, as an example. The household staff all belong to one family. Only the fieldhands are single men."

Hunter nodded thoughtfully, for it was becoming increasingly easy to imagine himself spending a great deal of time at the Barclay plantation. A young woman as affectionate as Melissa would prompt lengthy stays, but he knew she was far too pampered a lady to find happiness visiting a Seneca village. No, if they were to fall in love, then he would have to become part of her world, as she would never be comfortable in his.

While that was a daunting thought, he liked the company of white men, and did not think living amongst them would create any great hardship for him. Besides, he could return home as often as he chose. To continue to come and go as he pleased was precisely how he intended to live his life, and he was certain he could keep Melissa too content to complain about his habits.

"Does Ian Scott intend to marry your sister?" he asked suddenly.

Because that question bore no relation to the subject Elliott had believed was under discussion, he was understandably perplexed, but recovered quickly. "He might. I really can't say. Melissa has always been popular and I don't believe she is any more fond of Ian than she is of her other beaus."

"There are other men interested in her?"

"Of course," Elliott insisted with a hearty chuckle. "Young women as pretty as Melissa are always eagerly sought after."

Not wanting Elliott to discover he had a serious interest in Melissa just yet, Hunter deliberately pretended his curiosity about the comely blonde had been satisfied. "What about Alanna? Is she too shy to have beaus?"

"I spend a great deal of my time worrying about her," Elliott confided unhappily. "She's so dear to us, but perhaps we've sheltered her more than we should. When she first came to us, she was so easily frightened, that I'm afraid we spoiled her terribly. She isn't demanding now, of course, but still, if we'd done more to encourage her to be as independent as Melissa, she might not be as shy as she is today."

Hunter cleverly turned their discussion to the subject of the Ohio Valley, but he remained preoccupied with how best to impress Melissa so that she would be anxiously awaiting his return. When she displayed an annoying indifference to him at supper, he was not only dismayed, but disgusted. He could readily understand her reluctance to openly display her feelings for him, but thought ignoring him completely was a poor way to behave. He held that sorry opinion until they left the dining room to go across the hall into the parlor, and she brushed by him to slip a tightly folded message into his hand.

Believing it to be a fervent plea for a meeting later, Hunter's spirits soared. Then he had to bear an agonizing wait as Rachel and Melissa treated them all to another harpsichord recital. It wasn't until everyone retired to bed that he finally had a chance to read the note. He was ashamed not to have thought of a way to get a similar message to Melissa, but as soon as the house was quiet, he went down to the dock where she had suggested they meet.

By the time she finally appeared, Hunter was thoroughly sick of waiting for her. "Did you think I would stand here all night?" he scolded, but when he drew her into his arms and discovered she was wearing only a light shawl over a cotton nightgown, his anger dissolved in the heat of desire.

Melissa reached up on her tiptoes to kiss away his frown. "I'm sorry. It took forever for Alanna to fall asleep and usually she's asleep before I've finished brushing out my hair."

"Would she tell your parents if she discovered you'd left the house to meet me?"

"No, I don't believe so, but I'd never hear the end of it from her."

"What does that mean?"

"She'd not approve and she would try to talk me out of seeing you."

Melissa had let her hair fall free, and Hunter slid his fingers through the fair curls at her temples to keep her face pressed to his as he kissed her. He then wrapped her in an affectionate embrace. "Are you afraid she'll convince you that seeing me is wrong?"

Melissa responded with a throaty giggle. "I already know it's wrong," she teased, "but I'm here anyway."

She felt so good in his arms that Hunter rested his chin atop her head and continued to hold her close. "Why is it wrong?" he asked.

The warm softness of his buckskins invited her caress, and Melissa rubbed against him with the unabashed joy of a contented cat. "Why?" she murmured seductively. "It's wrong because the envious people who want to keep lovers apart constantly say it's wrong. That's the only reason I can see."

That she would refer to him as her lover was all the encouragement Hunter required. He relaxed his hold on her to allow her the freedom to step back slightly, and then kissed her again with the same demanding affection she had welcomed so eagerly that afternoon. He slid his hands to the small of her back and pressed her hips against his. He wanted her, and that blatant gesture made his need shockingly plain.

Although captivated by him, Melissa knew better than to give in to Hunter, and when he ended a lengthy exchange of deep kisses to provide an opportunity for them both to take a much needed deep breath, she slipped out of his arms. "I can't stay," she whispered dramatically, as though having to leave him tore her heart in two. "Meet me here again tomorrow night."

Shocked that she would even consider leaving him now, Hunter delayed an instant too long before reaching out to catch her arm, and she easily eluded him to escape into the night. Left too disappointed to do more than moan, Hunter vowed not to waste a second of their time talking the next evening. It would be his last opportunity to be with Melissa for several months, and he intended to leave her with such exciting memories, no other man would ever win her heart.

As was her custom, Alanna left the house early the next morning, but Melissa slept late and when she finally awakened, her late-night tryst with Hunter lingered in her memory with the vague sweetness of a dream. She was certain she had met him, but to her mind, the encounter had been far more innocent than the one beside the road, which was precisely how she had intended it to be. She had sought only a few passionate kisses, and surely, despite Hunter's ardor, he could not have expected her to give more.

She was a lady after all, and he was an Indian brave, albeit an immensely appealing one. Where her mind had been the previous day on their ride home from Williamsburg she could not explain, but she was in full possession of her faculties now. A brief exchange of fevered kisses certainly made for a memorable interlude, but falling in love with an Indian would bring only tragedy, and she would certainly not disgrace herself with such an unsuitable match.

Melissa had left her bed, but was still wearing her nightgown and stretching languidly when her mother came to her door. Completely unburdened by guilt, she greeted Rachel warmly. "It looks like another lovely day. Tell me what to do for tonight's party."

"I'd appreciate your help in arranging the flowers," Rachel replied. "Then I'd like for you to convince Alanna to join us at supper tonight. We've had ample opportunity to observe the Indian scout, and he's no savage. Besides, Lieutenant Scott has promised to bring along two of his friends, and I'm hoping she'll like one of them."

"I asked her only yesterday if she would like to meet one of Ian's friends, but I'd no idea two had already been invited."

"What did she say?"

"She gave her usual reply. She doesn't care if she ever meets a man and falls in love." Melissa picked up her brush and began to brush the tangles out of her hair. "I don't think I'll mention Ian's friends. I'll simply insist she be at dinner to tell Byron and Elliott goodbye. If I make it sound as though they'll be insulted if she stays away, she can't refuse to eat with us. After all, we're just asking her to walk down the stairs, not to attend a party in town."

Rachel gave her clever daughter a hug before turning toward the door. "Perfect, I knew you'd think of a way to convince her to join us. I'll be out in the garden when you're dressed."

"Yes, Mama." Very pleased with herself, Melissa moved to the dressing table and smiled at her reflection in the mirror. Ian had kissed her cheek a time or two, but now she wondered if he knew how to kiss as well as the Indian. If not, she would most certainly teach him. Not that night, of course, but soon.

After a day of Melissa's inspired coaxing, Alanna found herself agreeing to wear one of her cousin's fancy satin gowns. She chose a pale blue dress Melissa seldom wore, but the fact that she was several inches taller was readily apparent when she smoothed the skirt into place over a hoop and a dozen petticoats. Even encased in silk stockings, her slender ankles looked horribly unattractive to her.

"Oh, dear," she complained. "This doesn't look right at all."

Melissa stepped back to survey the problem and clucked her tongue impatiently. "That you have no beautiful gowns designed to fit you is your own fault, Alanna. Perhaps now you'll come with me on my next visit to the dressmaker's. It's high time you had more elegant clothes. You think just because you seldom leave the plantation you needn't dress well, but what about all the times we have guests? Hasn't it ever oc-

curred to you that Mother and Father are embarrassed to have
you look so neglected? It reflects very badly on them, you
know."

Having never once considered that her choice of apparel
was anyone's business but her own, Alanna was horribly embarrassed by her cousin's scolding. "Oh, no, I never thought—"

"No, of course not," Melissa chided. "You are too lost in
yourself to worry about how we look to our friends. Well, that
can't be helped tonight, but if you remain seated, or take care
to stand behind me, no one will notice your gown is of an
improper length. You look adorable otherwise, so let's go on
downstairs and enjoy the party."

Alanna gave her skirt a tug in a vain attempt to find another
couple of inches of material that just wasn't there. At least the
sky blue slippers were the right size, so any anguish she might
suffer was purely mental. A final glance in the mirror revealed
a young woman who appeared more uncomfortable than adorable, but Alanna had agreed to go to dinner and forced herself
to follow Melissa down the stairs.

It had been the prospect of dining with Hunter which had
upset Alanna initially, but when she saw Ian Scott coming
through the front door with two other young British officers,
she panicked. She would have run right back up the stairs had
Melissa not clamped her hand around Alanna's wrist and refused to let go. Trapped, Alanna took a fortifying breath, and
telling herself that at least these unexpected guests were not
Indians, she managed to respond to the introductions with a
shy smile which completely charmed the Englishmen.

Hunter stood back, content to observe the festivities rather
than participate. He had not expected Alanna to come to supper,
and when she first appeared, he did not immediately recognize
her. One of Melissa's ribbon-and-lace-trimmed caps sat atop her
curls, and the blue gown was so flattering that for an instant he
saw only a lovely young lady, rather than Alanna. When he did

realize who she was, he managed a smile rather than an awkward gape, but Alanna appeared not to have seen him.

Knowing that he would not be ignored later that night, was all that kept Hunter from striding out of the Barclays' home, when Melissa appeared no more interested in him than she had been at supper the previous evening. He was pleased to see that she included Alanna in the conversation, and gave as much attention to Ian Scott's friends as she did to Ian. Soon after the British officers' arrival, two young women joined the party. Brunette sisters from a neighboring plantation, Sarah and Robin Frederick barely spoke to the Englishmen, before hurrying over to Byron and Elliott to chat.

When supper was announced, Hunter found himself seated with Byron, Elliott, and the Frederick sisters on one side of the table, with Alanna, Melissa, and the three British officers on the other. Because he had a clear view of Melissa between the silver candelabra and crystal vases filled with colorful cut flowers, he took his place without complaint. The other young men at the party were dressed in military uniforms, but he was not ashamed to attend in his buckskins. He was proud of who and what he was, but as always eager to learn, he kept a close watch on his companions and studied their every move.

Lacking Hunter's natural self-confidence, Alanna twisted her napkin into a tight knot during the blessing. The young man on her left, Graham Tyler, was the most talkative individual she had ever met, and she savored every second of her Uncle John's lengthy prayer, as it forced the young man to be silent. She did not want to be rude to him, but thought he must surely know that conversations required more than one person's comments to be successful. The other officer, Stuart Harnett, appeared to be a taciturn individual, and she thought it a shame that they had not been seated together, since neither would have pestered the other with needless conversation.

As the food was served, Alanna pretended to be listening

to Graham and assiduously avoided looking in Hunter's direction. She was proud of herself for being there for Byron and Elliott, and hoped that with all the guests present she and the Indian would not have to exchange a single word. Others at the table addressed questions to him and he gave intelligent replies, but she had already known he was bright, and that did not make him any the less difficult to accept.

Unmindful of Alanna's worries, Melissa had an absolutely wonderful time the whole evening. Despite the presence of Alanna and the Frederick sisters, Ian was especially attentive, which was enormously flattering. She failed to notice that Hunter disappeared after supper somewhere between the dining room and parlor. It wasn't until Byron suggested their mother provide the music for dancing that she looked around and found him gone. Doubting that he knew any of the charming country dances she and her friends loved, she dismissed him from her mind, until after a marvelously entertaining evening their guests departed and she and Alanna went upstairs to bed.

Alanna was exhausted. "Will you please ask Ian—no, *beg* him—not to bring Graham Tyler here ever again? The only time he ceased talking was when he was forced to pause for a breath."

"Really? I didn't notice. He dances very well."

Noting her shyness, Elliott had been Alanna's partner for the first dance, and between her considerate cousins and the enthusiastic Graham Tyler, she had danced more that evening than she had her entire life. She sank down on her bed and kicked off her slippers. "I suppose he does," she reluctantly agreed. "He's not unattractive either, but my ears positively ache from the sound of his voice."

"Perhaps he was merely nervous. You're very pretty, Alanna. It's only because you bury yourself here that you aren't surrounded by suitors."

In Alanna's mind, suitors were inexorably linked to propos-

als of marriage, weddings, and babies, which was a most unsettling sequence. Preferring not to encourage the direction of
her cousin's thoughts, she covered a wide yawn, then rose, and
began to remove her gown. By the time she got into bed, she
was half-asleep, and when Melissa left their room twenty minutes later, she did not hear the door close behind her.

Melissa thought she was the first to reach the dock that
night, and when she didn't immediately see Hunter, she was
insulted. She would have returned to the house, had he not
stepped out of the shadows within seconds of her arrival. He
had already removed his shirt, and the moonlight sculpted his
muscular frame with a haunting perfection that left her staring
in awestruck wonder. She might have asked him where he had
been most of the evening, but he didn't give her the chance.

Hunter was tempted to scold her for giving Ian more attention than she had given him that night, but decided there were
far better ways to spend his time. He caught her in a joyful
embrace and, delighted to find her again wearing only her
nightgown and shawl, he turned his welcoming kiss into a
seductive demand for total surrender. Melissa was soft and
warm, her petite figure perfect in all respects; her weight provided a slight burden when he lifted her into his arms. He
doubted anyone else would visit the dock that night, but there
was a secluded spot shielded by a hedge nearby, and it would
provide the privacy he craved.

Melissa hadn't been carried since she was a child. Excited
by the strength of Hunter's embrace, she wrapped her arms
around his neck and again freed his hair from the cord at his
nape. When he placed her on her feet, she leaned against him
to savor the warmth of his broad chest. In the next instant, he
pulled her down into the grass. Had she realized how much
he wanted, it would have already been too late to protest, but
his kiss muffled any objection she might have wished to make.

Determined this time to keep Melissa with him until he was

ready to send her away, Hunter's kisses were slow and deep. His caresses were tender, his touch knowing and sweet, and when he slipped his hand beneath her nightgown and slid it up the smooth skin of her bare thigh, she was too lost in his affection to push him away. He ran his hand over the gentle swell of her hip, tilting her body toward him. It was a simple matter then to separate her legs with his knee, and his fingertips brushed the soft cluster of curls nestled between them.

Far from random in his approach, Hunter knew how to please a woman, and precisely where an easy touch could create exquisite longings he was only too willing to satisfy. He soon felt Melissa tremble with desire, as he continued to explore her most tantalizing secrets with a slow, circling motion. He paused occasionally to dip his fingers into the sweet feminine nectar her body had created to ease his way, and silently rejoiced that she would welcome him so eagerly. When he could no longer delay making her his own, he loosened his belt with one hand, shoved his breeches aside, and plunged deep within her. As her body convulsed with the shock of his forceful thrust, he was stunned by the realization that she had been a virgin.

The blissfully romantic moment shattered by searing pain, Melissa tried to cry out, but Hunter's hand closed over her mouth before she had uttered more than a tiny wail. Betrayed by her own desires, she choked back her sobs, but she knew this time she had blithely encouraged Hunter to take her much further than she had wished to go. She stared up at him, and rather than a handsome man with flowing black hair, she saw only a savage, and knew that should anyone ever learn what they had done, her reputation would be irrevocably ruined. Heartbroken by her own willful folly, she waited for Hunter to speak.

"You should have told me I would be the first, and I would have been much more gentle," Hunter whispered. "I love you, and you belong to me now." He raised his hand from her mouth, but kissed her before she could reply.

He began to move with slow, shallow thrusts, which he hoped would not cause her any additional pain. No longer responsive, Melissa lay still in his arms until he had found his own release, even if he had not provided her with the pleasure he had intended. Mistaking Melissa's horrified sense of shame for merely shy wonder at the power of love, he pulled his clothing back into place and helped her to her feet.

"I want to shout with joy, but I know we must be quiet. Remove your nightgown and wash in the river," he encouraged.

Not wanting to return to her room with any lingering trace of his loving to incriminate her, Melissa allowed him to help her out of the white garment, and then walked down to the river's edge and waded in. The water's chill made her shiver, but that was such a slight discomfort compared with her overwhelming sense of guilt, that she scarcely noticed it. For one terrifying moment, she considered drowning herself, but swiftly abandoned the idea. If she never told anyone what had happened that night, never admitted it to a single soul, no one would ever suspect that she had lost her virginity. Now knowing precisely what to expect on her wedding night, she was confident she could portray a virgin so convincingly that her new husband would believe her to be a chaste bride.

When she left the water, Hunter was waiting to help her again don her nightgown. It had gotten pushed up around her waist before he had entered her, and bore no telltale stains to give away her secret. The instant she was dressed, she turned toward her house, but Hunter reached out to stop her and handed her the shawl she had forgotten.

"Making love will be much better when I get back," he promised. "You will enjoy it as much as I do then."

Melissa dared not tell him that she would never spend another second alone with him, for fear he would complain so loudly he would wake her family. What if he then demanded her for a wife? she agonized. She had been raised to wed a fine gentleman who would give her the same prestigious social position and pampered life her parents had provided.

Unable to bear the possibility she had jeopardized her whole future by foolishly encouraging an amorous Indian's passions, she raised up on her tiptoes to kiss him goodbye, and then fled toward the safety of her home. By the time she had reached her bedroom, she lost her tenuous hold on her composure and had to muffle her sobs with the shawl she had almost carelessly left at her lover's feet.

Unable to tame an ecstatic grin, Hunter remained at the dock, watching the moonlight play on the river and remembering the delectable softness of his beloved's fair skin. He had never expected to fall in love with a white woman, but Melissa Barclay was so irresistibly appealing, he had not been able to help himself. He would have to move far more slowly with her parents than he had with her, but he intended to take Melissa for his wife, and for her sake, he wanted their consent. While he was certain they had never imagined having a Seneca son-in-law, he would strive to make them proud.

Four

Melissa struggled against the paralyzing fear that all her bright hopes for an advantageous marriage and blissfully happy life had vanished along with her virtue. She was only eighteen, but all because of an irresistibly appealing Indian brave, her whole future lay in jeopardy. Her tears became hoarse, choking sobs as she weighed the necessity of keeping the shame of her disastrous flirtation with Hunter a secret, and the horrible possibility of it being discovered. She would never tell, never even hint that there had ever been anything whatsoever between them.

But would Hunter be equally discreet? she agonized.

What were the chances he would keep the shocking details of their friendship to himself? Clearly he was a proud man, but if anything, she had minimized whatever compliments Byron and Elliott had bestowed on his talents. He was no braggart, but was that because he had simply not had anything as tantalizing as his affair with her to prompt a boast? Perhaps sleeping with a white woman was the most exciting thing he had ever done, and he would be eager to tell everyone he knew just how easily he had seduced her.

No! she fought to convince herself. He was too clever a man not to realize Byron and Elliott would not allow him to talk about her as though she were a common trollop. Her brothers would beat him senseless—if not much worse—should they ever hear him speak of her in a disrespectful fashion. A fresh wave of tears followed that thought, for surely she had betrayed her brothers' trust that night, when she had betrayed herself.

"Melissa?" Alanna called from her bed. "Are you sick?"

Oh yes! Melissa longed to blurt out, but she dared not. She could not take the chance of drawing even the slightest bit of attention to herself. She felt as though anyone with a sharp pair of eyes would see her sinful secret, and brand her a harlot. To her way of thinking, she had merely made a stupid mistake, but unless she could forever keep the scandalous moment buried deep within her soul, her life would never be the same because of it. Hastily searching for an excuse for her tears, she found one she hoped Alanna would believe.

"No," she responded wistfully. "I'm just so dreadfully worried about Byron and Elliott."

Alanna sat up and swung her legs over the side of her bed. "But why? They're grown men, who know how to look after themselves."

"Yes, but they've never gone out looking for trouble as they are now, and I'm so afraid they'll find it."

Touched by her cousin's anguish, Alanna left her bed, lit the lamp on the nightstand, and then went to Melissa's dresser to fetch her a handkerchief. "You mustn't carry on so," she said. "Your brothers are intelligent men. I doubt they'd go into the Ohio Valley if they didn't believe in what they're doing, and their ability to succeed."

Alanna had proven to be so gullible, Melissa became positively inspired. She sat up and made a great show of blotting her tears. "That's just the problem," she complained. "They are too confident, and that folly could place them in great danger."

Alanna had never seen Melissa is such a pitiful state. "I think I ought to wake your mother," she said. "Perhaps you'll find her advice more comforting."

"Oh no! We mustn't bother Mother. If she hasn't realized

that Byron and Elliott are putting themselves in terrible danger, then I don't want to risk upsetting her."

Stymied as to what else to suggest, Alanna sat down on the edge of Melissa's bed. "It sounds as though the trip will be long and tiring, but it doesn't necessarily follow that it will be as terribly dangerous as you fear."

"But it can't help but be dangerous!" Having just convinced herself of the peril, Melissa's worries doubled. She had hoped Hunter's friendship with her brothers would prevent him from speaking ill of her, but what, God forbid, if something actually did happen to them? With loyalty to Byron and Elliott no longer a factor, would Hunter feel free to say whatever he chose about her? She bent her knees to provide a comforting resting place for her cheek, and wrapped her arms around her legs. She tried to catch her breath, but tears continued to pour down her face.

Never having realized her cousin was even capable of such abject despair, Alanna sat quietly observing her. She did not doubt that Melissa was dreadfully unhappy, but that she would weep so pathetically over her imagined fears for her brothers' safety just didn't seem plausible. Both young men had made similar trips with the militia, and she couldn't recall Melissa being even the slightest bit upset on any of those occasions. What was different now?

Her first thought was that Byron and Elliott had not been traveling with Hunter in the past. Could Melissa's endless stream of tears be because of the Indian? Was she heartbroken because a man she had insisted meant nothing to her was leaving? Not wanting to upset her cousin with a repeat of their last conversation in which Melissa had stubbornly denied any interest in the Indian, Alanna kept those thoughts to herself. As far as she was concerned, Melissa could weep and sob over Hunter as long as she wished. Alanna was too grateful he would be gone in the morning to complain.

"Would some tea help?" Alanna asked.

"How can you be so incredibly shallow as to believe a cup of tea would ease my pain?"

"It was only a suggestion."

Alanna was such a bashful girl, and when she looked away, Melissa realized how insensitive she had been to snap at her. "Please forgive me. At any other time the offer of tea would be most appreciated, but tonight, well, it just isn't enough."

"Brandy then?"

"Yes! Some of my father's brandy would be enormously helpful. Will you fetch me some, please?"

Alanna would have been happy to get whatever Melissa wished, rather than listen to her cry until dawn. She lit a candle to light her way, and went downstairs to her uncle's study. He kept a crystal decanter of brandy and matching glasses on a tray on the corner of his desk. She had never sampled it herself, but knew that her uncle regarded brandy as being of great value when he was troubled. Hoping Melissa would find it equally soothing, she poured a few drops into a glass, then added several more, and carried it upstairs. Melissa hadn't moved in the time she had been gone.

Alanna handed her the glass. "I believe this is supposed to be sipped."

Melissa eyed the scant quantity she had been given, fearing it would not be nearly enough. A quick taste revolted her completely, but the numbing warmth as the potent liquor spread throughout her body were remarkably pleasant. She finished the final sip in a hasty gulp and handed the empty glass to Alanna.

"Thank you. I feel better already."

Alanna set the glass aside on the nightstand. Not really wanting to believe that Melissa cared for an Indian, she probed the excuse for her tears with deliberate subtlety. "You seemed so happy last night at the party. When we prepared for bed, you didn't express any worries about Byron and Elliott. Did you have a bad dream about them? Is that what happened?"

Melissa had no choice, but she didn't relish lying to her cousin. It had not occurred to her to blame her drastic change in mood on a dream, but the suggestion was too good to waste. "Yes, that's precisely what happened. Perhaps the dancing was more tiring than usual. All I know is that I awoke overcome with both sorrow and fright. It's sweet of you not to scold me for being silly."

"It isn't silly to want the best for your brothers."

"No, of course, it isn't, but some would call me foolish for carrying on so." Melissa's handkerchief had become as soggy as a washrag, and Alanna brought her another. She thanked her between sniffles. "Let's try and get back to sleep, if we don't, we'll look awful in the morning when we tell the boys goodbye."

And Hunter, Alanna added silently. She would be ecstatically happy to wave goodbye to him. If Melissa felt differently, it would not matter, for the Indian would undoubtedly be gone long enough for her to forget him. Not that her cousin was fickle, of course, but she had never favored one beau for more than a few weeks. Alanna put out the lamp and got back into bed, content in the belief Hunter would soon leave their home, and with any luck, absent himself forever.

Melissa rearranged her pillows and attempted to find a comfortable pose, but despite the lingering warmth imparted by the brandy, she was still too restless to find peace. With but a tiny bit of imagination, she could feel the seductive sweetness of Hunter's caress, and the passionate hunger of his kiss. He had worked a sensual magic she had not even known existed, until the first time his lips had brushed hers and created the desire she had only dreamed of in romantic fantasies.

The memory of that sunlit ride made her cringe, and she drew her hand across her mouth, while wishing she could erase all trace of Hunter as easily from her mind. It was not only her mind which clung to his memory, however, but her whole body that recalled the warmth of his smooth, bronze skin, and the rapture of his touch. If only she had had sense enough to stop there, before he claimed her innocence as easily as he had her reason. She sighed dejectedly, certain she had been lost from the moment their eyes had met on the dock. She had seen only a handsome savage, when what she should have recognized in his dark gaze was the reflection of her own doom.

Depressed beyond further tears, she knew she would not get to sleep that night, for how could she rest, when in the space of an evening she had come so close to destroying her whole life? She had been incredibly weak, and the resulting pain that tore at her conscience was far too high a price to pay. If only she were certain no one would ever learn how foolish she had been, then she could go on as though no mistake had been made.

Tragically, the change in her had been too profound to mask with the pretense that she had suffered no such epiphany. She would no longer have a frivolous outlook, that she now feared had bordered on the childish. Instead, she was eager to alter her habits, to curb the flirtatious manner which had always made her so popular, for it had been her undoing.

Popularity no longer concerned her. What she wanted now was a cloak of respectability so thick that no breath of scandal could ever dislodge it from her shoulders. She would have to be careful though. She could not change her behavior so abruptly it caused comment, and drew curiosity and speculation. No, she would have to make the changes she desired slowly, with deliberate caution, so no one would ever suspect how badly she had strayed from the path she ought to have followed.

With that plan clearly in mind, Melissa slipped from her bed to wet a washcloth in the pitcher of water on the washstand. When she lay back down, she placed it over her eyes to reduce the swelling. She intended to look her best in the morning, and she dared not appear as though she had spent most of the night crying. After all, why would Melissa Barclay have any reason to be sad, when she was so pretty and popular? she asked herself. Why indeed?

The next morning, Alanna was astonished to discover Melissa had gotten up before her. She dimly recalled a Christmas morning when they were children, when Melissa had beaten her out of bed, but that had been the only other time. Thinking it was no wonder she had overslept after the party and Melissa's late-night bout of tears, Alanna grew worried she might not be dressed in time to bid Byron and Elliott farewell.

She left her bed and hurried to the window, but there was no sign of activity on the dock. Byron's *bateau* was still there, although it did appear to be partially loaded. Not wishing to be mistaken for lazy on such an important morning, she dressed so hastily she was still donning her cap as she ran down the stairs.

Standing in the hallway, Elliott stepped forward to catch Alanna around the waist and swing her off the bottom step. "Where are you off to in such a rush?" he asked.

Nonplussed, Alanna drew away. "I was afraid I'd miss saying goodbye to you."

Amused by the sweetness of her excuse, Elliott had to fight the impulse to tease her again. "Didn't you know I'd not leave without a kiss from you?"

There had been a time when Alanna would have thrown her arms around his neck and hugged him, too, but now that she was grown, such an affectionate display no longer seemed appropriate between them. While she also loved Byron, she and

Elliott had always shared a special rapport. He was as protective as an older brother, and had always made her feel dearly loved.

"Well, I'd hoped that you wouldn't," she admitted, "but the others might not have bothered to wait for me."

Entering the hall from the dining room, Hunter could not help but overhear Alanna's remark, but when she shied away from him, he thought better of saying that he would also have waited to kiss her goodbye. A pretty blush filled her cheeks and, while she was again dressed in simple homespun fabrics rather than satin and lace, he thought her as pretty as she had been at dinner the previous evening.

He was in exceptionally high spirits, but like Melissa, did not wish to make anyone curious as to the reason, and so tried very hard to behave as he always did. "I was just going upstairs to get my things," he said as he slipped by her, but she failed to reply. Thinking perhaps his comment had not required a response, Hunter took no offense, but it felt very strange to have made love with Melissa, while Alanna would not willingly offer a kind word. He had observed the sharp differences between the two young women upon first meeting them, but he hoped by the second or third time he visited the Barclay home, Alanna would drop her reserve.

As he reached his room, Hunter decided he would not insist upon friendliness from Melissa's family, but he believed he had a right to expect courtesy, and Alanna still had a difficult time with that where he was concerned. He had already packed his few belongings and, after slinging them over his shoulder, he gave the room he'd occupied a final glance. From the elaborately carved cornice to the highly polished pine floor, and every piece of furniture it contained, it was as fine a room as could be found in Virginia, but to Hunter, it held none of the warmth of home.

A long house afforded Seneca families the finest of forest

accommodations, and it was that unique oneness with the earth that Hunter missed. In his view, the Barclay mansion squatted on the land like an overgrown toad, rather than being a part of the natural scene as a long house was. If his visits to the plantation proved to be as frequent as he hoped, perhaps he would ask permission to build a long house nearby. Melissa and he would then have a perfect place to meet.

For the present, however, the construction of a home was not his utmost concern. He might have felt out of place in Melissa's house, but not in her arms, and enchanted by her, he was anxious to see her again. They had made no plans before parting, but he was confident she would share his wish to keep their love a secret for the time being.

A slow smile played across his lips as went down the stairs. As long as Melissa did not keep their love a secret from him as well, he would not complain.

Seeking excuses to leave the house, Melissa took on more chores that morning than she usually handled in a month. First she went to the laundry to make certain all of her brothers' clothes had been washed, pressed, and returned to their rooms. Then there were favorite dishes she asked Polly to prepare for their breakfast, and she took the cook with her to the smokehouse to search for the choicest side of bacon. The henhouse was on the opposite side of the barn, and while she had not gathered eggs in years, she made a point of doing so now.

Finally, noticing several of the camellia blossoms in the bouquet on the dining room table were tinged with brown, she rushed out to the garden to replace them. She had just finished arranging the flowers for the breakfast table, when she heard her brothers descending the stairs. Believing Hunter would be with them, she again left the house, and this time walked down to the stable where the horses used to Alanna's pampering snickered softly for the apples Melissa was too preoccupied to dole out.

Knowing she was far too nervous to swallow a single bite, she sat in the cool darkness of the stable until she was certain breakfast would be over. Then she walked out on the dock and watched the ducks paddling by with their downy babies, intending to stay there until the young men were ready to leave. Frequently fed from the dock, upon sighting her the mother ducks led their broods in close and, expecting breakfast, quacked eagerly. Equally eager for something to do, Melissa dashed back to the kitchen for bread, and met Hunter on her second trip to the dock. Too frightened to think clearly, she clutched the stale loaf Polly had just given her as though she were as desperately hungry as the ducks.

"I was just going to feed the ducks," she told him.

Melissa was wearing the same attractive blue dress she had worn the day he had arrived, and Hunter again thought her a beauty, but she was blushing so deeply he could not help but laugh. "I'm taking my things to the *bateau*," he announced, "so we can walk there together." He then leaned down to whisper, "You needn't look guilty. Love is no cause for shame."

Melissa had known she would have to speak with him that morning, but she had hoped there would be others present to keep their conversation from taking such an intimate turn. To her way of thinking, there was an enormous difference between the cherished beauty of love and the lustful desire that had led her astray, but she was not about to lecture Hunter on her views. She just wanted him gone.

"I'm not ashamed," she denied bravely. "It's just difficult to see you and not dwell on how soon you'll be gone."

"Then you will miss me?"

Melissa dared not look up at him, when she knew his dark eyes would be radiant with a teasing light. "Yes, I'll miss you terribly," she promised, although the lie pained her deeply. "Won't you miss me?"

They had reached the dock, and Melissa began tearing off hunks of bread and tossing them out to the ducks, who dove to catch them. Believing the pieces to be too large, Hunter took the loaf from her hands and broke off a tiny bit. "The ducklings need smaller bites," he explained as he threw one out into the river.

"Yes, of course. How silly of me." Melissa let him keep the bread and, moving closer to the edge of the dock, pretended to look for fish. In another hour he'll be gone, she told herself. Surely she could convince everyone his visit had left her unchanged for that long. She sent a sidelong glance Hunter's way, and found him studying her with the knowing gaze she feared might haunt her for the rest of her days.

"Stop it!" she hissed.

"Stop what?"

"Stop looking at me like that."

"Like what?"

He was caressing her body with a heated glance she could actually feel and, although she was fully clothed, he made her feel naked. A fresh blush filled her cheeks. "As though I were some delicious morsel you couldn't wait to eat."

Hunter licked his lips, and it was a far more suggestive gesture than she had ever shown him. Mortified by such blatant disrespect, a painful lump formed in her throat. Clearly the Indian cared nothing for her feelings, and why would he, when she had behaved like a wanton? She turned her back on him and bit her lip to force away the monsoon of tears that threatened to drown her in remorse. Her life was ruined, and the man who had caused her disgrace was laughing at her! Could there be any worse punishment?

Wondering what had become of the enchanting belle he had admired, Hunter tossed the last of the bread to the ducks and then walked up behind her. He slipped his arms around her waist and pulled her back against him. She was wearing a floral scent that teased his senses, and he regretted having to leave her. Believing his departure was troubling her, too, he offered the only reassurance he could.

"I'll come back as soon as I'm able. Think of that day rather than this, and don't be sad."

Responding to his affectionate hug without thinking, Melissa placed her hands over his, but she would anticipate his return with dread rather than longing. She closed her eyes, and surrounded by his warmth, wished he were any man other than the one he was. If only he were a British officer, or a planter's son, or a frontiersman with a European heritage. If only he had been someone she could have been proud to love, rather than a seductive savage whom she ought to have avoided with Alanna's zeal.

"Melissa?"

His hushed whisper increased her shame, for he ought not to have ever addressed her in terms less formal than *Miss Barclay.* She pushed away his hands and turned to the side where she had ample room to escape him. "Please, the others will be here soon, and we dare not arouse their suspicions."

"Is that all you want to say to me?"

His sullen frown inspired the words she knew he wanted to hear. "No. I'd like to talk with you all day, to learn about your home and family since you know all about mine, but there's no time." Praying someone would be approaching, she looked toward the house, and to her immense relief, she saw Elliott crossing the lawn. "Look, Elliott's ready to go."

"I'm not."

"Then you'll have to get ready!"

Hunter shook his head, but remained silent rather than increase her agitation. He reminded himself that making love was new to her, and her shyness around him was understandable. He crossed to the *bateau* and knelt to rearrange the gear it already held, to make room for his own.

"Mother's looking for you," Elliott called out to Melissa.

"Why?" Melissa rushed to him, and then, catching herself, stepped back.

For an instant she had looked terrified, but just as quickly her expression reflected mere puzzlement rather than fright, leaving Elliott unsure of what he had really seen. "I'm sure nothing's wrong," he told her. "Maybe she has presents she wants you to give us."

Seizing control of her emotions, Melissa responded with a saucy smile. "I think we'll save the presents for your return."

Seeing her parents crossing the lawn, followed by Byron and Alanna, Melissa continued to play the carefree young woman they would all expect to see. Her voice was tinged with the proper regret at her brothers' departure, but otherwise her mood appeared to be as sunny as the spring day. After ascertaining that her mother had merely wanted her to come to the dock to wish her brothers farewell, she stood between her parents and added her own best wishes for a safe journey.

When it came time to leave, Hunter thanked the Barclays for their hospitality, then bid Melissa and Alanna a polite goodbye. He did not linger as though he expected the same show of affection they gave Byron and Elliott, but promptly turned away and joined the two young men in the *bateau*. He did not glance back as they shoved the boat away from the dock and began to row, but he hoped if Melissa's eyes were brightened by tears, they were for him. After the passion they had shared, she had been strangely shy that morning, but his hopes for a joyous welcome upon his return overshadowed his concern.

John and Rachel waved until their sons' boat was well out into the river, before going back to the house. Melissa and Alanna, however, waited on the dock until the *bateau* had rounded the bend and was no longer in view. With the unabashed glee of a condemned man who's just won a pardon, Melissa drew in her first deep breath of the morning. Hunter was gone, and no one suspected a thing. She was so relieved, she might have leapt into the air with a jubilant shout had Alanna not been there to watch and wonder why.

"It's always fun to have them home, isn't it?" Melissa enthused. "We really ought to have more parties like the one we hosted last night. There's no reason to wait for Byron and Elliott to entertain, when I like having company so much, and I think you're finally beginning to enjoy it as well." She looped her arm through Alanna's, but rather than match her stride, Alanna hung back, pulling her to a clumsy halt.

"Last night you wept yourself into a deplorable state over your brothers' safety," Alanna reminded her. "Yet you just bid them goodbye as though they weren't going any farther than Newport News, and now you want to talk about parties?"

Alanna had made a point of observing the Indian that morning, but she hadn't seen anything untoward from him or Melissa. Perhaps her fears had made her overly cautious around him, but that didn't explain Melissa's constantly shifting emotions. She still felt something was wrong, but with Melissa's stubborn reluctance to confide in her, she doubted she would ever learn what it was.

An adept conversationalist, Melissa hastened to distract her cousin from pursuing such insulting questions. "After you fell asleep, I realized you were absolutely right. Byron and Elliott are capable men, who can handle whatever dangers they encounter. So I ceased to worry." She flashed a beguiling smile, and continued as though she had not been interrupted.

"If Graham Tyler was too talkative, what did you think of Stuart Harnett? Did you like him better?"

Startled by Melissa's abrupt change of subject, Alanna looked out toward the river. The current was brisk, but her cousins were as at home in a *bateau* as they were on land,

and she wasn't worried about them either. As for Hunter, she had never been so happy to see a guest depart. Now, if she could only banish the wretched memories he had stirred, her life would regain the tranquility she craved. It took her a moment to recall what Melissa had asked.

"He's very quiet, but whether he's shy, or merely unimpressed with me, I can't say. Whatever his reason, it really doesn't matter, because I'm not interested in him."

Melissa called upon whatever store of patience she possessed in an attempt to deal with her cousin. Rather than scold her, she grew flippant. "I think you actually enjoyed yourself last night, and you're just too stubborn to admit you had fun."

Alanna smoothed out her apron, then began to fidget. "I wasn't miserably unhappy, that's true, but there's a difference between attempting to be polite to our guests, and having fun."

"All you need is more practice," Melissa insisted. "It's such a lovely morning, let's sit out here by the river and talk for a while." She led the way onto the lawn, seated herself in a graceful heap of petticoats and lace, and patted the grass at her side.

"The morning is bright and clear," Alanna agreed, "but I don't think I'm going to like your topic of conversation."

"Nonsense. Let's talk about the young men we know. It isn't too soon for either of us to begin thinking about marriage. It's a shame Jonathan Frederick didn't wait for me. I loved him dearly, when I was a little girl."

"I remember that," Alanna said, and hoping to keep Melissa talking about herself, she joined her on the lawn. "How many children do he and his wife have now?"

"Four at last count," Melissa replied, "but they'll probably have a dozen in as many years." She named several other young men, friends of her brothers that she had known all her life. At one time or another she had kissed them all, but none of those brief infatuations had deepened into love. "Do any of them appeal to you?"

"I don't believe they even know I exist."

"Then you do like them? Or one of them at least? Tell me which one, and I'll make certain he and his whole family are invited to supper soon."

"That would be a waste of everyone's time. I like them all, but not in a romantic way."

Melissa reached over to pluck Alanna's cap from her curls. "Perhaps you'd prefer an older man. What about Randolph O'Neil? Whenever we see him at church, he always greets you far more warmly than he does me."

While flattered by that observation, Alanna disagreed. "I'm sure you're mistaken, besides, Mr. O'Neil must be in his forties, isn't he?"

"So what? He has beautiful blue eyes, and he's as trim as a man half his age. He's a successful merchant, and owns a fine home. He was widowed several years ago, so he must be lonely. I think he'd make a fine husband for you."

Alanna grabbed her cap back, but kept hold of it rather than again cover her hair. "Doesn't he have a daughter older than we are?"

"I'd forgotten all about her," Melissa mused thoughtfully, "but she needn't concern you, since she's married with a home of her own. What was her name? Sharon? Karen? Well, whatever it was, I believe she lives in Maryland, so she'd give you no trouble if you married her father."

"Melissa, I'm not going to marry Randolph O'Neil!" Alanna couldn't help but laugh at the thought, although she considered Mr. O'Neil a very nice man. She really didn't believe that he went out of his way to speak to her every Sunday, but even if he did, it was undoubtedly because he was being kind. "Why don't you consider him for yourself, if he'd make such a fine husband?"

"It's not such a bad idea," Melissa agreed. "I'm sure he'd treat me well, and he can afford to buy me whatever I want. A woman would be wise to consider those assets, when selecting a husband."

"Well, of course, no one would encourage you to wed a man who was impoverished, or one who would treat you badly," Alanna replied. "What about Ian? You've not grown bored with him these few weeks, the way you usually do with your beaus. Isn't he a good prospect?"

Melissa could not hide her admiration for the British officer, and this time her smile was sincere. "Yes, Ian's so charming I can't help but like him. He has fine manners and appears to be from a respectable family, but he can't hope to come into a large inheritance, or he'd not have gone into the military."

"Perhaps not, but he could always leave the Army, and your father would loan him the money to buy land or invest in a business, if you asked for his help. Shouldn't marrying the man you love be your first concern?"

The possibility she might be viewed as no longer worthy of a fine man's love brought a renewed threat of tears, and Melissa rose to her feet to hide them. By the time she had arranged her skirt and petticoats into flattering folds, she had shoved all thought of her regrettable affair from her mind, and overcame them. "Yes," she finally cautioned, "but a woman ought to take care to choose the right man to love."

Alanna coiled her hair atop her head, and covered it with her cap before rising. "Is it possible to choose whom to love?"

"It has to be," Melissa replied. Determined to find Alanna a beau, she was seized with the sudden inspiration to request Ian's help in the matter. After all, he liked Alanna, and it would be a wonderful—and totally selfless—excuse to see him. Charmed by the cleverness of her idea, she guided Alanna up

to their room, where they discussed the much needed additions
to her wardrobe. For a few hours at least, Hunter actually was
forgotten.

Five

In Newport News, Hunter and the Barclays left their small *bateau*, and along with other members of the militia boarded a sailing ship bound for Alexandria. The voyage north through the Chesapeake Bay and then up the Potomac River was neither long nor difficult, but Hunter did not enjoy the company he was forced to keep. The Barclays were officers, intelligent, educated men who were able to appreciate people of different cultures, and he had been proud to be their friend. Sadly, the recent recruits traveling with them to join the Virginia regiment were unsophisticated country boys. Most kept their distance, as Alanna had, but a few taunted him with insults they believed him too stupid to comprehend.

Once they began their journey over land, Hunter's duties as a scout would keep him constantly moving ahead of the regiment. That fact had at first prompted him to simply ignore the jokes told at his expense, but he had paid close attention to those telling them. He soon learned Vernon Avey wasted no opportunity to make others look foolish. He was a surly fellow, mean-spirited and belligerent. In his late twenties, he was one of the older recruits, but made no effort to set a good example for the younger men.

Vernon was shadowed by Willis Hoag and Hank Jepsen, whose loyalty bought them immunity from his vicious taunts. Like birds perched along the peak of a roof, they lined up at Vernon's elbow, ready to double-over with laughter whenever he chose someone to ridicule. Because none of the recruits were seafaring men, simply traversing the deck without stumbling and falling was a challenge. Cleverly avoiding drawing ridicule upon himself, Vernon spent his time leaning back against the rail, where from a secure footing he provided a malicious commentary on the mishaps befalling those who could not easily cross the deck with a sailor's rolling gait.

While none of the accidents he found hilarious were serious, being humiliated by Vernon was so painful that the men began to avoid him. Frustrated by the diminishing supply of fodder upon which to feed his sarcasm, Vernon shifted his target to Hunter. The Indian was too agile to call clumsy, and too handsome to draw criticism for his looks. He was Indian, however, and that fact inspired Vernon to plummet to new depths of tastelessness.

Hunter could excuse such insufferable ignorance for just so long, but after a particularly demeaning remark about the length of his hair, he crossed the deck, stood close, folded his arms over his chest, adopted an impassive expression, and stared down at the man who had spoken it. Vernon's blond hair, light brows, and pale lashes provided little definition for his features, which not even his mother would describe as attractive. His eyes were a pale blue and reminded him of a fish, Hunter laughed to himself before offering a jest of his own.

"Even a fish has sense enough to know when to shut his mouth. If you're not that smart, then I will shut yours for you."

Vernon looked to Willis and Hank for protection, but both men had begun to sidle away when Hunter had first approached, and clearly he was on his own. Infuriated that an Indian would dare to make fun of him, he doubled his fists at his sides and threw out his chest. He was skilled at making light of the misfortunes of others, but his usually sharp tongue failed him, and all he succeeded in doing was puffing himself up until he resembled an amorous bullfrog during a midnight serenade.

Hunter waited, his feet braced should he have to block a punch, but Vernon lacked the courage to hit him. Finally the fair-haired bully looked away, his expression still defiant, but his silence damning. Hunter could have walked away then, but he didn't. He kept staring at Vernon until he finally broke away from the rail and, still not hazarding a glance up at him, scurried back to the stern, where the men gathered there hurriedly moved aside to avoid him. Still not content, Hunter turned toward Willis and Hank, but his challenging stare prompted them to flee to the bow.

Hunter had learned from experience that once he had proven a man lacked the courage to repeat a joke to his face, he would have no more trouble with him. Unfortunately, there always seemed to be another man willing to test the limits of his patience. Had one of those belligerent clods—rather than the Barclays—approached him and offered a job as a scout, he would have refused it. Byron and Elliott had always treated him with respect, however, and it was his loyalty to them that kept him from quitting as soon as he reached the bottom of the gangplank in Alexandria. He had not complained of the way he had been treated, and he was surprised when Elliott apologized for the troops' lack of manners.

"Give them a couple more days," he encouraged the Indian. "Seeing how easily you move through the forest will put a stop to their teasing faster than anything I could say."

"It's not my skill they're questioning," Hunter replied. "They're laughing because I'm Indian, and no matter how far I lead them, I will be Indian still."

Unable to contradict him, Elliott looked to Byron for a response, and his older brother quickly obliged. "These men were hired to fight, not think, and that accounts for their lack of judgment. If they ever stopped to consider the differences between you, they'd quickly realize you're worth at least three of them, and none of them wants to face that."

Hunter turned to look back at the troops filing off the ship. Even if they weren't bright, they were young and strong, but none had impressed him as being invaluable to the Ohio Company's cause. "Only three?" he asked. "A Seneca brave is easily worth twice that."

Elliott's eyes widened at Hunter's boast, and amused, Byron feigned a punch to his brother's ribs. "He's teasing you. Now come on, let's report in and make certain Washington hasn't left without us."

Hunter followed, but he made no more immodest boasts when he was introduced to Col. Joshua Fry, the Oxford-educated Englishman commanding the Virginia regiment, or Lt. Col. George Washington. He had heard the Barclays speak of Washington several times, but they had not mentioned he was only twenty-three years old, or of such an imposing height they would all have to look up at him. That Washington would make a splendid target was Hunter's first thought, but he was favorably impressed.

After questioning Hunter to satisfy himself the scout was familiar with the terrain they would cover, Colonel Fry announced his intention to remain in Alexandria to drill half the regiment, while Washington went on ahead with the rest of the troops. They would take supply wagons and follow the trail paralleling the Potomac River to the Ohio Company's storehouse at Will's Creek. From there, Washington would use pack animals to cross the Alleghenies and reach the fort they believed to be under construction at the junction of the Monongahela and Allegheny rivers.

Not wishing to appear ignorant, Hunter drew Byron aside. "Who is building the fort?" he whispered.

"Capt. William Trent. He's an Indian trader from Pennsylvania. He's in charge of the Ohio Company's post at Redstone Creek. Do you know him?"

"Yes. He's an honest man."

"Governor Dinwiddie agrees, and asked him to gather volunteers to build the fort, but Washington's the one who chose the location. There's an Ensign Ward with Trent, and they should have the fort completed by the time we get there."

Barring interference from the French, Hunter thought to himself. "Your troops can't become lost on the way to Will's Creek. I'm going to go on ahead and meet you there."

"No, you'll stay with us," Byron argued.

So as not to create a scene in front of their superior officers, Hunter waited until the Barclays had been dismissed to repeat his request, but the minute the three of them were alone, he made the reason for his decision clear. "You'll be following the river, so I won't be needed until later," he explained.

"No, that's not true," Byron insisted. "I'll admit our troops are a surly lot and unused to discipline, but that will soon change. By the time we reach the Ohio Valley, they'll have learned how to follow orders. They'll also have learned how greatly we rely on you. But if you leave us now, they'll have no opportunity to observe your skill."

"I don't need anything from them," Hunter reminded him. "They are the ones who need me."

Byron nodded. "Yes, that's certainly true, and while they don't appreciate that fact as yet, we do. I'm asking you to stay with us, but if I have to, I'll make it an order."

Hunter laughed. "I'm not one of your soldiers."

"Perhaps not, but you have given your word that you'll scout for us, and I expect you to keep it."

"You may be the ones to release me from that promise."

Confused, Byron looked toward Elliott before replying. "I know you won't get us lost, so why would we dismiss you?"

Hunter wore his knife in a beaded sheath on his belt. He

rested his palm on the hilt as he spoke. "I demand the same respect as a white man, and because you give it, we have become friends. Some of your troops are not as generous, and it might cost them their lives. Am I worth that risk?"

The seriousness of Hunter's expression conveyed his conviction, and Byron understood the Indian was speaking about conflicts which would be an almost certain eventuality. It was not simply a matter of pride either, for there were men who equated Indian scouts with hunting dogs, and he was no more tolerant of such blatant prejudice than Hunter. "I heard that you put Vernon Avey in his place without having to strike a single blow. I think you'll be able to handle similar problems without bloodshed."

"And if I'm not?"

With that question, Byron had been pushed too far. "What do you expect from me, permission to kill whomever you dislike?"

"No, merely permission to defend myself."

"Every man has that right."

"Even an Indian?"

"Yes!"

Satisfied for the moment, Hunter nodded before turning away, but he intended to pursue their discussion until Byron agreed that taking a white bride was also among an Indian's rights.

Byron waited until he could not be overheard to speak to his brother. "Have we made a mistake?" he asked. "After all, what do we really know about Hunter?"

Elliott was understandably confused by Byron's apparent change of heart. "If you had reservations about his character, we shouldn't have taken him home with us. But except for the fact he didn't bother to excuse himself before leaving the farewell party, he was the perfect guest."

The thought of Hunter dancing with the delightfully demure

Frederick sisters was so amusing, Byron could not help but smile. "That was probably our fault. He was undoubtedly too embarrassed to admit he didn't know any of our dances."

"Even if he had, would the girls have danced with him?"

"Alanna surely wouldn't, but Melissa probably would have. As for Sarah and Robin—" Byron paused a moment and then shook his head. "No, they would have gone home early rather than have danced with an Indian brave."

"Then it's a damn good thing he had sense enough to leave, rather than risk spoiling the party, so I'll not fault him for a lack of manners. Now let's just see he stays with us when he's in camp, and that ought to minimize the danger of anyone offending him." Elliott clapped Byron on the back, and the matter settled, they turned their attention to other duties.

For the first couple of nights after Hunter had left their home, Melissa lay awake until the pale pink rays of dawn filled the sky. It was only then that the burden of her dreadful secret lifted long enough for her to sleep, but her tortured soul filled her dreams with taunting memories of a dark-eyed man whose kisses were divine, and she awoke as exhausted as when she had gone to bed. She had successfully pretended to be in good spirits for her family's benefit, but on Sunday morning, the prospect of attending church and attempting to fool the whole town was too much for her. She complained of a severe headache and remained in bed while her parents and Alanna went into Williamsburg. She could hear the servants moving around downstairs, making the preparations for Sunday dinner, but while the familiar sound of their voices should have been reassuring, it was not.

Melissa drew in a deep breath and exhaled with a sob. If only she could sleep, she knew she would be much better able to cope. Brandy had helped one night, but she dared not rely on

it. Not only would her father notice it was disappearing too fast,
she knew men had nothing but contempt for women who drank.
There were men who frequently got so drunk at the Raleigh
Tavern they could not sit their horses to ride home, and no one
thought less of them, but should a woman ever become tipsy, it
was a cause of endless gossip and shame. She had trouble
enough without inviting the kind brandy could bring.

Her mother had brought her a cup of camomile tea before
leaving for church, and although it had grown cold, Melissa
sipped it slowly. She did not really have a headache, so it did
not matter what she took to cure it, but she knew she could
not continue to live indefinitely in such a miserable state. It
was a great pity she hadn't felt well enough to attend church,
because Ian Scott was usually there, and she did so want to
see him. Just the thought of his charming smile brought a tear
to her eye, and she had to set her teacup aside. She lay down
and tried to think only of Ian, for his sweet teasing had always
amused her. She would never need him more.

At Melissa's urging, Alanna wore another of her cousin's
stylish gowns to church, and while she made a sincere effort
not to glance in Randolph O'Neil's direction during the service, she nevertheless found herself doing just that. Each time
their eyes met he would nod and smile, while she would blush
and force her attention back to her prayer book. Merely curious, she had not meant to encourage him, but at the end of
the service, when everyone gathered in front of the church to
talk before going home, he hurried to her side.

"Good morning, Miss Barclay," he began in an enthusiastic
rush. "I don't recall your ever being as beautiful as you are
today."

Uncertain whether or not that was a compliment, Alanna
hesitated a moment too long before replying. "Thank you."

Her delay made Randolph realize his remark had been ambiguous, if not just plain stupid, and he hastened to apologize. "Not that you don't always look pretty, of course, you do, but usually, well, I guess what I mean is your gown is especially attractive today. Pink is a very becoming color."

Melissa had been right, Alanna noted, for not only was Randolph O'Neil a nice man, his eyes were a vivid blue. Had he been closer to her age, she would have thought him handsome, but all she saw was a dear man who was old enough to be her father, and that precluded any romantic possibilities, had she wanted them, which she didn't. She liked him though, and it showed in her smile.

"I'm afraid I've neglected my wardrobe the last few years. This is Melissa's gown, and I'll tell her how much you liked it. I'm hoping to have some new gowns made soon, and I'll remember that you said I looked nice in pink."

Completely captivated by Alanna's quiet charm, Randolph strove to make an intelligent reply, but John Barclay spoke to him first and when he turned to respond, Ian Scott and Graham Tyler came forward to talk with Alanna. He had to step back to make room for them, and his opportunity to impress her was lost. Alanna had a maturity that appealed to him, and determined to get to know her better, he concentrated his efforts on strengthening his friendship with John and Rachel.

"Why didn't Melissa come to church?" Ian asked.

By comparison, Ian's greeting made Randolph's clumsy compliment appear devoted, and while Alanna could see by the Englishman's expression how worried he was, she could not excuse his rudeness. "I'm very well, thank you, and how are you?" she replied.

Flustered for an instant, Ian quickly recovered. "Good morning, Alanna. I didn't mean to ignore you, but when I saw you and not Melissa, I couldn't help but be concerned. Is she ill?"

Rather than speculate on the cause of the continued distress

Alanna had watched Melissa hide from others, she provided Ian with a concise report, and then added a suggestion. "I'm sure she'll feel better by this afternoon, should you wish to call on her."

"Do you really think so?"

"Yes, I do." Graham Tyler had been staring at her throughout that exchange, and she had not meant to exclude him. "Good morning, Lieutenant."

"Good morning, Miss Barclay," Graham greeted her, his grin wide. "You were so lovely in blue the other evening, but now I think pink is truly your color. Perhaps pastels flatter all blondes, but—"

Alanna attempted to feign interest as Graham continued to describe her as a fair beauty. He was attractive, and his gray eyes sparkled with admiration as he spoke, but she simply did not care to hear what he had to say. Although Randolph O'Neil was speaking with her uncle, he was still looking her way, and she began to regret letting Melissa talk her into having new gowns made. Not that she wished to embarrass her aunt and uncle with her old clothes, if truly she had, but if new gowns brought more unwanted attentions, then why should she buy them?

Her aunt and uncle had a great many friends, and it seemed as though each and every one wished to speak with them that morning, giving Graham an extended opportunity to talk with Alanna. His discussion of ladies' fashions reminded him of his three sisters, each of whom had her own interests, which ranged from playing the harp, and raising ponies, to painting watercolor seascapes. They sounded as though they might actually be delightful young women, but Graham described them in such minute detail, Alanna was again bored witless rather than entertained. When finally her uncle announced it was time to leave for home, she bid Graham goodbye in mid-sentence and hurried to their carriage.

As soon as Alanna arrived home, she traded Melissa's gown

for one of her own. When new, the fabric had been a deep rose hue, but now it was faded to a soft shell pink. Comfortably worn, it required neither hoop nor an extravagant number of petticoats, and she wished she had worn it to church rather than a satin gown. Melissa was still in bed, and Alanna encouraged her to rise.

"Ian was disappointed not to see you at church. I think he may come by this afternoon. Of course, if you're still in bed, your mother won't allow him to come upstairs to see you."

Melissa threw back the covers. "Well, why didn't you say so?"

"I just did."

"I mean sooner, the instant you came through the door." Melissa raised her hands to her hair, felt the wild disarray of her sleep-tossed curls, sat down at her dressing table, and quickly went to work with her hairbrush. "Was he invited to dinner?"

"No, there will just be the four of us." Thank God, Alanna thought. She didn't remember Randolph O'Neil ever coming there to dine, but he had spoken with her aunt and uncle for so long, she would not have been surprised had he been invited that day. She walked up behind Melissa.

"You were right about Mr. O'Neil. He does like me more than I had realized. Is there a polite way to discourage a man's attentions that won't offend him?"

Melissa shot her cousin an exasperated glance in the mirror. "The man is absolutely perfect for you. Why would you want to discourage him?"

"I realize women usually wed men several years older than themselves, but—"

"Father is a dozen years older than Mother."

"Yes, I know, but even if Randolph were only twelve years older than me, I still wouldn't be interested in him."

"Whom do you like best, Randolph or Graham?"

"Randolph."

"Then you do like him," Melissa teased.

"Yes, I like him, but not the way you like Ian. As for Graham, I didn't think he had left any subject uncovered at the party, but this morning he told me more about his sisters than I will ever need to know."

Melissa leaned closer to the mirror to study her reflection. Despite her indiscretion, her prettiness was undimmed and reassured, she made Alanna a promise. "When Ian arrives, I'll invite him to stroll through the garden, and I'll make it plain to him that you'd rather not see Graham again. He might be with Ian today, but since this will be the last time, you can be nice to him, can't you?"

"I'd sooner throw myself into the river and drown."

When Melissa had contemplated just such a dire fate, she had been serious, and she did not find Alanna's comment in the least bit amusing. "Jokes about suicide are in extremely poor taste, Alanna. Don't make another."

Because they were so close in age, Melissa seldom spoke down to her, and predictably, Alanna rebelled. She left their room and went downstairs to ask her aunt's advice on how a young lady might tactfully rid herself of a boring admirer.

To Alanna's delight, Ian came calling alone that afternoon, and she went down by the river to read a favorite book while Melissa entertained the British officer. After daydreaming about Ian all morning, Melissa had been so thrilled to see him she had almost wept. As soon as they left the parlor to take a stroll in the garden, she reached for his hand.

"I'm so happy you came to see me today. We had such a wonderful time the other night, and I had hoped that you'd come to call on me again soon."

Ian was accustomed to Melissa's every gesture being flirtatious, but there was something else in her manner that day. Had he not known her better, he would have thought it desperation, but in the case of such a popular young woman, he discounted the possibility as absurd. As they entered a long row of azaleas, he pulled her around to face him and reached out to touch her forehead lightly.

"You don't feel feverish," he exclaimed. "To what do I owe this sudden enthusiasm for my company?"

Well aware of how thin a line existed between appealing femininity and a pathetic demand for attention, Melissa played her part with stunning success. She glanced down shyly, and then stared up at Ian through the dark veil of her lashes. It was one of her most irresistible poses and, predictably, Ian's expression instantly turned adoring.

"Is it wrong of me to admit how much I've missed you?" she asked.

"Certainly not, but—"

Melissa placed a fingertip on his lips. "No, don't say it," she whispered. "If you can't return my affection, just go, you needn't embarrass us both by putting your rejection into words."

Ian could scarcely believe his ears. Having been invited to Melissa's home, he was the envy of every man he knew, but he had been Byron and Elliott's friend first, not hers. He knew that she found him amusing, but he had never thought anything serious would come of their flirtation, when she could have her pick of Virginia's wealthy men. But if she had fallen for him—which he dared not hope—he would never refuse her love.

Watching her closely, he raised her hand from his lips and placed a kiss in her palm. When her eyes began to fill with tears, he felt he had his answer. There was an old oak tree not ten feet away, and he led her around to the far side, where they couldn't be observed from the house. He doubted her parents were spying on them, but he did not want to take the chance of being banished from their property either. He knew he ought to recite some bit of romantic poetry, but all he truly wanted to do was kiss her, and when she came into his arms without the slightest hesitation, he did.

Ian's first tentative kiss was warm and tender, but Hunter had taught Melissa the thrill of passion, and she was no longer satisfied with such a sweet gesture of devotion. She raised her arms to encircle his neck, relaxed against him, and then ran the tip of her tongue over his lower lip, seductively coaxing him into abandoning all sense of reserve. She wasn't merely acting, for she did truly care for him, and her affection was sincere.

Never guessing the enchantress in his arms had been tutored by a savage, Ian opened his mouth to slide his tongue over hers and, hungry for the taste of her, kissed her with the wild abandon she had so skillfully inspired. Lost in desire, he stood balanced against the gnarled old tree, so captivated by the woman he adored, that not a single thought of her purpose entered his mind. He noticed only the tantalizing fragrance of her perfume, the silken softness of her skin, and the delicious taste of her kiss.

Melissa, however, was all too aware of the warmth of the day, the shrill cry of a mockingbird overhead, and the roughness of Ian's red coat. She had not been aware of a single such distraction when Hunter had kissed her, but while Ian's kiss was definitely pleasant, it was not nearly as exciting as the Indian's had been. She thought perhaps with practice they would reach the thrilling accord she had found at Hunter's first touch, but when Ian paused to catch his breath after more than a dozen kisses, she felt just as detached as during the first.

The hint of tears still glistened in Melissa's eyes, and believing she had somehow misunderstood him, Ian pressed her cheek close to his chest as he spoke. "I'm not nearly good enough for you. You know that, don't you?"

She was standing in a British officer's arms, but failing miserably to forget a forbidden romance with an Indian, and Melissa knew she wasn't nearly good enough for Ian. He saw only the attractive young woman he had admired, but inside she felt far from worthy of his love. She slid her arms around his waist and held on tight. She knew she could fool him, forever if need be. The question was, why had she ever thought she could fool herself?

"Melissa?"

"Hm?"

Ian gave her another joyous hug. "Have I spoken too soon?"

To Melissa's way of thinking, he had not spoken soon enough to save her from a lifetime of shame. There was always the river, but death frightened her far more than living a lie. She couldn't speak, but when she looked up at Ian, he bent down to kiss her again, and not expecting more than the sweet sensation she had felt before, she was no longer disappointed. She felt safe with Ian. She knew she could depend on him, and he would never betray her trust. The next time he drew away, she found it easy to smile.

"Was I unforgivably bold?" she asked.

"Not at all. Was I?"

Melissa reached up on her tiptoes to kiss him. "No, but I think we ought to continue our walk."

She tried to slip out of his arms, but Ian refused to release her. "Wait a minute," he scolded. "I realize I've gone about this all wrong, but if the love that flavors your kiss is real, shouldn't I ask for your father's permission to marry you? If he's going to refuse me—which he well might—I'd rather he did so today, before leaving you becomes impossible."

Melissa had not expected to prompt a proposal from Ian so soon, and while she was grateful for it, she wasn't ready to involve her parents as yet. "I'm positive my father likes you, but we haven't known each other long, and I don't want him to object to you for that reason. Let's give him a few more weeks to appreciate what a fine man you are, and then when you approach him, there will be no danger that you'll be refused."

"And if he gives his permission, is there any danger you'll refuse me?"

While Melissa dared not admit what thoughtful consideration she had given the question, Ian was her first choice, and she wanted him to know it. "If I give you my answer now, will you become so insufferably conceited that I'll wish I'd kept you guessing?"

Charmed as always, Ian began to laugh. "You know me very well, don't you?"

"I should hope so," Melissa replied with mock seriousness. "It's not every man I kiss as passionately as I did you." That in truth, his affection had left her emotions untouched, was something she would never admit. She liked him enormously, and surely her feelings would soon deepen into love. "Let's go down by the river. The view's very beautiful, and there are several secluded spots were we might stop and talk without fear of interruption."

Ian caught her hand and let her lead the way. "Yes, we really do have a great deal to discuss, don't we? I had hoped only to see you this afternoon. I'm really not prepared to present a plan for the rest of our lives."

"Must we be so serious? Can't we simply enjoy the beauty of the day, and the fun of being together?"

Relieved, Ian was quick to agree. "Whatever you like, my darling."

Melissa gave his hand a squeeze, but his skin didn't tingle beneath her touch the way Hunter's had. That was another disappointment she shoved aside and hid with a smile. Ian had such a warm and appealing personality, she wanted to love him so badly, she was positive she would in time. As they neared the dock, she saw Alanna seated close by and finally remembered her promise.

"Graham Tyler appears to be quite taken with Alanna, but he simply overwhelms her with endless conversation. Do you suppose he might change, if you mentioned her preference for more introspective men?"

Recalling how easily Alanna had put him in his place after church, Ian shook his head. "Alanna ought to make that point herself. It would only be meddling if such a suggestion came from me. Stuart doesn't say more than three words a day, but I didn't see her giving him much encouragement at the party."

"No, they didn't take to each other either. Do you know someone else, another officer Alanna might like as much as I like you?"

"I've no idea what your cousin would like, but you've met everyone at one time or another at church, and so has she. She can make her own choice. You needn't be so concerned about Alanna. She's shy, but very pretty, and I'm certain she'll find someone to love before long."

Knowing Alanna's reluctance to encourage suitors, Melissa did not share Ian's optimism. Fearing he was becoming cross with her, she chose a shaded path where her lavish kisses soon distracted him so completely, he could not even recall a mention of Alanna, much less Melissa's desire to find her a beau.

Six

In a rare lazy mood, Hunter lay back in a thickly cushioned bed of bluegrass, and gazed up at the clouds slowly skimming by. Predictably, George Washington's portion of the Virginia regiment was making steady progress along the trail to Will's Creek, and the scout's days had been as uneventful as he'd feared. Understanding his restlessness, Byron and Elliott had dropped their insistence that he trudge along with their men during the day, and allowed him to roam free, as long as he ate his meals in camp and slept there at night. He had begun hunting to supplement their rations with fresh meat, but that took only a few hours each morning, leaving him long afternoons to fill on his own.

While no one expected to encounter French troops this near the coast, it was always a possibility, and Hunter went out each dawn to make certain the day's march would not end in an ambush. So far, he had found no sign of an imminent threat, but that morning he had seen a wolf, his clan symbol. Sighting a wolf might mean nothing, since the forest was their home, but this one had been larger than most. His behavior had also been peculiar, for rather than fleeing when Hunter had come over a ridge and startled him, he had remained motionless for several seconds.

They had stared at each other, feral yellow eyes locked with calm brown, until the wolf had lifted his head as if responding to an unheard cry, and loped away into the pines. If the wolf's presence on the trail were mere coincidence, then it meant nothing, but if it had been a warning, Hunter knew he would be wise to adopt a far more cautious attitude. He closed his eyes to recapture the brief scene in his memory, and envisioned it with astonishing clarity.

The wolf had not simply possessed a greater size than most, his glossy gray coat had retained its winter thickness into the spring, and his fangs had been wickedly sharp. There had been no fear in his gaze, but instead, a light that signaled recognition. Extraordinary in every way, Hunter now believed the wolf had to have been a messenger, bringing a warning he'd be a fool to ignore.

Sitting up, he scanned the surrounding valley for some sign of trouble, but it was as peaceful a place as any he had ever seen. The gentle breeze was fragrant with spring blossoms, and sweetened by the song of the meadow lark. Lulled by such tranquil beauty, Hunter again stretched out on the grass. He had been warned, but whatever danger lay ahead would not come that day.

His thoughts strayed to Melissa, but shimmering with reflected light her image danced in his mind and refused to come clear. That bothered him badly, for he wanted to recall the passion they'd shared in all its splendor. He could remember the bright sparkle of her blue eyes, the softness of her blond hair, and the delicacy of her touch, but he could not picture the sweetness of her expression as she had reached up to kiss him.

Blaming that failure on the fact that his most stirring memories of her were lit by moonlight, Hunter was annoyed rather than worried, but he hoped by the next time they parted, Melissa's image would fill his mind as surely as her love filled his heart.

* * *

Alanna turned slowly as Sally Lester fitted the waist on the first of her new gowns. Melissa might have shamed her into wearing prettier clothes, but she was far from happy about it. She told herself that at least the skirts would be of a fashionable length appropriate for her height, but she dreaded the thought of drawing attention to herself. It was Melissa who sought the constant thrill of admiring glances, not her.

She had been complimented when wearing blue and pink, but the fabric of this gown was a glossy white printed with such charming bouquets of violets, she could almost smell their delicate perfume. The moment she had seen the striking floral material on the bolt, she had reached out to touch it; delighted that something in the dressmaker's shop appealed to her, Melissa had encouraged her to buy it. Now that the dress was ready for the final fitting, Alanna thought it so exceptionally pretty, she doubted she would ever want to wear anything else.

"You ought to have lavender slippers to wear with this gown," Sally advised, "and keep it scented with lavender sachet."

"We'll buy some lavender perfume this very day," Melissa enthused. "You never wear perfume, Alanna, and it adds so much to a woman's appeal."

First new clothes, and now perfume? "You sound like you're baiting a trap," Alanna replied.

Both Sally Lester and Melissa laughed, but clearly they agreed it was a woman's natural right to capture the attention of an attractive man by whatever means she chose.

Alanna ignored them for the moment and stroked the folds of her skirt with a reverent touch. This was the first time she could recall being excited about having a new dress. Her aunt and uncle had always been generous, but she had never shared Melissa's fascination with clothes, and couldn't remember any particular favorites. It was the floral print she liked so much about this gown, for the violets held a shy sweetness that touched her heart.

"What about the yellow gown?" Melissa asked. "Will you have that one finished by next week, too?"

"Yes, Miss Melissa, I surely will."

"Good, then Alanna will have no excuse to miss any of the fun of the Publick Times."

Alanna made a face at her cousin. Twice a year, in April and October, Williamsburg was the site of fairs, races, and fabulous parties to mark the convening of the General Assembly and courts. The inns were filled with men from distant plantations, while their women boarded with friends, and the entertainment provided for them was continuous. Alanna enjoyed the fairs and watching the auctions in Market Square, but the prospect of having to attend parties or—God forbid—the ball at the Governor's Palace, was more than she could bear.

"I've always gone to the fairs and auctions," she reminded Melissa.

"Yes, I know you have, but that's not what I meant. This year you're old enough to go with us to the more lavish parties, and I'm going to insist you attend the governor's ball."

"I should have gone with Byron and Elliott," Alanna sighed sadly. "I'd much rather fight the French, than pretend I enjoy dancing."

Sally Lester assumed Alanna was teasing and began to giggle. "You can't mean that, Miss Alanna. The yellow satin gown will be perfect for the ball. You and Miss Melissa will be the prettiest girls there."

Alanna watched Melissa's smile widen into a triumphant smirk, and knew her cousin would talk her mother into insisting she attend whatever function the family chose to enjoy. Uncle John was a member of the Assembly, and always received more invitations than he could accept, but he had never insisted that she go along. Perhaps at seventeen she was too old to be left at home, but she wished she had been given more than a week to get used to the idea.

"Do you make more beautiful gowns for us than you do for your other customers, Mrs. Lester?" Alanna asked.

"All my gowns are equally lovely," Sally claimed. "But unfortunately, not all of Williamsburg's womenfolk are as beautiful as you and Melissa."

Alanna was used to everyone referring to Melissa as a beauty, but doubted that she deserved equal praise. Glancing toward the dressmaker's mirror, she saw a pair of green eyes that were too large for her face, a nose that was passably cute, and lips that formed only a hesitant smile. That certainly didn't add up to beauty in her mind. She and Melissa bore a slight resemblance, it was true, but her cousin's features were usually animated by radiant smiles, and Alanna never felt any such joy. Sally Lester was merely being kind, she decided, and it was a relief rather than a disappointment.

As the two young women left the dressmaker's, they found Randolph O'Neil walking their way. Alanna would have darted into the shop next door, but it was apparent he had already seen them, and he didn't deserve to be treated rudely. Melissa gave Alanna a playful nudge in the ribs, but had no time to tease her before he greeted them.

"Good morning!" he called out when he was still several feet away. "Please tell your mother that I have just received some crystal vases I think she might like. I hope that you'll have time to come in and have a look at them while you're in town."

He had addressed his remark to Melissa, but he was looking at Alanna, and she could not help but blush. Randolph O'Neil sold elegant imported merchandise and jewelry, and Rachel Barclay was one of his best customers. On her infrequent visits to town, Alanna had always enjoyed browsing through his shop, but that had been before he had taken special notice of her. Now, she would have avoided his place of business so as not to encourage the interest she couldn't return. Melissa, however, felt differently.

"We have a few other stops, and then we'll be there," Melissa promised with the sparkling smile she used on all men, and satisfied he would see them again soon, Randolph continued on his way.

Melissa turned to watch him. "I swear that man becomes better-looking each time I see him. I'll bet he's only forty-two or three. I still think he's perfect for you, and if you're nice to him, he's sure to give us better prices."

"And what will he expect in return?" Alanna questioned hoarsely.

Melissa eyed Alanna with an incredulous glance. "He can expect whatever he wishes, Alanna, but you don't ever have to respond with more than a polite word and a smile." Melissa had always given Alanna the benefit of her advice, but she no longer felt like much of an expert in romance. She had hoped for a chance meeting with Ian that morning, but she hadn't seen any British officers on the street. Fatigued from lack of sleep, she raised her hand to cover a yawn, then made light of it.

"The warmth of the day is making me sleepy. Let's hurry up with our errands, so we'll have time to visit with Mr. O'Neil before we go home."

Alanna didn't argue, but she had already made up her mind to be honest with Randolph and, should the opportunity arise, she'd tell him he would never be more than a friend. Unfortunately, the chance did not present itself. He welcomed them cordially to his shop, but confined his remarks to the exquisite wares he had on display. Other than referring to her Aunt Rachel's tastes while showing off the crystal vases, he didn't make any comments of a personal nature, prompting Alanna to wonder if perhaps she hadn't just imagined him being especially attentive after church.

She then grew all the more self-conscious, and when Randolph walked them to the door, she found it difficult to look up at him as she said goodbye. His smile was warm rather than overly eager, convincing her that she had allowed Melissa's imaginative interpretation of his interest in her to influence her opinion of him. They had brought a small wagon and she hurried toward it, climbed in, and might have started for home without Melissa, had her cousin not called out to insist she wait.

"I'm sorry," Alanna exclaimed, "but romantic intrigues are simply too much for me. When we come back to Sally's, I'm going to park the wagon by the back door, so I can slip in and out without anyone else knowing I've come into town."

"You are such a silly goose," Melissa chided. "Both you and Randolph are so painfully shy, I doubt anything will ever come of your friendship."

"Good."

Melissa watched Alanna slap the reins on the horse's rump to speed his pace, and wondered as she frequently did, how they could have such differing attitudes when they were blood relatives. In the next instant, she envied her cousin, for Alanna would never have become involved with an Indian brave—or any man for that matter—with the disgraceful haste she'd displayed. She closed her eyes briefly and repeated a silent prayer for divine protection from future indiscretion.

"I do hope Byron and Elliott are all right," she then remarked. "They're scarcely backwoodsmen, like the men with Captain Trent."

Alanna was ashamed of how little thought she had given to her absent cousins. "Maybe they've never skinned a bear, but they know how to ride and shoot. I'm sure they're fine officers, too."

"Yes, they must be."

The next time Alanna glanced toward Melissa, she was asleep. That was such an unusual occurrence she didn't know what to make of it. Melissa had always had boundless amounts of energy, and even after long evenings required no more than a brief nap the next day. They hadn't been up late the previous evening though, so she couldn't understand why Melissa was so tired. Perhaps she wasn't sleeping well, but she hadn't complained after that one night of tears. If anything, she had been almost too cheerful, displaying what appeared to be a forced gaiety at times.

When they reached the gate at the end of the lane leading to their home, Alanna gave Melissa's shoulder a gentle shake. "Wake up, we're home."

Startled, Melissa's eyes flew open, and she quickly straightened up. She barely recalled leaving Williamsburg, so she knew she had slept all the way home. "I'm sorry. I wasn't very good company for you, was I?" she asked.

She and Melissa spent most of their time together, but Alanna knew neither of them confided wholly in the other. Their personalities were simply too different for them to ever be as close as some sisters or best friends were. Melissa might be overly concerned with impressing others, but Alanna knew she could draw an equal amount of criticism for being too distant, so neither of them was perfect.

"Is something wrong?" Alanna asked. "I know you're concerned about your brothers, but if you've another problem, with Ian perhaps, or someone else, I could at least listen, even if I might not be able to provide any helpful advice."

Alanna's expression reflected not only a compassion which invited such a confidence, but also an innocent sweetness that made confiding in her impossible. How could Melissa ever admit what she had done, when the enjoyment of a man's affection was so completely out of Alanna's realm of experience? Melissa ground her fingernails into her palms to force back her tears.

"I haven't been sleeping well, but I think it's just a combination of the boys leaving, Ian's attentions, and the excitement of the upcoming Publick Times. Now let me get the gate."

Melissa hopped down from the wagon before Alanna could question her response, but she feared she was going to have to be much more careful. Alanna could sense the distress she hid from her parents' eyes, so she would have to bury her secret even deeper. Perhaps Ian would come to see her that evening, and with his laughter reflected in her eyes, no one would perceive her pain.

When they reached Will's Creek, Hunter was astonished to find William Trent in residence, but the captain had left forty men with Ensign Ward, and had complete confidence in their ability to construct the fort on their own. In Hunter's opinion, forty men might be sufficient to build a fort, but it certainly wouldn't be enough to defend it. The French had thousands of soldiers in Canada, and if they chose to invade the Ohio Valley, Hunter knew one small fort would cost them no more than a few minutes' delay.

Because no one turned him away, he had stayed close as the officers discussed their plans, but when none expressed any fear of the French, he again thought they had a feeble grasp of the situation. With his sighting of the wolf still in mind, he was about to say so, when Washington announced he intended to move his reinforcements to the new fort with all possible haste. Hunter relaxed then. At Governor Dinwiddie's behest, Washington had gone to Fort Le Boeuf near Lake Erie in December, to insist the French remove themselves from territories belonging to the king of Great Britain, and it was apparent he understood that the threat posed by the French was very real indeed.

His initial impression of the intelligence of the young lieutenant colonel confirmed, Hunter went to bed eagerly anticipating the next part of their journey. From Will's Creek, it was one hundred forty miles to the new fort. They would be traveling through dense forest now, and crossing two mountain ranges, innumerable hills, and fording fast-moving streams. It would not be an easy trip, but this was the exciting kind of traveling Hunter relished, where a man had to rely on all his skills to survive.

The next morning plans were still being made, and the troops were taking a much needed rest, but Hunter wasn't tired and left camp early to scout the trail. He had not gone far when he heard someone moving up fast behind him. Not wanting company, he stepped into the trees to let them pass. When Vernon Avey and his two cronies trotted by, Hunter was tempted to laugh out loud. They had no reason to enter the forest, but if they were tracking him, they would soon turn back, and he remained hidden to see what they would do.

Vernon was positive the scout hadn't left camp more than three minutes ahead of them, but when they reached a long level stretch and there was no sign of the Indian on the trail ahead, he stopped abruptly. "The devil's vanished," he announced in disgust.

"Maybe he took another path," Hank suggested.

Vernon cuffed him hard. "Fool! There ain't no other path."

"Then he must be traveling much faster than we are," Willis argued. "Come on, let's hurry."

"I'll decide what we'll do!" Vernon didn't waste a second, however, before continuing on down the trail at a near-run. Hank and Willis exchanged a knowing glance before following, and the three men traversed another hundred yards before giving up their pursuit.

"He must have left the trail to hunt," Vernon finally surmised. "We'll have to jump him in camp. After dark there won't be no witnesses, and we can say he came after us."

"Who'd believe that?" Hank asked, and this time he was smart enough to duck out of Vernon's way before he got hit.

"Everyone will believe it!" Vernon insisted. "The word of

three white men will be taken over an Indian's, and with any luck, there won't be enough left of the bastard to talk."

Hank and Willis pondered that possibility a moment, and agreed. "Sure. Whatever we say will be believed, but we ought to get our stories straight first, just to make certain we're convincing," Willis suggested.

Vernon herded them back along the trail as he continued to plan. "We'll say he wasn't watching where he was going, and plowed right into us. We backed off, but he came at us again. All we was doing was defending ourselves."

Hunter waited until the three soldiers were within ten feet of him to step out into the path. Startled, they slammed into each other. Tripping over Willis's feet, Hank would have fallen had Vernon not caught him by the scruff of the neck. They had left their muskets in camp, so Hunter wasn't worried about getting shot, but if they wanted a fight, he was ready.

"Did Washington decide I need help to scout?" he asked. "Or are you three just lost?"

Vernon had first planned to overtake Hunter in the woods and beat him senseless before the Indian knew who had hit him, but standing face-to-face with the brave, he lacked the courage to carry out his underhanded plot. He still loathed him though, and tried to make Hunter start the fight he was aching to have. He moved a step ahead of his friends.

"We was looking for you," he said.

"Why?"

"We don't like Indians who think they're better than us!"

Hunter eyed Vernon coldly. This was the first time anyone had come after him after he had put them in their place, but Hunter wasn't surprised that Vernon hadn't learned his lesson in one session. "Can you name a man who doesn't?" he asked.

Outraged by that sarcastic taunt, Vernon nearly strangled on a snarl, but it was Willis who carried him forward as he lunged for Hunter. With the finesse of a matador, the Indian stepped aside, and both Willis and Vernon landed facedown on the dusty trail. Cursing each other they struggled to get up, and when they succeeded, they found Hunter observing them with an amused smile.

"I'm going to kill you!" Vernon shrieked.

"No, you can only try." Hunter appeared relaxed, but he had shifted his weight forward to the balls of his feet, and was ready to block any punch Vernon might throw. He had learned how to fight with his fists at William Johnson's trading post, and he had never been beaten. "There isn't room here on the path. Let's go back to camp and settle our differences there."

Camp was the last place Vernon wished to go. "There's plenty of room for what I want to do to you!"

Hunter motioned for Vernon to come forward. "Show me you can do more than talk."

It was the cool disdain the Indian displayed that sent Vernon into a blind fury. He threw himself at Hunter, and again found his target shifting, while he was in midair. He put out his hands, but still landed so hard he knocked the wind out of himself. He lay gasping on the path and wondering how the Indian had managed to elude him again.

"Coward!" he gasped.

"I'm not the one crawling in the dirt," Hunter pointed out. He nodded toward Willis and Hank. "Carry your friend back to camp, and I'll fight all three of you there." With that he turned his back on them and walked away with a long, confident stride. He had yet to meet a white man who could throw a knife with sufficient accuracy to stab him in the back, so that possibility didn't alarm him. His hearing was as acute as his eyesight, and while he appeared to have forgotten them, he was listening to their every move.

Hank was on the verge of tears. "Get up! Get up!" he cried. Terrified he would have to fight Hunter alone, he yanked on the back of Vernon's shirt.

Willis was too angry to care what happened to Vernon. He'd gone along with him when they were going to jump Hunter together, but he sure as hell didn't want to fight the savage alone. Of the three of them, he might be the tallest and have the longest reach, but that didn't mean he was much of a fighter.

"I never should have let you talk me into this," Willis decried. He stepped over Vernon and started back down the trail toward camp. "Hey, Indian!" he called out.

Hunter glanced over his shoulder.

"I've got no quarrel with you," Willis assured him. "The fight's off, you understand?"

"But why? I'll have to fight three men, and you only one."

Willis shook his head sadly and kept right on walking. "Two men, count me out."

Hunter doubted that he would have to fight anyone. Vernon was right where he had left him, finally on his feet, and simultaneously brushing off his clothes and pushing Hank's hands away. They presented a comical sight, but Hunter didn't discount the danger of anyone that filled with hatred. He now knew Vernon would sneak and hide, hoping to strike back at him from ambush, rather than approaching him directly. If they did fight the French, he was going to make certain he knew where Vernon was, to avoid being shot in the back.

"Hurry up, Vernon," he called to him. "I want this fight over by noon."

A knot of fear-laced anger choked off any response Vernon might have wished to make, and shoving back the last of Hank's attentions he started off down the trail, his fists clenched and his shoulders hunched, as though he were heading into a fierce wind. Muttering curses under his breath to inspire courage, he attempted to convince himself he actually had a chance to beat Hunter in a fair fight.

Willis was the first to emerge from the trail. As he entered the camp, he turned and began to walk backwards, so as not to miss a second of the excitement he was sure was coming. Other soldiers took note, and came forward to surround him. "There's gonna be a fight," he announced with a near-hysteria that some mistook for pride.

Hunter had no sooner set foot in the camp, when men began to shout out their bets. That brought Elliott over, but Hunter had no intention of allowing him to stop what he hoped would be his last confrontation with Vernon. Vernon arrived then, with Hank trailing several paces behind.

"Stay out of this," Hunter asked.

Elliott had already caught the gist of what was about to occur, but he hadn't decided what ought to be done. A lieutenant with minimal military training, he knew the men weren't supposed to fight amongst themselves, but they appeared to be so eager for the contest, he wondered if he ought not to allow it. He was no more impressed with Vernon than Hunter was. In his view Vernon was a bully, who could use a good whipping. When he looked at it that way, the fight seemed like a damned good idea.

"Clear a space!" he shouted, and the troops immediately moved back to form an irregular ring. The men who'd been cleaning their muskets, or were otherwise occupied, came forward now and crowded in behind the first men on the scene. Soon the entire camp was straining to see who would win. That one of the participants was a bully no one admired, and the other an Indian brave whom no one really knew, didn't hamper the crowd's enthusiasm in the slightest. The bloodier the fight, the better, was their only view.

Hunter removed the quiver and bow he'd had slung across his back, then peeled off his buckskin shirt, and tossed it aside. He heard appreciative murmurs for his well-muscled torso, and nothing but snickers when Vernon removed his coat and shirt. His body was pudgy rather than lean and fit, and while his face, neck, and hands were tan, the skin of his chest and back was as pale as a fish's belly. Hunter shook his head, certain this wasn't going to be much of a fight.

Such blatant disrespect wasn't lost on Vernon, and again abandoning his strategy in favor of a furious rage, he came for Hunter with his hands outstretched, clearly going for his throat. Hunter stood his ground until the last second. He then stepped aside and brought the heel of his hand down on Vernon's left forearm in a brutal blow that shattered both bones with such a sickening *crack,* it instantly silenced the crowd's cheers.

Vernon slid to a stop, looked down at the unnatural bend in his arm, and let out a pathetic wail. He sank to his knees, cradled his broken arm against his chest, and began to sob. Embarrassed by such an unmanly display, the crowd dispersed into a dozen smaller groups, where the men who had bet on Hunter collected their winnings, while those who had backed Vernon, muttered in disgust.

Hunter picked up his shirt, pulled it on, and slung his quiver and bow over his shoulder. He then turned to Elliott. "He ought to have a splint on his arm."

The fight had been over so quickly, Elliott wasn't certain what he'd seen, but it was clear Vernon was in a bad way. "I shouldn't have let you fight him," he bemoaned aloud. "I didn't realize what you'd do."

Hunter shrugged. "I would have fought him with my fists, but he wanted to throttle me."

Afraid he'd be criticized for allowing the fight, Elliott glanced around anxiously, but all he saw reflected in his troops' faces was admiration for Hunter. Then he noticed his brother, William Trent, and George Washington. They were chuckling amongst themselves, so he knew they'd seen the fight and weren't outraged by the result. He breathed a sigh of relief and then shouted for a couple of men to carry Vernon into the storehouse, where he'd receive what medical attention they could provide. Then he confided in Hunter.

"I doubt you'll hear so much as a cross word after this, but please—don't let it happen again."

"It was a fair fight."

"Not really, not when you were so much better than Vernon."

"He was the one who issued the challenge," Hunter informed him. "He followed me into the woods with Hank and Willis. They didn't mean for me to come out."

"What?"

"You heard me." Hunter stared at his friend.

"I'll court-martial them."

Hunter knew Willis regretted his association with Vernon, and Hank had abandoned him when he'd been injured. He was positive it wasn't their plan anyway. "Willis and Hank don't matter, and Vernon's in enough trouble. Just take care of his arm."

Elliott might have continued to argue, but at that instant his attention was diverted by a disheveled band of men who came streaming out of the woods. Tired and dirty, they shuffled into the clearing, their gait slowed by the burden of defeat. Frontiersmen dressed in buckskins, they were led by Ens. Edward Ward, the British naval officer Captain Trent had entrusted with the building of the fort.

Grateful to have reached Will's Creek, many of the dust-covered men sank to the ground, while the ensign explained how they came to be there to George Washington. For the second time that day, the troops formed a close circle, so as not to miss anything. The ensign had had a one-hundred-forty mile trek on which to practice his report, and physically spent, he gave it with little emotion.

"We were attacked by at least a thousand French troops. They must have had three hundred canoes and sixty *bateaux*. They rolled their cannon up to our stockade, and their com-

mander, the Sieur de Contrecoeur, demanded our surrender."
The outcome of their confrontation obvious, he paused only a
moment. "As soon as we had left, they began tearing down
our fort to construct their own."

A low moan emanated from the troops, for all appreciated
the depth of the disaster Ensign Ward had described. Washington had insisted that a fort placed where the Monongahela
and Allegheny rivers joined to form the Ohio River, was vital
to the defense of the Ohio Valley. That it had fallen to the
French as soon as it was built, meant war with France was
inevitable.

Hunter heard the troops' sorrowful murmur, but it was followed by the howl of a wolf that went unnoticed by the others.
He glanced toward the forest, expecting to see the beast which
had crossed his path, but a squirrel scrambling up a pine tree
was the only animal in sight. He had heard the wolf though,
as clearly as he had seen him. His howl had signaled the coming of war, and death.

Seven

.The ballroom of the Governor's Palace was ablaze with the light of a thousand candles, but so crowded that the dancers frequently toured the adjacent gardens not simply for a breath of fresh air, but to have a chance to breathe at all. Melissa's hand rested lightly on Ian's arm as they strolled down a secluded path, but her mood was agitated in the extreme. Her monthly flow was now six days overdue, and this was the first time she had ever been late.

That she might be pregnant was so abhorrent a thought, she could not bring herself to accept it. Her guilty conscience had caused her to suffer a great deal of distress, and quite naturally her body's delicate rhythm would be affected. That was a plausible excuse for the delay in what had previously been a predictable sequence. That she could not sleep well was undoubtedly a factor also. She had already been nearly exhausted by guilt, and now with this additional worry, she was grateful to have an hour or two of sleep a night.

She followed Ian numbly, unmindful of where he was leading her. He was a fine man, and her admiration for him had continued to grow. He had been her escort at several parties that week, and he had also brought her to the ball. They had not discussed their future as yet, but Melissa was counting on him to provide the safe haven she craved more urgently with each passing hour.

They had left the others far behind, and while they could still hear the music, they had no fear of being seen or overheard. Ian drew Melissa into his arms. "I love you," he whispered.

"I love you, too," Melissa responded easily, but she clung to him with a desperation she could no longer hide. She was badly frightened, and drank in his attentions as though she were dying of loneliness.

She responded to each of his kisses with increasing passion, until he had to take a step back in an effort to restore control to her emotions as well as his own.

Melissa's pretty blush had matched the pale rose satin of her gown while they were dancing, and now, bathed in Ian's affection, she could feel the heat of that charming glow clear to her toes. He was looking down at her with an adoring glance that filled her with hope, and in an instant, she knew precisely what she wanted.

"Let's get married," she begged.

Surprised by her sudden enthusiasm for marriage, Ian cocked his head slightly. "I was willing to ask for your hand two weeks ago, but you asked me to wait. Has your father had enough time to regard me as a serious suitor?"

Actually, her father had no idea her current romance was more serious than any of the others, and when she considered the reason for his view, she was deeply embarrassed by how many frivolous flirtations she had enjoyed. In the last week, both her parents had gone out of their way to see that she renewed her acquaintances with the sons of Virginia's most prominent planters. If she were totally honest with herself, she knew they would prefer her to wed one of them, any one of whom could provide a secure future.

It was not security which concerned her most however, and she was dreadfully afraid she did not have the weeks, or months, it might take to wring a proposal from a man of her parents' choosing. Even if she did receive an unexpectedly prompt proposal, as she had with Ian, the elaborate wedding both families would insist upon planning would still be several months away.

"My father likes you, of course, he does, but I know that he'd prefer me to wed one of his friends' sons. Being around them this past week has put ideas in his head that I really don't want him to have. If you asked for my hand now, he might forbid me to see you again. We dare not take that risk."

"I'll be promoted to captain soon, and that ought to impress him. I could wait until then."

"No!" Melissa threw herself into Ian's arms, and when he enfolded her in a warm embrace, she blurted out what she truly wanted. "I think we should elope tonight."

Stunned by her request, Ian loosened her hold on him and held her at arm's length. He had not the slightest doubt that he loved her, but her suggestion struck him as preposterous. "You can't possibly mean that."

Terrified that he was going to refuse her, Melissa began to cry. "Do you want to see me wed to my father's choice, rather than you?" she sobbed. "Don't you love me at all?"

"Melissa, stop it," Ian scolded softly. "You mustn't cry. Of course, I love you. That's why I want you to have the beautiful wedding you deserve, not some hasty elopement that will set all of Williamsburg gossiping for years. I'm thinking of your reputation, beloved, and you should, too."

Fearing her reputation was already beyond salvaging, Melissa pulled free of his grasp. She was too upset to care that she might be risking his contempt rather than winning consent for an elopement, and she lashed out at him, "You don't love me! You couldn't, or becoming my husband would mean more to you than what some gossiping shrews might say about us." She turned away from him then, and too distraught to return to the ball, she ran on through the darkness toward the trees that formed a natural boundary to the palace grounds.

Ian had not realized Melissa was so high-strung, but he

dared not waste a moment considering the sensitivity of her temperament, when she could so easily become lost or badly hurt, if she stumbled and fell. He raced after her and overtook her in a matter of seconds. Taking care not to trip her, he reached out and grabbed her around the waist to bring her to a halt.

"Let me go!" Melissa wailed.

"Never," Ian swore, and he easily subdued her defiance with a flurry of impassioned kisses.

Taking refuge in his affection, Melissa clung to him and kissed him with such stirring ardor that he longed to grant every request she could ever make. He would have made love to her there, but she was a fine lady, and he respected her far too much to strip her of her beautiful gown and take her in the damp grass. He struggled to contain her excitement as well as his own, and when he had succeeded in calming her with gentle caresses and tender words of devotion, he made his plans aloud.

"If we go to the priest at Bruton Parish, he might send someone to summon your parents, but the chaplain of our regiment is a young man whom I believe I can persuade to perform a wedding ceremony tonight. What shall we do then? Every inn in town has three men in a bed. I can't take you to my barracks. Where shall we go?"

Melissa searched her mind for only an instant. "Take me home! We can leave a note for my parents in their carriage, telling them we've eloped. Then we can spend the night in one of the guest bedrooms on the third floor. No one will know we're there, and in the morning, we can greet everyone at breakfast as husband and wife."

That was such an audacious idea, Ian needed a moment to appreciate the beauty of it. Then his face lit up with a smile Melissa could see even in the darkness. He grabbed her in a boisterous hug, lifted her off her feet, and let out a wild whoop.

"By God, we'll do it!" he cried. He replaced his bride-to-be on her feet, took her hand, and led her back toward the Governor's Palace, intent upon beginning a marriage he prayed would overflow with the exquisite joy they'd share that night.

Alanna was the first to note that Melissa's absence from the ballroom had grown to an unseemly length. Fortunately neither Aunt Rachel nor Uncle John had missed their daughter's presence in the crowd. They had been dancing and talking with friends on the opposite side of the room for at least fifteen minutes, but Alanna was certain Melissa and Ian had been gone much longer. Perhaps they were merely strolling in the gardens and had lost track of the time, or had stopped to talk with friends, but whatever their excuse, Alanna feared their long absence from the party would draw severe criticism.

Graham Tyler had waited patiently for the opportunity to dance with Alanna again, and he was disappointed that she seemed so preoccupied. When she apologized for forgetting the steps of the dance which she had performed perfectly in her own parlor, he could no longer pretend that she was enjoying herself as much as he. "Would you rather have some punch, or visit the gardens?" he asked.

"Some punch first, and then the gardens?"

"Whatever you wish."

Alanna took his arm, as they slowly made their way toward the refreshment tables where punch was being served from ornate silver bowls. The berry-flavored beverage was overly sweet and rapidly losing its chill, but she sipped it without complaint. Melissa had insisted upon dressing her hair with pomatum and powdering it white, and suddenly catching sight of herself in a mirror, Alanna realized she had become so concerned about Melissa that she had completely forgotten her earlier fears of looking ridiculous. Her apprehensions now returned to increase her discomfort tenfold.

"Yellow is definitely your color," Graham enthused. "You're as radiant as sunshine, and I like your hair styled that way, too."

"Thank you, you're very sweet to say so."

Despite her compliment, Graham thought her distracted glance anything but appreciative. "I don't please you, do I?"

Mortified that he would ask her such a personal question, Alanna nearly dropped her cup and, to avoid such an embarrassing accident, hurriedly set it aside. She knew that in her place Melissa would open her fan, peer over it with a coquettish glance, then close it with a flourish to give him a tap on the chest, before reassuring him he was one of her favorite people on earth. Alanna was not Melissa, however. She could neither tell him flattering lies, nor the blunt cruelty of the truth.

"We scarcely know each other, Lieutenant," she said instead. "Could we visit the gardens now, please? I saw Melissa and Ian go outside some time ago, and I'm beginning to become concerned about them."

Instantly realizing how badly he had embarrassed her, Graham hastened to apologize. "I'm dreadfully sorry, Miss Barclay. I didn't mean to presume, or assume, that I had any right to inquire as to your feelings. Please forgive me."

"You're forgiven. Now could we please visit the gardens?"

"Oh yes, of course. I didn't mean that I wouldn't escort you through the gardens, regardless of your feelings for me."

Exasperated nearly beyond endurance, Alanna shot Graham such a withering glance that he immediately offered his arm rather than endless apologies, and led her outside. The air was several degrees cooler here, and caressed her flushed cheeks like a welcome splash of spring rain. "It was becoming unbearably warm in there, wasn't it?" she asked, as she peered down the main path hoping to catch sight of her missing cousin.

"Yes, it was." Fearing that he would unintentionally insult

her again if he said more, Graham clamped his mouth shut. He envied Ian then, for Melissa's charm was apparently endless, while Alanna was so shy, any effort to draw her out ended in failure. He still liked her enormously though.

There were more than a dozen couples touring the gardens, but Melissa and Ian weren't among them; Alanna didn't know where else to look. "They can't have just disappeared," she mused fretfully.

"Perhaps they were returning to the ballroom on another path, while we started down this one. Would you like to wait here while I go back inside to look for them, or would you prefer to come with me?"

Alanna sat down on the adjacent bench. "I'll wait for you here, thank you."

Not surprised by her decision, Graham returned to the ballroom alone. He skirted the fringe of the dancers, assessed the groups clustered near the windows, walked by the refreshment tables again, and then began to inquire as to whether or not any of their friends had seen Ian or Melissa in the last half hour. When he received only shrugs and denials rather than any encouraging news, he began to worry, also. He knew Ian was fond of Melissa, but could he have lured her away from the ball so intent upon romance that he'd been unmindful of how quickly her presence would be missed?

Discouraged that he had nothing to report, he returned to Alanna. "I'm sorry, but I can't find them. Do you think we ought to tell her parents?"

Alanna gave her head such a violent shake that her side curls tickled her cheeks, and she hurriedly brushed them back into place. "Good heavens, no." Alanna didn't know what else to suggest, however, and drew her skirt in to make room for Graham beside her. He promptly sat down and folded his hands together, rather than reach for one of hers.

"Could they have left for another party?" he asked.

While there had been several entertainments from which to choose on other nights, the Governor's Ball was the only one she knew of taking place that evening. "We weren't invited to any other parties. I don't believe there are any."

"Maybe they had a fight. Could she have gone home?"

"I don't recall Melissa ever fighting with any of her beaus, and even if she and Ian had had words, she'd not have left the ball."

"Are you sure?"

Alanna considered his question more thoughtfully this time. Melissa had been strangely anxious of late, and Alanna was forced to admit that perhaps she couldn't successfully predict what her cousin might have done. "Well, it would have been unlike her to leave without telling her parents, and asking me to come with her."

"All right, then let's assume she didn't go home. Ian likes to play billiards at the Raleigh Tavern. Could they be there?"

"Do men frequently invite ladies into the billiard room?"

"No, but with so many people here at the ball, things could be different tonight."

The Raleigh Tavern was at the other end of town, and Alanna doubted Melissa would have wanted to walk all the way there in her ball gown. "Thank you for trying to help, Lieutenant, but I really don't believe they would have gone as far as the Raleigh. Perhaps I'm being very foolish. As long as Melissa is with Ian, I'm sure she'll be safe, regardless of where they've gone."

"Yes, Ian always behaves as a gentleman, and I know he's fond of Melissa."

"Maybe we'll find them among the dancers," Alanna prayed aloud. "Would you mind going back inside?"

Graham leapt to his feet. "Not if I can dance with you again."

Ashamed that she hadn't been as gracious with him earlier, Alanna apologized, but as they danced they kept watching for

Melissa and Ian, and came to the quick conclusion that the couple just wasn't there.

As the musicians paused for a break, Rachel Barclay came to Alanna's side. "Have you seen Melissa?" she asked. "Our dear friends, the Harleys, are here, and I want her to speak with them."

Alanna fully expected Graham to blurt out how long they had been looking for Melissa, but for once he remained silent. "Why no, Aunt Rachel, I've not seen her."

"She must be in the garden. Well, you come with me then, dear. Will you excuse us, Lieutenant? The Harleys haven't seen Alanna in years, but I know you'd prefer to dance."

"Why no, I'd be honored to meet your friends," Graham assured her.

Alanna was surprised to discover she was relieved by Graham's presence, and her aunt didn't seem at all displeased to have him accompany them to the far corner, where her husband stood talking with an elderly couple. Alanna only dimly recalled their faces, but she greeted them warmly, as though she regarded them as fondly as her aunt and uncle did.

All too soon, however, her uncle excused himself in another attempt to summon Melissa, and Alanna had scant hope that he'd be able to find her. She and Graham exchanged a fearful glance, and when John Barclay returned alone, they steeled themselves for what would surely be difficult questions. At first, John was merely perplexed rather than angry, but when Alanna finally confessed Melissa and Ian hadn't been seen for at least an hour, he grabbed Graham by the arm and they went off to conduct a thorough search for the missing couple.

Although embarrassed that they could not account for Melissa's whereabouts, Rachel pretended not to be in the least bit concerned as she bid the Harleys farewell. She and Alanna moved down the side of the large ballroom to the first open space. Rachel then began to fan herself with furious strokes, while Alanna fidgeted nervously by her side. When Randolph O'Neil approached, greeted her aunt, and asked her to dance, she was much too upset to accept.

"I'm so sorry, but Melissa seems to have disappeared. I'm sure she hasn't really disappeared, you understand. It's just that no one has seen her for a while. Would you be so kind as to help my uncle look for her? She was with Lieutenant Scott a while ago, and now no one can find them."

Randolph had spent the earlier portion of the evening dining with a friend, and now bitterly regretted not arriving earlier. "I'd much rather dance with you," he readily admitted, "but I'll do whatever I can to find Melissa, and perhaps you'll have time for me later."

"Yes, of course, thank you." Alanna was relieved Randolph had accepted her excuse graciously, and hoped that with another pair of eyes, Melissa would promptly be found.

A few minutes later, John Barclay returned alone to his wife and niece. His lips were set in a thin line, and his brow deeply furrowed. He slipped his arm around Rachel's waist, nodded toward Alanna, and calmly announced a sudden desire to depart, but both women hung back.

"I'll explain everything once we reach the carriage," he added in an insistent whisper. "Please, let's just go."

"What's happened to Melissa?" Rachel asked fretfully.

"Nothing." John stubbornly refused to say more before leaving the palace. Andrew McBride, Polly and Jacob's son, had driven the Barclay carriage that night, and had brought it up to the door. As soon as they were all comfortably seated inside, John signaled for Andrew to get underway, and pulled an envelope from his breast pocket. "I came out to the carriage to ask Andrew to help us look for Melissa, and found that she'd left this note with him. She and Ian have eloped."

Stunned, Alanna gasped sharply, but her heartbroken aunt began to weep as though she had just been told that her dear daughter was dead. Alanna hurriedly found her a handkerchief, but her kind gesture only intensified her aunt's mournful sobs.

"Rachel, please." Unsympathetic, John leaned forward as he spoke. "You don't think I plan for anyone else to learn of this ridiculous elopement, do you? Melissa could have had any man she wanted. Why in God's name would she have chosen some penniless soldier?"

"She must love him," Alanna mused aloud, but the threatening look she received from her uncle discouraged further speculation.

"Did Melissa tell you what they intended to do tonight?" John asked.

"No, sir, she didn't."

"You've no idea where they've gone?"

"Absolutely none."

John sat back and eyed his niece with a suspicious glance. "You swear you weren't privy to their plans, and yet you didn't inform us immediately when you couldn't locate them. I think you're lying to me, Alanna, and I shan't forgive it."

"Oh, Uncle John, I wouldn't lie to you and Aunt Rachel," Alanna swore.

Convinced that was only another blatant prevarication, John refused to believe her. He looked away and ignored her for the remainder of the trip home.

Just as Ian had predicted, the chaplain was easily convinced to perform a marriage ceremony. Due to the lateness of the hour, Ian presented Melissa with his own onyx signet ring, and they were pronounced husband and wife within thirty minutes of leaving the ball. He then hired a carriage for the journey to Melissa's home and, in the comfort of the lumbering vehicle, he held her in his arms and kissed her until neither of them could recall ever being apart. Once they reached their destination, he bribed the driver handsomely to return to Williamsburg without divulging where he had gone, or who his passengers had been. None of the Barclays' servants slept in the main house, and as the couple entered, it seemed eerily quiet.

"We dare not light any candles," Melissa whispered. "Someone might see the light and come to investigate."

"That's fine with me. I don't want any company other than yours."

"I want to bring some wine upstairs with us. We ought to toast ourselves, don't you think?"

Ian was already so drunk with desire, he doubted he could taste it. "If you don't insist that my tributes to your beauty rhyme, I'll be happy to answer each of your toasts with one of my own."

"No, I know you're a soldier rather than a poet." Melissa went into the dining room and returned with a bottle of a neighbor's peach wine she knew to be especially potent, and two crystal goblets which she handed to Ian to carry. She then led him up the stairs. When they reached the second floor, she paused again.

"I want to go to my room first for a nightgown."

Ian didn't argue, but he planned to strip her nude as soon as she joined him in bed. He waited at her door as she fetched the gown. The room held a subtle hint of her perfume, and its teasing assault of his senses increased his impatience to make her his own. When she returned to him, he shifted the goblets to one hand, grabbed her in a fervent embrace with the other, and kissed her long and hard.

Breathless when he finally broke away, Melissa pleaded softly, "Can't you wait until we're upstairs?" Despite her complaint, she was thrilled by his eagerness to consummate their marriage, for it meant he would be all the easier to fool. When they reached the third floor, she made her choice without conscious thought, and guided him to the room Hunter had occu-

pied. Once inside, she turned the key in the lock to assure
their privacy, then asked him to pour the wine.

It took a moment for Ian to locate a table, but once he had,
he opened the bottle she handed him, and filled both goblets.
"Thank you for becoming my wife," he offered rather shyly.

Melissa pretended to take a sip of her wine, and was pleased
when Ian nearly drained his goblet. She promptly refilled it.
"Thank you. That was a fine toast. I knew you could do it.
Now let's drink to a long and happy life."

Again, the wine only caressed Melissa's lips, while Ian took
a generous swallow. She pretended to refill her goblet, then
replenished his. "We should also hope for prosperity, don't
you think?"

"Yes, indeed." The peach-flavored wine was too sweet for
Ian's usual tastes, but that night it seemed perfect. When
Melissa gave him more, he took a generous sip. "We ought
to wish for bright and beautiful children."

"With us as parents, they will certainly be both intelligent
and handsome." Melissa touched the lip of her goblet to Ian's
and he took another drink without noticing that she hadn't.
She was ashamed to be resorting to alcohol to facilitate her
plan, but dared not risk bedding him sober. He obliged her
request for toasts with several more, and when he began to
get silly and giggle, she knew his perceptions were no longer
clear enough to allow him to see her for what she truly was.

"I think you've had enough," she said as she took his goblet
and set it aside. "Will you help me remove my gown, please?
Be careful," she cautioned. "I shall have to wear it again in
the morning."

Pleasantly tipsy, Ian leaned down to kiss her bare shoulder.
"I've never been a lady's maid," he apologized. "You'll have
to tell me what to do."

With a deliberately languid pace, Melissa provided suggestive directions, and they peeled away her gown, then her hoop-

skirt and the first layers of petticoats. She had only to think of Alanna to portray a virginal shyness Ian never questioned, but she also led him on with her well-practiced charm. She leaned close to brush the tips of her breasts against his chest, and then drew away as though her motions were the natural ones required of disrobing, rather than a seductive dance meant to further cloud his already befuddled mind.

"Do you plan to come to bed in your uniform, Lieutenant?" she asked as she again stepped free of his arms.

Ian had not appreciated how much time Melissa would need to disrobe, and he was aching to make love to her. That he would have to remove his clothes first was only a minor annoyance. "Certainly not," he assured her, but he was grateful the room was too dark for her to see what he feared was an ungentlemanly haste, or how clumsy he had become.

"Water!" Melissa suddenly remembered. "We'll need water in the morning, and there's none in the pitcher. I'll get some while you undress."

Ian was about to argue that the morning would take care of itself, when he realized she might have a greater need to bathe than he. Not wishing to be inconsiderate, he did not object, but he moaned softly as Melissa hurried away. Because he would have no change of clothes, he lay his uniform coat across a chair to keep it from becoming wrinkled, and placed his wig on top. He discarded his shirt and boots, but remained in his pants. Enough moonlight entered the room for him to believe the bed looked wonderfully inviting, and he turned down the covers as he waited for his bride. When she came through the door carrying the now-filled pitcher, he hurried to relock it behind her.

"I simply took the water from my room rather than go out to the well, but it's directly below this one, and I heard you drop your boots! We must be more careful. We don't want Alanna to hear us when she comes home."

Ian followed Melissa to the washstand, wrapped both arms around her waist, and gave her another enthusiastic hug. His words were slightly slurred as he made a heartfelt vow. "I want to make love to you all night long, and I don't care whether or not Alanna hears us."

"My goodness, I had no idea making love created such a racket. Isn't it as quiet as kissing?"

"Not if you're enjoying it, and I do so want for you to enjoy it," he promised.

"Well, so do I," Melissa replied. She eluded him for a moment to cast off the last of her lingerie, and donned her nightgown. She then crossed to the bed, where the snowy white linens suddenly brought home the enormity of her deceit. She was nearly overcome with anxiety, and couldn't bring herself to climb in. When Ian again came up behind her, she knew he could feel how badly she was trembling.

"I'm frightened," she admitted, knowing he would never guess why.

Ian wanted to promise that he'd not hurt her, but he knew it would be a lie. He'd not want to, not mean to, but the pain was inescapable. His heart too full of love to say anything at all, he helped her into the bed, tossed his pants aside, and then joined her. He drew her into his arms, meaning to be gentle, patient, and tender rather than demanding, but when Melissa responded to his first tentative kiss with the same unabashed joy she'd displayed in the palace gardens, all his good intentions were lost.

He slid his hand under her gown to caress her bare thigh, and she leaned against him, silently coaxing him to trace each of her lush curves. The fullness of her breast filled his palm with rounded perfection, while beneath his fingertips the pale pink crest puckered like lips eager for a kiss. Wanting to taste as well as touch, Ian tugged on her gown, and Melissa pulled it off over her head.

Whether it was her own natural flavor or the lingering taste of the peach wine, Ian thought she was absolutely delicious. He suckled at her breast, and then returned to her lips for more devouring kisses. He had been fascinated by Melissa from the hour they had met, and that he had somehow performed the miracle of making her his wife surpassed the wildest of his dreams.

Melissa felt no such elation. Her mood now one of total despair, she ran her fingers through Ian's brilliant red curls and remembered another man whose long, ebony hair had streamed through her hands in a silken cascade. She didn't want Hunter to be a part of her wedding night, but the more ardent Ian became, the more impossible it was to force the Indian from her mind. It was Ian she wanted to love, but there was no magic in his caress, and his clumsy sweetness could not distract her from the pain that filled her heart.

Too excited to delay any longer, Ian entered her in a heated rush, and, without having to act, Melissa recoiled with an anguished cry. It was her body's instinctive response to the husband she knew she should have welcomed lovingly; overwhelmed with shame, she began to sob. If her innocence had died with Hunter, it was the natural joyousness of her spirit which died now, and she would forever mourn the loss.

Terrified that despite his best intentions, he had given their marriage the worst of beginnings, Ian tried without success to dry Melissa's frightened tears. Failing, he craved the release her fervent kisses had promised too greatly to withdraw without succumbing to that need. He completed the act required to make them husband and wife, but he was devastated that she had not shared his bliss. He held her cradled in his arms, and prayed that he had not ruined their chances for happiness.

Melissa knew she was behaving very badly, but she couldn't stop crying. It wasn't until she heard her parents' carriage roll through the yard that her fears of facing them finally silenced her hoarse sobs. She then lay silently trembling in Ian's arms, her heart broken in a thousand jagged fragments. The morning would only bring more lies, for somehow she would have to convince her family that she was happy to be Ian's bride. She did not know where she would find the strength.

"I'm sorry," Ian whispered.

Melissa raised her hand to his lips. "No, you mustn't apologize."

"But I should have—"

"No!" This time Melissa silenced him with a kiss. They lay cuddled together as her parents and Alanna entered the house, and, more than a little drunk, Ian soon fell asleep. Her conscience hurting badly, Melissa was far too anxious to rest. For as long as she could remember, she had been diligently tutored to be a rich man's bride. She had been encouraged to captivate men with the flirtatious ways which had betrayed her with Hunter.

She still blamed herself for that indiscretion, for surely Indian maidens didn't flaunt their charms the way she had with him. Hunter hadn't known it was all an amusing game she had never meant to carry so far. No, he had simply fallen prey to the wiles that had brought her so many devoted suitors. Virginia boys all knew the rules, however, and enjoyed flirting without believing it meant anything more than momentary fun.

Brushing away a last tear, Melissa knew exactly how costly her brief romance with Hunter had been. But Ian was a fine man, although he wasn't rich, she knew he would do his best to give her a good life. If it wasn't the elegant existence she should have had, the fault would be entirely hers, not his. Drained of all emotion, she prayed that by marrying Ian she had not merely compounded her mistake. Then, shoving that wretched thought aside, she vowed to be such a good wife to him, he would never feel cheated of the love she now doubted she could ever truly give.

Eight

With her marriage to Ian, Melissa had expected to instantly replace her dread with hope. Instead, she had sunk even deeper into despair. When the dawn brought enough light for her to study her new husband while he slept, she was again moved to tears, but hurriedly brushed them away. By sheer force of will, she convinced herself that the time for weeping was over. She wanted their marriage to mark not only the beginning of their life together, but a return to the laughter and joy she and Ian had shared in the past.

She had always admired his vivid coloring, and considered him a remarkably handsome man. Even asleep, his even features radiated the strength of character which had drawn her to him. He was so honest and good, and what was she? Not even the sharpest-tongued gossip could revile her with worse names than she had already called herself.

Unable to bear the thought of their next conversation taking place in bed, she slipped from Ian's arms cautiously, so as not to disturb him. She knew she had the wine rather her affection to thank for the depth of his slumber, but she planned to make good use of it. Her nightgown lay in a wrinkled heap on the floor; she quickly wadded it into a tight ball and shoved it under the bed. Later, when she mentioned it had been stained, she knew he would believe her. It would be a lie, but preferable to splattering the bed with chicken blood while he slept.

She was glad she had remembered to fill the pitcher, and

washed before donning her lingerie. She would have preferred to shampoo her hair rather than recomb her pomaded curls, but she would need warm water for that and would have to see to it later. She and Alanna had helped each other dress for so many years that neither had ever had a maid. She missed her cousin now, and wondered who would be helping her with her clothes from now on.

Once dressed, Melissa sat down by the window, propped her arms on the sill, and looked out toward the river. The ducklings she and Hunter had fed would soon equal their mothers in size, but the little families still presented a charming sight swimming along in undulating lines. She glanced over her shoulder at Ian, who remained lost in his dreams. He was her family now, but she hoped that the rest of her relatives wouldn't be so angry with them for eloping that she was disowned. That would be unspeakably cruel, after all she had suffered of late. Of course, they were unaware of her problems, and would continue to be blissfully ignorant of them, but she did not want to lose their love.

At least an hour passed before she heard anyone stirring downstairs. It was Sunday, and she assumed the household routine would continue undisturbed, and that everyone was preparing for church. Would they be praying for her and Ian to be granted many blessings, or mourning the loss of a daughter? Not eager to discover which choice they had made, she enjoyed the beauty of the sunlight on the river, and hoped Ian would sleep until noon.

Ian did sleep nearly that long, and when he awoke with an excruciating headache in a pale green room he didn't recognize, he let out a low moan.

"Good morning, my darling," Melissa called to him, "although by now it may be afternoon."

At the sound of Melissa's voice, Ian sat up with a start, causing his already aching head to throb even more painfully.

He raked his hand through his curls to sweep them off his forehead, and stared at the beautifully gowned young woman seated by the window. "Melissa?"

"I didn't realize there was any danger that you might forget my name, especially not after last night."

"Last night," Ian repeated, and the echo of his voice sent a fresh wave of pain rumbling through his head. He could recall attending the Governor's Ball, but then his memories grew faint. He struggled to bring them into focus, and then felt even worse.

"My God, did we get married?"

"Have you come to regret our marriage so soon?"

Ian leaned forward and propped his head in his hands. "Where did you get that peach wine? I fear it's lethal."

Melissa had not sipped more than a few drops and didn't share his pain. "It was a gift from a neighboring plantation. You seemed to enjoy it last night."

"I must have." Ian was positive marriage was one of the most significant events in a man's life, but he'd not realized how easily a few glasses of wine would wipe the memories from his mind. "Would you please bring me my pants?"

Melissa plucked them from the chair where she had placed them that morning. She handed them to him and then returned to her chair by the window, to provide him with the necessary privacy to dress. From that safe distance, she took refuge in practical matters. "There are so many things we need to discuss. Where are we going to live?"

Ian rolled out of bed, nearly fell, but caught himself and hurriedly pulled on his pants. Expecting some evidence of their passion, he glanced back toward the bed, but when the wrinkled sheets bore no trace of their union, he was in too much pain to care. He pulled the spread up in a hasty attempt to make the bed and then sat down on it.

"I don't know," he replied. "I'll try and rent us a house in town until we can build one, but I don't feel up to discussing real estate today. I'd rather just go back to sleep, but I can't leave you to face your parents alone."

Melissa rose and went to him. "I'm sorry. I wouldn't have suggested we toast each other last night, had I known how badly you'd feel today."

Ian took her hands and pulled her close. "You needn't fear you've married a drunkard. I'll not make this great a fool of myself ever again."

Melissa had to bite her lower lip to prevent her ravaged emotions from betraying her. "You're no fool. Don't even think that."

Ian had not expected her to take his remark so seriously. "Thank you, but I know just how wretched I feel."

"We often have guests during Publick Times. Fortunately for us, this is one of the few springs that we haven't, but these bedrooms are always kept ready. There's shaving soap, a razor, water, although I'm sorry it's cold."

Taking her remarks as a gentle prod, Ian slid off the bed. "Yes, my dear, I'll make myself presentable."

"Don't wear your wig. Your hair is really too beautiful to hide."

"Do you really mean that? I've always thought it was hideous."

Melissa's pretty blue eyes widened in surprise. "No, it's certainly unusual, although not for a Scotsman I don't suppose, but it's a very attractive shade." She reached up to kiss his cheek. "I like your freckles, too."

"My God, woman, you've become absolutely shameless with your flattery."

"I think every woman ought to flatter her husband," Melissa protested, "and I intend to keep right on flattering you."

Despite the pain of his headache, Ian longed to take her back to bed, but knew he would have to face her parents first. "I shall strive to deserve it then," he responded with a mock bow.

He walked over to the washstand, and she returned to the window. He poured himself a drink first to rid his mouth of the awful taste of peach wine, and then added water to the bowl. As he scooped it up in his hands to wash his face, he had a startling recollection of tears, and his heart fell. He couldn't remember much of the night, but now recalling Melissa's heartbreaking sobs, he glanced toward her.

She was gazing out the window, smiling slightly, and from the affectionate way she had greeted him that morning—or afternoon, if that were the case—she wasn't displeased with him. He debated with himself a minute, and then decided there were some questions that were better left unasked. If his wife wished to pretend their wedding night had gone well, when all he could remember was wine and tears, then he would not challenge her on it. He was touched that she would try so hard to make the day seem like any other, when in truth they would probably never face a more difficult conversation than the one they would soon have with her parents.

That he had seldom felt worse wouldn't help any either, and he forced himself to concentrate on shaving, but he laughed to himself as he recalled Melissa's comment about his freckles. He was twenty-six years old, and he had more freckles than most ten-year-old children, and Melissa liked them! He would thank God every day of his life for sending him a wife whose love was truly blind.

Neither John nor Rachel Barclay had felt up to attending church services that morning, but they had gone anyway and insisted Alanna accompany them. They left while the last notes of the recessional hymn were still echoing through the nave and, without lingering to speak with friends, rode home in the same sullen silence with which they had arrived. When they walked through their front door and found Melissa and Ian waiting in the parlor, Rachel again burst into tears, while John fought to control his temper. Alanna saw the protective way Ian's arm encircled her cousin's waist, and envied the newly married couple their love.

They had been downstairs only a few minutes, and Ian had scarcely had enough time to prepare, but he seized the initiative and spoke first. "I want to apologize to you both for any anxiety we may have caused you last night. I know what we've done must seem selfish, and perhaps it was, but we had been discussing marriage for several weeks, and felt we were ready to take that step. I love your daughter dearly, and you have my word that I'll give her the best of lives."

John Barclay's vision was clouded with a scarlet mist exactly matching the coat of Ian's uniform. "Anxiety?" he repeated in a hoarse croak. Ignoring his new son-in-law, he addressed his remarks to his daughter. "Anxiety does not begin to describe the suffering you've brought your mother and me. Barmaids and scullery maids elope, but the well-bred daughters of respectable families, which ours most certainly is, do not elope! Now I want both of you to sit down, and we'll try our best to undo the terrible mess you've made."

"Our marriage is no mess," Melissa argued.

"Sit down!" John bellowed.

"I'll not allow you to shout at my wife," Ian replied.

"She is also my daughter, young man, and I'll shout at her all I please."

"Not in my presence you won't, or we shall have to leave," Ian insisted.

Rachel placed her hands over her ears. "Please, I can't bear the sound of strident voices. Let's all sit down and discuss things calmly."

Alanna wondered if she ought to go, after all, the discussion at hand didn't really concern her, but she was too curious to excuse herself, and when her uncle didn't demand that she leave, she moved to the closest chair. Ian and Melissa chose the settee, and John and Rachel took the chairs across from them. For a long moment, the two couples simply stared at each other, but then John spoke in a more reasonable tone.

"How many people know of your marriage?" he asked.

"The chaplain who performed the ceremony, and the two soldiers who served as witnesses, but I asked them to keep our wedding a secret until you'd been informed," Ian explained. "We've not told anyone else. Have you?"

"Certainly not," John quickly denied. "Lieutenant Tyler and Randolph O'Neil helped us look for you, but when I found the note you'd left with Andrew, I told them Melissa had been taken ill and gone home."

"You lied to them?" Melissa asked.

"Of course, I lied to them," her father scoffed. "Do you think I'd brag about the fact you'd run off with a soldier?"

"I am an officer, sir, not a common foot soldier."

"I'll agree. There's nothing common about you, Lieutenant, not from your bright red hair to your total lack of regard for my daughter's reputation."

"I have the highest regard for your daughter's reputation, but must I remind you that I'll not allow you to criticize my wife?"

John waved aside Ian's feisty defense. "You're a virile young man. May I assume having the marriage annulled is no longer an option?"

"Father, how could you?"

"Hush, Melissa. It's Ian who has to answer."

For an instant, Ian wished there were bloodstained sheets he could flap in his father-in-law's face. Instead, he squeezed his bride's hand more tightly, and replied with a knowing smile, "Believe me, sir, we're legally wed."

"Where did you spend the night?"

"In the green guest bedroom," Melissa volunteered.

"My God!"

Rachel reached out to pat her husband's arm. "Please don't shout, darling."

Astonished, John eyed his wife with an incredulous glance. "This is a sad day for the Empire, if Ian is a fair sample of the King's officers!"

"It was my idea," Melissa rushed to explain. "We wanted to be here to speak with you today."

John mumbled a string of unintelligible curses before regaining what little hold he had on his composure. "Outside of this room, there are only three men who know of your marriage. Is that correct?"

"Yes," Ian agreed.

"Then you will tell them to maintain their silence, and we shall simply announce your engagement," John said. "After a suitable interval, you'll be wed in a proper ceremony, and no one need ever learn that it is your second wedding, rather than your first."

Not having expected such a reaction, Ian was taken aback for a moment, but then he turned toward Melissa, and spoke before she could object. "You know I'm concerned about what people will say. I think we should give your father's suggestion serious thought."

Melissa had a major objection, and she didn't mince words in voicing it. "As my father so tactlessly asked, we are husband and wife, Ian, and I may have already conceived a child. Our elopement may cause a stir, but it will be minor compared with my marrying you in a few months when my condition might be noticeable, and the subsequent birth of our first baby occurs prior to our nine-month anniversary."

John Barclay fixed his daughter with a piercing stare. "Is

this the real reason you and Ian were in such a great hurry to wed? Are you already with child?"

Overwhelmed with guilt, all color drained from Melissa's face, while Ian objected violently to that insulting question. His courage bolstered her own, and she felt no need to even hint at the truth. After all, she was only a week overdue now, and surely that wasn't time enough to confirm a pregnancy. "Ian is a gentleman, Father, and he has always behaved as such with me. In fact, our elopement was my idea, not his, so you mustn't blame him."

"I blame you both for not having more sense," John complained.

An uncomfortable silence ensued, and it was Rachel who finally broke it. "We can plan the wedding for a month from yesterday. Then if you should have a child eight months later, we'll say he's four weeks' premature. A month isn't really sufficient time to plan a wedding, but since Byron was born just nine months after your father and I were wed, I don't think we should gamble on having the luxury of more time. Perhaps we can say that you anticipate being transferred elsewhere, Lieutenant. That's certainly plausible, isn't it?"

"Yes, if the situation in the Ohio Valley worsens, I could easily be assigned elsewhere."

"I think we should discuss this in private, Ian," Melissa urged. "It's too important an issue to decide in haste."

"Unlike your wedding!" John reminded her.

Ian chose to ignore that ill-tempered outburst. "Will you excuse us, please?" he asked.

John rose and gestured toward the door. "Certainly, take all the time you need. We'll wait dinner for you. After all, we don't want to compound the problems of one hasty decision with another equally foolish choice."

Ian helped Melissa to her feet. She glanced toward Alanna, and knew by the hurt she saw in her cousin's expression just how upsetting their elopement had been for her. "I'm sorry," she whispered as they passed by her chair. "I would have told you our plans had there been time, but it was all very romantic and spontaneous."

Alanna nodded, then looked toward her uncle to see if he had heard Melissa's apology. When he looked away, she knew that he had, but it didn't appear as though he would offer her an apology of his own. She understood his preoccupation with Melissa could be blamed for his shocking lack of manners, but that didn't make her feel any better.

Because they had enjoyed previous walks down by the river, Ian led Melissa along the path that crossed the lawn. "At least your father didn't try and shoot me," he teased. "I'm taking that as a good sign."

"Let's not make light of our situation," Melissa begged. "It isn't in the least bit funny."

"I'm sorry if my attempt at humor was misplaced." By the time they'd reached the river's edge, Ian's mood was as serious as hers. "Please don't misunderstand me. I'm not sorry that we got married," he assured her, "but you know I wanted you to have a big wedding so all your family and friends could be there to celebrate. I think we should agree to your father's plan, and keep our elopement a secret. A month isn't an unreasonable amount of time for us to wait to live as man and wife."

While Melissa knew that a month might not seem like long to him, she dared not give him any reason to doubt the child she feared she was carrying was his. "I believed you to be a man of integrity, Ian."

"Only believed? You don't believe it still?"

"Not when you'd hand me back to my father, as though you regretted taking me for a wife."

"I'm doing no such thing."

Melissa knew she was pushing him, but she couldn't help

herself. "If you'll deny we're wed, then that's precisely what you're doing."

Melissa wore such a heartbreaking look of rejection, Ian instantly pulled her into his arms. "No, all I'm doing is attempting to set everything right: to see you have a proper wedding, and to make a better impression on your parents. Please consider my side for a moment, Melissa. I don't want your parents to despise me for the rest of their lives. I don't want to be an outcast, who's ignored at every family gathering and treated as though I don't exist.

"If I can win your parents' approval by merely agreeing to marry you again in a month, then I'm willing to do it. We needn't be apart. In fact, I'll make it a condition for our consent to your parents' plan. I'll insist upon spending the nights here with you, but for propriety's sake, I'll return to town before dawn. Will that make you happy?"

His promise to spend the nights with her was all Melissa needed to be swayed to his point of view. She waited a long moment to make him believe she was silently debating the issue, however, and then looked up at him and smiled. "Yes, if I don't have to wait a month to actually *be* your wife, then I'll pretend we're only engaged, because that's the best choice for you. I do so want for my parents to love you, too."

"Did you really think I could stay away from you for a month?"

"Well, I'd certainly hoped not, but I'm glad that you don't intend to promise my father that you will."

"He'll never get that kind of promise out of me." Ian sealed his vow with a kiss, took her hand, and started back toward the house. "Let's suggest we make our plans over dinner. I'm so hungry, I can barely stand."

Melissa felt queasy rather than eager for food, but she smiled, relieved that Ian had proved to be as thoughtful a husband as she had hoped, she actually began to look forward to planning a formal wedding. She was smiling as they returned to the parlor, but not for long.

"Because I want what's best for Melissa," Ian told the Barclays, "I'll agree to marry her again in a month's time, but I'll not forgo the privilege of being her husband until then. I want to spend the nights with her here as often as my duties permit, but I'll return to Williamsburg well before dawn, so our engagement will appear suitably chaste. If that's not agreeable to you, then Melissa will leave with me now, and there will be no second wedding."

John clenched his fists at his sides. "You claim to want what's best for my daughter with one breath, and then deny it in the next. This is my house, Lieutenant, and I'll not allow you to use it for trysts!"

Ian nodded slightly, and then offered Melissa his arm. "Shall we go then, dearest?"

Without a second's hesitation, Melissa slipped her arm through his. "I'm sorry, Mama. I know you would have given us a lovely wedding, but we're already married, and can't agree to live apart."

Rachel turned to her husband. "She's right, John. They *are* married, and allowing Ian to visit her here isn't condoning trysts. That word doesn't apply to a married couple."

"Rachel!"

"I don't mean to appear disloyal," Rachel assured him, "but Melissa is Ian's wife, and shouting won't change that."

Alanna moved to her aunt's side. She dared not enter into the argument, but her gesture made it plain whose side she favored. When her aunt responded with a determined smile, she was certain her uncle would soon be forced to give in. With four of his family against him, he would be exceedingly foolish not to.

"I'm hungry," he announced instead. "Let's have dinner and talk about this later."

Ian shook his head. "I'm sorry, sir, but I wouldn't feel comfortable sharing your food, after you've ordered me out of your house."

John regarded his son-in-law with a darkly menacing stare. "You have more courage than sense. You realize that, don't you?"

Ian squared his shoulders proudly. "I married your daughter, sir. That ought to be proof of my intelligence."

"What does your father do?"

"He's one of London's finest barristers, sir."

"You're misplaced in the military, Lieutenant, when you've obviously inherited your father's skill at argument."

"Is that meant as a compliment, sir?"

It was Ian's disarming grin that dissolved John's objections to his plan. "All right," he finally agreed. "You may stay here if you must, but I'll expect you to keep your word and be out of here well before dawn."

"You have my word on it, sir."

"Good." John gestured with flourish. "Now let's have dinner together, and try to speak in a courteous fashion while we do."

"It will be no problem at all now, Papa," Melissa assured him. She left Ian's side to give her father an enthusiastic kiss, and then nearly skipped into the dining room on her husband's arm. Everything was going to work out beautifully, she just knew that it would, but she still didn't feel much like eating.

By the time they retired to the guest bedroom that night, Melissa was so exhausted, she could barely see. Ian, however, was in high spirits. He drew her into his arms and danced around the room, before pulling her down beside him on the bed.

"It's going to be difficult to keep our marriage a secret," he confided, "but at least I can brag about our engagement. That will have to do for now. What kind of a ring would you

like? I'd buy sapphires to match your eyes, but if you'd like
rubies or emeralds, just say so."

"You needn't buy me an expensive ring, Ian. I know your
salary isn't generous, and we'll have a great many expenses
when we set up housekeeping."

Ian frowned slightly. "My family isn't poor. In addition to
being one of London's finest barristers, my father is also one
of the most successful, as was his father before him. We have
more money than many of the men who sit in the House of
Lords. I chose the army because I craved adventure, but there
will probably come a time when I'll join the family law firm.
Would you like to live in London?"

Ian had saved Melissa from a fate too ghastly to contemplate, and she would have agreed to live with him anywhere.
"London would be very nice," she replied.

"You'd rather stay here in Virginia though, wouldn't you?"

"Only if you would."

"You needn't be so agreeable, my love. You can tell me the
truth."

Melissa flinched slightly at the mention of that word, but
she didn't hesitate to confide the truth of her feelings in this
matter. "My family is here, so yes, staying here would be nice,
but your family is in London, and you shouldn't have to give
them up for me."

"I haven't given anything up to marry you," Ian assured her.
She had bathed and washed her hair that afternoon, and he
removed her cap to free her golden curls. They smelled like
sunshine. "You didn't answer my question about your ring. Do
you want a sapphire, or not?"

Melissa had never considered the question and needed a
moment to do it properly. "Because I wear so much blue, a
sapphire would be very nice, thank you."

"I'll buy you a ring tomorrow then. Now, let's not waste
another minute of tonight."

Ian slid off the bed, and took Melissa's hands to pull her to her feet. "I'm certain I'll do much better helping you to undress tonight."

"Oh wait," Melissa begged as she backed out of his embrace. "I'll need another nightgown. The one I had on last night was stained so badly I had to throw it out."

Ian looked puzzled for a moment, but then understood what she meant, and believed that when he had made love to her, the nightgown had been soiled rather than the bed. He brushed her request aside. "You won't need a nightgown tonight, anymore than you did last night. Now come back here, and I'll help you out of your gown."

"But I'll need something to wear in the morning, after you're gone," she reminded him.

"Wear your chemise."

Relieved by how easily she had been able to refer to the stained nightgown, Melissa ceased to argue. Very pleased with herself, she turned her back and lifted her hair out of his way. His fingertips brushed her nape, and she shivered slightly. As always, he was very gentle and sweet, but she stopped him when he reached her chemise.

"Now you must help me," he suggested.

"What? You can't reach the buttons on your shirt, or unhook your belt buckle?"

"No, I'm much too tired to undress myself tonight."

"You certainly don't look tired. How's your headache?"

"It was gone by mid-afternoon, but I still need help in getting undressed."

"You can at least remove your boots, can't you?"

Ian shook his head. "That would be much too taxing for me."

"You scarcely look incapacitated, Lieutenant."

"Humor me."

A teasing wink convinced Melissa to do just that. "Sit down, and I'll help you with your boots. After all, I can't have you sharing my bed while wearing them."

"I agree. That would be ruinous to the linens." Melissa gave his right boot a hearty yank and then, remembering Alanna was directly below them, she set it down carefully rather than dropping it, and reached for his left. "I think you must be very spoiled."

"Terribly." Ian waited until she had peeled off his socks to stand. "The buttons on this shirt are so tiny, I have difficulty finding them."

"I don't recall your ever being this clumsy, Ian."

"It's the strain of marriage, madam. It will do that to a man."

"How tragic. It's not permanent, I hope."

"It could be, if I don't receive the proper care."

Melissa had his shirt unbuttoned now. His chest was covered with crisp red curls, while Hunter's golden bronze skin had been hairless. Why had she again thought of him? she wondered. Hunter was gone, and he ought to have been forgotten. She reached up on her tiptoes to kiss Ian. When he wrapped his arms around her waist to pull her close, she relaxed against him.

"How marvelous," she exclaimed. "You've recovered from your clumsiness."

Ian stepped back and made an ineffectual pass at his belt buckle. "No, I'm still all thumbs. You'll have to keep helping me."

Melissa unfastened the buckle. "I may be able to help you undress tonight, but you'll have to dress yourself in the morning."

"You'll not get up to help me?"

"There's no reason for me to wake up before dawn."

Again Ian pulled her close for a kiss. "I'll give you one then."

Melissa slipped her arms under his open shirt to hug him. His skin had an inviting warmth, but still no magical tingle. She rested her cheek on his chest for a moment, but when she closed her eyes, Hunter's bright smile flashed in her mind. Startled, she clung to Ian all the more tightly.

"I know you enjoy making me laugh, Ian, but we are going to be all right together, aren't we?"

Ian stroked her hair lightly. "Of course, we are. We're a perfect match." Intent upon proving that, he scooped her up into his arms and carried her to the bed. The linens were fresh, and he lay her down on them before turning away to douse the lamp. Despite his earlier protests, he had no difficulty removing his pants. He would not have forced her to look at him nude, but he could not help but feel that she must be curious about how men are made. She did have brothers, but that did not mean she had ever seen them without their clothes.

He lay down beside her, reached for her hand, trailed her fingertips down his chest, over the taut muscles of his stomach, and then lower still. She didn't try and pull away, which rather surprised him. "That feels good. Leave your hand there," he whispered.

Melissa felt him grow hard, but it was no surprise to her. She caressed him lightly, and then pulled his hand between her legs. "It feels good to me, too," she explained. "You showed me last night."

Ian couldn't recall their wedding night in sufficient detail to know what he had shown her, but her seductive tone convinced him he must have pleased her. That's all he wanted: to please her, since she delighted him so. He enticed her out of her chemise, and then kissed her luscious breasts, while he continued to tease her with a gentle touch that coaxed a grateful moan from deep in the back of her throat.

He moved over her then, and brought their bodies together with a smooth, sure thrust that seemed strangely familiar. Knowing it couldn't have been that easy the previous night, he thought he was remembering other women and, ashamed of himself, promptly banished the thought. Melissa was the only woman he would ever want, and he gloried in the warmth of her response, and fell asleep snuggled in her arms.

Ian's tender loving left Melissa languidly combing his curls, rather than euphoric, but knowing he had not questioned her virginity relieved her of a heavy burden of dread. He was the dearest of men and, even if she never loved him with the enthusiasm he had shown her, it would be another of her secrets, rather than a truth that would cause him pain.

Nine

The forest had always been Hunter's home, and he had roamed it with the effortless enthusiasm of a deer, but now that the French had entered the Ohio Valley, and clearly intended to stay, he grew far more cautious. He had always taken his early morning patrols seriously, but now that a confrontation with advancing French soldiers could come at any time, he became acutely aware of the possibility that men out scouting for the French might see him. He would have thought himself a great fool if he were taken prisoner, and he intended to avoid such a humiliation.

Now, before moving forward, he climbed the tallest tree and scanned the horizon for telltale wisps of smoke that would indicate a campfire. There were still men trapping furs, so smoke in itself might only mean their presence, rather than that of troops in the area. Whether or not there were campfires which needed to be investigated, he remained aloft to study the terrain thoroughly. He was searching for anything unusual: birds that suddenly took flight, or a waving motion in the foliage caused by frightened animals fleeing human pursuit.

Each morning his careful observation failed to disclose any ominous signs, but he continued to exercise care when he began to explore on foot. He relied not only on the sharpness of his eyes and ears, but also on his intuition to warn him of danger. Certain he would sense the presence of the enemy before they could be seen or heard, he often sat quietly and waited for the forest to reveal its secrets. It was only after he felt its natural calm remained undisturbed, that he returned to camp.

Washington's men were carving out a road wide enough for wagons and cannon, and their progress through the mountains was tortuously slow. Because the French had cannon, Hunter understood the British need, but he envied the ease with which the French had floated theirs down the Allegheny River. In his view, the French had far too many advantages, but he had to admire the courage of his traveling companions when, according to Ensign Ward, the force that opposed them was nearly ten times their size.

Hunter heard his name being called as he entered camp, and turned to see a burly young man approaching. No one had dared to bother him since the day he had broken Vernon Avey's arm, but he was instantly on guard. "What do you want?" he asked.

"Whoa, Indian, there's no reason for you to get mad at me. My name's Thomas McGee. Some of us were talking this morning, and we got to wondering who's the best man in camp with an ax. Now I said the only way to settle that question is to have a contest. We find trees of equal size, and see which man can fell his first. Some of the men think you would win, others don't, but a difference of opinion is what makes a contest exciting. You want to try it?"

Anxious to see the competition, men had already begun to gather, but Hunter didn't feel like doing such hard work just to entertain them. "What do the officers say?"

"There's no reason to bother them," Thomas replied. "We're supposed to be chopping down trees, aren't we?"

That was certainly true. All the men were working from dawn to dusk to widen the trappers' path through the forest. How two of the trees were removed couldn't be of much interest to their officers, but Hunter had another objection. "Are the men going to place bets?"

Thomas was shocked. "Well, of course, they're going to make bets!" he answered. "That's part of the fun."

"I'll do it, if I'm given a quarter of the money won on me," Hunter offered.

"A quarter! Hell, nobody will agree to that."

Hunter shrugged. "Then have someone else do it."

The men began to voice their opinions in the matter, and it soon became apparent that without Hunter, there would be no contest, and their spokesman had to give in. "All right, you get your quarter of the amount won on you. Is there anything else you want?"

"Yes, I want to choose the trees, as well as my ax, and I want time to sharpen it."

A respectful murmur passed through the crowd, for now everyone realized that Hunter was not merely strong, but also clever. "We've already chosen the trees, but I guess you can pick two others, if you don't like them. As for the ax, each man ought to work with his favorite, and they ought to be sharp."

"Do you want to do this now?"

"Sure, as soon as you're ready."

"Who's the other man?"

"Carl Schmidt, you must know him."

Having heard his name, Carl pushed his way through the crowd. He was a brawny young man with a ready smile, good-natured and strong, but not overly bright. He walked up to Hunter and offered his hand. He was the same height as the Indian, but easily outweighed him by thirty pounds. Big and tough, his grin showed what he thought of his chances of winning.

Hunter shook Carl's hand, but quickly released it. "Make them give you a quarter of the money, if you win," he urged him.

Carl turned to Thomas McGee. "If he gets a quarter, don't I get a quarter, too?"

"Of course, Carl," McGee assured him. "We'd not cheat you."

Carl believed him, but Hunter doubted he would have seen any money had he not asked for it. Carl had already selected an ax, and Hunter went through the others, carefully judging not only the weight, but also the feel of the handle. When he found one he liked, he sat down and sharpened the blade with a whetstone. Ignoring the men standing around discussing the match, he worked with a methodical rhythm until the ax had a sharper edge than it had possessed when new.

He then set the whetstone aside and stood. Thomas McGee immediately came over to lead him down the trail to the pine trees he'd chosen, and while the trunks were not so thick as to make the contest exhausting, they were too closely spaced to suit Hunter. He shook his head and, after a careful search, pointed out two others of approximately the same girth, but standing farther apart.

"These are better," he announced without detailing his reason.

"Trees is trees, Indian," Thomas scoffed, but he didn't argue with Hunter's selection, and neither did Carl.

When they were ready to begin, Carl wore a look of intense concentration. He spread his legs to assume a carefully balanced stance and raised his ax to shoulder height, while Hunter was completely relaxed, apparently not caring who won. While the majority of bets had been placed on Carl, Hunter had nearly as many vocal supporters, and they began to cheer him on as soon as Thomas McGee gave the signal to begin.

In a matter of seconds, the difference between the two men became clear. Carl was slamming his ax into the tree with the agitated frenzy of a crazed woodpecker, sending chips of bark flying in all directions, while Hunter worked in an easy rhythm that sliced more deeply into the heart of the tree with each cleanly swung stroke. Had the trees been saplings, Carl might have succeeded in felling his first, but these trees required not speed, but endurance, and as he tired, Carl gradually began to slow his furious pace, while Hunter continued to swing his ax low and hard at the same steady rate. When his tree was the first to fall, no one was surprised.

Hunter then gestured graciously for Carl to continue. With his face red with both embarrassment and effort, he struggled to chop down his tree. When Carl had finally accomplished his task, Hunter offered his hand. While Carl shook it, he couldn't look the Indian in the eye, and turned away to hide his tears. Hunter had expected to win, and felt no real elation in his victory or any sympathy for Carl in his loss.

"I'd like my money now," he told McGee.

Clearly in awe, Thomas counted it out and handed it to him. "Where did you learn to use an ax?"

"I am Seneca," Hunter reminded him. "Our children play at chopping down bigger trees than these."

Thomas considered that reply for a moment, and then shook his head in dismay. "Somehow, I doubt there's much you can't do."

If Hunter was aware of any gaps in his knowledge, he didn't share them with Thomas McGee. Instead, he smiled and, carrying his winnings and ax, walked back toward camp, while the men who had bet on him kept on cheering.

The noise of the contest had drawn Byron's interest, and he met Hunter on the trail. "It looks as though you're as good with an ax as you are at fighting."

"That's not difficult."

"Try and be careful," Byron warned. "The men are working hard, and they can use a little fun, but don't let them talk you into anything you'd rather not do. The men you beat won't forget how foolish you made them look."

Unable to work, Vernon Avey had remained back at Will's Creek, so Hunter wasn't concerned about him. As for Carl Schmidt, he had not seemed hostile, just disheartened that he had lost. "I know you and Elliott are my only friends here," he confided. "I don't trust any of the others."

"You can trust Washington," Byron assured him.

"Perhaps."

"Just remember what I said. Every man you beat will harbor a grudge against you, and in time that might grow to be a dangerous number."

Thinking that by then he would be a very wealthy Indian, Hunter could only smile rather than shiver in dread.

Alanna didn't have to ask Melissa if she enjoyed being married, because she had never seen her look happier. At the same time, there was a disconcerting difference in her cousin that she couldn't name. One moment she seemed more mature, more thoughtful, and in the next, wistful to the point of tears, although she never actually cried.

The announcement of her engagement to Ian and their plans for a May wedding had brought enthusiastic good wishes rather than censure, when his military service was given as the reason for their haste. Aunt Rachel's friends were all eager to help. The Frederick sisters, along with Alanna, were to be bridesmaids. The only regret was that Byron and Elliott would be unable to attend.

Melissa was intent upon having a whole new wardrobe by her wedding day, and Rachel, Alanna, and she spent almost as much time at Sally Lester's shop as they did at home. There were fabrics to select, as well as endless yards of lace and pretty ribbons which had to be chosen for the subtlety of their color and fineness of stitch, followed by many hours of fittings. For Alanna, who had had scant interest in clothes a month prior, it was all a bit overwhelming at first, but she soon got caught up in the fun, since so much of it was focused on Melissa, rather than her.

She could sit back and watch her cousin preen, without feeling any uncomfortable assault on her own shyness. She was content simply to watch, and to occasionally offer an opinion, while Melissa and her mother made so many demands Sally Lester's staff was kept sewing until their fingers bled. Melissa was going to have not only a beautiful wedding, but a wardrobe any woman in Virginia would envy.

One afternoon, Randolph O'Neil was waiting outside the dressmaker's shop. "Good afternoon, ladies. Would you care to join me for tea?" He gestured toward the elegant tearoom across the street. Renowned for its delectable pastries, it was one of Rachel Barclay's favorite places, and she readily agreed.

"How sweet of you to invite us, Mr. O'Neil. We'd love to join, you." Rachel took his arm as they crossed the street, leaving Melissa and Alanna to walk together.

"I should have told her he's interested in you," Melissa whispered.

"That would be cruel," Alanna argued. "They're friends, and I'm sure he must like your mother very much. She has both beauty and charm, and I have neither, besides, she spends a great deal of money in his shop."

"He was waiting to see you, not her," Melissa insisted. "I saw him walk by Sally's shop at least three times. Just watch."

With what appeared to be merely a random choice, Randolph seated himself between Alanna and Rachel. Amused, Melissa winked at her cousin, and then directed her comment to Randolph. "Ian and I hope you'll be able to attend the wedding, Mr. O'Neil."

"I'm looking forward to it," he assured her. "Your cousin owes me a dance."

Noting Alanna's blush, Melissa couldn't help but probe. "Really, and why is that?"

Expecting Alanna to explain, Randolph hesitated a moment, but when she appeared to be too shy to speak, he did. "I asked her to dance the night of the Governor's Ball, but unfortunately you'd been taken ill, and Alanna had to leave early."

Rachel was not at all pleased by Randolph's mention of that night, and hurriedly changed the subject. "You'll be able to dance until dawn at the reception, Mr. O'Neil. Now tell us just what sort of things you'll be carrying in your shop in the fall. I know Melissa and Ian are sure to receive a great many beautiful wedding gifts, but I'd like to give them something special for their first Christmas together."

"It won't be a surprise if he suggests things with me listening, Mama."

"She's right," Randolph agreed, "but I'll look for something especially nice, and save it for you."

"Thank you." Rachel reached out to touch his sleeve as she spoke. Their refreshments were served then, and for the next few minutes, the conversation centered upon how delicious they were. She was a perceptive woman, and noted just how frequently Randolph's glance strayed toward her niece. She was accustomed to men admiring her daughter that openly, but he was the first who had ever shown an interest in Alanna and that he was one of Williamsburg's most prosperous merchants delighted her.

She did her best to involve Alanna in the remainder of the conversation, and as soon as they had bid Randolph goodbye and entered their carriage for the ride home, she reached out to pat her niece's knee. "I didn't realize Randolph O'Neil was so taken with you. Do you like him, too?"

Alanna felt as though she were being shoved in a totally wrong direction, and mentally dug in her heels. "He's attractive and personable, Aunt Rachel, but other than as a friend, I've no interest in him. I won't be impolite, but I shan't encourage his affection, when I can't return it."

Distressed, Rachel pursed her lips thoughtfully for a moment, but her expression soon brightened. "Don't you worry, sweetheart. Weddings are the perfect place to meet eligible men, and perhaps one will please you."

Alanna glanced out the window rather than argue, but she didn't want to be pleased. She just wanted to be left alone.

In anticipation of their marriage, Ian rented a house on Francis Street, and a thrilled Melissa promptly took Alanna to see it. It was a charming, white frame cottage with green shutters, and while it was very small compared with the home in which she had grown up, Melissa couldn't wait to move into it. Supplied with the minimum in furnishings by the owner, it provided Melissa with ample opportunity to express her own tastes in decorating.

"I'll wait until after the wedding to buy what I want," she told Alanna, "because we're sure to receive many lovely things as gifts, and I don't want to duplicate them, but I want this house to be as perfect as Mother's."

"I'll help you with the garden," Alanna volunteered. "You've never liked working with flowers as much as I do."

"That's certainly true, thank you. I want to plant azaleas and camellias across the front, and a rose garden in the back. I suppose I'll have to raise a few vegetables, but they're no trouble, are they?"

"No, and won't Ian help you?"

"Yes, I'm sure he will. This is only a temporary home, of course. We'll build one of our own soon, but since we've told everyone we're marrying now because Ian may be transferred, we can't buy land and start building a house. Everyone would consider us either daft or liars, if we did."

"What if Ian really is transferred?"

"Then I'll go with him," Melissa replied. "Did you think I'd let him go off by himself?"

"No, of course not. I just wondered if you'd made some plans."

Melissa feared she'd been too curt. "I'm sorry. It's just that

I'm so excited about the wedding, that it's difficult to think about anything else, and I certainly don't want to begin worrying about being parted from Ian."

"I'm going to miss you," Alanna confided. "We've been together since we were children, and—"

"And now it's time to grow up," Melissa enthused brightly. "Please don't become maudlin over my marriage. I want everyone to be as happy as Ian and me. Now come on, let's go, we've so much to do and—" She turned toward the door and, suddenly growing dizzy, Melissa reached out to grab Alanna's hand to steady herself.

"Melissa, what's wrong?"

Melissa took a deep breath and let it out slowly. Ian was gone when she awakened in the mornings, so he was unaware that she had begun to experience morning sickness. Now it seemed dizzy spells were going to plague her, too. "It's nothing, just the excitement is all. I'm fine."

She looked too pale for Alanna to believe her. "I think we better sit down and rest a minute. You really don't look well, and you don't want to be ill for your wedding."

Melissa didn't feel up to protesting her cousin's suggestion. She sank down into the nearest chair, leaned back, and closed her eyes. Only a few days remained before the wedding, and she wasn't worried about missing it. "Can you keep a secret?"

"Yes, but if it's something important, perhaps you ought to tell Ian or your parents rather than me."

"Oh, Alanna, you're so incredibly naive, but it's charming. Truly it is." She sat up and, after a suspenseful pause, confided in her. "It's too soon for me to be sure as yet, so please don't tell anyone, but I think Ian and I will become parents as quickly as my mother and father did."

Rather than respond with the excited squeal Melissa had expected, Alanna had to look away. The mention of a baby had brought such painful memories of her sisters and brother, that she needed a moment to shut them out. They had been beautiful children, and she tried always to think of them as angels surrounded by the glory of heaven, rather than as she had last seen them. It was a struggle, but finally she found a smile.

"Does Ian know?"

"No, not yet, and don't you dare tell him either! This is my news, and I'll share it with him when I'm certain. I had to tell you because there are times, like a few minutes ago, when I'm not quite myself, and I don't want you to worry. I'm sure it's perfectly natural."

"Shouldn't you speak with Dr. Earle?"

"Having a baby isn't like being sick, Alanna. There's no need for me to consult a physician. I'm feeling much better already."

The color had returned to Melissa's cheeks, so Alanna didn't argue, but she still felt uneasy. Melissa was right, it was time to grow up, but somehow she thought she had already done that a long time ago.

Melissa's wedding day was slightly overcast at dawn, but by the time she, her parents, and Alanna were dressed and ready to leave for the Bruton Parish Church, the skies were clear. May was always an exceptionally pretty month, and that year it was especially fine. It would be a glorious day for a wedding, and no effort had been spared to make Melissa and Ian's memorable.

Rachel had been too busy supervising the preparations to have time to consider the meaning of the day, but once she was seated opposite her daughter in the carriage, she could no longer stifle her tears, prompting her husband to scold her in a teasing fashion.

"This is supposed to be a happy occasion," he reminded

her. "What will everyone think, if the mother of the bride is weeping throughout the ceremony?"

"They'll think me very sentimental, which I can't deny," Rachel replied.

Melissa was too happy to care what anyone said about her mother, but she hastened to defend her. "The wedding is going to be so beautiful, *everyone* will be moved to tears, and no one will think Mother is overly sentimental. I want to thank you both. Ian and I will never forget your kindness."

It was John who nearly choked on tears then. He took out his handkerchief and blew his nose to hide his discomfort, but both his wife and daughter understood the cause of his distress. For the past month, Melissa had remained at home, and her marriage had brought little change in their lives, but from that day on, she would be living with Ian, and her love and loyalty would belong to him. "Our home is going to seem empty without you," he finally managed to say.

"Just wait for the day when Ian and I come to visit with all ten of your grandchildren. Then you'll be happy to see me leave."

Amused by the thought of his lovely daughter surrounded by ten youngsters, all with Ian's bright red hair, John had to laugh. "When you put it that way, yes, I realize I ought to enjoy the quiet while I can. I wonder just how much longer you'll be with us, Alanna. You're so pretty today, we'll be lucky if someone doesn't run off with you, too."

"John, you hush about that," Rachel scolded. "One elopement was more than enough for this family."

Alanna was grateful her aunt had distracted her uncle so easily, but she could not even imagine herself becoming so enamored of a young man that she would consider marriage, let alone an elopement. She was thrilled for Melissa, but didn't expect to ever have a lavish wedding of her own. Perhaps it was because Melissa was already wed, but there had been very little in the way of confusion that morning. Their gowns had been laid out the previous evening, with every stocking and slip in its place, so they had been able to dress in less time than they had for parties. There had been no anxiety, no apprehensions, merely a calm commitment to giving this second wedding the look of a well-rehearsed formal rite.

Melissa and her family arrived at the Anglican church as the first of the guests began to appear. The priest had not been taken into their confidence, and before leaving the carriage, John reminded the women to keep their silence in that regard. "This is the day your marriage begins, Melissa, and none of us need ever admit otherwise. We'll ask for God's blessing today, but we've already been blessed, and I hope that for the rest of our lives, we'll never have to fool our friends and neighbors as we have this last month. Lies don't come easy to me, and I don't need more practice in using them. From now on, let's all endeavor to live lives where only the truth prevails."

"Amen," Rachel added.

Melissa nodded and, in her mind, her actions had all been governed by the truth. She cared deeply for Ian, and she intended to be all he would ever want in a wife. She took her father's hands as she left the carriage, and smiled bravely. "You'll never be sorry for this, Papa."

John had seen the love reflected in her eyes when she was with Ian, and didn't doubt her. He placed a kiss on her cheek and helped her adjust the fit of her veil. "I've never seen a lovelier bride. That's not to say that your mother wasn't a beauty, but today you look enough like she did on our wedding day, for me to mean that as a compliment to you both."

"Thank you, Papa."

The Frederick sisters and their parents arrived then, followed by additional guests; the bridal party entered the church to wait for the ceremony to begin. They heard the muffled conversation as the pews began to fill, and the deep tones of the organ as the hymns Melissa and Ian had chosen were played. John and Rachel smiled with memories of their own wedding, while Sarah and Robin Frederick looked forward to equally splendid ceremonies of their own. Melissa twisted the sapphire and diamond ring Ian had given her, and had only sweet thoughts of him. Alanna, with neither pleasant memories nor hopeful dreams, stood nearest the door and, when all the guests had arrived, conveyed the priest's signal to begin.

The church had been decorated with huge bouquets of white roses and camellias. Sarah, Robin, and Alanna were dressed in gowns of ice blue taffeta with the iridescent sheen of pearls, and Rachel was equally lovely in an exquisite shade of sky blue. The golden threads interwoven in the ivory satin of Melissa's gown reflected the sunlight streaming in the windows, framing her in a hallowed glow. The guests responded with appreciative gasps as her father escorted her down the aisle, but all she saw was Ian.

Recently promoted to captain, Ian's red coat was accented with deep blue lapels, generous amounts of gold braid, and two rows of brass buttons. His waistcoat, while bordered in gold, matched the cream-color of his britches. A pair of highly polished black boots and a sword completed his attire. Melissa had chosen blue for her bridesmaid's dresses, not simply because it was her favorite color, but because blue blended perfectly with the uniforms Ian and his friends would wear.

When Ian took her hand and winked slyly, she realized he was as calm as she. After a month as his wife, she was convinced they had been meant to be together, and repeated her vows in a confident tone that held no hint of tears. Ian was her choice, and if anyone had attempted to tell her how wrong her original reason for marrying him had been, she would have argued that today, her motive was the right one. When they were pronounced husband and wife for the second time, she was happier than she had ever thought she could be.

"I love you," she whispered.

Ian responded with a kiss, before escorting her up the aisle and out into the sunshine. The beauty of the day had convinced him they were the luckiest of couples, and would have a long and happy life together. He helped Melissa into the carriage for the ride to her home for the reception, and pulled her across his lap.

"Do you remember the last time we made this same trip together?" he asked.

"Yes, and while this wedding was all I could have hoped, I'm glad we didn't wait for today."

"So am I," Ian teased, and with a low growl he nibbled her throat. He was so lost in her he could not wait for the day to end to make love to her again, but when he suggested they put the carriage ride to a better use, she appeared to be shocked.

"My goodness, Captain, I'll thank you to keep such scandalous thoughts to yourself today. We are supposed to behave like a very proper bride and groom, and I don't want to give our friends any other impression. Besides, the ride isn't nearly long enough to make love to you as I'd like to."

Charmed by that promise, Ian ceased to complain, but he still would have liked to have made love to her right then and there. He told himself he would have a lifetime to make love to Melissa, but somehow he didn't think that would be nearly enough time either.

True to his promise, Randolph O'Neil came looking for Alanna as soon as the dancing began. The furniture had been removed from the parlor to create a small ballroom, and he led her out into the middle of the floor. The musicians had begun with a lilting minuet, and all around them couples traced graceful figures. Self-conscious as always, Alanna tried to remember to smile as she danced, so she would appear to be enjoying herself as much as her partner, but Randolph wasn't fooled.

When the first tune melted into the second, he kept hold of her hand. Along with a sumptuous meal, the Barclays were serving a rum punch flavored with pineapple and lemons, and he suggested they have a cup, then lured her outside where they could escape the crowd for a few minutes. "While I'm not as old a man as your uncle, I'm going to feel very foolish asking his permission to call on you. If you'd rather not see me, I'd appreciate your saying so now, as it will save me an embarrassing ordeal."

Amused by his plea, Alanna's smile was now genuine. "I've never had any callers, Mr. O'Neil, and I've no idea how to entertain you. Perhaps you would be saving us both an embarrassing ordeal, if you did not speak to my uncle."

Randolph laughed with her. "You see, you do know how to entertain callers. I can't believe that you haven't had any though. Of course, until recently, I seldom saw you except at church. I imagine other men lacked the same opportunity to impress you."

Uncertain what to say, Alanna frowned slightly. Where should she begin? she wondered. Should she describe how her family had been murdered, and explain how love and loss were so closely intertwined in her mind, she couldn't separate them? Surely that wasn't the kind of charming tale a young woman told to regale her suitors.

Alanna's expression revealed the answer she didn't seem to be able to put into words, and Randolph regretfully provided his own reply. "You'd rather I didn't call on you, wouldn't you?"

Alanna was close to tears. "It's not that I don't like you, Mr. O'Neil. It's just that I doubt I'll ever wish to marry and have children. There's really no need for me to entertain callers then, is there?"

"How old are you, Alanna?"

"Seventeen."

"That's rather young to choose a spinster's life, don't you think?"

"It's not really a matter of choice, Mr. O'Neil," Alanna argued halfheartedly.

"You're a lovely young woman," he leaned forward to whisper. "All you need is a little more time to grow up. I'll try and be patient. Shall we go back inside?"

Alanna knew her decision had nothing to do with age, but let the matter drop. "I think I'll stay out here awhile, thank you." He took her empty cup with him, and she turned toward the garden but she hadn't taken more than three steps before Graham Tyler appeared at her side. He was as splendidly attired as Ian and greeted her with a delighted grin.

"I've been hoping for a chance to speak with you alone. There wasn't time at the church, of course, with all the confusion to get everyone into carriages for the trip here. Now that I've finally found you, I hope that you might have a few minutes for me. If you'd rather dance, I'd be pleased to be your partner. I'll be happy to do whatever you'd like."

"Do you think that you could stroll through the garden without talking incessantly?" Alanna regretted that comment as soon as she had spoken it. "I'm sorry, that was very rude of me, but, Graham, *must* you be so talkative?"

Rather than being as badly embarrassed as Alanna had feared, Graham started to laugh. "I'm so horribly nervous when I'm with you, I don't have any idea what I'm saying. If you'd rather I just be quiet, it would be a great relief to me as well."

"Some men are too quiet, and that's upsetting, too." Alanna looked around hurriedly to make certain Stuart Harnett wasn't anywhere near. "Perhaps we could just stroll for a while, and wait until something interesting occurs to us. Then the conversation would be far easier for us both."

Unwilling to spoil what he considered a rare stroke of good fortune, Graham offered his arm, but he wisely kept his mouth shut.

Ten

Toward the end of May, Washington's men crossed the main range of the Alleghenies and camped in the shadow of the next barrier, Laurel Hill. The ground here at Great Meadows was level, covered in thick grass and bushes nourished by the waters of a small brook. The one hundred fifty men, who had labored so hard to cut a wide swath through the forest, were in sore need of reinforcements, but Colonel Fry had yet to arrive with the rest of the regiment. As for Captain Trent's frontiersmen, they had been so badly discouraged after the surrender of their fort to the French, they had wanted no more to do with the militia, and had resumed their solitary lives in the woods.

While the majority of the men remained at Great Meadows, Hunter and Elliott were with George Washington exploring the Youghiogheny, a branch of the Monongahela, when a messenger arrived from Monacatootha, the chief who had accompanied the young lieutenant colonel to Fort Le Boeuf the previous fall. Having been humiliated by the French when he had voiced the Indians' demands that they leave the Ohio Valley, he was a staunch ally of the British. Washington had every reason to trust him.

"Monacatootha says the French have left their fort in search of Englishmen to fight. They may be no more than twenty miles distant," Washington warned.

A decision was quickly made to return to Great Meadows

and, as the others started back down the river, Elliott drew Hunter aside. "You were hired as a scout, not a soldier. If you wish to leave, as Trent's men did, no one will call you a coward."

Hunter could not look at either Elliott or Byron without being reminded of Melissa. Neither was as blond as his sister, but their eyes were just as vivid a blue. He did not believe she would be favorably impressed if he were to leave her brothers to face the French alone, but he chose not to mention his desire to please her in his reply.

"I won't leave before my job is done, and you still need me to track the French."

"Well, yes, that's true, but—"

Hunter rested his hand lightly on Elliott's shoulder. "I don't carry a musket, but that doesn't mean I don't know how to fire one."

Elliott studied the Indian's sly smile, and readily guessed its meaning. "You're probably the best shot in camp, aren't you?"

"Do you want to arrange a contest?"

Elliott had to laugh. "No, not yet, but I'm glad you'll stay with us. I think you'll bring us luck."

"You are going to need it."

"Yes, I know. Now come on, let's hurry. We don't want to be left behind."

Hunter was not concerned about falling behind and becoming lost, but he could see Elliott was, and hurried him along rather than tease him about it.

Great Meadows was surrounded by wooded hills and on one side furrowed by a gully. As soon as his scouting party returned to camp, Washington set part of his men to work deepening the gully to form an entrenchment, while the others cleared the open field of shrubs to prepare for battle. Rather than help with that effort, Hunter went out to search the woods for the advancing enemy. At dusk he returned to the meadow where most of the men were too excited to eat, but he helped himself to the rice and salt pork the cooks had prepared, and went to sleep early.

The next morning he again scoured the woods for some sign of French soldiers, but returned to camp without having gathered any valuable intelligence. He knew they were coming, but apparently they were moving much slower than anyone had anticipated, or perhaps they were circling wide to approach them from an unexpected direction. Whatever their plan, Hunter did not like it anymore than he relished the thought of battling them on a wide plain, where the only cover was a shallow ditch.

The next morning, Christopher Gist paid them a visit. He had served as a guide on Washington's fall expedition, and now lived at a settlement on the far side of Laurel Hill. He had traveled a dozen miles to bring important news.

"There must have been fifty Frenchmen at my house yesterday. They would have stolen everything had the Indians who care for the place not been there. You've enough men here to defeat them easily."

Volunteers were plentiful, and with Gist's directions, seventy-five men went out to search for the French, but they had no better luck than Hunter had in finding them and, discouraged, returned to camp before nightfall. Soon after, another messenger arrived from Monacatootha, who had found suspicious tracks and believed he had discovered where the French were hiding. Taking forty men, Washington led this search party himself. It was now dark and raining, but the men followed in a weary procession that lasted until dawn.

Blessed with greater stamina than most men, Hunter traveled fast and stayed near the head of the line, but occasionally he would drop back to make certain Elliott was still with them. The rain had turned the narrow path into a slippery quagmire that tugged at the soles of the men's boots one minute, and then turned slick as a wet mirror the next. In the darkness, men who stumbled and lagged behind soon found themselves lost in the dense forest, and unable to call out for help for fear of alerting the French, they had to huddle alone until dawn. When Washington at last arrived at the place where Monaca-tootha was camped with a dozen of his warriors, seven of his soldiers had been lost.

Eager to fight the French, two of Monacatootha's warriors led the way; again traveling in single file, the men of the Virginia Regiment and their Indian allies followed the suspicious tracks to a rocky ravine. Finding a small force of French soldiers encamped there, Washington gave the order to fire. While one Canadian managed to escape, within a few minutes ten of the Frenchmen were killed, including the ensign, Coulon de Jumonville, who was slain by Monacatootha. The fury of the fighting was enough to prompt the surviving twenty-two men to surrender.

Splattered with the blood of their slain comrades, and terrified, the captured men hurriedly explained that they had been sent by the Sieur de Contrecoeur, the commandant of Fort Duquesne, the newly constructed fortress named for the Governor of New France, which now stood on the site originally occupied by Ensign Ward. They swore they had been on a peaceful mission, to deliver a summons warning the English to withdraw from lands belonging to the King of France, or be forced to go.

"How do you expect us to believe you meant to deliver such a summons, when we found you hiding in a ravine?" Washington asked through his interpreter. "Clearly you are spies, not messengers."

"No, that's not true!" one of Frenchmen protested. "We left Fort Duquesne five days ago with orders to deliver the summons to the first Englishman we met. We observed your camp, and as ordered, sent two men with word for Contrecoeur that we intended to speak with you. We were camped here, awaiting his reply."

"That makes absolutely no sense," Washington scoffed. "You were told to seek out any Englishman, but to notify Contrecoeur before you actually approached him?"

"Yes, sir. Those were our orders."

Washington glanced toward Elliott, who shook his head. Such contradictory orders were absurd, unless Contrecoeur had meant to respond with whatever force would be necessary to enforce the summons. If there were a thousand men at Fort Duquesne, why hadn't he sent more than thirty-five in the first place? Washington felt that his first impression was correct: he had surprised a party of spies, who had been told to mention a summons should they be caught. Disgusted, he marched his prisoners back to Great Meadows under heavy guard.

Their return with French prisoners was greeted with celebration, but fearing a swift reprisal from Fort Duquesne, Washington quickly channeled his troops' energy into building a log stockade, which was aptly named Fort Necessity. Monacatootha arrived with a woman known as Queen Alequippa, and more than two dozen braves and their families. Their force still dangerously small, however, Washington sent Christopher Gist to Will's Creek to urge Colonel Fry to bring up the rest of the regiment.

Gist returned with the sad news that Colonel Fry had fallen ill and died, but the remaining three companies of the regiment soon marched into camp, swelling Washington's force to three hundred. They were followed by a company of British regulars from South Carolina, commanded by a Captain Mackay. Mackay's commission had been granted by the king, and he was unwilling to take orders from Washington, who had been appointed by the governor of Virginia. The soldiers under his command were no more cooperative, and refused to work without extra pay.

Hunter watched the antagonism mount between the industrious Virginians and the slothful troops under Mackay's command, knowing such a feud would aid the French rather than anyone in their camp. When George Washington announced that he intended to leave Mackay at Great Meadows, while the Virginia Regiment extended their road over Laurel Hill to Christopher Gist's settlement, Hunter was the first man ready to leave. Like the Virginians, he preferred the strenuous work of hacking out a road wide enough for wagons and cannon, over watching the men fight amongst themselves while waiting for an attack.

Resolute in their purpose, the regiment crossed the dozen miles to Gist's settlement, and then again set to work creating a defensive entrenchment. Reports from French deserters provided the distressing news that the already well-manned Fort Duquesne was expecting reinforcements. When Indians appearing to be friendly to the British brought warnings of an attack by vast numbers of Frenchmen, Washington sent for Mackay and his troops.

With Gist's house serving as their command post, it was soon decided that the surrounding hills would provide the French with a murderous advantage, and all retreated to Great Meadows over the newly widened road. With but a few packhorses, the Virginians were forced to carry most of their provisions on their backs and drag the swivel guns, which they relied upon for defense, during the arduous two-day walk. As usual, Mackay's men were of absolutely no help. On July 1, 1754, they returned to Fort Necessity, too exhausted by their travels to retreat farther.

July second was spent in reinforcing the barricades of the crude, square fort. The men had fresh beef to eat, but little else, and their store of ammunition was small. Monacatootha's scouts had reported that the French were rapidly approaching with nine hundred soldiers, supported by countless numbers of Indians. It was clear to all that they were ill prepared for a long siege against a vastly superior force. Rain added to the dismal nature of their outlook.

The enemy was first sighted at mid-morning on July third. Washington advanced to meet them on the plain in front of the fort, but the wily French scattered and opened fire from the cover of the two adjacent hills. Washington then ordered his troops to drop back to the entrenchment, but, caught in a crossfire, they could inflict little damage. The rain continued to fall, at times rendering the visibility so poor they could not even see the enemy, let alone shoot one. They mounted the swivel guns on the rampart, but there was so little cover for the gunners, they were unable to maintain steady fire.

"We don't have much powder left," Elliott warned.

Their plight had been so dire all day that Hunter wasn't greatly alarmed. Unwilling to face certain defeat, Monacatootha and his braves had withdrawn before the fight had begun, but Hunter had not even considered leaving with them. He raised up slightly, took careful aim, and fired. Through the drizzling rain and smoke he saw a Frenchman fall, but he quickly ducked his head before he became a target.

"When we run out of powder, I'll do what I can with my bow."

Elliott doubted there was a braver man among them. "You don't even look tired," he murmured in awe.

"This is no time to be tired!"

"I realize that, but, Lord, I'm weary." Elliott removed his hat momentarily to pour the water off the brim. Nearby a man who'd been wounded lay sobbing, while his friends tended him in the mud. Elliott glanced over at him and shuddered. "I didn't think it would be this bad."

"I did," Hunter replied. He rose up again, and this time took aim at an Indian he recognized as an Abenaki. The brave suddenly turned toward him, and the intensity of the hatred reflected in his gelid gaze caused Hunter to hesitate a second too long. In the next instant, the rain swirled around the Abenaki in a dense wave, and unwilling to waste a shot on a man who might duck for cover, Hunter dipped low without firing.

"Where's Byron?" he asked.

"He's on the other side."

The shooting was no less intense there, but Hunter believed Byron would survive. Hoping for a second shot at the Abenaki, he eased up again, but when he heard one of the French call out, he sank back down out of range and yanked Elliott down beside him. "The French want to talk. Hold your fire."

Washington knew as well as any of his men just how desperate their situation was. One hundred of his force of three hundred eighty-four had been too sick to fight, and in the day-long battle, another hundred had become casualties. Not wanting the French to send a spy into their midst to make such a report, he declined their offer to talk. It wasn't until the French commander suggested he send an officer to them, that he finally agreed. He had only two men who were fluent in French, one, an ensign, was wounded, so the other, Captain Vanbraam, a Dutchman, had to go.

When Vanbraam returned, Hunter stood at Elliott's elbow to hear the French proposal. "The French commander is Coulon de Villiers. He says his brother, Coulon de Jumonville, was the ensign killed when we captured the spies. While clearly he's come for revenge, most of his terms are reasonable." The discussion which followed was lit by a candle frequently extinguished by the rain, but by midnight, terms agreeable to both sides had been reached, George Washington signed the surrender, and freed his French prisoners.

Early the next morning, Fort Necessity was abandoned. During the battle, all the horses and cattle had been slain, so any soldier able to help carry the wounded and sick was obliged to do so. They had been accorded the honors of war and left accompanied by drums with their flags waving proudly. They had been allowed to keep their muskets, and one of the swivel guns, but it was a pathetic parade which would have to cover the fifty-four mile route back over the Alleghenies to Will's Creek.

Among the able-bodied, Hunter was carrying a severely wounded man on his back, when several volleys of musket fire rang out farther down the line. Fearing they had again fallen under attack, Hunter did not wait for an order. He eased the wounded soldier down onto the grass at the side of the road, and hurriedly reassured him that he would soon return.

Terrified that he would be forgotten, the injured man reached out to grab Hunter's arm, but caught only a handful of fringe. "No, don't leave me," he begged.

Hunter pried his fingers loose. "If there's trouble, I must stop it before it reaches you. Now let me go." He watched the fear in the soldier's eyes turn to confusion, but at last he gave a feeble nod and Hunter got away. Others were also attempting to dodge the wounded and make their way to the rear, but Hunter was among the first to reach those in need of aid.

The troops at the end of the column had been set upon by Indians, and when Hunter saw the Abenaki brave he had missed shooting during the battle, he screamed, "Coward! You attack the wounded rather than men who can fight!" He raised the musket he'd been given, intending to send the brave straight to hell, but a badly wounded soldier chose that instant to stagger to his feet and blocked the shot.

"Blind Snake is no coward!" the Abenaki shouted, and waving a bloody scalp, he followed his fleeing band into the trees.

Hunter started after them, but Byron caught up with him and hauled him back. "No, stay. We can't spare you," he ordered.

Hunter looked around at the bloody scene. In the surprise attack, two of the men wounded in the previous day's battle had been murdered and scalped, and several others appeared near death. The medicine chest had been reduced to splinters, and the medicines which would have eased the wounded men's pain had been ruined.

"The Abenaki are no better than vultures," he complained. "Let me go after them."

"No," Byron insisted again. "We may have seen only a few of a much larger war party, and I'll not risk losing you. The French may be unable to control their Indian allies, but I'll not tolerate the same wild streak in you."

Outraged by that undeserved taunt, Hunter stepped back and regarded Byron with a newly suspicious gaze. "I would never stalk a retreating army to kill their wounded. Indians are like white men. Some have honor and others do not." Disgusted that Byron would compare him to murderers, he threw his musket at his feet. "Keep your weapon. I'll have no more need of it."

Hunter turned away, and Byron called out to him. "Where are you going?"

"I have a man to carry."

Byron knew he'd just made a terrible mistake, but the responsibility of caring for so many sick and wounded men in the wake of a humiliating defeat was weighing heavily on him. He bent down and picked up Hunter's discarded musket, and having more than enough grief on his hands for the present, he vowed to make peace with the Indian later.

It was July 4, 1754, and having vanquished all English resistance, the French now dominated the Ohio Valley.

Ian bathed Melissa's flushed face with a cool washcloth and then rocked her gently in his arms. "You shouldn't be this sick every morning, sweetheart. I want to send for your doctor."

"No." Melissa clung to her husband as she sought a way to avoid a physician's scrutiny. She was three months' pregnant, but it had been only two months since their wedding at Bruton Parish Church. "We'd have to confide in him about the elopement, and he's sure to tell others."

"Then we'll consult someone who's more discreet, but I can't bear to watch you suffer like this."

"It's not supposed to last more than the first few months."

Ian scanned the crowded bedroom Melissa had been attempting to decorate. He had hired a woman to come in each day to cook and clean, but Melissa wouldn't let her touch the clutter. He admired his wife's ambition, but doubted she would ever arrive at any order, while she felt so poorly. Between the abundant wedding gifts and her subsequent purchases, the bedroom was filled to overflowing, while the rest of their home remained as stark as the day they had moved in.

Just looking at the mess made him nauseous, but he didn't want to discuss his frustration while she was sick. "I doubt it's just the pregnancy that's making you ill. I think it's something more."

Alarmed, Melissa sat up slowly. She had never given Ian any reason to doubt her babe was his, but she was terrified that he might have somehow guessed the truth. "What do you mean?" she asked.

"I fear I've expected too much of you. While I'll readily admit the responsibility for your condition, I also deserve the blame for encouraging you to work so hard on our home. It's no wonder you're not well. I think it might be a good idea for us to move back to your parents' house for a while. I'll do what I can to straighten everything out here, and when you're feeling better, you can provide the finishing touches."

Relieved that he hadn't grown suspicious, Melissa gave her husband a loving hug. "I've made a dreadful mess of things here, haven't I?"

"No, not all," Ian lied. "You're going to create a beautiful home, but this just isn't the time to do it."

"But I want to stay here."

"Yes, and so do I, but not if it's making you ill."

"The house is really no trouble, Ian." Melissa caught herself then, for their home provided the perfect excuse for the black moods that often overtook her without warning. She could be merely straightening a pair of curtains, or pouring a cup of tea, and suddenly she could feel Hunter's presence so strongly she would turn toward the door, fully expecting to find him standing there. She had told herself repeatedly that now that she was married to Ian, Hunter could never do her any further harm, but her imagination continued to play tricks on her.

She sighed softly and rested her forehead against Ian's. "No, you're right. It's foolish of me to try to accomplish everything at once. I really should be more careful, take things easier, and concentrate on having a healthy baby. Perhaps a week or two at my parents' home will be all I'll need to get over this awful queasiness."

"At least you never feel sick at night."

Melissa sat back to study her husband's rakish grin. His loving left her feeling wonderfully content, and she was as pleased as he was that their nights together hadn't been ruined by the nausea that plagued her days.

Aware of their daughter's pregnancy, John and Rachel readily welcomed her and Ian back into their home, for it was plain at a glance that the once-vivacious young woman was unwell. Without criticizing their son-in-law, they provided her with every comfort, and encouraged the young couple to remain with them until after their baby's birth.

Alanna had been lonely while Melissa was away, but now that every conversation led to talk of babies, she found being around her difficult. They had always had their own separate interests, but now Melissa was preparing for motherhood with the same enthusiasm she had shown when planning her wedding, while Alanna was still absorbed in the simple pleasures she had always found there on the plantation. Alanna did try to take an interest in the tiny clothes her aunt and cousin had begun sewing, and because she was good with a needle, they welcomed her help.

Melissa held up a tiny nightgown. "Are babies really this small?" she asked.

"I used the same pattern for your brothers' clothes," Rachel reminded her. "You'll be surprised by how quickly your baby will outgrow them though."

Alanna was seated near a window to take advantage of the light, and as she knotted her thread and cut it, a long-forgotten memory suddenly became clear. She hadn't been old enough to be of any real help to her mother before her sisters had been born, but she had been able to do simple sewing by the time her brother arrived. Her mother had cut out tiny garments for him and done the seams, but Alanna had put in the hems. Her work couldn't have been very neat, but her mother had given her lavish praise.

Many an afternoon she and her mother had spent their time sewing, while the babies slept. Her mother had told her wonderful stories, and on more than one occasion, they had spent more time laughing than sewing. Those had been the happiest days of her life. Alanna didn't realize she was crying until her aunt spoke to her.

"Alanna, dear, what's wrong?"

Embarrassed by her tears, Alanna quickly wiped them away. "My mother and I used to sit together and sew, the way we are now. I'd not thought about it in years, but the last things we made were my brother's clothes."

"I remember you called him Chris. Was that for Christopher or Christian?" Melissa asked.

"Christian."

"Christian Scott would make a fine name," Melissa decided, after repeating it a few times. "If we have a son, I'll ask Ian if we might call him that."

"What a sweet idea," Rachel enthused. "I know we seldom speak of your family, Alanna, but they've not been forgotten."

That Melissa would even consider using her brother's name touched Alanna deeply. "Thank you," she murmured. "Do you have a name picked out for a girl?"

"No, we've really given no thought to names, but let's try and find some pretty ones now. I liked your sisters' names, Margaret and Mae, but perhaps you'd rather I didn't use those names, so that you could. After all, we don't want to give our children the same names, or they would never know who should answer when they are called."

"You should feel free to choose whatever names you please," Alanna assured her. "I've no plans to wed and have a family, so I'll have no need of names."

Rachel and her daughter exchanged an exasperated glance, for they had heard Alanna express the same sorry sentiment before, and had believed her then no more than they did now. "Let's just wait and see," Rachel mused thoughtfully. "We've seen a great deal of Lieutenant Tyler of late, and perhaps you'll grow fond of him."

Since the wedding in May, Graham had been far less talkative and much better company, but Alanna had never flirted with him, nor given him any reason to believe they were more than friends. She only saw him on Sundays when he came to the house for dinner after church, but it had always been with Melissa and Ian, and she considered him more Ian's friend than hers. She had seen sly glances pass between her cousin and aunt, and wondered if she had somehow given them the wrong impression, then Graham might misunderstand her views, too.

The following Sunday Graham was again invited to come for dinner, and Alanna felt uneasy throughout the meal. If Graham had mentioned that he would like to ask for permission to call on her the way Randolph O'Neil had, she would have had the perfect opportunity to explain she had no desire for beaus. He had not done so, however, and it struck her as absurd to announce to a man who had never expressed an interest in courting her, that she had no wish to become his wife.

She looked up to find him watching her and tried to smile. The night of the Governor's Ball he had commented upon her reluctance to be with him, but she had been so worried about Melissa disappearing, she had brushed his question aside. Such haste to avoid personal topics now seemed unforgivably rude, but she was grateful he had not expressed his feelings again. After dinner, when he asked if she would like to join Melissa and Ian for a walk down by the river, she felt relaxed enough around him to accept.

Melissa and Ian walked only as far as the river's edge, however, before they chose a spot to sit and rest, but at Graham's urging, Alanna led him toward a winding trial that bordered the river for miles. It was wide enough for two people to walk side by side comfortably, and they strolled for some distance before Graham spoke.

"I know compliments make you cringe, but that dress is one of my favorites. The violets almost appear real."

"Thank you. I don't mean to cringe, Lieutenant. I'm sorry if I've offended you in the past."

"If you'd offended me, I'd not be with you here now, would I?"

"I'm afraid I know so little about men that I'm not sure."

Thinking she was teasing him, Graham laughed. "I keep forgetting that you're a year younger than Melissa. You're so much more mature in your attitudes that I thought you were the eldest, until Ian explained otherwise."

"You've talked to Ian about me?"

"Of course. I can't believe that you and Melissa haven't once talked about me."

Now it was Alanna who couldn't suppress a smile. "Yes, I'll admit upon occasion we have."

"And what do you say?"

Alanna knew Graham was providing her with the perfect opportunity to confide her desire to remain unmarried, but at the same time, she feared expressing it would be as rude as many of the other thoughtless remarks she had made to him. "I'd really rather not say," she finally replied. "This has been an especially pretty summer, hasn't it?"

Graham stopped abruptly and, afraid Alanna would walk right on by him, he put out his arm to stop her. "Please, if you would only give me some slight hope that you like me, it would mean so much to me."

Graham's expression was painfully sincere, but Alanna could not begin to understand how desperate he felt. "I do like you, Lieutenant. You're a very nice man."

"If a bit too talkative?"

"I shouldn't have said that."

"No, I disagree. You must always tell me precisely what you think and feel, or I'll never learn how to please you."

"Is pleasing me so very important to you?"

"Oh, yes, you mean the world to me."

Graham was attractive, pleasant, and kind, but Alanna felt not the smallest stirrings of affection for him. Melissa and Ian were always touching, hugging, and kissing, if they thought no one was watching them. She understood how much pleasure each received from being with the other, because it was obvious in their expression and manner, but she felt no such joy with Graham.

"I do like you as a friend, Graham. Please don't ask me for anything more."

Graham took that small concession on her part as a victory and his expression lit with triumph. He leaned over and gave her cheek a quick kiss, and then took her hand to continue their walk. "I'm grateful you want me for a friend," he said. "I don't mean to pry, but there isn't another man you like better, is there?"

Alanna shook her head. "You're simply impossible, aren't you?"

"Where you're concerned I am. Now please answer my question. Is there someone else?"

"No," Alanna assured him quickly, and again he flashed a wide grin. She knew other women considered him handsome. The Frederick sisters certainly did. He was bright, too, during dinner he always entered discussions with her uncle with a confidence born of knowledge of the subject. He was undoubtedly a fine prospect for a husband, but as she walked by his side, her conviction to avoid marriage never wavered.

Eleven

Byron offered an apology to Hunter before they reached Will's Creek, but it was coolly shrugged off and their relationship never resumed its former warmth. While the Indian and Elliott had grown closer during the four months they had served together, Byron came away from the experience feeling bitter and alone. When their *bateau* reached their plantation dock one hot August afternoon, he felt none of the elation of his last visit home.

Elliott was in only marginally better spirits than Byron, but he was consoled by the fact that their defeat was common knowledge throughout the colonies, so they would not have to disclose the wretched news themselves. It was a small comfort, but he clung to it. Both he and Byron had lost weight, and their faces no longer retained any trace of youthful softness. They had left home as exuberant young officers of twenty-one and twenty-three, and returned home hardened veterans of what they now regarded as a futile campaign.

Unlike the Barclay brothers, Hunter had not been burdened by the guilt of defeat. He had done his best under the worst of circumstances, and took pride in it. He would have preferred to return to Virginia with exciting stories of their victory to entertain Melissa, but lacking those, he knew there were other far more pleasurable ways for them to pass their time.

While Byron and Elliott climbed out of the *bateau* slowly, he leapt over the side and had to fight the impulse to run up the path to the house, shouting Melissa's name. After waiting four long months to see her, any further delay was excruciating, but he had to adopt an impassive expression, as though his visit were without the special significance Melissa's presence gave it.

John and Rachel hurried down to the dock to greet their sons, and Alanna followed along closely. They were all enormously relieved to see Byron and Elliott had returned home unharmed, and greeted Hunter politely. "Did you get my letters?" Rachel asked. "The one you sent from Alexandria made no mention of Ian and Melissa, so I feared none of my letters reached you."

"Mail delivery was haphazard at best, Mother," Byron explained. "Was there a particular reason you wrote to us about them?"

Rachel turned to her husband. "You know I wrote to them."

"Yes, my dear, but it's no wonder they didn't get the news of the wedding."

"Wedding?" Elliott asked. "Are Melissa and Ian engaged?"

"They were married in May," Rachel rushed to explain. "It was a wonderful wedding, and we missed you both terribly. That's not the only news though, we'll have a grandchild in January!"

Byron and Elliott were quite naturally surprised to learn of their sister's sudden marriage and expected child, but Hunter was stunned to hear the woman he loved had wed another. Angry tears stung his eyes, and as he turned to hide them his gaze met Alanna's. She had undergone such a dramatic change since April that he almost didn't recognize her. She could no longer be mistaken for a servant, now that she wore an attractive gown and lace-trimmed cap. Her manner was confident rather than timid. Afraid she could see his pain, he turned back to the *bateau* and began unloading it.

He had expected to have to hide his feelings until he and

Melissa could be alone, but love would have been far easier to conceal than the despair he now felt. He heard John Barclay curse the lack of support from other colonies as a factor in their defeat, and realized that whatever sorrow he displayed would be mistaken for the same anguish Byron and Elliott were making no attempt to disguise. They were merely discouraged, however, and he was heartbroken.

By the time he had set the last piece of luggage on the dock, Hunter had his emotions under firm control. He would not scream and plead when he saw Melissa, he would simply ask her to explain why she had made love to him, and then wed another. She was a passionate woman, and he was not surprised she and Ian had conceived a child so quickly, but that was a small insult compared to the betrayal of her marriage.

It wasn't until they reached the porch and he saw Melissa waiting at the door, that her motives instantly became clear. She may have been wed only three months, but the fullness of her bosom and thickening at her waist made it plain her journey toward motherhood was further advanced. When she avoided his glance, he knew with a devastating certainty that her child was his.

He dropped his belongings on the porch and, unable to offer a coherent excuse, walked away.

"Hunter?" Elliott called.

Hunter turned back to wave, but kept on walking. He had been a full-grown man at sixteen, and in the last eight years he had known several woman as intimately as he had known Melissa, but none had touched his heart. Sweet memories of the stolen moments they had shared had never left his mind, but obviously her thoughts had seldom, if ever, strayed to him. That he had given her a child apparently meant nothing to her, or she would have sent for him, and he would be her husband rather than Ian.

He remembered Ian as a likable young man with a friendly

smile, but there was nothing remarkable about him. He was white, of course, and apparently that was all that had mattered to Melissa. She had chosen to wed an English gentleman rather than an Indian brave. He was accustomed to white men attempting to take advantage of him, but this was the first time a white woman had succeeded in doing so, and he had never felt so humiliated. Melissa had used him, perhaps merely to satisfy her curiosity, and then gone on to Ian.

Torn by the desire to turn his back on Melissa forever, and the equally strong need to confront her, Hunter ran along the river until he had taken the edge off his rage. He then began to play out scenes in his mind, in an attempt to find words that would convey his disgust in a manner Melissa would never forget. There was nothing he could say that would be too mean after what she had done to him, and he practiced insults until he was certain his would ring in her ears forever.

With their father's encouragement, Byron and Elliott described their recent adventure, but Alanna excused herself at the first mention of bloodshed. While she had listened to her cousins' tale, she had been haunted by the memory of Hunter's agonized expression when he had learned of Melissa's marriage. He had tried to hide his pain, and had succeeded with the others, but she was far more observant. She could appreciate his need for solitude, but at the same time, she did not want him to suffer needlessly.

As she started across the lawn toward the dock, Alanna could not help but marvel at the improvement in her attitude since Hunter's first visit. She had been terrified of him, not for who he was, but simply for *what* he was, and that had been most uncharitable of her. Due to her aunt and cousin's encouragement, she was more comfortable in the company of others now, and because she felt she owed him an apology, she thought this might be the perfect time to give it. As she had suspected, he was down by the river, but he had left his buckskins and moccasins on the dock and was swimming. Not wanting to embarrass either of them, she turned back toward the house, but Hunter had already seen her and called out her name.

Alanna turned around slowly. "I wanted to speak with you, but it can wait."

Hunter reached the dock in three long strokes, but remained in the water. He flipped his hair out of his eyes. "Did Melissa send you?" he asked.

A sense of obligation had prompted Alanna to deliver an apology, but she was surprised by how much his question hurt. "No, I'm sorry to disappoint you, but I had a message of my own."

Hunter cursed his own stupidity for even imagining Melissa might have sent her cousin in her place, but he wasn't so lost in his own misery that he didn't notice the sudden change in Alanna's mood. The newly confident young woman who had stood before him only moments before had disappeared, and in her place he saw the same sad, sweet waif he had known. "I'm sorry. I didn't mean to disappoint you either. Turn around, and I'll come out and dress."

Alanna did as he asked, but what had struck her as a good idea when she had left the house, now seemed a fool's errand. Like so many men before him, Hunter was infatuated with Melissa, and he wouldn't care what Alanna had to say. He probably wouldn't even hear it. When he touched her shoulder, she jumped in surprise, but managed a faint smile as she turned toward him.

He had donned only his britches, and the water dripping off his hair was rolling down the muscular planes of his chest in slippery trails that caught her eye, and made it difficult for her to meet his gaze. The deep bronze of his skin added to the aura of masculine perfection, and while she knew she was staring, he was so attractive it was impossible not to. This was the first time she had seen him as a man rather than a dreaded savage. That he would prove to be so appealing was such a shocking sensation, she fought to force it away, but she had to clasp her hands tightly to resist the temptation to reach out and touch him.

Thoroughly distracted, she could scarcely recall why she had come looking for him. Finally, she began haltingly, "The last time you were here, my memories governed my behavior, and I was very rude to you. You didn't deserve it, and I wanted to tell you how sorry I am."

Alanna's expression was so painfully sincere, Hunter had no difficulty believing her. He now doubted that Melissa had meant anything she had told him, but Alanna impressed him as a woman whose emotions couldn't be hidden to enable her to lie. "The fault was mine, too," he replied.

"Oh, no, it was not," Alanna argued. "You were very kind, and I simply wasn't able to appreciate it. I know I must have hurt your feelings, and I'm so sorry."

Hunter frowned slightly. "Most people do not even realize Indians have feelings."

Alanna glanced back over her shoulder and, seeing no one in view, hastened to add another thought. "Please, you mustn't judge Melissa too harshly. Men have always adored her, but I fear she seldom took their attentions seriously. It's plain that you like her, and I understand why finding she's married Ian would disappoint you, but you mustn't dwell on it. Whatever casual flirtation you shared is over. She loves her husband dearly."

To have such an innocent creature lecture him on love was more than Hunter could bear. He reached out to grab her shoulders and replied in a tone she could not mistake for anything but rage. "You know nothing of what happened between Melissa and me. I'll stay here only one night, and I want you to tell Melissa I have to see her alone. She knows when and where to meet me. If she refuses, tell her I'll have a long talk with Ian in the morning."

When Alanna was too frightened to speak and simply stared at him wide-eyed, Hunter shook her. "Do you understand?"

Trembling badly, Alanna managed a nod.

"Good. Now repeat it. What are you going to say?"

Alanna had to swallow hard to force back her fear. "You want Melissa to meet you tonight. She's supposed to know when and where. If she doesn't, you'll talk with Ian in the morning."

Satisfied, Hunter dropped his hands to his sides and stepped back. "Deliver my message, and there will be no further need of apologies between us."

"No," Alanna swore as she backed away. "It's you who owes me one now." Panicked, she picked up her skirts and ran toward the house. Ian was expected home soon, and Melissa had gone upstairs to their bedroom to rest until he arrived. Alanna knocked lightly at their door, and waited for her cousin's welcoming call before she entered. Still shaking badly, she took the precaution of locking the door to insure their privacy before she approached the bed.

She studied her cousin's expression closely as she repeated Hunter's demand, but Melissa showed not a flicker of interest, let alone dread. "He's furious with you," Alanna warned, "and if there's something you'd rather he didn't tell Ian, I think you ought to get up and speak with him now."

Melissa covered a wide yawn. "I'll do no such thing, and I don't want you talking to him again either. Because he was my brothers' friend, I tried to be nice to him when he was here in April. Obviously he misinterpreted my friendliness for something more. It's unfortunate, but I won't compound the problem by talking with him now, or sneaking out at midnight either."

"Is that when you met him before?"

Aghast at the secret she'd just revealed, Melissa sat forward and attempted to save herself. "No, of course not. That was what he asked though, so I'm sure that's what he means now."

Recalling the vehemence of Hunter's tone, Alanna was amazed by her cousin's calm. "What is it he's threatening to tell Ian?"

"I've no idea," Melissa insisted. "The man's a savage. He might make up any wild tale, but don't worry, I'll speak to Ian, so there won't be a problem no matter what Hunter says."

Hunter had reacted as though he had a right to feel betrayed, but he had terrified Alanna, and she found it impossible to plead his case. "I hope he does leave tomorrow."

"So do I. I wonder why he bothered to come."

Alanna made an easy guess. "Apparently he thought the trip was worth making. I wish you could have seen his face when your mother said you'd married Ian. He may have meant nothing to you, but it was plain you meant a great deal to him."

"He's an Indian."

"He's also a man who cares about you."

Melissa raised her hand to massage her forehead. "Please, Alanna, no more. I'm not feeling well, and I don't think I'll come downstairs for supper. Will you please ask my mother to send up a tray."

As Alanna unlocked and opened the door, she heard Ian coming up the stairs. "Shall I make that two trays?" she asked her cousin.

"Yes, please do." Melissa held out her arms to welcome her husband with an enthusiastic embrace. "That awful Indian is here again, and somehow he thought that I liked him. I'm so embarrassed that he could have mistaken my friendliness for affection, that I'd rather not sit at the same table with him. Do you mind?"

Alanna closed the door before Ian replied, but she had the uneasy feeling she had just witnessed a performance that would have done a professional actress credit. She would have liked to have provided an excuse herself and also eaten in her room, but unwilling to take such a cowardly option, she forced herself to join the family. Her apprehensions proved unfounded when there was nothing threatening in Hunter's manner during the meal, and as they left the dining room for the parlor, she stepped close.

"I gave Melissa your message."

Hunter barely nodded his appreciation, and because Melissa had not asked Alanna to convey a reply, she kept their conversation to herself. John wanted to hear more about the skirmish with the French, and she and Rachel excused themselves and went to their rooms, rather than listen to any more of the disastrous tale. Once there, however, Alanna found it impossible to prepare for bed. She knew she ought not to be so curious about what had transpired between Hunter and her cousin, but Hunter's anger and Melissa's denials had left her aching to know the whole story.

She was still dressed and wide-awake when she heard her uncle and cousins come up the stairs. She listened at her door, expecting to hear them tell Hunter good night before he went up to a guest room on the third floor, but apparently he wasn't with them. Had he decided not to spend the night? she wondered. Or had he merely gone to meet Melissa?

She opened her door a crack, and sat down where she would be sure to hear anyone passing by her room. She sat nervously fidgeting in the dark, and prayed that any footsteps she heard would be Hunter going upstairs to bed, rather than Melissa sneaking out to meet him. She had nearly nodded off when the clock in the parlor struck midnight. Instantly alert, she rose and moved to her door. In the next instant she felt rather than heard Melissa tiptoe past her room.

Alanna did not mean to spy on Melissa, but she did not think her headstrong cousin ought to meet Hunter alone either. She waited a few seconds to allow Melissa to reach the bottom of the stairs, and then followed her outside. The moonlight reflecting off her white nightgown created a ghostly image, and Alanna had no trouble keeping her in sight. She followed at a discreet distance, but realizing that Melissa was headed for the dock, she swung around to the south and approached through the trees bordering the river. She was too faraway to overhear Melissa's conversation with Hunter, but she could at least keep an eye on her cousin and run to her aid should she need it.

Unaware that they were being observed, Hunter rushed forward to greet Melissa. He drew her into a warm embrace and kissed her with a demanding passion meant to inspire the truth. Rather than welcoming his affection as she had in the past, however, Melissa was coldly unmoved by his ardor and stood stiff in his arms. When he released her, she wiped the back of her hand across her mouth.

"I'm a married woman," she stated proudly, "and I've come to tell you goodbye. I've already spoken to Ian about you, so you can just forget making any vile threats. He'll never believe you."

Hunter grabbed her arm to again pull her close, and slid his hand over the slight swell of her belly. "Does the fool believe this babe is his?"

"It is his," Melissa swore.

"Not if you were wed in May."

"We were secretly married a month earlier. That's when the child was conceived."

Her golden hair glowed in the moonlight, but her features were shadowed, and Hunter recalled how many nights he had lain awake trying to see her face clearly in his mind's eye. He had remembered her blue eyes had the bright sparkle of the sun and her fair skin the cool beauty of the moon, but now he saw her as no more than the pale reflection of his own desires. Cold, heartless, that she had deceived him so easily filled him with shame.

"You were with me in April," he reminded her.

"That was no more than a foolish mistake I shan't repeat."

"Neither will I," Hunter responded with equal bitterness, "but how can you be certain who fathered your babe?"

Melissa knew the truth, but she had buried it so deep in her soul that she could not admit it to anyone, least of all to him. She wrenched free of his grasp and began to back away. "Don't try and make trouble for me," she warned. "If you even hint to anyone that I so much as kissed you, I'll swear you raped me. My honor is as precious to my family as it is to me, and you'd not live to stand trial for the crime."

Shocked by the venomous hatred dripping from her words, Hunter forgot the string of ugly insults he had practiced, and merely shook his head in disbelief. "Is it really me you despise, or yourself?"

"You! Now go away and don't ever come back!"

Hunter didn't try and stop her when she ran from him. Instead, he turned toward the river and wished with all his heart that he had had the sense not to climb out of the *bateau* the first time he had visited the Barclay plantation. That had been his first mistake. His affair with Melissa had been another, but he vowed there would not be a third.

The brevity of Melissa's meeting with Hunter had assuaged Alanna's fears for the moment, and she hurried back to her room. She did not know what she had expected, but if Melissa and the Indian could settle their dispute so quickly, then she tended to believe her cousin's story had been closer to the truth than his. Grateful that Hunter would be gone in the morning, she climbed into bed and promptly fell asleep.

Accustomed to waking early, Alanna's late night vigil did not prevent her from following her usual routine and going out to the stable shortly after dawn. She swung open the door and nearly tripped over Hunter, who lay asleep in the straw piled just inside. She hesitated a moment, thinking the sudden burst of light would awaken him, but he continued to sleep undisturbed.

He had impressed her as being a proud man, and she wasn't surprised that he hadn't wanted to sleep in the house. Melissa had undoubtedly dismissed him with a remorseless vigor that had to have left him feeling both abused and bitter. His happiness wasn't her responsibility, anymore than Melissa's probable cruelty, but she could not help but feel sorry for him.

She knelt in the straw and reached out to touch his shoulder. "Hunter, it's morning, wake up," she urged.

Exhausted, Hunter came awake slowly, and because it suited his dreams, he mistook the blond woman silhouetted against the open doorway for Melissa. He reached out to grab her arm, pulling her off balance and into the straw beside him. He closed his eyes as he kissed her and her initial reluctance to respond inspired rather than discouraged him. Peeling away her cap, he wound his fingers in her curls so she'd not escape his eager kisses, and he tried with a tenderness he'd not shown her at midnight to rekindle the passion they had shared all too briefly.

Taken completely by surprise, Alanna was so shocked by the Indian's sudden passion for her that she didn't have the presence of mind to struggle. Instead, she placed her hands on his chest and pushed against him with such a light touch it went unnoticed. Whenever Graham leaned down to kiss her, she turned her cheek, and therefore she was unprepared for a man who lacked such elegant manners, and instead took what he wanted. His insistent kisses weren't in the least bit unpleasant though, and her initial dismay gradually turned to a ready appreciation of what Melissa must have liked about him.

She savored the sweetness of his adoring kisses until she realized he had transferred his affections from Melissa to her with unseemly haste, and, unwilling to be a substitute for her cousin, she summoned the anger to shove him aside. "Yesterday it was Melissa you wanted, and now it's *me?* I had no idea men could be so fickle."

Finally realizing his mistake, Hunter let out an anguished moan. He sat up quickly and handed Alanna her cap. "You must forgive me," he begged. "I didn't see you clearly, and I thought you were Melissa."

For a few magical moments, Alanna had believed Hunter's enthusiastic affection was real. To learn that they were both victims of a silly mistake filled her with a sickening sense of disappointment. That the love which had flavored Hunter's kiss had been meant for her cousin, hurt far more than what she had interpreted as mere fickleness had.

"If I'm supposed to be flattered by that, I'm not," she blurted out as she struggled to stuff her hair under her cap.

Hunter watched her beautiful green eyes fill with tears and gestured helplessly. "What should I have said? Most people say my English is good, but there are times when I choose the wrong words."

"Or the wrong woman?"

"Please, don't laugh at me."

It was Hunter who now looked ready to cry, and Alanna feared she was treating him as badly as Melissa had. "I'm not laughing at you, certainly not. But even if I *had* been Melissa, you ought not to have grabbed me like that. What if she had come to tell you goodbye and brought Ian with her? At the very least he would have yanked out a handful of your hair, pulling you off her. I shudder to think what he would have done next. It's too dangerous for you here, Hunter. You've got to go."

They were both kneeling in the straw, but when she made no move to rise, neither did he. As before, her concern seemed real, and he longed to confide in her, to make her understand he had every right to be there, but he hadn't forgotten Melissa's threatened accusation of rape. He had not the slightest doubt that she would tell such a damaging lie either. It would not only be Ian he would have to fight then, but Byron and Elliott as well. If by some miracle he did survive the combined fury of their anger, he knew his claims that Melissa had willingly lain with him would never be believed in court. He did not know what the punishment for rape might be, but he was positive he didn't want to risk finding out.

"Melissa married the wrong man," he said instead.

"You were here only a few days in April. How could you have thought she might marry you?"

Again, Hunter dared not speak the truth, but despite the fact that neither he nor Melissa had made any promises, he had believed in the unspoken vows of her love. Now all Melissa displayed toward him was contempt, but in April, he would have sworn she loved him. He sighed unhappily. "I have money to pay for the *bateau*. Will you give it to your uncle?"

"No, you needn't pay for a boat. We have several, and one more or less won't be missed."

"I forgot how rich you are."

Alanna recoiled at the resentment in his tone. "My uncle has worked hard for everything he owns, and he's known for his generosity to others. Won't you need some food to take along? Come with me. Let's go to the kitchen and see what provisions we can find."

"You won't take my money?"

"No, of course not. You're Byron and Elliott's friend."

Hunter rose to his feet, and with a graceful tug pulled her up beside him. "Have I ruined things with you, so that we can't be friends?"

That his passionate kisses had been meant for Melissa no longer seemed important in light of his obvious pain, and she responded with a smile. "Yes, I'd be proud to be your friend.

Elliott has nothing but praise for you, and I believe it's well deserved."

"Byron thinks I have a wild streak, and had he seen us a few minutes ago, he would know he was right."

He flashed a charming grin but there was definitely a wildness about Hunter that went far beyond his buckskins and long flowing hair. She doubted that white men were such passionate creatures, but that was not a subject she cared to discuss. "Let's get the food I promised," she said instead.

Amused by her haste to see him gone, Hunter followed her out of the stable. He had not slept more than an hour or two, but he wanted to be on his way, and he would rest later. He went into the house to fetch the things he had left in the room he hadn't used. He could not help but wonder if it was mere coincidence that Melissa and Ian now occupied his former room. Then he realized he was giving Melissa credit for a depth of feeling she did not possess. She had undoubtedly chosen the green room for the beauty of the view, not out of fond memories of him.

He walked out of the brick mansion and did not look back. When he reached the kitchen, he found Alanna had filled a bag with enough provisions to see him home; he again offered her money, and she again refused. He slung the bag over his shoulder and carried it down with the rest of his belongings to the dock. When Alanna came with him, he knew he ought to do more than thank her for her kindness.

"I should not have yelled at you yesterday," he began. "I made a great many mistakes here, and I am sorry for the ones that hurt you. You may need to find me someday. If I'm not at William Johnson's trading post on the Mohawk, he will know where to find me."

Alanna could not imagine such a circumstance arising, but she thanked him anyway. "Melissa and Ian will move into town after their babe is born. If you came back to see Byron and Elliott, you wouldn't have to see her."

For a fleeting instant, Hunter wondered if she wasn't really asking him to come back to see her. Then he decided such a delusion was absurd. She was merely being kind, and he would expect no more, nor did he want it. The pain of loving one white woman had been more than enough for him. Still, he couldn't resist the impulse to kiss her goodbye. He slid one arm around her waist and pulled her close.

"This time I know it's you," he whispered before his lips caressed hers, but the sudden jolt of pleasure as she responded warmly made him long for far more. Melissa's betrayal had left him with an aching sense of loss, but he felt only wonder as he finally released Alanna and climbed down into the *bateau*. She remained on the dock, and he kept looking toward her until she was lost from view. He stopped rowing then and, unable to contain the pain of his shattered dreams and a love that could never be, he let out a mournful cry that was mistaken for the howl of a wolf from the shore.

He had made another terrible mistake, he realized. He had blamed Melissa for marrying the wrong man, but he now knew he had fallen in love with the wrong woman, so the fault was entirely his. Sick with loneliness, he began to row again, but he could not outdistance the pain.

Twelve

"What do you mean he's gone?"

"I'm sorry, Elliott, but Hunter left hours ago." Alanna could see how disappointed her cousin was, but there was little of her last encounter with Hunter that she cared to repeat. Now that she looked back on it, she didn't know where she had found the courage to wake him, but she was glad that she had. Seizing upon what she could confide, she explained she had given the Indian some food and a *bateau* and seen him on his way.

Elliott was still perplexed. "I know he meant to stay with us awhile. What could have happened to change his mind? He didn't go straight up to bed when we did last night. Could he have gotten in a fight with someone? Did he have any cuts or bruises?"

Knowing how uneasy she had felt listening to what had surely been half-truths from Melissa, Alanna couldn't do the same to Elliott. "Please don't share this with anyone, but he was infatuated with Melissa. When he found out she had married Ian, he had no reason to stay."

"Melissa?" Elliott repeated numbly. "Oh no, Hunter couldn't have become another of her adoring beaus!"

"Why should he have been different from any other man? Believe me, it happened, but please don't mention anything I've said about Hunter to Melissa or Ian. She's already embarrassed to tears, and it would only make Ian jealous, when there's no need."

Elliott shoved his hands into his hip pockets. "Damn it all," he mumbled. "Nothing's going right for us. Absolutely nothing."

Alanna hated to see him so badly discouraged. "You're alive and well, and you've not fallen in love with a woman who's married to someone else, so you've more reason to rejoice than be sad."

When stated in those terms, Elliott was ashamed of himself. "Guess I did sound pitiful, didn't I?"

"I've done that, too," Alanna admitted.

Alanna had always understood him better than anyone else in the family, and Elliott started to hug her, but then suddenly grew shy and settled for just squeezing her hand. "Thanks for helping Hunter, but if he's ever here again and wants to just up and leave, come and get me."

"All right, I will," Alanna promised, but she doubted they would ever see Hunter again.

Hunter sold the *bateau* in Newport News, and then booked passage to New York on the first ship whose captain did not try to overcharge him simply because he was an Indian and was not expected to know the difference. From there he traveled on a barge up the Hudson River to the junction of the Mohawk. He had been gone from William Johnson's trading post for nearly six months, but the trappers who frequented the place remembered him.

"We thought you was dead, Indian," one called out.

"Not yet," Hunter replied. He swiftly discovered being in familiar surroundings wasn't the same as being home. Johnson had work for him organizing the supplies he stocked, but all it required was a strong back, and he completed it in a few hours each morning. He would begin trapping again in the fall, but until then he spent his idle hours building a small long house.

It was easiest to peel sheets of bark from elm and hickory trees in the spring, but he managed it even in late summer. After he had pounded the bark flat with stones, he tied it to the frame he had constructed of logs and poles. Mud filled any crevices in the bark walls, and hides draped over the ends formed the front and back doors. Poles lashed to the rafters added more than enough storage space for his few belongings. He built platforms along the walls to serve for both seating and beds, while the space underneath provided ample storage for the furs he would gather.

Once the house was finished, he considered making a trip home to the southern shores of Lake Ontario, but then lacked the enthusiasm to actually go. His father was dead, and his mother had taken a second husband whom he had never liked. Rather than share his dismal view of their stepfather, his two sisters were overly fond of the man. The whole family was content with the old ways, and ridiculed him for learning English and seeking adventure in the white man's world. He knew he ought to go home once in a while, but he had become so uncomfortable around his family, that he decided to avoid them a while longer.

A loner by nature, he was used to passing a good deal of his time lost in his own thoughts. Whenever memories of Melissa came to mind, he would angrily shove them aside. There were women who hung around the trading post. Women he had once found amusing, but now he saw them for the coarse whores they were, and wanted nothing more to do with them.

He had been spoiled by the dream of love, although it had only been an illusion, and now nothing less would satisfy him. Melissa had never been worth loving, but he now knew there was another young woman who was. Unfortunately, Alanna was no more likely to fall in love with him than Melissa had been, and he fought to suppress the sweetness of his memories, and to forget her as well.

Hunter had just finished stacking sacks of cornmeal one morning, when he heard the sounds of voices raised in an argument coming from out front. Fur trappers were an obnoxious lot and fights were frequent. Curious as to the cause, he went outside to watch. When he found Peter Bright, a young fellow he had always liked, being badly beaten by Ben Murdock, a man twice his size, he didn't wait for someone else to stop the uneven match. He stepped between them and gave Ben a forceful shove.

"Settle the matter another way," he ordered.

Infuriated, Ben pushed back. "Stay out of this, unless you want your nose broken, too!"

Hunter laughed. "Do you really think you can do it?" he asked.

Already in a rage, Ben swung for Hunter, but missed. The dozen or so men standing around began to take sides; seizing the opportunity to get away, Peter Bright ran up the steps of the trading post and hid inside. Hunter had learned how to fight on that very ground, and none of the blood spilled had ever been his. He held up his fists in a taunting pose, but again moved agilely aside when Ben lunged for him.

"Stand and fight!" Ben yelled.

"Like this?" Hunter asked, as he came in close and punched Ben square in the face, before the bully had a chance to react. When Ben started to yowl in pain, Hunter slammed his fist into him again. He then dodged Ben's efforts to wrestle him to the ground, by constantly moving he presented the much slower man with an impossible target, while he landed increasingly brutal punches at will.

His face a bloody mask and his vision blurred, Ben started to stagger. Hunter finished him off with a series of punches he timed to the chorus of cheers from the small crowd. His knuckles would be sore for a couple of days, but otherwise he walked off unharmed. The men who had watched him were too impressed to drift away, and ignoring poor Ben, who lay sprawled in the dirt, they began to plot how a talented Indian might make them all some money with his fists.

"So what do you say, Indian?" they asked him later.

Hunter was ready for them. "I won't fight more than once a week, and I want a quarter of the money won on me."

Ten minutes of hushed debate preceded a grudging agreement on that point. "And what if you lose?"

Thinking that one of the stupidest questions he had ever been asked, Hunter shook his head. "Then none of us will make any money, will we? The first time I lose, I quit. I won't fight again, if I ever get hurt."

"Well now, we don't see as how one loss could hurt you much. Besides, we'd all want a chance to win back whatever we'd wagered."

Hunter backed away. "No. Those are my terms. One loss and I quit."

Forced to accept Hunter as a man of his word, the group finally gave in, then scattered to look for a man foolish enough to fight an Indian brave for a cut of the winnings the hapless challenger would probably never earn.

That autumn, Alanna would often recall the sunlit morning when Hunter had bid her an affectionate farewell, for it marked a beginning as well as an end. He had shown her but a brief glimpse of how glorious love was meant to feel, but it was a priceless lesson. That it had come from an Indian brave was only one of its remarkable aspects. Perhaps they had simply been sympathetic to each other's sorrow, but whatever the reason, Alanna knew that for a few precious seconds they had shared a closeness she had never achieved with another human being, and it was impossible to forget.

Neither would she forget his involvement with Melissa.

While her cousin never mentioned his visit, it had left her irrevocably changed. She continued to prepare for her baby's birth, but without her former joy. The expected improvement in her health did not occur, and she grew increasingly demanding and petulant. She gave up the hope of returning to the house Ian had rented in Williamsburg, and spent her days curled up on the settee in the parlor. When the Publick Times came again in October, she had neither the energy nor interest to attend any of the parties and fairs.

The whole family was concerned about her, but none spoke their worries aloud, as though giving voice to their fears would not simply confirm them, but somehow also bring them to fruition. Byron and Elliott had left the militia and were helping to run the plantation. The Frederick sisters were frequent guests, but not even their sunny temperaments helped to lift Melissa's dark moods.

Graham Tyler visited each Sunday, but he spent as much time talking with Alanna's relatives as he did with her, in an apparent attempt to court the whole family. He did not press her for the affection he sensed she was still reluctant to give, but strove to be a true friend to her. If he ever despaired of his lack of progress, he never shared it with a soul.

Hunter was never mentioned, but his abrupt departure had left everyone curious. Byron feared he was somehow to blame. Elliott wrote to his Indian friend at William Johnson's trading post, but received no replies and, discouraged, finally gave up the effort to correspond.

Ian pulled on his coat and adjusted the fit across his shoulders, before walking over to the bed. All their friends believed their baby was due in January, but December was the true date. It was now early November, and, unable to find a comfortable pose, Melissa was having trouble sleeping. She had been discontented before, but now she was downright irritable, and while she never blamed him for the discomfort caused by her condition, he still felt responsible. The resulting guilt made him hate to leave her each morning; at the same time, he couldn't wait to get away.

"Do you have plans for the day?" he asked.

"Only to survive it. Is it foggy again?"

"Yes, but perhaps it will be clear by afternoon."

Melissa huddled down into the covers. "It's gotten cold too early this year. I don't even want to get out of bed."

"Then don't. The servants will pamper you as always, and your mother and Alanna are good company. You never lack for anything."

"No, that's not true."

Fearing she would begin a litany of complaints ranging from clumsiness to boredom, Ian leaned down to kiss her goodbye and strode from the room. He felt disloyal, but he did not want to risk losing patience with his wife and making a thoughtless remark he would soon regret. Beside himself with worry, when he entered the stable and saw Alanna feeding the horses, he delayed his departure for Williamsburg to speak with her.

"Melissa and I used to laugh constantly, but she no longer finds my sense of humor amusing. I know she doesn't feel like herself, and I try to be understanding, but I don't know how much more of this I can take. At first I thought she was depressed by the nausea, but when that went away, her swollen figure began to upset her. I keep telling her that she's beautiful still and assuring her that she'll be slender again after the baby comes, but that doesn't help at all. I thought this was supposed to be a happy time, but obviously I was wrong."

"Does she ever complain about me?" he asked. "If she regrets our marriage, I don't know what I'll do."

"Oh no, Ian, I'm sure she doesn't. Think of how prettily

she smiles, when you come home each evening. You needn't doubt her love."

Anticipating a lengthy chat, Alanna sat down on an overturned barrel. She scuffed the toe of her slipper through the straw and immediately thought of Hunter, but that was a private thought, rather than one she wished to share. "Melissa was seldom ill before last spring. She's not a patient person, and I'm sure feeling poorly all these months has been extremely difficult for her."

"It's been difficult for us all," Ian complained. "I miss the charming young woman I married, Alanna. I miss her terribly."

"You don't have much longer to wait for the baby."

"That's true, but what if she's still not happy? What if there's something more that's bothering her?"

"What else could there possibly be?" Alanna asked.

"That's precisely the problem. I don't know. We were so close at first, and now, well, I don't expect her to want to make love when she feels so awkward, but—" Ian noticed Alanna's blush and realized he had said too much. "I'm sorry if I embarrassed you, but everyone knows married couples make love."

"Perhaps you should be talking to my aunt, since I know nothing about making love or having babies."

"Rachel just pats my sleeve and whispers *Patience,* whenever she notices my frustration. Damn, maybe it's this blasted fog that's depressing everyone. I'm lucky my horse knows the way to Williamsburg, for I'd not find the place on my own."

"You're careful, aren't you?"

"Yes, Lord knows what would happen to Melissa, if anything happened to me."

Not liking the morbid turn of their conversation, Alanna slid off the barrel and went to the open door, but all she saw was the gray mist that had rolled off the river and clung to the earth for nearly a week. The tobacco crop had all been harvested, and the leaves were drying in the curing sheds out of the reach of the dampness, but she wasn't immune to the chill and shivered slightly.

"You're getting cold. Hurry on back to the house. Melissa probably won't get out of bed today. I appreciate how much time you spend with her. I haven't thanked you enough."

"She's been good company to me all these years. I don't mind."

"Thank you, anyway."

Ian leaned down to brush her cheek with a light kiss. His touch was as sweet as Graham's: warm, friendly, but nothing more. Finished passing out apples, Alanna returned to the house. She and Melissa had begun having breakfast together, and she carried their tray up to the green room. Melissa had brushed out her curls, but left them falling free rather than styling them atop her head and covering them with a cap.

"You look wonderful. How do you feel?" Alanna asked brightly.

"Like one of the dairy cows ready to have twins."

"Wouldn't twins be fun?"

"Only if *you* were to have them." Repelled by the idea, Melissa hurled her sterling silver-handled hairbrush toward the dresser. The edge caught the corner of the mirror, and both girls jumped at the sharp report as it cracked. "Oh, no, now look what I've done. The day's barely begun and already I've ruined it."

Alanna left the breakfast tray on the nightstand and went to the dresser. "You mustn't be so melodramatic. You've scarcely ruined the whole day. Look, when I rearrange your perfumes and lotions, the crack doesn't even show."

"The mirror's ruined, Alanna. Tell mother we need a new one."

Alanna wasn't used to being ordered about, but she curbed the impulse to tell Melissa to do it herself. "If I think of it later—which I probably won't—I will. Now let's have breakfast before the eggs get cold."

When handed her plate, Melissa took a couple of bites, then lost interest in food. "I'm not hungry."

"Well, I am."

"That's right. Go ahead and eat all you want. You'll not end up being as wide as a cow."

Readily sharing Ian's frustration, Alanna had finally heard enough. "You don't even remotely resemble a cow, Melissa. Your skin has a vibrant, healthy glow and you've never been prettier, but must you be so insufferably conceited? Don't you realize you're making everyone miserable with your constant complaints? You're having a baby, not dying of some dreaded disease. Why can't you be happy about it? Whatever became of the blanket you were knitting, did you finish it?"

"No."

"Or the booties?"

"No."

"Well, why don't you work on them today?" Alanna reached for Melissa's plate and placed it on the tray. "Stay in your nightgown if you want, but let's go downstairs."

"No, I want to stay here."

Alanna sat down on the edge of the bed. "If you don't care about the rest of us, have you stopped for even a minute to consider what you're doing to Ian?"

Fearing the worst of complications, Melissa was chilled to the marrow by that question. She clutched the sheets as she sat forward. "What do you mean? What has he said to you? Tell me."

Alarmed, Alanna quickly apologized. "I'm sorry. I didn't mean to upset you so badly. All I meant was that he's worried about you. More than any of us, he wants you to be happy."

"Happy," Melissa whispered. When had she last been truly happy? Perhaps it had been at their wedding, when the wretched pretense that had become her life had been so much easier to maintain. As if able to read her thoughts, the babe kicked her, but she didn't need to be reminded of his presence. She prayed daily for a daughter with her fair coloring and blue eyes, but the male child who appeared in her dreams was as dark as his father. Alanna had begun to eye her with a peculiar stare, and she couldn't abide that.

"I do think of Ian, constantly, but I just wasn't ready to have a child so soon."

"But you were so excited at first."

"That seems like a very long time ago. When I was slim and pretty."

When Melissa didn't continue, Alanna said what she thought she should. "You're still a beauty. You mustn't be so concerned about the changes in your figure, when they don't bother Ian at all."

"So he *has* spoken with you. What did he say?"

Melissa appeared to be eager to hear it, but Alanna veiled the truth. "He said that he loves you very much. That's all."

Relieved by that thought, Melissa relaxed against her pillows. "He does really love me, doesn't he?"

"Yes, of course, he does. How can you doubt it?"

"Forgive me." Suddenly Melissa wanted to be alone. "I didn't sleep well or I wouldn't be behaving so badly. I think I'll try and nap for a while. Do you mind?"

"No, not at all. Shall I wake you at noon?"

"Yes, please do."

Melissa closed her eyes, but the strain of their conversation still showed in her face. Sorry that she had been of such little help, Alanna carried the breakfast tray downstairs and then outside to the kitchen. "The eggs were delicious, Polly. Melissa just wasn't hungry."

Polly wiped her hands on her apron and eyed the remnants of Melissa's meal with a suspicious glance. "This is real odd,

Miss Alanna. She ought to be eating *more* than usual, not less. How's her poor baby gonna thrive, if she don't eat?"

"She eats, Polly." Dismissing the cook's worries, Alanna left the kitchen and went out into the garden to cut some chrysanthemums for a bouquet to brighten Melissa's room. She supposed the moist air was good for the plants, but she was as tired of the foggy days as Ian. She was moving down a row of mums, when she spotted a scrap of paper caught in the leaves. She unrolled it to find a fragment of a carefully drawn map with notations in Elliott's handwriting. Will's Creek was marked, and she recognized it as a souvenir of their failed expedition against the French.

Why would he have torn up the map and thrown it away? she wondered absently. Unwilling to do the same, she slipped it into her pocket. The valiant effort to stop the French had been important, even if it hadn't been successful. Her thoughts turning again to Hunter, she wondered what he was doing, and if he had found an Indian maiden as eager for his loving as he had been for Melissa's. She plucked another bright yellow chrysanthemum and prayed that he had.

Hunter had not merely fulfilled his backers' expectations, he had exceeded their wildest dreams. He had proven himself to be not only a very talented fighter, but one with endless reserves of rage he could not only tap into at will, but skillfully control to defeat every man who had mistakenly assumed an Indian would be dumb and slow. He had left one man with a shattered wrist, and another with a dislocated shoulder. He broke most opponents' noses, and inflicted cuts and bruises that were so deep they took weeks to heal. As for Hunter, as his reputation grew, his only visible scars were on his hands.

Emotionally, however, his carefully nurtured aggressiveness was becoming increasingly difficult to channel solely into scheduled bouts. Once regarded as aloof, he was now considered surly. Where before he would have walked around a group of men, he now walked right through their midst, and none dared call him rude.

His long house was kept warm by the heat from the fire pit dug into the center of the dirt floor, and his bed was comfortable, but there were nights when the villainy of his thoughts kept him awake until dawn. He had continued to suppress thoughts of Melissa as unworthy of his attention, but the anger of her betrayal fed the worst part of his nature with an unceasing stream of bitterness. Hatred created in him a superbly determined fighter, but each day he felt diminished as a man.

The first time he heard the howl of a wolf echoing on the crisp autumn air, he knew the beast was again calling to him. Death was approaching, but life now held such little appeal, he began to welcome its end.

Melissa went into labor a few minutes past midnight on November eleventh. She had dreaded the ordeal of childbirth, not for the pain it would bring, but for the damning truth which she feared she would no longer be able to conceal. Believing she had until early December before that inevitable horror overtook her, she was as unprepared as the rest of the household to give birth prematurely. Her mother had told her labor would begin slowly with only mild discomfort, but the pain that tore through Melissa's insides ripped her from her dreams with terrifying zeal.

She grabbed for Ian and shook him. "Ian, it's time!"

Still half-asleep, Ian's first thought was that he had overslept, but as he opened his eyes, he saw no hint of dawn at the windows. "Time for what?" he asked.

Frightened nearly out of her wits, Melissa grabbed for his hair and yanked him awake. "It's the baby. Get help."

Wide-awake now, Ian was in such a hurry to leave the bed, he got tangled in the sheets, but after slipping and sliding, anchored his feet firmly to the floor. He lit the lamp and then peered at his wife's agonized expression. "It's too soon," he blurted out.

A second pain caught Melissa, and she grabbed a pillow to muffle the scream it wrenched from her lips. She had never thought of herself as a coward, but she hadn't been warned that the pain of childbirth would be so intense, and already on edge, it completely unnerved her. "Do you think I'm lying?" she gasped.

"No, obviously not." Ian yanked on his britches and ran downstairs to wake her parents and Alanna, but his panicked pounding on their doors brought Byron and Elliott out into the hall as well. The Englishman had scared all five of them so badly they beat him back up the stairs. Rather than being comforted by her family's presence, Melissa began to cry huge tears.

"My darling, you mustn't carry on so," Rachel warned. She smoothed back her daughter's hair and patted her shoulder lightly. "First babies take hours to arrive. When did your pains begin?"

"Just now, but—" Melissa doubled over as another one tore through her.

"They're only a few minutes apart," Ian explained, as he moved to his wife's side. "Send Andrew for Doctor Earle. I don't want to leave her, or I'd go myself."

"We won't need him," Rachel cooed sweetly. "I'll get Polly to help us instead. She's delivered more babies than Dr. Earle."

"I want the doctor," Ian insisted.

John touched his arm, "If her pains are coming so fast, there isn't time to send for him, Ian. Now try and settle down a bit. There have been plenty of babies born in this house: Byron, Elliott, Melissa, and my brother and I, just to name a few."

Alanna and her sisters had been sent to the neighbor's house on the day of her brother's birth, and she had no memories of it, but reacted to the tension in the room with her old fright. "I'll get Polly," she called, as she started down the hall. Barefoot, she ran from the house without taking a lamp or candle, then nearly lost her way in the dark. The McBrides lived a quarter of a mile down the road that ran through the plantation, but Alanna sprinted the whole way. When she reached it, she pounded on the door with both fists, instantly waking all the McBrides.

It was Jacob, wearing a tattered nightshirt, who opened the door. "Lord, Miss Alanna. What's wrong?"

Alanna hurriedly explained why Polly was needed, but she didn't wait for the cook to get dressed before she started back to the house. When she reached the third floor, her aunt, uncle, cousins, and Ian were still clustered around the bed. "Polly's on the way," she informed them. "Don't you think Melissa needs more room to breathe?"

"Of course, she does," Rachel agreed. She pushed up the sleeves on her nightgown before waving toward the door. "John, you take Ian and our boys downstairs and keep them entertained. Despite the way Melissa is carrying on, I don't think we'll see our grandchild before dawn."

"I don't want to leave," Ian argued.

Barely recovered from the throes of another anguishing pain, Melissa still made her wishes known. "Please, Ian, just go," she begged.

When the young man failed to move, Rachel took it upon herself to usher him toward the door. "She wants you to go, son, and believe me it will be better for the both of you, if you do." When they reached the door, she leaned close to whisper. "She'll do just fine. Don't you worry. She's just always loved attention is all."

Ian looked over his mother-in-law's head for a final glimpse of his wife. He still wanted to stay with her, but afraid he would only be in the way rather than of any help, he succumbed to Rachel's insistent gestures and went downstairs.

Alanna remained at the open door waiting for Polly, but she cast frequent glances toward the bed, where Melissa continued to weep and moan. "Try and have courage. Babies are born everyday," she called.

"Not to me," Melissa cried.

Rachel tugged on her daughter's arm. "Come on, get out of bed. Your labor will go faster, if you walk a bit."

"That's impossible." But Melissa obeyed. She held on to the nightstand, then her mother's arm, and tried to take a few steps. "Something's wrong, Mama. It shouldn't hurt this bad, I know it shouldn't."

"I never told you it wouldn't hurt," Rachel reminded her. "You won't be able to remember any of it, once the baby comes. I can promise you that. No woman would ever have more than one child, if she could remember the pain."

Polly reached the landing in time to hear that remark, and clucked her tongue as she came through the door. "What are you telling that child, Miss Rachel?"

"The truth is all."

Swiftly taking charge, Polly sent Alanna for towels to protect the bed. "Bring us a kettle, too, and we can make hot water for tea in the fireplace right here. We'll need us some warm water later to bathe the baby. Better add another log to the fire."

Alanna was kept busy supplying Polly with all she required, but she was frustrated the practiced midwife could do so little to calm Melissa and ease her pain. One hour slipped by and then two, but despite the frequency and harshness of Melissa's pains, Polly described her as being only in the first stages of labor. "You mean this could go on all night?" she asked.

"You want to go back to bed, Miss Alanna? This could easily take until noon."

Melissa was again lying curled up on the bed. She looked worn out, and Alanna couldn't leave her. "No. I'll stay, but isn't there something more we can do?"

Polly shook her head. "Just wait is all. Now where are the baby's clothes?"

"On the dresser, and the cradle's all ready, too. It's sitting there in the corner."

"Oh, yes, I remember that pretty cherry wood cradle from when Miss Melissa was small. You were such a pretty baby, child."

Melissa was beyond caring how attractive she might have been. Engulfed in another wave of pain, she no longer had the strength to do more than whimper. For the first time it occurred to her that born early, her baby might not survive. If his frail little body were whisked away and laid in a tiny coffin before Ian saw him, then her secret would be safe. It was an awful thought, and even to save herself, she couldn't wish the infant dead, but she feared that if he was suffering as badly as she, he couldn't possibly survive.

To go through this terrible agony for nothing was a horrid possibility. She heard her mother and Polly talking softly, but she could no longer make out their words. Through a veil of tears, she saw Alanna, still in her nightgown, hovering near, and gestured helplessly for her to come closer.

"Don't let Ian see the baby," she begged.

"Melissa, what are you saying?"

Melissa reached out to catch her cousin's wrist in a feeble grasp. "I want to show him the child. Only me. Promise."

"Yes, if that's what you want." Alanna remained by the bed, but Melissa closed her eyes and didn't speak again. She had grown so pale, Alanna called Polly. "Please, come look at her."

Polly wrung out a cloth in the bowl on the washstand before she approached the bed. She used it to wipe Melissa's face, and then she, too, grew alarmed. "Miss Melissa, honey? Look at me." When there was no response to her request, she drew back the covers.

The lower half of Melissa's nightgown was soaked with blood.

Polly began to scream. Rachel fainted. Alanna's mind played a cruel trick on her, sending her back in time to an afternoon eleven years earlier. She had a bunch of wildflowers in her hand, and was humming softly as she came through the front door of her home, but the safe haven she had expected was gone, and she was greeted by a nightmare that had taken years to recede.

It wasn't until Ian shoved her aside that she realized she was no longer a terrified child, but the stench of death filled the room, and she feared her dear cousin was already gone.

Thirteen

"Your wife's hemorrhage couldn't have been anticipated or averted, Captain. Had I been at her bedside, I would have been as helpless as you were to save her. It's a miracle you had the presence of mind to save your son. You ought to be more than just grateful for his birth, celebrate it. Had you not been so quick to act, you would have lost them both. What a terrible tragedy that would have been."

Too numbed by grief to benefit from the physician's comfort, Ian could only stare at him blankly. "You should have been here," he agonized. "I never should have entrusted Melissa's care to a cook. That was my mistake, and it cost Melissa her life."

Dr. Moses Earle was a man of inexhaustible patience. He explained again, and then once more. By the third telling, Ian finally seemed to understand that his wife had been doomed from the instant the hemorrhage had begun, and no physician—no matter how talented—could have saved her. He then gestured toward Ian's bloodstained garb.

"I want you to get out of those clothes. After you've had the opportunity to bathe and dress, come back and sit with Melissa awhile. Talk with her. Tell her how much you'll love your son. I truly believe that she'll hear you, and talking will be a comfort to her, as well as you."

"She was only eighteen."

"You're not much older, are you, son?"

"I'm twenty-six."

"I'll not insult you by suggesting you'll fall in love again someday, but I know Melissa would want her child to have a loving mother. Talk that over with her, too. Now go on and clean up. I'll see that Melissa's body is prepared for burial, while you do. When you come back, everything will be ready."

Alanna breathed a small sigh of relief as Ian shuffled out of the room without pausing to look at the newborn infant, who lay tenderly cradled in her arms. She was seated in a rocking chair near the window, and the early morning light illuminated the child clearly. After freeing the babe from his dead mother's womb, Ian had thrust him into Alanna's hands and taken no further notice of him. At first, with the baby covered in his mother's blood, she had not recognized him, but now that he had been bathed and dressed in the tiny garments his late mother had made, his heritage was unmistakable.

He was a handsome child with a startling shock of ebony hair, deep brown eyes, and skin of a gorgeous golden hue. When Hunter had complained that Melissa had married the wrong man, Alanna had not realized he had such a strong justification for his view. She knew exactly when he and her cousin had been together: the night in early April when Melissa had awakened her with agonized sobs she had blamed on concern for her brothers. It was obvious now Melissa hadn't been crying for Byron and Elliott, but for herself.

That had merely been the first of Melissa's lies. Now Alanna could not help but wonder if she had ever spoken the truth in the last eight months. It was now obvious why Melissa had insisted upon being the one to introduce Ian to her son, but what had she meant to tell him? Surely she would not have tried to convince Ian the babe was his, but would she have told him more lies, or provided the damning truth at long last?

Alanna glanced up to find Polly had returned. She and Dr. Earle were hovering over Melissa's body, working to prepare her for her final journey to the grave. They had all expected the day to bring the joy of new life, not the pain of death, and no one had even glanced at the babe nestled in her arms. He was small, but perfectly formed, and his eyes shown with a bright, eager light. He was sucking on his fist, and Alanna began to worry how they would feed him.

"Dr. Earle," she called softly.

Startled, the physician turned. "My goodness, I'd quite forgotten that you were seated there. What is it, Alanna?"

"We need some way to feed Melissa's son."

"Yes, of course, a wet nurse must be found without delay. When I go back into Williamsburg, I'll see who I can find."

"Charity Wade cares for infants," Polly offered.

"Yes, she'll do," Moses Earle agreed. "It might be a good idea for me to take the baby to her, until arrangements can be made to care for him here."

Alanna tightened her hold on the babe. "No, I want to meet her first and see her home, before I entrust Christian to her care."

Dr. Earle approached Alanna's chair. "Is Christian the name Melissa had chosen?"

"Yes, he's named for the brother I lost in infancy."

"How prophetic," the physician mused, "for now he's lost his mother." He leaned over, peeled away the blanket to get a better look at the child, and then, shocked by his dark coloring, straightened up abruptly. "I know an Indian's babe when I see one. What's going on here?" he asked.

Shocked by the doctor's question, Polly came close to get a good look at Christian. "Mother of God," she gasped, and quickly crossed herself. "What are we going to tell the Captain?"

"It won't matter what we tell him, because he's never going to claim this child."

"I believe Melissa meant to tell Ian the truth," Alanna explained. "But I don't know how to put it, when he's already heartbroken over losing her."

"Do you know the father?" Moses Earle asked.

That was not a question Alanna wanted to answer, but the doctor was a trusted family friend, and she could not bring herself to lie. "Yes."

"I'm right, aren't I, he's an Indian brave?"

"Yes, but I think I ought to discuss the matter with Ian and let him decide if he wishes to make that known."

"Yes, of course," the physician agreed. "There's also Melissa's parents to consider. They won't be pleased to learn their darling daughter was unfaithful to her husband."

"She wasn't unfaithful to Ian, Dr. Earle. She was with Christian's father before she married."

"He's a bastard then!" Polly moaned.

"Please, Mrs. McBride," Moses scolded, "his dear mother's body is not even cold."

"Forgive me," Polly begged, but she again crossed herself.

Taking note of the cook's horror, Dr. Earle rocked back on his heels. "I don't know Ian Scott well, but I would not want to compound the pain of any grieving widower by presenting him with a child who obviously wasn't his. I think we should leave here right now, Alanna, and take Christian to Mrs. Wade's. It may be an entirely unnecessary precaution, you understand, but I think we ought to do all we can to safeguard his life, when it cost his mother her own."

"Ian wouldn't harm an infant," Alanna argued.

"Not intentionally perhaps, but newborns are fragile. If Ian were to become enraged, and shook the child, or knocked him from your arms, the tragedy would occur before you could stop it. Let's not take that risk. Get dressed, gather up some clothes for the boy, and let's go."

Uncertain what would become of the babe in her arms, Alanna rose slowly. "Polly, wrap Christian's clothes in one of the small blankets, and take them out to the doctor's carriage for me, please."

While the cook hastened to do her bidding, Alanna carried Christian downstairs to her room. She laid him in the middle of her bed, and hurriedly pulled on one of the faded dresses hanging at the back of her wardrobe. She had no dark attire suitable for mourning, but the somber colors of the old dress mirrored her mood far better than any of her new garments did. Melissa had not shared the room in months, but the sight of her bed called forth memories Alanna could not tarry to savor. When she went downstairs, she found Dr. Earle waiting for her in the hall.

"I cautioned Polly not to say anything about Christian, ever. To trust a servant not to gossip is foolish I know, but I do believe I convinced her to hold her tongue temporarily at least. I gave Rachel enough laudanum to keep her sleeping most of the day. John's sitting with her. Ian is still getting dressed, but let's be on our way before he attempts to stop us."

The urgency of the physician's tone frightened Alanna, but she hoped Christian was more in need of nourishment than protection from his family. Byron and Elliott were seated in the parlor, and she paused at the doorway while Dr. Earle spoke with them. Depressed beyond tears, neither appeared to possess the energy to argue with what he had to say.

"Alanna is coming with me to take the baby to a wet nurse in town. It will be better for everyone, if you don't have the bother of an infant in the house for the next few days."

Moses and Alanna had already reached the yard when Elliott caught up with them. "I don't want Alanna to be stranded in town. I'll saddle a couple of horses and follow you, so she'll have a way to come home."

"Thank you. I've been so concerned about the baby, I'd not thought about getting home."

Embarrassed by her gratitude, Elliott just nodded and loped off toward the barn.

"Elliott's a very considerate young man. What do you intend to tell him?" Dr. Earle asked the moment they had gotten underway.

"The truth," Alanna replied, "or at least what I know of it."

"One look at the babe will tell Elliott all he needs to know."

"Perhaps not."

"Don't romanticize what happened, child. What Melissa did was wrong."

The rocking motion of the carriage had lulled little Christian to sleep, and Alanna relaxed her hold on him slightly. "Yes, and she paid dearly for it. I've not had time to cry for her, but I don't want you to consider me unfeeling."

The doctor glanced over at Alanna and noted the sweetness of her expression as she studied the sleeping child. "You ought not to get too attached to the boy. Ian won't want him, and I doubt that his grandparents will either. Might be best for all concerned, if he goes to a family that will welcome a child. He's half-white, and with the proper upbringing, his Indian blood might not even be suspected."

Alanna was aghast at the doctor's words. "How could you even imagine that my aunt and uncle won't want their daughter's child? They took me in when I was orphaned, and treated me as one of their own."

"You were kin, Alanna."

"Well, so is Christian! Just look at him. He resembles Melissa as closely as he does his father."

Moses regarded the infant with scant interest. "All I see is an Indian's bastard, and that's all anyone else is going to see. If you object to finding him a home with white folks, what about giving him to his father to raise? Indians are far more generous in their views, and won't ridicule him for having white blood. The reverse isn't true."

The thought of handing Melissa's son—or any infant—to Indians to raise was more than Alanna could bear. "That wouldn't please Melissa," she argued.

"Melissa is dead."

"Yes, I know, but it wouldn't be what she would have wanted, had we asked her."

"I saw her only a couple of times in the last few months, and because it was so unlike her, I couldn't help commenting on her nervousness. Now I understand that she had good reason for it. What could she have planned to tell her husband?"

"She didn't take me into her confidence, but I know she had faith in Ian's love. Had the request come from Melissa, I think he would have accepted her child."

"You're dreaming again, Miss Alanna. Captain Scott couldn't be that great a fool."

"Is a man a fool to adore his wife and raise her son as his own?"

"In this case, he certainly would be."

Alanna couldn't agree. "You've a harsh view of the world, Doctor."

"I'll admit it. Comes from watching pretty eighteen-year-olds bleed to death. Such tragedies will harden any man's heart, or drive him mad."

The doctor fell into a sullen silence and didn't speak again until they had reached the outskirts of Williamsburg. Elliott had caught up with them, but he was riding along behind the carriage rather than alongside it, and could not overhear him. "Have you ever wondered why your uncle doesn't own slaves?"

"I've been told that he freed all the plantation's slaves, when my grandfather died."

"That's true, but you don't know why?"

"I believe he objects to slavery on moral grounds."

"Oh, yes, he certainly does, but not for the reason you might believe. Your Uncle John and your father weren't the only children your grandfather sired, but the others were all born in the slaves' quarters. I won't say mixing with slaves isn't a common practice among plantation owners, because it is, but it broke your grandmother's heart, and hastened her death by at least a dozen years."

Alanna felt a sudden chill of apprehension. "Are you saying that my uncle would be unlikely to accept a grandchild with mixed blood?"

Moses nodded. "Not just unlikely, dead set against it is probably closer to the truth."

Stunned by that revelation, Alanna looked down at Christian. Truly she did see the sweetness of Melissa's features, even if he did have Hunter's black hair and golden skin. She patted his bottom lightly. *Don't you worry,* she assured him silently. *Your Cousin Alanna won't abandon you.*

Alanna had expected Charity Wade to be a matronly woman with silver hair and an ample bosom, but she was a thirty-year-old with thick auburn hair and the reed slim figure a lifetime of hard work imparts. Widowed when she was pregnant with her third child, she supported her family by caring for other women's infants. She answered Dr. Earle's questions with intelligent replies; a perceptive person, she noted Alanna's questioning glance.

"I can tell what you're thinking," she confided with a saucy smile, "but a woman doesn't have to have tremendous breasts to nurse, does she, Doctor?"

"No, Mrs. Wade, she doesn't. Now, the lad's not even a day old and without a mother. If you take him in, it might be only temporary, but then again, it might be for some time."

Charity caressed Christian's cheek. "He's as handsome an orphan as I ever did see. It's high time I weaned Jamey, so I can take good care of him. What do you say, Miss Barclay? I understand it's up to you. I'm real fond of this little house, but if you want me to live at your place, I could do it. Provided that you've room for my children, too, of course."

Charity smiled often, and although small, her home was a model of neatness and order. Her children were clean and handsomely dressed, although their garments were far from new. Alanna could find no reason to refuse to hire Charity, and it was obvious she needed the employment as a wet nurse, yet she hated to leave Christian in another woman's care.

She kept him snuggled in her arms as she described his situation. "Quite naturally, Christian's father and grandparents haven't had time to accept his mother's death. Until they do, and can make decisions concerning his welfare, I'd like to leave him with you. I'll want to come visit him often, perhaps every day. I won't be able to leave him here with you, if that's not acceptable."

"My goodness, Miss Barclay, we'll be happy to have you come visit. I love company as much as I love babies. Besides, babies thrive when they have lots of people fussing over them. You come to see him anytime you want. We'll be here."

Relieved by Charity's enthusiasm, Alanna relied on the doctor to set a fair wage and agreed to bring the first week's payment the following day. She kissed Christian's cheek, placed him in Charity's arms, and left the little house while she still could. Elliott was waiting out front, but Dr. Earle caught Alanna's arm to delay her departure.

"Think about what I said, Miss Alanna. Send the money with Elliott tomorrow. It won't do for you to become too fond of the babe, when likely as not he'll have to be given away."

Sickened by what she prayed was unnecessary advice, Alanna pulled away without replying. "Would you like to meet Mrs. Wade and see the baby before we go?" she asked her cousin.

Elliott shook his head. "I know it's not his fault Melissa's dead, but I can't help blaming him. You were right to get him out of the house. Everyone will feel the way I do."

"How can you talk that way about your own nephew? Do you think Melissa would be proud to hear it?"

Ashamed of himself, Elliott looked away, but he didn't apologize. "I can't help the way I feel."

Alanna hiked up her skirt so she could ride astride, and quickly mounted the dapple gray mare Elliott had brought for her. "I've always thought I could depend on you," she said.

"You can!"

"No, not when you're so quick to forget how much Melissa meant to us."

Elliott urged his bay gelding into place beside Alanna's mare, before he replied in a voice that was choked with tears. "I loved my sister. Everyone did. I don't mean to sound cold, but I need time to grieve for Melissa, before I start worrying about her son."

Alanna gave him all of ten minutes. By then they were far enough out of town to avoid being interrupted, and she confided in him before she lost her courage. "Hunter wasn't just smitten with Melissa," she began, "and while she stubbornly denied having strong feelings for him, she must have."

"Why are you bringing him up now?"

"When you finally feel up to looking at little Christian, you'll know why. It's not a coincidence that he bears such a striking resemblance to Hunter."

Appalled by her comment, Elliott pulled his bay to an abrupt halt. "My God, Alanna, what are you saying?"

Alanna drew her mare around to face him. His stricken expression made it difficult for her to continue, but she needed his help too badly to soften, or delay, the truth. "Hunter fathered Melissa's child. They were together the night before you all left to join George Washington."

"That can't be!"

"Do you want to ride back to Mrs. Wade's and see for yourself? Dr. Earle recognized Christian as being half-Indian the instant he saw him. What are we going to do, Elliott? I don't want to tell Ian Christian isn't his son, but the first time he sees him, he'll know. He's smart enough to recall Hunter was here in April, and he'll also remember that Melissa refused to see him when he came back with you in August. She snuck out of the house to meet him that night though. I saw them."

Elliott felt sick. "Just what exactly did you see?"

"I didn't spy on them as they were making love, if that's what you're thinking. They talked only a few minutes, and then she returned to the house. The next morning, he left."

Elliott didn't want to believe Alanna's claims, but fearing they were true, he turned his bay off the road, and slid off its back. He stumbled through the dry grass and fell as much as sat down. He rested his head in his hands and began to weep with huge racking sobs. Alanna left her horse to graze beside the bay and hurried to his side, but when she put her arms around his shoulders, he shoved her away.

"Leave me alone. I don't want to hear any more of your evil tales."

Shocked by his insult, Alanna sat back and rested her hands lightly on her thighs. "I'm not telling malicious stories, Elliott, and you know it. I think Hunter fell in love with Melissa, and maybe she loved him, or thought that she did, for a few days at least. He certainly wasn't anything like her other beaus, and maybe that was his appeal. She eloped with Ian just two weeks later, so I doubt that she could have been certain she was carrying Hunter's child.

"Think how frightened she must have been all these months. I suspected something was wrong. I asked her more than once what was bothering her, but she would never admit that she had reason to be upset. It shouldn't have ended like this, Elliott. Melissa shouldn't have died and left us with this awful secret."

Ashamed to have wept in front of her, Elliott dried his tears on his sleeve. "But she did die."

"Yes, she did, and you and I are going to have to decide what to do. I don't want to tarnish Melissa's memory in her parents' eyes, or Ian's either, but we can't keep the truth about Christian's father a secret indefinitely."

"The babe was born early, wasn't he? Maybe he'll die."

"Elliott!"

"I'm sorry, I know that's an awful thing to say, but it's better than having everyone learn Melissa was a—" Unable to speak the distasteful word that came to mind, Elliott fell silent.

"A what? A foolish young woman who fell prey to her own romantic dreams? That's all Melissa was. She wasn't wicked. She just fell in love with the wrong man, became frightened, and denied it."

"I thought that she loved Ian. Ian certainly thought so."

"Yes, I'm sure that she did. The last words she spoke were about him."

"What did she say?"

"She wanted me to promise that she would be the one to show the baby to Ian."

"Then she must have known Hunter was the father."

"Yes, it seems likely."

"This is all my fault then. He was more my friend than Byron's. I'm the one who invited him home, and he repaid me by seducing my sister."

"Have you forgotten what delight Melissa took in flirting? I think Hunter might be the one who was seduced."

Elliott couldn't accept her view. "No, I know Hunter far better than you do, Alanna, but it's obvious I didn't know him nearly well enough when I brought him home. I admired his confidence, his courage. He was the only Indian who didn't desert us when the French attacked us at Great Meadows. Most of the men were afraid of him, and with good reason, but I considered him a friend. I wonder if he was laughing at me."

"I think Melissa broke his heart, and no, he was never laughing at you." Alanna rose to her feet and offered her hand. "Now come on, let's get back home. I'm sure we're needed there."

Once standing, Elliott kept hold of Alanna's hand. "Do you suppose we could find a blond baby somewhere, and swap him for Hunter's bastard?"

"I couldn't give Melissa's baby away, not even to save her reputation."

Elliott pondered her comment a moment, and then nodded. "I'll try and think of him as Melissa's child. Maybe that will help. Let's do whatever we can to keep everyone away from Christian, until after the funeral. We can provide Melissa with a peaceful burial, if little else."

"Yes, that's a fine idea. Let's just concentrate on laying her to rest. There will be plenty of time later, when everyone is feeling stronger, to reveal the truth."

Elliott brushed his dear cousin's cheek with a light kiss and, grateful that she was such a sympathetic young woman, he poured out his love for his sister the whole way home.

Ian had insisted upon having Melissa dressed in her wedding gown for burial, but Byron and Elliott had had to ply the young widower with brandy until he passed out before her body could be placed in a coffin. Even in death she was a rare beauty, and none of her family could bear to watch as the lid was nailed in place, and she was lost to them forever. That a young woman who had been so full of love and laughter had died so suddenly, robbing them of the opportunity to tell her goodbye, had left them all heartbroken and heavily burdened with despair.

The ride to the Bruton Parish Church for the funeral was

one of the saddest journeys of Elliott's life, but he kept a close watch on Alanna. The rest of his family was too distraught to recall that she had already buried five of her loved ones, but he did not want Melissa's death to send her back into the fearful silence of her first years with them. Hoping that she would be reassured by his presence, he sat beside her in the carriage and held her hand.

Despite her cousin's worries, Alanna's thoughts were not focused on the past, but on the present, and how best to shield an innocent babe from what was surely to be the worst of scandals. Ian had not even inquired about his son; viewing his pain, Alanna hoped he did not ask to see Christian for several weeks. Perhaps by then he would be strong enough to accept the truth, and she would have found a way to relate it without breaking what was left of his heart.

She squeezed Elliott's hand as they reached the church, and his responding smile warmed her clear through. The day was overcast and cold, with a threat of rain. Melissa deserved better, but none of her friends had deserted her. The church was full, just as it had been for her wedding, only today the hymns were all sad laments rather than joyful tunes, and many people were too overcome by sorrow to sing.

With his father-in-law on one side and Byron on the other, Ian made it through the service without weeping as pitifully as he had at home, but his sagging shoulders and vacant stare made his suffering plain. Surrounded by mourners, his thoughts were filled with memories of his dear wife. He had expected to be with her for a lifetime, never suspecting the years she had been allotted would be so tragically few. He strove to appear courageous to honor her memory, but inside, all he craved was an early death, too.

Rachel fainted at the graveside, and John carried her back to their carriage, leaving Elliott and Alanna to help Byron look after Ian. Even after it began to rain and the other mourners hurried away, Ian refused to leave the cemetery. It wasn't until Byron took his arm in a firm grasp and physically forced him to go, that he was led away.

Once Byron had Ian seated in their carriage, he made what he thought was an excellent suggestion. "I think we ought to visit the wet nurse and see Christian. The poor little tyke hasn't had any visitors except Alanna, and that's not right. We have to make arrangements for his christening, too."

Rachel had recovered from her faint, but just barely, and the mention of her grandson brought back the all too vivid memories of Melissa's death, and she couldn't suppress a shudder. "No, please, Byron, this just isn't the time. Our friends will expect us to be home to receive condolence calls, and we can't disappoint them. The boy will have to wait."

"I'm not suggesting a lengthy visit, but we ought to at least look in on Christian whenever we're in Williamsburg," Byron argued.

"That's enough," John cautioned. "Your mother is right. We're all cold and wet, and this isn't the time to be anywhere but home."

"It ought to be Ian's decision, not yours," Byron chided. "Ian, what do you want to do?"

Ian just shook his head.

"You see," Rachel insisted. "He wants to go home, too. Now let's go. I don't want to lose any more children to pneumonia."

Obviously distressed, Byron sat back in his seat and folded his arms across his chest. When the carriage lurched into motion, he glanced out at the falling rain rather than attempt any further conversation with his companions. Alanna squeezed Elliott's hand, and he nodded. It was time they shared Melissa's secret with Byron, but guests were already arriving by the time they reached home, and there was no opportunity to do it.

Sarah and Robin Frederick were the first to ask to see

Melissa's son. "He was born early," Alanna reminded them, "and he's really too small to have visitors as yet."

"Nonsense," Byron contradicted. "Sarah and Robin were Melissa's closest friends, and I'll be happy to take them to see Christian. We can go tomorrow, if the weather clears. Do you want to come with us, Elliott?"

"Someone ought to stay with Ian. I don't think he should be left alone."

Alarmed, Sarah stepped close and lowered her voice to a hushed whisper, "You don't think he'll harm himself, do you?"

"I don't want to give him the chance."

"Well, if Elliott has to stay here with him, couldn't you come with us, Alanna? I know Melissa would expect us to take an interest in her son. Have godparents been chosen?" Robin asked.

"Yes," Alanna surprised herself with that answer. "Elliott and I will have that honor."

"When was that decided?" Byron asked.

Readily understanding Alanna's reasoning, Elliott was quick to take her side. "You mustn't be insulted. Alanna and I simply have more time to devote to Christian than you do. That's all."

"Is that what Ian said?"

Unconsciously mimicking one of Melissa's gestures, Alanna laid her hand on Byron's sleeve. "We're doing our best to ease Ian's burden, but if he would like to choose other godparents when the time comes to christen Christian, we'll step aside. Now let's not argue. We need to pay attention to our guests."

"Alanna's right," Elliott insisted. "So many people have brought food. Why don't we have something to eat?"

Byron watched Elliott link arms with both of the Frederick sisters, then moved in front of Alanna to prevent her from following them. "Wait just a minute. Mother didn't want us to stop and see Christian, and something's made you equally reluctant to take others to see him. Is there something wrong with the baby? Is that why you don't want him to have visitors?"

Alanna wished Elliott were still with her, but left on her own, did her best to stall him. "It's really too crowded in here to talk. Can we discuss this later?"

"There is something wrong, isn't there?" Byron glanced over her head to survey the crowded parlor. "You're right, it's much too crowded here to talk. Let's go upstairs to my room."

"Your room?"

"Don't look so shocked. You're like a sister to me, and I'll not try and seduce you."

"I know that. It's just that this is such an awkward time to discuss anything and—"

"Right now, Alanna. Come with me."

Not wanting to create a scene, Alanna managed a few shy smiles as she followed him to the stairs, but she dreaded every step. Byron was only two years older than Elliott, but he had always been the more serious of the two, and he and Alanna had never been close. Explaining to him was going to be every bit as difficult as speaking with Ian, and she didn't have nearly enough time to phrase her words carefully before he shut his door behind them.

"Is the babe sickly?" he asked. "If you don't expect him to live more than a week or two, then we all ought to hurry on over to see him, rather than wait until he's dead, too."

Alanna glanced around the room, started toward the chair at the desk, and then decided she would rather stand. "Christian appears to be a healthy little boy. He is small, of course, but that's to be expected, since he was born a month early."

"I thought he was due in January, not December."

"Oh, yes, I'd forgotten you and Elliott were never told about Melissa and Ian's elopement."

"What elopement?"

Byron now had his hands on his hips and looked ready to

wring the truth out of her, if she didn't hurry up in telling it. She explained the secrecy about the elopement had been his father's idea, and that Ian and Melissa had agreed to go along with it and have a second wedding. The rest of her tale was far more difficult to tell.

"I know you loved Melissa."

"I asked you to tell me about the baby, Alanna, not my sister."

"First you must promise me not to tell Ian what I'm about to tell you, until he's far stronger than he is now. Will you give me your word?"

"I thought you said the baby was healthy?"

"His health isn't the issue. Now will you give me your word, or not?"

"You should know better than to have to ask."

"Forgive me then, but this is too important a subject to be bandied about."

Byron crossed the short distance between them, and placed his hands on her shoulders. "Are you never going to satisfy my curiosity? Must I ride into Williamsburg and have a look at the child?"

Feeling as trapped as Melissa must have, Alanna tried to state the facts calmly, but when she revealed that Christian was Hunter's child, Byron reacted even more emotionally than Elliott. For several seconds he simply stared at her, too shocked to speak, but then he shoved her away and bolted from the room. She ran to the door and watched him sprint down the stairs and out the front door. She didn't have to wonder where he was going, she knew, and she couldn't let him go alone.

Fourteen

The black taffeta gown Sally Lester had provided for the funeral was far too expensive and elaborate an outfit to wear on horseback, and Alanna went to her room to change into one of the comfortably worn dresses she wore for riding. The earlier rain had gradually diminished to a heavy mist, and while her cloak was still damp around the hem, it would keep her warm and dry. With the hood drawn up to cover her curls, she thought she could succeed in leaving by the back door without being observed, until Graham Tyler called her name.

Obviously concerned about her, he was frowning slightly. "Surely you're not going out again?"

Alanna had seen Graham among those at the church, but she hadn't spoken with him. She had been at Charity Wade's the morning he had come to the house after learning of Melissa's death, but Ian hadn't felt up to seeing anyone and he had been sent away. He had made the effort to console his friend, however, and she admired his thoughtfulness.

"I have to go back into Williamsburg. Byron's gone to see the baby, and I need to be there."

"I have a carriage for the day, I'll take you."

"That's very kind of you, but then you'd have the bother of bringing me back home. I'd rather ride, and then I can return home with Byron."

"There's no reason for you to risk falling ill by riding in

the rain. I'm free for the whole day, and it will be no trouble for me to bring you back here."

Alanna was in too great a hurry to argue with him. "All right, thank you. Can we leave right now, please?"

"Of course." Graham turned to gesture toward the front door, and Alanna hurried by him. Outside more than a dozen carriages were parked in a single row, and while he found his immediately, it took him several minutes to locate the driver who, along with the other drivers, had been invited into the kitchen to keep warm.

"I'm sorry to keep you waiting," he said. "It's a shame Byron has already left, or we could have all ridden together."

"It was a hasty decision on his part. I'm sorry to have drawn you into it."

Graham had taken the place beside her and reached for the blanket lying on the opposite seat. "Here, let's wrap this around ourselves, so we don't become chilled. It will do little good if I keep you out of the rain and then still allow you to fall ill."

"I'm seldom ill." Alanna wasn't used to being fussed over, but she soon realized what Graham had really wanted was an excuse to cuddle up close. He was a sweet man, but his timing was so incredibly poor she couldn't abide it. "We buried Melissa only this morning, and I'd rather not be fondled."

Mortified that he had offended her, Graham moved aside several inches. "Forgive me if I seemed too forward, but it's been difficult for me to keep my feelings to myself all these many months. We met last spring and—"

Graham had recently been promoted, and Alanna remembered to use his new title. "Captain, please. I've never encouraged your affections, nor misled you in any way. Perhaps you ought to tell your driver to turn around, and I'll get into town on my own as I'd originally planned."

"No," Graham responded too sharply. "I'll behave myself."

He looked thoroughly miserable, but Alanna was more concerned about how Byron might behave at Charity's house. Byron had a temper, but she prayed he would not vent his anger on a helpless babe. "Melissa's death is not our only problem," she explained. "There's also her son's welfare to consider. I shall undoubtedly be preoccupied with his care for several months, if not years, and you ought to find yourself a young woman who can devote herself solely to you."

"I'll decide what's best for me. Besides, the babe is rightfully Ian's responsibility now, not yours."

"You saw how he looked today. He doesn't even remember he has a son."

"He loved his wife dearly, so his grief is natural, but it will lessen over time, and he'll take more of an interest in their child."

"A young widower with a commission in the King's army? It's unlikely."

"I think you're underestimating Ian. He's not one to shirk his responsibilities. He'll want to provide for his son. He's kept up the rent on the house he and Melissa lived in briefly. He can well afford to live there, and hire a housekeeper and nanny to make a home for the boy."

Reluctant to spin a web of lies as intricate as Melissa's, Alanna nodded rather than argue. She had given the driver Charity's address on Nicholson Street, and when they reached her house, Byron's horse was tethered to the gate. "Would you mind waiting here?" she asked. "Mrs. Wade wasn't expecting us, and I don't want to trouble her."

"I'll do whatever pleases you."

Alanna was merely exasperated by his abject adoration and hurriedly left the carriage, as soon as the driver had opened the door. The front door of Charity's house was slightly ajar, and Alanna could see her children playing on the rug in front of the fireplace. Hearing adult voices coming from the back room, she rapped lightly and then entered.

"Hello, children, where's your mother?"

The eldest boy ran to get her, and Charity appeared almost immediately. She was holding Christian in a frantic grasp. Byron was right behind her. "This man claims to be the babe's uncle. Is that true?"

"Yes, Melissa had two brothers, Byron, whom you've just met, and Elliott."

"I know I told you I'd be happy to have visitors, but I'd expected them to display better manners."

"I've not been rude," Byron contradicted.

"That, sir, is a matter of opinion."

"May I hold Christian?" Alanna asked.

"You sure may. Do you want to hang your cloak on a peg?"

Alanna left the long garment hanging by the door, scooped Christian from the wet nurse's arms, and then nodded toward the bedroom. "May we use the back room for a few minutes, please?"

Charity nodded and stepped aside without glancing in Byron's direction. "I'd just finished feeding Christian, when this gentleman arrived. If you rock him, he'll go right to sleep."

The small bedroom held a double bed, a cluster of small beds for the children, and the cradle where Christian slept. Alanna sat down in the rocking chair, and looked up at Byron. "There was no need to upset Charity. She's been very good with Christian."

Byron looked around for another chair, but there wasn't one. Too weary to stand, he sank down on Charity's bed. "How long do you plan to allow this farce to continue?"

"I wouldn't describe what we've done for Melissa's son as a farce."

"Just who is 'we'?"

"Dr. Earle, Polly, and Elliott. They were the only ones who knew this is Hunter's son rather than Ian's, before I told you."

"You'd not have told me if I hadn't insisted upon seeing him though, would you?"

"You would have been told today, after all the guests had left."

"How thoughtful of you. Did you intend to tell my parents then, too?"

"No. This was as great a surprise to me as it is to you, Byron. I knew Melissa seemed troubled, but I didn't even suspect that she could have such a terrible secret. If I've not handled things as well as I should have, it's been because there's been no time to plan. Elliott and I wanted Melissa to have a proper burial, before we took anyone else into our confidence. We were only trying to help you ease Ian's grief, not exclude you."

Byron raked his hand through his rain-soaked hair. "You must realize there are some who will say she ought not to be buried in hallowed ground."

"I know people can be cruel."

"Good, then you'll be prepared for whatever gossip will surely come. As for a christening, that's out of the question. The babe's a bastard, and no priest will welcome him."

"Melissa was a married woman, Byron, and a married woman's children are considered to be her husband's, are they not?"

"No one is ever going to believe that's Ian's child."

"The lace-trimmed christening gown your mother showed us before Christian was born has a matching cap. If he wears that, it will cover his hair, and if he's asleep, no one will see the color of his eyes. He's a very pretty child. That's all anyone will notice."

"You intend to lie to the priest?"

Alanna had not thought about the christening until now, and she needed a moment to perfect her plan. "No, it won't be necessary to say anything more than that we want Melissa's son baptized. The priest married her and Ian, and he'll assume this is Ian's child. We needn't disabuse him of the idea."

"No, I'll not stand for it. We have to tell everyone the truth—my parents and Ian, today."

"But Byron—"

"Yes, I know, they are already heartbroken, so how can I even suggest we add to their burden with the truth about the child? Look at it this way, they could not feel any worse, so there's no reason to delay revealing what we must. My sister died giving birth to an Indian's bastard. If that destroys anyone's love or respect for her, then so be it. As for the babe, I'm going to send for Hunter. If there's anything left of him after Ian and I get through with him, then he can take his son and go."

Alanna wrapped her arms more tightly around the tiny babe. "No! You'll not give Melissa's son to Indians to raise. How could you even make such a vile suggestion?"

"After what happened to your family, how can you want to raise an Indian's brat?"

"He's Melissa's child," Alanna repeated.

"A moment ago you were insisting that legally he's Ian's son. I think you're right. As Melissa's husband, the boy is his." Byron paused a long moment. "But Ian's so sick with grief, I'm not certain he'll even understand what we're saying when we try to tell him. It would be better for all concerned if we let everyone think Christian had died. There are childless couples who would adopt him. Perhaps Dr. Earle knows of a good family."

"Now who's sanctioning lies? How can you want to give away Melissa's son? I know she would have willingly raised *yours.*"

"*My* son would have been white."

Alanna felt sick. "I won't let you give Christian away. I never intended to hide the truth from Ian indefinitely. He loved

Melissa. He may find it in his heart to raise her son as though he were also his."

"I think he'd sooner kill himself."

"Then you can't tell him the truth tonight! One tragedy is more than enough for our family to bear."

"What do you call that brat in your arms, if he isn't an even greater tragedy than losing Melissa?"

Recoiling from his malicious tone, Alanna looked down at Christian, but she saw another baby boy with the same name and choked on her tears. "You didn't see what the Abenaki did to my baby brother, Byron. You didn't see how they killed him, or the others."

"Oh God, Alanna." Byron had never heard the manner of their deaths described, but he had been twelve years old when she had come to live with them, and his imagination had painted the horror she had witnessed in sickening detail. He slid off the bed and knelt beside the rocking chair. Alanna had seemed the strongest of them all since Melissa's death, but he now understood her love for the infant had inspired the bravery he had admired.

"That's not your little brother, Alanna. He's Ian's responsibility, or if he refuses him, Hunter's. He doesn't belong to you."

Alanna understood Byron's reasoning, but it didn't matter to her. She might not have given birth to Christian, but she loved him as a mother would. He was sound asleep, and she didn't object when Byron picked him up gently and placed him in the crib. He then gave her a hand and pulled her to her feet.

"Let's just go home. Neither of us feels up to handling this disgrace today. What we need is something to eat, and a good night's sleep. You and Elliott and I can decide which course to follow in the morning."

Alanna nodded, and Byron slipped his arm around her waist and led her into the front room. Charity had been seated, but she rose and hastily straightened the folds of her apron. She was attractive, but her mouth was set in a firm line that readily conveyed her lingering displeasure. Byron had to admire her pride, when her circumstances were obviously humble.

"I'm sorry if I seemed rude, Mrs. Wade, but burying my sister was the most difficult thing I've ever had to do. Thank you for all you're doing for her son. If you need anything, for yourself, or your own children as well as Christian, be sure to let us know."

Surprised by that burst of generosity, Charity thanked him and hurried to fetch Alanna's cloak and helped her on with it. "Be careful on your way home. A wet road is a treacherous one."

"We're always careful," Alanna replied absently, but truly, the dangers of a slippery roadway were infinitesimal compared to the impossible situation in which Melissa had left them.

When they reached the carriage, Graham swung open the door. Alanna entered on her own, but Byron didn't want her to be alone with the English officer. "If you've no objection, I'll tie my horse to the back of the carriage and come with you," he said.

Knowing he had wasted his opportunity to impress Alanna on the way into town, Graham welcomed his company. "Please do," he replied, but he found the journey back to the plantation with two silent companions an equally difficult trip.

Hoping to avoid being overheard, Byron, Elliott, and Alanna met after breakfast the next morning in Byron's room. As the eldest, Byron considered it his duty to take charge of matters. "I won't pretend that I'm not disappointed in Melissa, because I am. She wasn't raised to behave in such an immoral manner, and her shame will undoubtedly taint the whole family. The question is how to minimize that damage."

"I disagree," Alanna was quick to interject. "The only question worth asking is what is to become of Christian?"

"Just hear me out," Byron asked. "I don't have the slightest doubt that Melissa loved Ian. Do either of you?"

"No," both Elliott and Alanna agreed.

"Fine, then what we've got to do is convince Ian to raise Melissa's son as his own. Perhaps he has relatives in England to whom he can send the child. Having never seen Melissa, they'll believe whatever they're told, and assume Christian resembles his mother."

"He does!"

"I certainly don't see it," Byron said, "but whether he does or not doesn't matter, as long as Ian's family believes that he does."

"And when he's grown?" Alanna inquired. "What if he comes to visit us? Will we tell him the truth then?"

"No, of course not," Byron declared.

Elliott was growing increasingly uneasy. "Ian isn't up yet this morning, but I doubt he'll feel any better than he did yesterday. How are we going to broach such a delicate subject with him?"

"I thought of little else all night," Byron admitted. "I think I should talk to him about the boy in general terms, and see if there is someone to whom he can entrust his care. Then, in a week or two, when he's used to the idea of raising Melissa's son, we can explain the truth, and ask him to accept Christian out of love for her."

"I don't think Ian should be misled another day," Alanna argued. "Melissa's affair with Hunter had to have been brief, and she married Ian so shortly thereafter, he was clearly her first choice."

"Wait a minute," Elliott cautioned. "Maybe we're all worrying over nothing. Ian might already know the truth. He and

Melissa seemed so close. Isn't it possible that he's known all along that her child wasn't his?"

Byron dropped into a chair and stretched out his legs. "Is that possible, Alanna? Could Ian already know the secret we're all so afraid to reveal?"

Alanna needed only a moment's reflection before she shook her head. "No, I think that's too remote a possibility to consider."

They were all startled by a knock at the door, but Byron quickly recovered. He called out, and his mother peeked into his room. "What are you all doing in here?" she asked.

Rachel was dressed in black, and the stark contrast between her gown and her fair coloring heightened her prettiness. That Melissa had resembled her so closely now seemed an eerie coincidence. Byron rose to welcome her to his room. "We're all worried about Ian, Mother, but we didn't mean to neglect you."

"You haven't, and I'm glad you're all together, because I'm also frantic with worry over Ian. I've tried to lift his spirits by encouraging him to talk about his son, but he shows not even a glimmer of interest. It's as if the boy doesn't even exist!"

Alanna looked to Byron and Elliott, who seemed equally unable to respond.

Rachel noted their exchange of anxious glances, but misinterpreted the cause. "Yes, it upsets me, too, dears," she said. "I'm not certain we should trust him with the boy."

Elliott took his mother's arm and led her over to the bed. "Sit down a minute. We need your help." He glanced over his shoulder at Byron and Alanna. Both nodded, and he cleared his throat as he tried to find the words which he feared would break his mother's heart. Thinking such an unexpected truth ought to be delivered with care, he started and stopped several times, but finally revealed that her grandson was not Ian's after all, but the son of an Indian who had been a guest in their home for less than a week.

Devastated by the recounting of her daughter's indiscretion,

Rachel's reaction was far worse than her sons had anticipated. She covered her mouth with her hand as though she feared becoming ill, and Elliott quickly sat down beside her and drew her into his arms. "He's still Melissa's baby, Mother. Try and think of him that way."

Rachel had already been pale, but now her skin lost even the hint of color. Several minutes elapsed before she was able to speak between choking sobs. "Send for your father," she ordered. "Do it now."

Fearing that they had made a very bad mess of an extremely difficult situation, Byron strode from the room, but soon reappeared with John, who had been working downstairs in his study. The strain of the last few days showed plainly in his face, and had aged him beyond his fifty-two years. Seeing his wife's obvious distress, he immediately went to her; Elliott stood up to make room for him.

"Oh John," she sobbed, "they're saying such dreadful things about Melissa. Make them stop."

"What's going on here?" John asked crossly. "Why have you upset your mother?"

This time Byron delivered the fateful news. His expression was solemn, his tone soft, his words as tactful as he could make them, but his father appeared to be no more inclined to believe him than his mother. "It's the truth, Father. I've seen the child."

John Barclay refused to accept the fact that his only daughter had flaunted the high moral values he had striven to instill in his children. He regarded the possibility that she could have lost her virtue to an Indian brave as gross and scandalous speculation. "It can't be true!" he cried out. "Melissa would never have stooped so low. She was a virtuous young woman, and I'll not allow any of you to say otherwise."

"But Father—" Byron began.

"Silence! Not another word is ever to be spoken against

Melissa, and I absolutely forbid you to repeat that hideous tale to Ian." He helped his wife to her feet and, after casting angry glances at his sons and niece, escorted her from the room.

"Damn it all!" Byron swore. "How can he even imagine we'd fabricate such a disgusting story?"

Alanna recalled Hunter's eagerness for a message when she had interrupted his swim, and disagreed with Byron's choice of words. "I don't think love ought to be described as disgusting."

"It couldn't have been love."

Alanna inclined her head slightly. "I think Hunter really did love Melissa, but we'll never know whether or not she loved him."

"She couldn't have," Byron repeated. "She barely knew the man."

"No, Alanna's right," Elliott argued. "I'd rather think Melissa did love Hunter, no matter how briefly, than to believe that she slept with him simply out of curiosity or lust."

Thinking them both romantic fools, Byron just shook his head and left the room.

"It never even occurred to me that they wouldn't believe us," Elliott said. "What shall we do now? You heard what father said about telling Ian, and he's so upset with us, I don't want to cross him."

"We won't have to do anything," Alanna mused thoughtfully. "One day they'll visit Charity Wade's, and the truth of Christian's parentage will be impossible to ignore."

Too restless to sit down, Elliott began to pace in front of Alanna's chair. "I don't mean to embarrass you, so please forgive me if I do. I've just always assumed that my mother explained everything a young woman should know to you and Melissa. But is it possible that Melissa didn't understand the consequences of being with a man?"

Alanna knew precisely to what sort of a conversation with her aunt Elliott was referring. Rachel had been vague to the point of obscurity, but Polly McBride had answered Alanna's and Melissa's questions in a straightforward manner. "From what your mother told us, she seems to have little understanding of procreation, despite having had three children, but Polly made things clear. Melissa knew what she was doing. It might be comforting to believe that she was too innocent to understand, but that just wasn't the case. She was as sophisticated as she appeared."

Elliott's shoulders slumped slightly. "It was just a hope."

"Save your hopes for Christian. I'm going to ride into town to see him. Do you want to come with me?"

"I guess it's high time that I took at look at him, isn't it?"

"You are his uncle."

"I'd forgotten that. Let's go."

Alanna was grateful for his company, and for the next week, the pair were the only visitors little Christian had. Byron asked about the little boy, but his grandparents did not. They appeared to be taking their cues from Ian, who asked no questions about anything, and when spoken to, replied with silent shrugs. When they all gathered for meals, he ate barely enough to survive. He got to sleep each night only with the aid of brandy.

Graham Tyler stayed away longer than he knew he should, but a week following the funeral, he finally came out to see when Ian would be returning to duty. Attentive servants had kept the young widower neatly groomed and dressed, but Graham was nonetheless astonished by the changes in his friend. Ian had always been such a good-natured man, but now his detached and sullen mood gave no hint of his former charm. When Ian made little attempt to follow his conversation, Graham hurriedly went to find Alanna.

"Ian isn't doing at all well," he complained.

"Yes, I know. We're very concerned about him."

"Has he seen his son?"

"No, not yet."

"Well, he can't just sit and stare off into space, while the boy grows up. Maybe if we took him into town and put his son in his arms, he would respond with a renewed sense of purpose."

"You're a very thoughtful friend, Captain, but your suggestion might simply create more problems. If you want to help Ian, why don't you just concentrate on him?"

"I thought I was."

"Well yes, of course you were. The weather's nice today, why don't you just encourage him to go out for a walk with you? Perhaps Ian might even like to go for a ride."

"Yes, it would do him good to get some exercise, wouldn't it?"

"Yes, I think so."

Wanting desperately to please her, Graham flashed a ready smile. "If I amuse Ian for an hour or two, will you have some time to spend with me?"

"Is this some kind of a bargain?"

"No, I really did come to see Ian, but I want to see you, too."

"Then yes, I'll invite you to stay for tea."

"Good." Pleased with himself, Graham not only succeeded in getting Ian to leave the house, he got him to agree to taking a ride. While Graham tried innumerable subjects in hopes of inspiring conversation, Ian remained listless. Finally deciding his original plan had been the best, Graham led his friend down the road into town. He had taken Alanna to Charity Wade's on the day of Melissa's funeral, and had no difficulty finding her house again.

"Come on in," he encouraged. "There's someone here I want you to meet."

Ian at first mistook the dwelling for a new tavern and, eager for a drink, swung down from his saddle, but after they had walked through the gate, he realized his mistake. "Wait a minute. I'm not up to meeting anyone."

"I promise this will be a brief visit. Come on, we can leave whenever you like."

"I want to leave now."

Graham Tyler was not easily discouraged. "Just a few minutes, Ian. You've got the time."

"I've nothing but time."

"No, you've something more." Graham had succeeded in getting Ian up on the front porch; he rapped lightly at the door. When Charity appeared, he quickly introduced himself as a friend of the Barclays. "This is Christian's father, Captain Ian Scott. May we see the boy?"

"Oh yes, do come in." Charity was delighted to invite the two handsome officers into her home, but when Ian removed his hat, she was startled by his bright red hair. "Forgive me, I didn't mean to stare. I'd assumed Christian resembled you, but now I see he must favor his mother."

Touched by that thought, Ian followed her into the bedroom, where Christian lay sleeping in the cradle. Charity pulled back his blankets slightly, so Ian could see him more clearly. "Would you like to hold him?" she asked. "He's a very good little boy, and spends most of his time sleeping."

Ian bent over the cradle, took one look at the precious infant, and straightened up abruptly. Thinking Charity must be caring for two babies and had confused them, he glanced around the room searching for another cradle but there was only the one. "There must be some mistake. This can't possibly be my child. Who told you that he was?"

Taken aback by his question, Charity grew flustered. "You were Melissa Barclay's husband, weren't you?"

"Yes, now answer me. Who brought you this child?"

"Alanna Barclay and Dr. Earle. I've had him since the day he was born."

"And when was that?"

"November eleventh."

Ian called for Graham, who had waited in the front room. When he entered, Ian pointed toward the cradle. "Do you have any idea whose child this is?"

As astonished by the golden-skinned, dark-haired baby as Ian, Graham shrugged helplessly. "Well, he certainly isn't yours."

"Gentlemen, you're frightening me. Miss Barclay visits the child every day. She was here this morning with her cousin Elliott. Byron has been here, too. None of them seem to think there's anything wrong."

"Oh, there's something wrong, all right," Ian assured her. "Alanna bears a close resemblance to my late wife."

Charity's eyes grew wide, for she had never known a blond woman and a red-haired man to produce an infant whose coloring presented such a stark contrast to them both. "I'm sure there must be some explanation," she mumbled.

"Yes, indeed, and I can't wait to hear it." Ian leaned down, scooped up the baby, and, holding him pressed close to his chest, carried him right out of the house.

"Captain Scott!" Charity called. "Be careful, Christian's not even two weeks old! Where are you taking him?"

Ian replied with a threatening glance that silenced any further objection, deftly mounted his horse, and urged him toward the plantation at a gallop.

Now understanding why Alanna had discouraged him from bringing Ian to see his son, Graham caught up to his friend. He tried to get him to slow down, but Ian was bent low, shielding the babe from the wind, and neither heard nor saw him. Mortified that his friend would so thoughtlessly endanger an infant's life, he stayed close, silently vowing to do whatever he could to save the lad, if need be.

Jostled awake and thoroughly terrified by the wild ride, Christian was screaming with all his might by the time Ian reached his in-laws' home. The outraged Englishman leapt off his horse and strode through the front door, where the whole family swiftly gathered to greet him, drawn by Christian's frantic shrieks. Rather than attempt to quiet the infant, Ian simply raised his voice to be heard above him.

"Whose child is this?" he shouted. "Surely he isn't mine and Melissa's."

As horrified as the dear babe, Alanna rushed forward to take Christian, but Ian held him aloft. "Oh, no, you don't. First you tell me where you got this child, because he sure as hell isn't mine!"

Rachel began to cry in a wail only slightly less pathetic than Christian's, while John stared at the screaming baby in shocked disbelief. Elliott hurried to Alanna's side, while his brother hung back. It was the most disgraceful scene imaginable, but Byron knew he wasn't the one to stop it.

"Ian's laid this one at your door, Father," he said. "If you can face the truth now, it's time you shared it with him."

John Barclay stood transfixed, unable to tear his gaze from the ebony-haired babe Ian now dangled in front of him. The child's face was bright red from the exertions of his screams, but his thick black hair provided clear confirmation of the scandal his grandfather had refused to believe.

"Give him to me!" John yelled, but Ian lifted Christian out of his reach, leaving the older man to claw the air wildly.

Appalled by the hatred that contorted his father-in-law's features, Ian turned to block him with his shoulder and laid the exhausted babe in Alanna's arms. "Here, you tend him. Come on, John, let's go into your study, where we won't have to listen to the noisy brat."

Ian grabbed his father-in-law's arm as he started down the hall. Wanting to make certain his father told the truth, Byron hurried to join them. Elliott dropped his arm around Alanna's shoulders and urged her to carry Christian into the parlor, but before she turned away, she sent Graham a glance which conveyed a lifetime of disappointment. Left in the hall with Rachel, who was now sobbing softly, Graham had no idea what to do. He knew he really ought to leave, but certain that the excitement had just begun, he helped Rachel into a chair in the dining room, sent a servant for tea, and prepared to remain for as long as it took to find out what had become of Ian's son.

Fifteen

While casting many an anxious glance toward the doorway, Alanna patted Christian's back gently and sang to him softly, until, soothed by her familiar voice and touch, he at last grew calm and fell asleep. She and Elliott couldn't overhear the conversation taking place in the study, but praying it was going well, she laid the baby across her lap and combed his hair through her fingertips.

"How could Ian have treated him so roughly?" she asked in a hushed whisper.

Elliott moved his chair closer to his cousin's. "Do you think Christian is all right? Should we take him to Dr. Earle's?"

"He was wrapped in his blankets, so he doesn't seem chilled, and he's breathing easily. I don't think he's suffered any physical harm, but it couldn't have done him any good to be frightened so badly. Babies need comfort and love, not to be tossed about and dangled in the air, like a tasty morsel meant for the hounds."

Elliott reached out to pat the sleeping infant's bottom. "He's still so tiny."

"Yes, and he's unlikely to get any bigger if Ian gets hold of him again."

"Perhaps we should take him back to Mrs. Wade's. He'll be hungry when he wakes, won't he?"

"Poor baby, he'll probably sleep all afternoon."

"Just to be safe, I think we ought to leave as soon as I can have the horses harnessed to the carriage."

"What could Ian have said to Charity? What if she's too upset to accept Christian back into her home?"

"Then we'll find him another wet nurse, but there's no point in fretting over problems that might not exist. For the time being, all we need do is—"

Elliott fell silent as Ian began to yell so loudly that they could hear him clearly through the study door. He was shouting at Byron, calling him a liar. Fearing the babe might again be snatched up to become part of what was clearly a heated argument, Elliott rose and helped Alanna to her feet. "Come on, let's get out of here while we still can."

Unfortunately, Ian was far more swift, and come running into the parlor before they had reached the door. "I can stand it if my baby died, but Alanna, please, please, tell me that's not Melissa's child!"

Tears were streaming down Ian's cheeks, and Alanna wished with all her heart that she could ease his torment, but she couldn't do it with convenient lies. "Melissa loved you. I truly believe she thought you would accept her child and raise him as your own."

Ian swayed slightly, and for a terrible instant, Alanna thought he might faint. Sharing her fear, Elliott rushed to his brother-in-law's side, but Ian shoved him away with a force that sent him reeling. "How can you speak of love after what that bitch did to me?" Ian asked. "Melissa was such a cunning liar, I never realized I didn't really have a wife. It's plain now it was all lies: the elopement, that night, our marriage. She made a mockery of our wedding vows, before they'd even been spoken."

"Oh Ian, you mustn't say such horrible things about Melissa," Alanna begged. "She loved you!"

Ian responded with a disgusted grimace. "I'm glad she's dead, or by God, I'd kill her for what she's done to me." He turned, and seeing Rachel and Graham standing in the hallway, he pointed at his mother-in-law. "Your daughter deserves to burn in hell forever," he shouted, "and you and everyone else in this house with her!"

Stunned by the sheer brutality of Ian's words, no one tried to stop him when he ran out the door. He leapt on his horse's back and rode away, leaving none of them untouched by his pain. John rushed to his wife's side and helped her to a chair in the parlor. Byron walked by Graham, and then gestured for him to follow.

"You've heard this much, you might as well hear the rest," he said.

John and Rachel suddenly appeared very old and frail. Alanna had always looked up to them, but now she saw them for the imperfect people they were. First they had lost their only daughter, and despite their best efforts to ignore the truth, it had caught up with them, irrevocably damaging the beauty of their memories. That they had been cursed by their son-in-law, as though they deserved his hatred, had crushed all that was left of their spirits. They sat together, shaken and hollow-eyed, waiting for someone else to speak.

Byron cleared his throat. "I'm afraid there simply is no considerate way to break a man's heart, but I would have given anything to spare Ian this new anguish. It's plain he'll not raise Christian. What are we going to do about the boy?"

"We'll raise him," Alanna proposed, "just as we would have any child of Melissa's."

Slowly emerging from his stupor, John heard Alanna's suggestion and reacted violently. "No! Make the Indian come for his son. All that has happened is *his* fault, and I'll not have his brat living with us as a daily reminder of it. Take the child back to the wet nurse, and leave him there until his father comes."

"But Uncle—"

"Don't you dare argue with me, Alanna. We'll tell everyone

the babe is sickly and can have no visitors, then when his father takes him away, we'll say he died. Ian can't talk about the babe without making himself look a fool, so Melissa's secret will be safe as soon as the babe is gone."

John Barclay was shaking with anger, and Alanna was not even tempted to argue with him. She carried Christian from the room. Elliott went to fetch the carriage, while she waited for him in the hall. When Graham walked up to her, she turned away.

"I really believed taking Ian to see his son was the best thing to do. I'd no idea the visit would provoke such terrible consequences. Can you ever forgive me?"

"We'd planned to reveal the truth about Melissa's son gently, in hopes that Ian would love him as dearly as he had loved her. Perhaps we would have failed, and his reaction would have been the same violently hostile one you observed, but now we'll never know. I can forgive you, but will Ian?"

"I doubt it. I always liked Melissa. I thought she was as nice as you."

"She was," Alanna insisted, but her eyes filled with tears, and she used the edge of one of Christian's blankets to wipe them away. "Why don't you go after Ian. He's the one who needs you now."

"I'd much rather ride into town with you."

"No, I'd not be good company. Please go."

"I am so sorry."

"Goodbye, Graham."

Despite having caused the day's disaster, the Englishman had no intention of giving up his quest to win Alanna's heart; he kissed her cheek lightly before leaving.

Night had fallen before Alanna and Elliott returned home, for it had taken them some time to satisfy Charity Wade's curiosity without divulging more than they wished her to know. She was fond of Christian, and relieved to have him restored safely to her care. They left her home after reassuring her Ian was unlikely to visit ever again.

"We should have told Charity not to admit any other visitors," Elliott worried aloud.

"I'll tell her tomorrow."

"You're not going to keep visiting the babe, are you?"

"Of course, I am. I realize I'm a cousin rather than his aunt, but I want him to feel loved."

Elliott held the front door open for her. "Come upstairs and help me write the letter to Hunter. I know you'll be able to explain the difficulty of our situation far more eloquently than I."

Alanna accompanied Elliott to his room, but she didn't want Hunter to come for Christian, so her heart wasn't in their task. "He hasn't answered any of your other letters. What makes you so certain he can read?"

"I've seen him do it many a time. I've also seen him write."

"Christian is too small to travel any great distance," Alanna reminded him.

"That will be a matter for Hunter to decide."

"He'll need to bring along a wet nurse."

Elliott went to his desk, sat down, and removed a sheet of stationery from the top drawer. "I doubt he'd recognize that term. I better just say he'll need to bring along a woman to nurse the infant."

Although hoping Hunter would never arrive, Alanna tried to appear helpful. "Yes, and tell him to bring plenty of blankets to wrap him in."

"I believe the Seneca use furs rather than blankets to keep warm."

"Well, whatever they use, tell him to bring plenty. Did Hunter have a house? Does he have anywhere to take Christian?"

Elliott dipped his pen into the ink. "Let's not overwhelm

him with questions, Alanna. How he chooses to raise his son really isn't any of our business."

"It most certainly is. Melissa isn't here to look after the boy, so we must."

Elliott turned around to face her. "You must be very disappointed in my parents. But, Alanna, they'd never love Christian, even if you somehow convinced them it was their duty to raise him. He's clearly part Indian, and they'd never be able to overlook that. I'm surprised that you can."

"So am I frankly, but Christian's heritage doesn't bother me at all. Now let's hurry up and write that letter. We better tell Hunter to send a reply, whether or not he's coming to Virginia. That way we'll be certain he received the letter and knows he has a son."

Elliott nodded thoughtfully, and they rehearsed each phrase before he wrote it, but they were both dissatisfied with their first effort and revised it repeatedly. Their final version was only a slight improvement, but convinced that they had done their best to convey sad and shocking news, Elliott sealed the envelope and addressed it to Hunter in care of William Johnson's trading post.

"This time I just know that he'll answer me," Elliott enthused.

But Alanna left his room praying that Hunter would feel as badly betrayed as Ian, and want nothing to do with his child.

The carefully prepared letter reached Hunter the first week in December. He carried it to his house unopened, and ashamed that Melissa's marriage had made it impossible for him to continue his friendship with Elliott, he tossed it into the fire unread. He liked Elliott, and was flattered by the fact that the young man still wished to write to him. His previous notes had been friendly and filled with humorous accounts of life on the plantation. Hunter had laughed as he had read them, but he had had nothing to say in return. When the letters had stopped coming, he had been saddened, but more than a little relieved.

He watched the flames blacken the parchment envelope, then spread through the single sheet of stationery, gradually reducing it to cinders. With the holidays coming, he supposed Elliott had thought of him, but he hoped this was the last letter he'd send. He added another log to the fire pit, and all that remained of the letter disappeared into the ashes at the bottom.

With the coming of autumn, all the men were busy trapping, and Hunter had not been challenged to any more fights. That suited him fine, for he intended to get in plenty of trapping himself that winter. He had gone out a couple of times, set a few traps, and had been amply rewarded for his trouble. By the spring he would have earned enough money selling pelts to take expensive presents home for his family, but he still was not certain that he would actually go.

The restlessness which had driven him away from home was still too much a part of him. A born warrior, he listened attentively whenever there was a mention of the French and English dispute over the Ohio Valley, but while he had been told London was sending more troops, they were not expected to arrive until spring. He was undecided as to whether he would again volunteer to scout, but the option held a definite appeal. While the pay wouldn't be nearly as good, there would be far more honor in going into battle against the French army, than simply fighting trappers each weekend for entertainment.

The weather was growing bitterly cold, and it would soon snow. Recalling the warmth of summer, Hunter moved closer to the fire. He had a few books for company, but with little hope that the coming year would be better than the last, he was far from content.

* * *

Ian requested a leave and sailed for England, but it was Graham Tyler who informed the Barclays of the officer's departure rather than Ian himself. The Scotsman had married their daughter and lived among them, but had not spoken with the family since the day he had fled their home in a rage, leaving them all feeling as abused as he. Hoping to spare the Barclays' further grief, Graham volunteered to gather up whatever Melissa and Ian had left in their rented house, and Alanna went along to help.

"Will Ian reach London by Christmas?" she asked.

"Yes, if the good weather holds."

"I wish I could have spoken with him before he left. Do you know when he's coming back?"

"I doubt that he will," Graham replied. "He lost too much here."

"Perhaps time will soften his heart. I can't bear to think of him hating Melissa, or the rest of us, when we all loved him."

Embarrassed by her mention of love because it did not include him, Graham carried a carton filled with crockery to the door, before replying. "Were you in town earlier today? I thought I might have seen you."

"Yes, my aunt and uncle disapprove of my visiting Christian, but they've not been so foolish as to forbid it."

"And if they did?"

"They'd be very wrong, and I'd have to defy them."

Alanna was refolding linens that had never been used, a task Graham thought particularly senseless, but he imagined she might feel as uneasy in her late cousin's former home as he did. "What if I asked you not to see the boy so often? Would you give my feelings any more consideration than your aunt and uncle's?"

Alanna set the last pillowcase aside. "Your feelings? What are you talking about, Graham? Why should you care how often I see my baby cousin?"

They were nearly finished with the sorting and packing, and Graham rushed to make his point. "People are beginning to talk, Alanna. Melissa's death brought your family enormous amounts of sympathy, and the suddenness of Ian's departure is understandable, but the fact that no one has seen the child is causing comment. I've heard rumors that he's deformed."

"Why would anyone say such an awful thing? You know that he isn't!"

"Yes, but I don't dare say that I've seen the boy, for fear I'll be asked questions I'd rather not answer. Weren't you going to send for Christian's father?"

"Yes, we did, but so far there's been no reply."

Graham nodded thoughtfully. "I'm sorry to hear that. I'd hoped he would be on his way here by now. Until he does arrive, I really wish you wouldn't spend so much of your time with Christian."

Alanna was amazed by what she regarded as completely unwarranted meddling in her affairs. She reminded herself that Graham was an officer and used to giving orders, but despite the splendid tailoring of his uniform and proud military bearing which imparted unmistakable authority to each of his gestures, she did not respond with the loyalty of his troops. "You have absolutely no right to make such a request, Graham. I wouldn't dream of telling you how you ought to spend your time."

"That's a completely different issue," he argued. "I believe there's something you haven't considered."

"Oh really? I can't think what it might be."

"What if a man were seriously interested in you, Alanna? You're so preoccupied with Melissa's child, he might fear the only way to win your consent for marriage was to agree to adopt him. Is it your intention to give such an impression?"

Graham was right, Alanna hadn't thought past her daily contact with Christian to the possibility of assuming responsibility for him permanently. She was of an age to marry, but Ian had rejected the prospect of raising an Indian's child so violently, that it had not even occurred to her that another man might have a more charitable view. "As I said, we've attempted to contact Christian's father. We'll have to exhaust that possibility, before any other plans can be made."

"My God, do you mean you'd consider taking the responsibility for Christian yourself?"

Alanna's pretty smile made her decision plain. "Why yes, I think it's a delightful idea. I have the money from my parents' estate. It isn't a great deal, but it would be enough to provide Christian with all he might need and a good education. He wouldn't be a burden to anyone."

Graham's eyes were a warm, soft gray, but narrowing now, they took on a steel-like glint. "Once you begin putting conditions on your love, I doubt there will be any end to them. If you'll demand a man adopt an Indian's brat to wed you, then you'll soon find another test for him to prove his devotion, and another. A man would be a fool to begin what would surely become an impossible series of challenges."

"You don't honestly believe that I'm such an unreasonable person, do you?"

"I don't know what to think anymore."

"Christian needs a home and family," Alanna replied. "I owe Melissa that much."

"How can you believe you owe her anything, after the way she behaved?"

Alanna picked up the stack of linens. "Please, I came here to help you clean up the house, not to listen to you criticize a woman who can't defend herself."

"You don't even see what you're doing, do you? If you wed a man to give Christian a father, you'll be repeating Melissa's mistake. You saw how bitter Ian was when he realized how he had been used. Your poor husband would soon feel exactly the same."

"I'll not listen to any more of this."

With her arms full, she couldn't move with her usual agility, and Graham had no difficulty blocking her way when she tried to get past him. "No, you'll listen to every word I have to say," he argued. "I love you, Alanna, but I can't go on hoping and praying that you'll come to love me, if that love is dependent on my willingness to raise another man's child."

"I'm thoroughly confused, Captain. Just what is it that you expect me to say, that should I fall in love with you, Christian wouldn't be part of our family?"

"Yes!"

"Now who's making unreasonable demands in exchange for promises of love? This whole conversation is ridiculous! Elliott's written another letter. Perhaps Hunter didn't receive the first. He could arrive any day."

"You can't possibly expect that renegade to come for his son."

"And why not? You only saw Hunter briefly the first night he was here last spring. How can you presume to know what he may or may not do?"

"He's an Indian!"

"I fail to see how that fact disqualifies him for fatherhood."

"If you think so much of Hunter, then why don't you marry *him?* He'd be the one man in the world who wouldn't resent the attention you lavish on Christian."

Aghast at that bizarre suggestion, Alanna simply stared at Graham for a long moment. Then she remembered the sweetness of Hunter's kiss, and her cheeks flooded with a bright blush. "I think the less said about Hunter the better. Now if you'll kindly step out of my way, I'll carry these things out to the carriage. Would you check to make certain there's nothing left to pack?"

Graham was too angry to respond, but he did move aside, and

with grim determination he searched the house, but found nothing that did not belong to the owners. "God damn," he murmured under his breath. He had finally told Alanna that he loved her, and her only response had been to ask him to move out of her way. He stormed out of the house, thinking that was precisely what he ought to have done several months ago.

While she was sorry they had quarreled that day, when Graham Tyler did not call on her again, Alanna understood his reasons and wasn't insulted. He had finally accepted what she had always known: that they simply hadn't been meant for each other. Always eager to gossip, the Frederick sisters kept her informed of the young women he escorted to holiday parties, until she finally convinced them that she really didn't care.

The holidays held such little joy for Alanna that year, that she left the Christmas service at church feeling as depressed as when she had entered. Elliott had helped her buy presents for Charity and her children, and they had delivered them earlier that morning, but that her aunt and uncle had not sent anything along for Christian, nor gone to see him, broke her heart. When the pair started toward the cemetery to visit their daughter's grave, she thought them hypocrites and didn't follow.

"Merry Christmas," Randolph O'Neil called to her.

Alanna recognized his voice, and smiled as she turned to face him. "Merry Christmas, Mr. O'Neil."

"I was hoping I'd have a chance to speak with you. Do you remember last spring, when your aunt asked me to find something special for Melissa and Ian's first Christmas?"

"Yes, I do, but sadly, they weren't able to celebrate it."

Randolph nodded. "I did find something, however, but before I could show it to your aunt, Melissa was gone. Then I couldn't decide if it would be unnecessarily cruel of me to mention it to Rachel, or if perhaps she wouldn't treasure the item even more.

I wonder, would you have time to come by my shop next week? I'd value your opinion, and perhaps you can help me resolve what has become something of a dilemma."

"I come into town every day to visit with the woman who's keeping Christian, and see how he's getting along. I'll be happy to stop in to see you, too."

"Thank you. I'd hoped you wouldn't think this insensitive of me. I'm not concerned about the cost of the item. I'd be pleased to give it to Rachel as a gift, if you think she'd like it."

"That's very thoughtful of you."

Randolph smiled slightly. "You've changed since our last conversation."

That had been at the wedding. It had been such a happy occasion, and now, Alanna couldn't bear to think of how greatly her family's circumstances had changed. "You're right. Nothing is the way it was last spring."

"For some things, that might not be bad."

Randolph's parting smile left Alanna wondering just what he meant, and she found herself thinking of him throughout what proved to be a long and solemn day. Byron and Elliott were as morose as their parents, and Alanna was grateful when they excused themselves right after supper and provided her with an equally fine opportunity to slip away. She went up to her room and began to read the copy of Henry Fielding's *Amelia* that Elliott had given her, until it was time to get ready for bed.

Alanna went to see Randolph O'Neil at her first opportunity. There were several customers in the shop, but he summoned clerks to see to their needs and escorted her into his private office. "How is your little cousin today?" he asked.

Randolph's expression was devoid of the hostility Graham had shown over her devotion to Christian, and Alanna was delighted to find his interest sincere. "He's very well, thank you. He's growing so rapidly, if I didn't visit him every day I'm sure I'd miss something."

"Yes, I remember when my daughter was small. Unfortunately, we had no other children, although we both wanted them very badly. Do you remember my daughter? I realize Karen is several years older than you, but I thought perhaps you might know her."

"No, I'm sorry I don't recall meeting her. I seldom came into town before last spring, so there are a great many people here in Williamsburg whom I've not met."

"I'm sure that will be remedied in the near future," Randolph predicted with an inviting smile. "Now let me show you the gift." He leaned down to open the bottom drawer of his desk and withdrew a leather box. He then removed the lid with care. "I know how much your aunt admires crystal, and this angel with silver wings is one of the most beautiful pieces I've ever seen."

He placed the angel on the corner of the desk where Alanna could appreciate it, but while she was equally impressed with its beauty, she had no idea how to advise him. "It's exquisite," she murmured.

"Yes, it most certainly is. The only question is: Would your aunt think it a fitting tribute to Melissa?"

The angel, who was glancing down at her demurely clasped hands, projected an air of serenity that Melissa had certainly never possessed while alive, and Alanna was afraid that should the name of Christian's father ever become common knowledge, her spirit would not be generally regarded as residing in heaven. As for the silver wings, they were highly polished, and yet so detailed, the softness of the feathers looked real. If not tended properly, those beautiful silver wings would tarnish, and knowing that symbolism would not be lost on her Aunt Rachel, Alanna decided against it.

"Truly, she is lovely, but my aunt is heartbroken over

Melissa's death, and I fear any reminder of the life she and Ian should have had, or even of an angel, would be unbearably painful for her. Thank you so much for showing her to me, but I think you should keep her for someone else."

Randolph frowned slightly, and for a moment he looked as though he wanted to argue with Alanna, but he apparently thought better of it. With the same care he had shown earlier, he returned the angel to her box and replaced it in his drawer. "I don't think I'll display her until next year. She's a Christmas angel, don't you think?"

"Yes, someone is sure to treasure her and see that she's passed down for generations. Perhaps she would make a nice gift for your daughter."

Randolph broke into a wide grin. "She has two little boys, so I don't dare give her anything that delicate, at least not for a while yet."

Thinking her visit had come to its natural end, Alanna rose from her chair. "I'm sorry I couldn't be more helpful."

Randolph moved between her and the door. "You needn't apologize. You gave me precisely the help I required. There is one other thing I'd like, though."

"Yes?"

"I'd like to see Melissa's little boy. I don't have much opportunity to be around my grandsons, and I'd just like to hold a baby once in a while."

Randolph O'Neil didn't fit Alanna's image of a grandfather any closer than she knew Christian would fit his expectation of Melissa's son. "I'm sorry, but the Barclays don't permit visitors."

"Oh, I didn't know that."

He made no effort to hide his disappointment, which made Alanna feel all the worse. "If it were up to me, I'd take you to see him right now, but when my aunt and uncle forbid it—"

Randolph raised his hands. "No, forget that I asked. It's just that I'd heard Captain Scott went home to England, and I thought the babe might enjoy an extra hug or two."

"Yes, I'm sure that he would. He's an adorable child."

"He would have to be."

Alanna waited for him to add a comment about Melissa, but he was regarding her with a sly smile that made it plain he was thinking of her. "Please, you're embarrassing me."

"Why, because I think you're pretty? Any man would."

"Thank you, but really, I must go."

Randolph reached for the doorknob, but hesitated to turn it. "If you're in town often, will you come to see me again? I should have offered you tea. I'll promise to have some ready the next time you're here."

Alanna's first impulse was to say no, but Randolph had such a warm and sympathetic manner, she really did want to see him again. "I don't want to become a pest."

"That will never happen."

"All right then, I will stop by again soon."

"Good." He walked her to the door, and again urged her to visit him soon.

Alanna found herself smiling all the way home. Randolph O'Neil was such a nice man, and he even liked babies. Would he like Christian, she wondered. Somehow, she thought that he would. Graham had insisted that she would be repeating Melissa's mistake, if she married a man simply to make a home for Christian, but what if the man knew exactly what she was doing, and did not object? What if he were a kind and gentle soul who would love Christian? Wouldn't the greater mistake be in *not* marrying such a man?

Then a truly horrible thought occurred to her: What if she were to marry Randolph, or someone like him, only to have Hunter appear later to claim his son? Then what? What a horrible mess that would be. After all, she was only a cousin, and he was the boy's father. Wouldn't that be the deciding factor?

"Damn it all, Hunter," she moaned. "Where are you?"

After dinner that night, Alanna waited until Elliott went upstairs to his room, and then she followed him. "We need to talk," she announced.

"Really, about what?"

"About Hunter."

Elliott ushered her into his room and closed the door. "I really thought he'd come as soon as he received my first letter. I don't know what to make of him now. Perhaps we expected too much."

"That's possible. I think we ought to go see him."

"You don't mean it."

"Oh, but I do. I think we need to confront him and settle the issue of who's to raise Christian once and for all. If he has no more interest in him than your parents do, we need to know it now, so that we can make arrangements for him to have a permanent home."

"Wait a minute. It's possible that Hunter has been away from the trading post trapping the last month or so, and that my letters haven't reached him."

"It's also possible that he just doesn't care."

"Yes, that's true, but I'd rather not go tramping through the wilds of New York in the dead of winter looking for him. Christian isn't even two months old. He's doing well with Charity, we can afford to wait awhile longer to hear from Hunter."

"And if we never do?"

"Well then, I'll go up to the trading post in the spring."

"I want to come along."

"My parents will never allow it."

Alanna lifted her chin proudly. "They don't want me visiting Christian, and I do that, don't I? I don't see why I should have to get their permission. I'll be eighteen by then. That's plenty old enough to make decisions for myself."

Amused by the fiery gleam in his once painfully shy cousin's eyes, Elliott had to laugh. "All right, if we don't hear from Hunter in three months' time, then we'll pay him a visit. Agreed?"

Alanna let out a joyful whoop, and then, fearing she had disturbed the rest of the house, she hurriedly adopted a sedate pose and shook his hand. "Agreed."

Elliott watched her practically skip out of his room, and shook his head in wonder at how much his dear little cousin had changed. When he had first brought Hunter home, Alanna wouldn't even talk to him, and now she was prepared to go all the way to New York to see the brave. Well, he was certainly looking forward to seeing Hunter, too, but for an entirely different reason. He knew the Indian was tough, but one of the Barclay men had to give him the thrashing he deserved, and by spring, Elliott thought he just might be able to do it.

Part Two

Sixteen

April, 1755

Elliott leaned over to tuck a stray curl under Alanna's cap. "You look tired," he said.

Alanna shook her head, then laughed when she had to cover a wide yawn. "What about you? I doubt that you've been able to sleep any better than I have, since we left home."

"It didn't even seem like home anymore."

Alanna looped her arm through Elliott's and rested her head on his shoulder. "Your parents miss Melissa terribly. Perhaps in time . . ."

"The problem isn't grief," Elliott interrupted. "It's shame. As for Byron, I don't think he's really been himself since last summer. He may have already rejoined the militia by the time we get back home."

Alanna had also noted the change in Byron, but she hadn't seen the same restlessness in Elliott. "What about you? Will you follow his example, if he's accepted another commission?"

"No. It's not that I don't believe in the British cause, because I do. I just don't want to be responsible for any more deaths. That doesn't sound very manly, does it?"

"Shouldn't a man's character be judged by the way he lives, not by how much destruction he causes?"

"That's a comforting thought, until you consider how much harm Hunter has done our family. If he's to be judged on the pain he's caused us, then he's already doomed to hell, if he believes in it."

That they would see Hunter soon, perhaps within the next hour, was causing Alanna nearly unbearable anxiety. She had lost count of how many times Elliott had written, half a dozen at the very least, but all to no avail. That winter she had watched Christian grow, while her confusion and despair had deepened. He was such a beautiful child. He seemed to have inherited Melissa's charm and his father's dashing good looks. She hoped that in addition to those blessings, he hadn't also been cursed with his parents' faults.

She had frequently recalled her few brief conversations with Hunter, but she could detect no hint of the cold indifference with which he had ignored Elliott's pleas for a response. If only he had written to say he had no interest in his son, it would have been enough to assure her she could raise Christian without the fear that he might someday be taken from her. But no, Hunter had not bothered to provide her with even minimal peace of mind.

"Randolph O'Neil will miss you terribly," Elliott teased.

Embarrassed, Alanna pretended to study the banks of the Hudson River, as she replied, "He's a wonderful man. Truly he is."

"Well, he certainly excels in patience. Either that, or he's beyond the age when desire makes something more than friendship enviable."

"That's unlikely. He's only forty-three."

"Only forty-three," Elliott mimicked. "You ought to be looking for a father for Christian, who's closer to your age."

The barge on which they were traveling was too crowded with freight to provide any place for Alanna to go to avoid such impertinent questions, but she certainly didn't enjoy them. "Is what I want so obvious?"

"It is to me, but then I know you better than any other man ever will."

"That's probably true, but what about you? Neither you nor Byron has seen much of Robin and Sarah lately."

Elliott understood she was merely trying to distract him, and placed his hand over hers to keep her close. "Have they complained to you?"

"They are too sweet to complain; however, they have hinted vaguely about neglect."

Elliott was amused by her choice of words. "I can't imagine them being all that vague."

"Perhaps I don't listen to them as closely as I should."

"Nor do I," Elliott admitted. After a long pause, he began a hesitant confession. "I've been thinking about something for quite awhile now. I've not said anything to you, because I knew that until we settled things with Hunter, you'd not accept a proposal from Randolph."

"He hasn't offered one."

"He has no idea where we've gone or why, does he?"

"I've had several opportunities to confide in him, and I do believe he'd be sympathetic, but no, I've not wanted to tell him the truth about Christian. I hope you won't consider me deceitful."

"You're the most trustworthy and honest person I know, Alanna, but there's a type of honesty I think you're avoiding."

"Is there more than one kind?"

"Yes. I don't think you're being honest with yourself."

Completely confused, Alanna hoped they would soon reach the junction of the Mohawk River. Then her fears that the inevitable confrontation with Hunter would be even more disconcerting than Elliott's perplexing questions caused her to shove the thought aside. "How could I lie to myself?" she asked. "Is that even possible?"

Elliott slipped his arm from hers, yanked off his hat to rake his fingers through his hair, than replaced it with an emphatic pat. "I know I'm your cousin, and perhaps you fail to think of me as a man, but damn it all, Alanna, I am one."

When he turned toward her, she was startled by the intensity of his gaze. It was the way Graham Tyler had looked at her upon occasion, but it made her far more uncomfortable coming from Elliott. It took her a full minute to comprehend what he meant; alarmed, her dismay grew to a near strangling apprehension. Apparently he considered himself a far wiser choice for a husband than Randolph O'Neil. She knew first cousins sometimes wed, but that he would even hint at such a possibility unnerved her.

"You're like a brother to me," she stammered.

Elliott wasn't certain just when he had stopped regarding Alanna as a sister, but he no longer did. "Does that mean you find it impossible to have romantic feelings for me?"

Alanna was so flustered by the direction their conversation was taking, she feared she might offend him, and that was the very last thing she would ever knowingly do. "Brothers and sisters aren't supposed to have romantic feelings for each other," she reminded him. "That's incest."

"I know what it's called, but we aren't brother and sister, regardless of how we were raised." When Alanna's blush deepened, Elliott finally realized how badly he was embarrassing her, and took a new tack. "Have you grown fond of Randolph? Do you have romantic feelings for him?"

Alanna saw no point in arguing that respect and friendship might eventually deepen into desire, because she didn't believe that they ever would. "Love isn't all that important to me," she explained instead. "It was all Melissa ever talked about, and—"

"Yes, and look what happened to her," Elliott agreed. "But we aren't discussing Melissa, we're talking about you and me."

"I do love you, Elliott, you know that I do, but—"

"But what? I'll treat you better than Randolph can ever hope to. The plantation provides an ample living for us all, so you'll never lack for anything. Can't you see I'm a more logical choice than an outsider to help you raise Melissa's child?"

Elliott's proposal was completely unexpected, but that didn't prevent Alanna from seeing the problems it created. "Your parents have never gone to see Christian, nor do they ask about him. If I do marry, it will be to make a home for him. What would your parents say, if we expressed a desire to raise Christian?"

That she would prefer to discuss Christian's future rather than the one he hoped they would share, annoyed Elliott, but he tried, not all that successfully, to be patient with her. "I've thought this through, Alanna. It won't be easy winning their consent for our marriage, but neither of us is easily intimidated, and if it's what we both want, then we'll eventually sway them to our point of view. As for Christian, I'd not try and separate you from the boy. I think my parents will come to love him in time. Of course, if we can convince Hunter the child is his responsibility, then that will be one less problem for us."

This time it was Alanna who spoke without thinking. "If Hunter takes Christian, then I'll no longer have any need of a husband."

"Is that a threat? Either I help you raise Christian, or you'll refuse my proposal?"

"Please, this is all so unexpected, and I need time to think! Melissa used to tease me because I had no wish to marry, but truly, I didn't consider marriage attractive until Christian was orphaned. You'll have to give me time to adjust to what you've said. What about Robin? She's been your sweetheart forever."

"No, she was merely my sweetheart until you grew up, and what she sensed as neglect was diminishing interest. I love you, Alanna, and I'm not going to hide my feelings another day."

He'd been a perfect gentleman on the trip. They'd occupied adjoining cabins on the ship from Newport News to New York, and again on the barge taking them up the Hudson River. He had been a charming rather than ardent companion, and she didn't want his mood or manner to change. She needed the comforting presence of a protective older brother, not the insistence of a passionate suitor.

"Have you spoken to your father about this?" she asked.

"No, I wanted to ask your feelings first."

Elliott's face was as familiar as her own, but Alanna found it difficult to look at him now, for fear he might mistake her confusion for rejection, putting an end to the closeness they had always shared. "Please, could we discuss this at another time? This won't be an easy visit, and I'm afraid I'm so distracted, I'm saying all the wrong things. What will Byron think?" she added suddenly.

"He'll be angry that I thought of marrying you before he did. Would you rather have him for a husband?"

Alanna was positive of her answer this time. "No!"

"Good. I've always known that you liked me best."

Flattered, embarrassed, frightened, Alanna didn't know how to accurately assess her emotions, but when the captain of the barge announced Johnson's trading post lay ahead, she was almost relieved that she would have to face Hunter rather than continue to discuss marriage with Elliott.

Hunter would have beaten Jonah Bramen as handily as he had all his other opponents, had he not caught a glimpse of Blind Snake in the crowd. Indians frequently came to the trading post, so sighting one wouldn't have jarred him, had it been any other brave. Distracted by that sharp jolt of recognition, Hunter failed to block Jonah's next blow, and suffered badly for his momentary lapse of attention, when Jonah's fist glanced off his right cheek and sliced through his brow. Blood began to drip into his eye, and he tossed his head to fling it aside.

Believing he was the first man ever to draw blood from the Indian, Jonah gave an excited whoop and waved to the men who were cheering for him. Hunter drew back, feigning pain and, fooled, Jonah dropped his guard slightly, giving Hunter the opening to come back at him with renewed ferocity. He slammed his fist into Jonah's solar plexus; when he gasped and doubled over, Hunter caught him on the chin with a teeth-rattling punch that buckled his knees.

His brief dream of victory brought to a painfully abrupt end, Jonah struggled to rise, but slipped on a piece of gravel and went down. Hunter moved astride the fallen man, planted his knees firmly on Jonah's shoulder blades, grabbed his hair, and yanked his head back. "Had enough?" the brave asked.

Jonah bucked and twisted in an effort to break free, but failed to dislodge the wily brave. He cursed loudly, and Hunter responded by grinding his face down into the dirt. "I'm not a patient man," the Indian revealed, before again pulling Jonah's head back at a dangerous angle.

His mouth full of sandy soil, Jonah spit and sputtered. Humiliated, he chose to give up rather than risk having his neck snapped by a foul-tempered Indian he had never expected to be so strong and fast. "Enough," he moaned grudgingly.

Hunter released him with another rude shove that sent Jonah's face slamming into the ground. The brave then rose and stepped away, but remained wary, just in case Jonah regretted his defeat and attempted another go at him. It wasn't until Jonah got to his feet and started off in the opposite direction, that Hunter began to relax.

Peter Bright handed Hunter a handkerchief. "That cut looks bad."

"It'll heal," Hunter insisted, but it was painful. He pressed the handkerchief against his brow to stem the flow of blood, while he searched the crowd for Blind Snake. He was positive he had seen the same evil snarl on the brave's face that he'd worn when he had waved a bloody scalp and shouted his name, but the Abenaki was nowhere to be found.

"Did you see an Indian here this afternoon?"

Peter looked puzzled. "Only you."

Peter was a good soul, but not the smartest man at the trading post, and Hunter didn't scold him for giving such a ridiculous answer. Not trusting the men who had organized the fight to give him a fair share, he waited while the money was being counted. It wasn't until he had pocketed his earnings that he turned toward the trading post, and saw Alanna and Elliott standing on the steps. He didn't know which of them looked more surprised, but what he saw in their shocked expressions looked close to disgust, and he knew they hadn't been favorably impressed to find him fighting.

He lifted the handkerchief from the cut, and when he felt no new blood oozing toward his eye, he stuffed the blood-stained square of linen into his belt. He picked up his shirt and carried it over to the bottom of the stairs. He eyed the Virginians with a suspicious glance, and waited for them to explain their reason for being there.

Elliott had seen enough of the fight to be reminded of the vicious streak Hunter had displayed last summer. He had admired the Indian's prowess then. Now, he thought him mean rather than courageous. "Didn't you receive my letters?" he asked accusingly.

"I got them."

"Then why didn't you answer?"

Hunter shook the dust from his shirt. "I had nothing to say."

Stunned by the inappropriateness of his response, Alanna could not help but stare. Physically, Hunter was still the same exceptionally handsome man—half-clothed, even more so—but his manner had changed so dramatically she scarcely knew what to expect. When he looked up at her, his icy gaze chilled her clear through.

"You had nothing to say about your own son?" she asked.

As surprised as when he'd first seen them, Hunter had to force himself to react calmly, rather than gape like a witless fool. "I have no children."

"I thought you said you got my letters," Elliott exclaimed.

Again searching for Blind Snake, Hunter glanced away, but there was still no sign of the belligerent brave. "I didn't read them," he finally admitted.

Alanna found it difficult to believe this aloof stranger was Christian's father, and she was deeply disappointed in him. When he had last bid her goodbye, she had actually believed that he really cared what happened to her. Apparently his kiss had meant nothing. "You told me if I ever needed you, to write to you here."

"You weren't the one who wrote to me."

His tone was insulting, and Alanna reacted with equal sarcasm. "You mean you would have answered had *I* written the letters rather than Elliott?"

Hunter continued to regard Alanna with an insolent gaze. He had not expected accusations from her, but there was a new pride to her bearing that had been absent in their last meeting. They had both changed in the intervening months, but he thought the difference in her an improvement.

"Yes," he replied. "I gave you my word. If you came all this way to hear me say I have no son, then I'm sorry for your trouble."

"You're not half as sorry as we are," Elliott declared. "Melissa's dead, and her son needs a father."

"That's her husband's concern, not mine."

Hunter had shown as little reaction to the mention of Melissa's death, as he had to the announcement of his son's birth. Alanna wondered if he was even listening to them. "The boy is clearly yours, Hunter."

No longer merely annoyed, Hunter's tone turned bitterly sarcastic. "No. Melissa swore to me the babe was Ian's."

Disgusted, he started to turn away, but Alanna hurried down the steps and caught his elbow. "Don't you care that Melissa's dead, or that you have a son?"

Her hand looked very small and white against the burnished copper of his arm. Knowing the color of their skin was the least of their differences, Hunter made no attempt to hide his distress, as he replied in a voice too low for Elliott to overhear. "Why didn't *you* write to me?"

That he would criticize the manner in which they had tried to contact him, rather than respond to the message their letters had contained, astonished Alanna. "You really don't care about Melissa or your son, do you?"

That she had ignored his question, incensed Hunter all the more. "Why should I? Melissa cared nothing for me."

Elliott walked up behind her, but Alanna wasn't content to allow him to handle what she feared was a rapidly deteriorating situation. Hoping that perhaps Hunter was as flustered by their news as she had been by Elliott's mention of marriage, she softened her tone. "Please, take some time to think about what we've said. Can we meet again later and talk?"

"I have nothing more to say."

"Well, we have," Elliott informed him coldly. "Go clean up and meet us back here in an hour."

Hunter didn't have to glance around the courtyard to know they were being observed. He could feel it. No one had dared come close enough to overhear them, and he did not want to present any curious bystanders with an opportunity to do so. "No, come with me to my house. We can talk there."

Alanna and Elliott hesitated a moment, but when Hunter turned away and did not look back, they followed. Not expecting an extended visit, each had brought only a small bag, and

Elliott carried them easily. Dismayed, Alanna whispered to her cousin, "How can he not care?"

Elliott just shook his head to warn her to be silent. Torn between the anger that made him want to rip Hunter limb from limb, and relief at the fact that the Indian had shown no interest in rearing his son, Elliott tried to decide how best to proceed. At the very least, he wanted Hunter's written statement that he was renouncing all claim to his child. Then, having provided Alanna with the assurance that she would be the one to raise Christian, he hoped he could convince her to become his wife.

When they reached his long house, Hunter held aside the hide draped over the doorway and gestured for them to precede him. Neither of his reluctant guests had ever seen such a dwelling, much less entered one, but they ducked slightly and stepped inside. With the only illumination coming from the coals glowing in the fire pit and the opening in the roof above, the interior was dim.

The contrast to the bright, sunlit rooms where Alanna hoped to raise Christian gave her a moment's pause. Gradually her eyes became accustomed to the darkness, and she noticed Hunter hadn't followed them into his home. She looked around and noted the bundles of furs rolled up beneath the platforms, which lined the walls.

"It looks as though Hunter has been busy."

Elliott set their luggage down on the nearest platform. "It isn't the first time. No one can call the man lazy."

Alanna was too embarrassed to respond to what was clearly a reference to the speed with which Hunter had seduced Melissa, and changed the subject. "Are we handling this badly?" she asked instead.

"Probably, but that may be the only way such a deplorable situation can be handled."

At a loss for what to do or say, Alanna perched herself down next to her valise. The months of dread were over, but Hunter's indifference had shocked and disappointed her. "I was so certain that he really cared for Melissa, but now . . ."

When she didn't continue, Elliott finished her sentence for her. "Now it's plain he cares for nothing but himself. We worked so hard on the wording of those letters and he didn't even read them. It's plain we care far more about Christian than he ever will."

Hunter entered before Alanna could reply. He had washed up outside, and his hair, still wet, was tied neatly at his nape. He'd shaken the dust from his pants, donned his shirt, and despite the cut through his brow, now looked the way she had remembered him.

"Why were you fighting?" she asked.

"Because I'm good at it."

"You wouldn't have been hurt, if you were all that good," Elliott pointed out.

Preoccupied, Hunter chose to ignore that taunt. "Do you remember the Indians who attacked the end of our column last July, and killed the wounded?"

"Of course."

"One of them was here this afternoon. I want to go look for him."

"Do it later," Elliott advised. "We've something far more important to settle right here."

Elliott sat down next to Alanna, but Hunter remained standing. "Let Ian settle it," the brave said.

"He's gone home to London," Alanna explained. "We hired a woman to look after your son, and waited for you to come for him. If you'd read our letters, you would have known that. Because you didn't respond, we felt we had to come here."

"You should have stayed home."

"Would you rather have never known that you had fathered a child?"

When Hunter looked away, apparently bored by her question, Alanna lost patience with him. "Christian is a beautiful boy. I know you'd be proud of him."

"Christian?" Hunter laughed. "I'd never name a son that."

Hoping that sarcastic boast could be construed as interest, Alanna tried again. "Christian was my brother's name. That's why Melissa chose it, but if you'd rather call him something else, you certainly may."

"I have no need of names, because I have no son."

Hunter was being flippant, and Elliott decided to adopt the same attitude. "Fine," he agreed. "Then you should have no objection to saying so in writing, so the boy can be adopted by another man."

Such a request struck Hunter as absurd. "If I swear the boy is not mine, and Melissa swore to me that he wasn't, won't you have to search for a man who will claim the child?"

"There is no other man," Elliott informed him. "The boy is clearly yours."

"But you want me to say that he isn't?"

"Forgive me if I confused you. All we need for you to say is that you have no wish to raise Christian. Then another man can legally assume that responsibility."

"Not Ian?"

"No, not Ian, although the boy owes his life to him, as it was Ian who delivered the child after Melissa died. It wasn't until later that he realized the baby he had saved wasn't his."

"Then Melissa lied to him, too."

"She was my sister, Hunter. Try and remember that."

Hunter looked Elliott straight in the eye. "She was a lying bitch, and any tears you shed for her were wasted."

Elliott leapt to his feet with his arms outstretched, clearly going for Hunter's throat, but the Indian backed away, drawing him outside where his home and possessions would suffer no damage during an exchange of blows. The small clearing in front

of his house formed a perfect arena, but after having had one
fight that day, Hunter had little enthusiasm for another bout.

Alanna followed the men outside. She had seen enough of
Hunter's fight with Jonah Bramen to fear that Elliott was badly
outmatched, but rather than unleash the brutality she had
glimpsed earlier, the Indian dodged her cousin's blows without
throwing any of his own. He was agile and escaped being hit
with apparent ease. She understood Elliott's wish to defend
Melissa, and made no move to interfere, but she looked around
for a fallen branch or anything else within reach, which she
might use as a club should the need arise.

When Elliott realized that Hunter wasn't going to do more
than defend himself, he dropped back. "What's the matter?
Won't you fight, if you're not being paid?"

"No. Melissa just isn't worth fighting over."

"You bastard!"

Outraged, Elliott changed his strategy and, rather than attempt to punish Hunter with his fists, he rushed him, grabbed
him around the waist, and wrestled him to the ground. He
managed to reopen the cut above the Indian's eye, but that was
the only harm he did him before Hunter grabbed his wrists,
threw him to the side, and scrambled to his feet. He glanced
toward Alanna, nodded, and again backed away.

Elliott rose just as quickly and would have gone after him
again, but this time Alanna rushed forward to stop him. "Look,
he's already hurt, and there's no point in continuing this until
you're hurt, too. It won't solve anything."

Elliott pried her fingers from his sleeve. "I won't let him
talk that way about Melissa. She's dead because of him, and
I don't intend to let him forget it."

Again, Alanna moved between the two men. "I doubt he
ever will, but what difference will words make to Melissa?
She'll never hear them. I thought we came here to provide for

Christian, not to avenge Melissa's death. Or were you just telling me what you knew I wanted to hear?"

Elliott continued to glare at Hunter, while he tried to decide how to answer Alanna's question without admitting she had guessed the truth. Finally he found a way. "I did come here because of the boy. Hunter's the one who started this. You ought to be angry with him, not me."

Alanna glanced over her shoulder at Hunter. The whole right side of his face was now awash in blood, and tending his wound was suddenly more important than convincing Elliott to stop trading accusations. "Come over here and sit down," she ordered brusquely. "It won't do any of us any good, if you bleed to death."

Hunter was beginning to feel sick to his stomach and when Elliott relaxed his stance, he ceased to worry about him. He followed Alanna back to the front of his house, and sat down beside the barrel of rainwater where he had washed up earlier. He still had Peter Bright's bloody handkerchief and handed it to her.

"Don't you have anything else?" she asked.

Hunter just shook his head and leaned back against the barrel.

Elliott stepped forward to offer his clean handkerchief. "Here, use this."

Alanna dropped Peter's soiled handkerchief and dipped Elliott's into the rainwater. After wringing it out, she knelt beside Hunter and held it against his brow. "You should probably have stitches."

Hunter replied with a distracted grunt.

"I suppose you think gruesome scars are handsome?"

She was only inches away, and when Hunter looked up at her, the concern mirrored in her beautiful green eyes surprised him. "You should have been the one to write," he said again.

"She had better things to do with her time," Elliott answered for her.

"Just you hush, Elliott," Alanna scolded.

"Can't you see what he's doing?" Elliott chided. "He's not content to have ruined Melissa's life. Now he's trying to do the same thing to you."

Unwilling to believe Hunter would ever consider seducing her, even if he felt up to it, which she doubted, Alanna rose, rinsed out the handkerchief, and used it to wipe the blood from Hunter's face. This time she took great care to concentrate on her task without really looking at him, but touching him brought a flush to her cheeks that wasn't due to embarrassment. His skin was warm, and his blood was as red as Melissa's. With that realization, his face began to swim before her eyes.

"I'm afraid I can't do this," she whispered, but before she could hand the handkerchief to Hunter, she fainted across his lap.

"Now look what you've done!" Elliott cried. He knelt beside Hunter, meaning to take Alanna from his arms, but the Indian pulled her into a tight embrace. "Let me have her," Elliott demanded. "I'll take her inside where she can lie down."

"No, she's better off out here in the air."

Thinking that might be true, Elliott still had an objection. "Well, it's certainly not going to help her any to wake up and get another look at you. Had someone split your head with an ax, I doubt you'd look worse."

Hunter handed Elliott the damp handkerchief. "Then rinse this out, and I'll take care of myself."

"She's my woman. You understand that?"

"I once asked Melissa if you two were in love. She said no."

"Well that was another of her mistakes, because we *are*." Elliott grabbed the handkerchief, decided it was beyond rinsing, and went inside the long house to fetch another from his valise.

Left alone with Alanna, if only for a few seconds, Hunter

leaned down to kiss her lips lightly. Thinking it might be the only opportunity he would ever have to take such a liberty, he quickly kissed her again, but when Elliott returned, he was staring off into the forest, rather than gazing at the beautiful young woman in his arms.

Seventeen

As the smokey haze of unconsciousness began to lighten,
Alanna gradually became aware of the tangy scent of pine
filling the air, and then the high-pitched chatter of squirrels
dashing from tree to tree in an endless game of tag. In a soothing contrast to their raucous rhythm, she felt the slow, steady
beat of Hunter's heart through his soft buckskin shirt.

How had she come to be in his arms? she wondered. That
was the last place she belonged, but his easy embrace was so
comfortable, she continued to lie still. He was tracing gentle
circles across her back, which felt too good to end; and she
was also far more tired than she had thought.

Hunter saw Alanna's eyelashes flutter slightly, but made no
move to shake her awake. He had not held a woman in a long
time, and she felt too warm and sweet to release until he absolutely had to. Elliott was talking about the need for him to
relinquish all claim to his son, but he was only half-listening.

After months of striving to banish any thought of the Barclays from his mind, he had been badly startled by the sudden
arrival of two of them, and most especially these two. The
news of Melissa's death had awakened painful memories, and
to talk of a son he would never see was nearly unbearable. He
allowed none of his anguish to show in his face, but he felt
every bit of it deeply.

When Hunter began to caress her nape lightly with his fingertips, Alanna opened her eyes. Not because his touch didn't

feel wonderful, it did, but she did not want to give him the impression that once awake she would welcome more of his affection. Obviously aware that she had been feigning unconsciousness for several minutes, he responded with an amused grin. Aghast that he would surely think she had been enjoying his caress, she struggled to sit up without touching him, but it was impossible not to rest her hands on his broad chest. When their eyes met, she saw something more than the hint of laughter in his dark gaze and, unwilling to explore just what it might be, she took Elliott's hand when he offered it.

Once on her feet, Alanna struggled to gather her composure. She pulled her cap back into place and adjusted the folds of her gown. It was a simple gray dress designed for traveling, but not for reclining in the dirt, and she quickly brushed away the leaves and soil that clung to her skirt. When she had run out of ways to primp, she spoke to her cousin rather than the handsome Indian who was still seated on the ground.

"I'm sorry, I don't know what came over me."

"You needn't apologize," Hunter assured her. "I'm not fond of the sight of blood either, especially when it's mine."

Still nonplussed, Alanna again turned to Elliott. "Where were we?"

Elliott relayed only what suited him. "You were scolding us both for behaving badly, but I'll put our argument aside if Hunter will." When Hunter nodded slightly, he continued. "Not knowing what would be available here, I brought writing materials. I think we can come up with a satisfactory statement in a few minutes time. After it's signed, Alanna and I will go back to the barge to be ready for the return trip to New York tomorrow."

Hunter thought that over for a moment, and then shook his head. "No, that's a poor plan. The crew of the barge will all be drunk tonight and Alanna won't be safe on board. Stay here with me instead."

"That's really very thoughtful of you," Alanna replied, "but the crew was respectful on the voyage here, so I'm not afraid of them."

"Did the captain allow drinking?"

"I really didn't notice. Did you, Elliott?"

Elliott scuffed the toe of his shoe in the dirt. "The crew were all sober, but Hunter's probably right. They're a rough lot, and once drunk, what few manners they have will undoubtedly disappear. Does the trading post have lodgings for travelers?"

Having recovered his strength, Hunter rose with an easy stretch. "They have a few rooms, but it's no place for a lady. I know my house isn't nearly as grand as yours, but you'll be safe here. I can hang hides to make a separate room for Alanna, so she needn't sleep with us. I have venison to roast for supper. Are you hungry?"

Elliott doubted that either of them were truly safe with Hunter, but if the frontiersmen who had been watching the Indian fight were a fair sample of the trading post's clientele, he did not want Alanna near that rude bunch either. Not pleased with the choice forced upon him, he tried to make the best of it. "Will you be comfortable staying here?" he asked Alanna.

"Is the trading post really so bad?" she inquired. "I saw several ladies there, and they didn't appear to be in any danger."

Hunter winked at Elliott. "Their kind never is, but no one else ever calls them ladies."

Now realizing that the women she had mistaken for trappers' wives were not a respectable sort, Alanna came to the same conclusion as Elliott. After all, he would be there, so she'd not have to be alone with Hunter. "It's very kind of you to offer us a place to stay. I hope we won't be in your way."

Hunter's gaze swept over her slowly before he shook his head. "I will enjoy your company."

Elliott was amazed by how easily the Indian filled a simple phrase with innuendo. He was anxious to leave, but first they had business to conduct. "To answer your question, we're both hungry, but I'd like to get the statement out of the way before supper."

"The barge will not leave until noon tomorrow," Hunter reminded him, "and I'd like some time to think. I want what is best for . . ." he paused to regard Alanna with a rueful glance, "Christian."

Impatient to have the matter settled, Elliott wasn't at all pleased by Hunter's request. Fearing he would risk losing the Indian's cooperation if he argued, however, he tried to smile as he agreed. "Of course. I didn't mean to rush you. There's plenty of time for you to come to a decision before we leave tomorrow. Now what can we do to help you prepare supper?"

"I don't ask my guests to cook. Rest, go to the trading post if you like. I'll call you when supper is ready."

Neither Elliott nor Alanna had any desire to peruse the trading post's wares, so they sat outside the long house talking quietly until it was time to eat. Hunter produced not only venison roasted to perfection, but corncakes dripping with maple syrup. He had ale for Elliott and offered to buy wine for Alanna, but she assured him it was unnecessary.

Alanna had not expected such a delicious meal, and paid Hunter a sincere compliment. "You're a marvelous cook. I wish all of Polly's meals were this tasty."

Seneca men did not cook unless they lacked a woman to handle the chore, and Hunter took no pride in his culinary skill. He uttered a distracted word of thanks and offered his guests another corncake, which both accepted. He had not been particularly hungry at the start of the meal, but the novelty of having company soon increased his appetite. It wasn't until they had all finished eating and he had gathered up the pewter plates and utensils, that he began to regret inviting them to stay with him. He had asked for time to think, but how could he think clearly with them there?

Alanna was fascinated by the way the fire's golden light sculpted Hunter's features with constantly changing shadows. For much of the meal he had appeared to be preoccupied, but she would not fault him for being less than a charming host. All of them harbored bitter feelings, but she was grateful she had been able to convince her male companions to behave as gentlemen. She doubted many people would believe an Indian brave was even capable of such courtesy, and especially not one who had seduced a white woman, but Hunter had an intelligence and depth she could not help but admire. She then began to wonder if Christian wouldn't miss out on a valuable part of his heritage, if he never knew his father.

"Hunter," she called softly. "Christian is as much your son as he is Melissa's, and I hope you won't think that we're forgetting that fact or being unfair to you. Is there a Seneca maiden you might marry to provide a mother for him?"

Unable to understand how Alanna could ask him something so personal, Hunter simply stared at her for a long moment. She was lovely, but it hurt to look at her when she asked such foolish questions. He had to swallow hard before he could force himself to reply, but his words still rang with contempt. "I wanted Melissa for my wife, but she did not want me for a husband and denied I was the father of her child. If I ever take a wife, it will be because she pleases me, not because I need her to raise Melissa's son."

Not having meant to revive his hatred of Melissa, Alanna hastened to apologize. "I didn't mean to insult you."

"No? What did you expect? Did you think I would welcome your advice? You're little more than a child. What gives you the right to tell me who I should take as a wife?"

"I said I was sorry."

"It's too late," Hunter informed her coldly. Unable to remain with his guests another second, he rose and left the long house.

Alanna turned to Elliott. "Was what I said as rude as he made it sound?"

"No, you weren't rude at all, but he's not like us, and you can't expect logical replies from him. Come on, let's find the hides he mentioned hanging as a partition."

"Don't you think you ought to go after him?"

"No, that will only make things worse. He'll probably be back in awhile."

"Where do you suppose he sleeps?"

Elliott gestured toward the platform where Hunter had sat during supper. "Over there I think. I'll take the one opposite his. That way you'll have the whole back of the house to yourself."

Alanna chewed her lower lip nervously. "Hunter is Indian. Why should the suggestion he wed an Indian maiden insult him?"

"Haven't you better things to think about than him? My proposal, for instance?"

They were standing in the narrow passageway which ran down the center of the long house, and when Elliott reached out to catch her in a fond embrace, Alanna couldn't escape him. His touch was familiar, bearing the comfort of home, but none of the almost magical excitement she had felt in Hunter's arms. He kissed her then, a soft, sweet, gentle kiss that left her totally unmoved. Had Hunter kissed her that afternoon, she knew she would still feel it, and guilt rather than pleasure brought tears to her eyes.

"Please don't," she begged.

Instantly, Elliott dropped his arms to his sides. "I didn't realize that my affection would disgust you."

"I'm not disgusted, not in the least," Alanna argued. "It's just that, well, I wish you'd give me some time to adjust to the idea you'd like to court me. I'd never even considered the possibility before today."

When stated that way, Elliott readily understood her reticence. "I'm sorry, I shouldn't have spoken so sharply to you. Let's just concentrate on getting Hunter's name on a statement for the time being. We can talk about us on the trip home."

Alanna had said earlier that day that love wasn't all that important to her, but that had been before she had seen Hunter again. He was as wrong for her as he had been for Melissa, but she couldn't deny the way he made her feel. His touch made her long to reach out and caress him, and she had not forgotten the kiss he had given her last August. How could a Seneca brave be more appealing than her own cousin? How could the black-eyed devil fill her with the desire another man might never satisfy? Why would the gods torment her so cruelly?

"Alanna? Are you all right?"

"No, I don't suppose that I really am," she admitted. "It was about this time last year that we met Hunter. It's been a truly awful year, hasn't it?"

Elliott turned away to fetch her valise. "The worst. Here, you take this, I'll find a rope we can use to suspend some hides. This house is really cleverly made. Did you realize that?"

Alanna saw only how dark it was, rather than the ingenuity of it. "I wonder if it's warm enough in winter?"

Elliott bent down to inspect the hides stored beneath the platforms. "I'll bet it's as cozy as a cave," he offered as he searched among them. "Here, these deer skins look long enough to use. Now where would Hunter keep a rope?"

"I thought I saw one outside."

"You're right, so did I." Elliott stepped outside and returned with the neatly coiled rope. He hummed softly to himself, as he stretched it between two poles on opposite sides of the structure. He draped the hides he had chosen over it, and stood back to judge the quality of his handiwork.

"That's a pretty flimsy wall, but it's probably more privacy than you'd get at the trading post."

Alanna wondered if Hunter hadn't deliberately been trying to frighten them, but she did feel more secure there than she would have staying in a rowdy inn filled with drunken sailors and frontiersmen eager to pay a woman for her favors. She wondered if a man as appealing as Hunter ever had to pay for a woman's attentions, and decided that was not a question she cared to have answered.

The hides covering the rear of the long house were secured only at the top, permitting an easy exit, and after telling Elliott she was going to prepare for bed, she stepped outside. Surrounded by dense forest, she breathed deeply and attempted to clear her mind of the distractions conjured up by thoughts of Hunter. Despite Graham Tyler's attentions, she was still dreadfully inexperienced when it came to men, and told herself that was undoubtedly why dealing with a man with Hunter's confidence was so unsettling. At least she would only have to pretend an indifference she didn't feel until noon tomorrow, rather than the rest of her life, but managing such a feat for even those few hours wasn't going to be easy.

Seeing her leaning back against his house, Hunter stepped out of the shadows and approached her. Her eyes widened slightly when she saw him, but he raised his fingertip to his lips to warn her not to cry out. He waited until they were mere inches apart to speak.

"Elliott says you're his woman now. Is that true?"

"I, well, that is—"

"Can't any of you speak the truth?"

"Of course, I can!" Alanna whispered defiantly. "It's just that I'm not sure what it is in this case."

Hunter caressed her cheek with his fingertip. "How can you not know if you are his?"

Her hands at her sides, Alanna gripped the hides covering

the doorway in a frantic clutch, and wished her emotions were as easy to hold in check. "If I have no right to inquire as to your marriage plans, then you certainly can't expect me to confide in you about mine."

"Why not? They might be the same."

The sun had already sunk below the trees, but the twilight was still bright enough to reveal Hunter's smile with alarming clarity. His lips were parted slightly, and when he leaned close, she thought he meant to whisper something, but instead he kissed her. She gave only the smallest cry, and that was muffled by his second kiss, or perhaps it was the third. She lost count as he traced a meandering trail of kisses across the soft swell of her cheek, then lingered at her temple. Next he drew her earlobe into his mouth, and sucked it gently before sliding his tongue down the smooth curve of her neck.

By then, he was wrapped around her as securely as a vine, and she still wanted him to come closer. His mouth returned to hers, his taste honey-sweet, and she welcomed him eagerly. He was kissing her as passionately as he had the morning he had mistaken her for Melissa, but now neither of them was confused as to his purpose. His tongue caressed hers until she feared she might drown in desire, but all too soon he drew away.

"You are as hungry for love as Melissa. Would Elliott want to marry you, if he knew you were just as faithless?"

Stunned to be insulted after she had welcomed his affection so joyously, Alanna raised her hand to slap the smirk from his face, but Hunter caught her wrist and twisted her arm behind her back. He pulled the hides aside and gave her a gentle shove.

"Now that I have you so eager, sleep with Elliott."

Alanna jerked free. "You despicable bastard," she mouthed silently.

Hunter blew her a kiss. "I love you, too," he answered.

Alanna ripped the hides from his hand to shut him out of

the long house, but fearing he might return for more of the delicious affection she couldn't refuse, she spent the night tossing in fitful slumber, tormented by a shameful dream in which she was scorned as a harlot by all of Williamsburg. When in the morning Elliott placed his hand on her shoulder, she sat up so quickly they bumped heads, causing them both to recoil in pain.

"I'm sorry, I didn't mean to frighten you," Elliott whispered. "It's early. You needn't get up yet, but Hunter just left, and I'm going to follow him. He took his quiver and bow as well as a musket he had hidden under his bed. Maybe he's only going hunting, but I'm afraid he might plan on staying away for several days, so that he won't have to sign a statement for us. After coming all this way, I'm not leaving here without one."

Alanna swept her hair out of her eyes. "Why didn't you stop him?"

"I awakened just as he was leaving, or I would have."

Alanna reached out to grab his arm. "Wait, I want to go with you."

"There's no need of that. You'll be better off staying here."

"No, I won't. What if Hunter's going home? Do you know where his tribe lives?"

"No, but—"

"You can't ask me to stay here all alone, when you don't know where you're going or when you'll be coming back. If I wouldn't have been safe staying at the trading post, then I certainly won't be safe here. Just give me a minute, and I'll come with you."

Initially, Elliott hadn't seen any reason to take Alanna along on what could be an arduous hike through the woods, but now understanding how frightened she was of being left on her own in a strange place, he reluctantly had to relent. "All right, I'll wait for you, but hurry."

Her head aching from lack of sleep and worry, Alanna rose

and hurriedly gathered up the clothes she had worn the previous day. Thinking her petticoats would only impede her progress, she didn't bother with them, nor with a corset. Making do with only her chemise and drawers for underwear, she donned the gray gown and was dressed in just a few minutes. She brushed her hair, coiled it atop her head, and covered it with a cap. Once outside, she splashed water from the rain barrel on her face, wrapped a shawl around her shoulders, and was ready to go.

"I'm afraid you're going to ruin your dress."

"I have others. Which way did he go?"

"Luckily the ground's damp, and I found the tracks of his moccasins. Come on, he went this way." Elliott reached out to take Alanna's hand, but the trail soon narrowed, and they had to travel in single file. Fortunately, she had no difficulty keeping up with him. Hunter was traveling northwest on a well-worn path, but after the sun came out and dried the ground, they could no longer be sure he hadn't left it.

It was now too warm for Alanna to need a shawl, and she tied it around her waist when they stopped at a creek to take a drink of cool water. They were walking at such a brisk pace, they had traveled several miles. "If we miss today's barge, when is the next one?" she asked.

"Not until next week." Elliott raised his hand to shade his eyes, as he looked up to judge the position of the sun. "We still have time to make it. If we can find Hunter, that is."

"Why does he have to be so terribly uncooperative?"

Elliott was touched by Alanna's troubled frown. "I used to think I understood him, but now I doubt anyone ever will. Clearly he's running from us, but we can't let him get away with it." Startled by a rustling in the shrubbery bordering the stream, Elliott reached for Alanna's hand and pulled her close.

"What was that?" she asked.

Hoping to identify the source of the noise, Elliott strained to listen, but it didn't come again. "I don't know. Perhaps only a thirsty animal, but we've tarried too long. Let's keep following the trail."

Again Alanna stayed close behind her cousin, but she was haunted by the eerie sensation that they were being watched. Rather than the familiar calling of songbirds and tittering of playful squirrels, the forest now seemed alive with mysterious sounds. A red-tailed hawk soared overhead in narrowing circles. It would not swoop down on her with its wickedly sharp talons, but she felt as vulnerable as the defenseless rabbit that was probably being stalked.

The sound of snapping branches, as though someone were hurrying through a pile of dry twigs, prompted her to grab Elliott's coattail. "Hunter, is that you?" she called out.

"Did you hear something?"

The forest was thick here, with not only dense stands of pine, but also hemlock, spruce, and fragrant cedar. Alanna scanned the fence of trees lining the trail, but saw only the primeval world through which they had passed. "It sounded as though someone were running, but they stopped, when we did."

Elliott had a knife at his belt, but no other weapon, and now fearing they had strayed too far from the trading post, he wished for a musket. "I think we better go back," he whispered softly. "There's probably no one else on this trail, but just in case there is—"

This time the rhythmic sound of running feet padding against the earth was unmistakable, but it was coming from the trail up ahead, and Elliott pulled Alanna off the path. Hidden by the lush green undergrowth, he could see who was approaching without being seen. When seconds later Hunter sped into view, the Virginian relaxed. He stepped out to block the way, and Alanna went with him.

"Wait, if you're going back to the trading post, we'll go with you," he said.

Appalled to come across his two guests wandering the forest unarmed, Hunter came to an abrupt halt. "You shouldn't be way out here," he scolded crossly.

"We can say the same of you," Alanna shot right back at him. "You knew we weren't finished talking. Did you think we'd just give up and leave without seeing you again today?"

His expression growing increasingly hostile, Hunter glanced over her head and peered through the trees. "I would have been back long before noon. I've been looking for Blind Snake, the Indian who killed our wounded. Have you seen anyone?"

Although doubting the excuse for Hunter's early morning jaunt into the forest, Elliott nevertheless told the truth. "No, we thought we heard something a minute ago, but it came from the other direction."

As Elliott turned to point, Blind Snake stepped onto the trail, a musket raised to his shoulder. Hunter dived into the underbrush carrying Alanna along with him, but before Elliott could reach cover, the Abenaki fired, and he was struck in the chest. He staggered backwards and fell, just inches from where Hunter had been standing.

"Elliott!" Alanna screamed. She fought to break free of Hunter's grasp to go to her cousin, but he held her fast.

"No! Wait!" he ordered in a frantic whisper. "I'll get him." Hunter had his own musket slung over his shoulder; speedily loading it, he stood and fired into the trees where Blind Snake had been hiding. Before the smoke cleared, he bent down to grasp Elliott under the arms and pulled him off the trail. Unharmed, Blind Snake fired a second shot that tore through the leaves just inches above Alanna's head.

"Keep down!" Hunter shouted, but the words had no sooner left his mouth than a shot coming at them from another direction ripped through the fringe on his sleeve. "We'll have to find cover," he warned, and seeing that the forest fell away in a rocky slope not ten feet away, he pointed toward it. "I'll fire at them again, you run for the rocks and stay there, understand? Elliott and I will follow."

Elliott's eyes were open, and praying he might not be as badly injured as she feared, Alanna nodded. The instant Hunter fired, she flung herself toward the rocks, half-running, half-swimming through the air. Reaching the slope, she fell to her knees as she scrambled down behind it, ripping her skirt, but managing to reach safety otherwise unharmed. Hunter then fired again, and quickly dropped to take a firm hold on Elliott. Moving in a low crouch, he sprinted toward the slope with his injured friend in his arms. A musket ball ricocheted off the rocks, spraying them both with sharp fragments, but they also made it down the far side of the slope without suffering further injury.

From here, Hunter could defend them, at least temporarily, but now knowing Blind Snake wasn't alone, he wasn't confident of his chances to keep his enemies at bay for long. Their situation desperate, he fumbled with Elliott's stock in an attempt to loosen the young man's collar, and Alanna leaned over to unfasten it in the back. She then pulled it away, and unbuttoned Elliott's bloodsoaked shirt to reveal the musket ball that had entered his chest just above his heart.

Hunter pushed her aside. "I can't have you fainting again."

Alanna couldn't deny that she was affected by the sight of her dear cousin's blood, but she was determined to find the courage not to fail him. "No, I'll be all right," she swore, and moved to take Elliott's hand. She gave his fingers an encouraging squeeze, but his response was feeble. Hunter folded the discarded stock, and placed it over the gaping hole in the young man's chest. When Alanna's gaze met his, the Indian shook his head, but she refused to believe Elliott was mortally wounded.

"Hang on," she begged. "We'll get help to take you back to the trading post, where a doctor can treat your wound properly."

With blood rapidly filling his lungs, Elliott had great difficult drawing a breath. "I have always loved you," he whispered.

He had lost his hat when he had been hit, and Alanna smoothed back his hair, before leaning over to place a kiss on his forehead. "I love you, too," she vowed. "Stay with me, Elliott, please try and stay with me." But even as she spoke, she watched the light in his blue eyes grow dim and knew he was already gone. His hand was limp, but she brought it to her lips to kiss him goodbye.

Without giving her more than that one second to mourn, Hunter grabbed her arm. "I'm sorry, but if we stay here, we'll be killed, too. Let's go."

"Go? But we can't leave him!"

"He's dead!"

"But if we leave him, they'll—" Alanna could not bring herself to describe how Elliott's body would surely be mutilated.

Hunter could see her anguish, and doubted anything he said would have any meaning. To stall for time, he reloaded and fired just to keep Blind Snake on his guard. Faced with the choice of carrying her or carrying Elliott's body in the hope they would live to bury him, he made the only decision that would be acceptable to her.

"I can carry Elliott," he offered, "but that means you'll have to look out for yourself. Are you strong enough to do it?"

"I shall have to be."

"If the choice becomes one of leaving you, or Elliott's body, I'll leave him."

"Yes, I understand." She hurried to button Elliott's coat to not only cover his gruesome wound, but to make him easier to carry.

Endlessly resourceful, Hunter took three of his arrows from his quiver and wrapped the tips in dried grass he pulled from between the rocks. He then lit them with the flint he carried in the pouch at his belt. He had to scramble up on the rocks and risk being shot, as he sent them in the direction he believed Blind Snake was hiding, but again escaped being hit. He did not expect to start any real blaze in a forest lush with the new growth of spring, but all they needed was a few minutes' confusion on his enemies' part to provide them with a chance to flee.

Again sliding down the slope, he handed Alanna his musket and bow, took a firm hold on Elliott, and slung him over his shoulder. His friend's body was no heavier than that of the last stag he had carried home, but it was not a burden he wished to take far. He was positive he had been Blind Snake's real target, but this was no time to carry an additional burden of guilt, and he forced such sad thoughts from his mind.

"They'll try and block our way back to the trading post, so I'm going north rather than east. I won't get us lost, but you must stay right with me. If we're fired on again, get down and take cover. If I'm hit, don't look back. Go south until you reach the Mohawk, and follow the river back to the trading post."

Elliott's head and arms were dangling down Hunter's back, but Alanna was certain she could focus her gaze on the Indian's legs rather than her poor cousin's body. "I understand. One of us has to survive to see that the men responsible for killing Elliott are punished!"

"The man's name is Blind Snake. Did you get a good look at him?"

Alanna nodded. His was a face she would never forget. He had been laughing when he had fired the shot that killed Elliott.

Hunter didn't waste another second before starting off at the fastest speed he could make. Had Elliott not already been dead, he would soon have expired from his wound, for Hunter made no effort to carry him gently. They were only minutes ahead of men he knew would not only mutilate Elliott's corpse as Alanna feared, but do far worse things to them while they were still alive.

Eighteen

Moving at a slow, even jog, Hunter stayed well away from the trail and cut his own path through the forest. Trying her best to keep up with him, Alanna held her side when it began to ache, and did not even consider begging Hunter to stop so she could rest. She did not understand how the Indian could maintain his steady pace mile after mile, when Elliott's body had to be growing increasingly heavier. Either he was incredibly strong, or through some Indian trick he was able to ignore the weight of his burden. Whatever enabled him to maintain his constant, measured step, she admired him enormously for it.

Fearing Blind Snake might be following close behind, she sent a furtive glance over her shoulder every few minutes. Smoke had come billowing up from the fires Hunter's flaming arrows had sparked, and she prayed that mischief had bought them the necessary time to escape. No more shots had been fired at them, and while she wanted desperately to believe that was a good sign, she knew Blind Snake might only be waiting for them to slow down and present an easier target. He was Indian, too, after all, and unencumbered by the weight of a dead body, wouldn't *he* be able to follow them no matter how far they went, or cleverly they attempted to fool him?

When Hunter finally slowed to a stop on the banks of a small creek, Alanna clung to a spruce sapling and struggled to catch her breath. "Are we safe here?" she was finally able to ask.

She looked exhausted, but Hunter knew they had not even

begun to test their endurance. "No, but we're leaving a trail even a child could follow. We must walk in the water to hide our tracks. Take a drink, but only a small one. From here, we'll go a mile or so upstream, and then look for a place to bury Elliott. We can disguise the fresh grave with leaves and branches, so it won't be disturbed."

"My aunt and uncle will want Elliott's body brought home."

"Then it is a shame they are not here to carry him." That bitter retort had leapt from Hunter's lips without forethought and he instantly regretted his sarcasm. "Later, when we are safe, I'll come back on horseback, or with others who can help me carry him to the trading post. For now, we'll just have to bury him as best we can."

Hostile one minute, thoughtful the next, Alanna didn't know what to make of Hunter, but she was too tired to object to his plan, and when he stepped into the middle of the creek, she followed. The water was icy cold. She had worn riding boots for travel rather than kid slippers, and she was now grateful she had made such a practical choice. The moss-covered stones at the bottom of the stream were slippery and slowed their pace, but she still came dangerously close to falling several times before they left the water.

Hunter chose a spot where they could step out onto a rocky bank to avoid leaving footprints along the muddy shore, and she followed carefully picking her way to make the most of his efforts to hide their trail. He took them perhaps a hundred yards into the forest, before he lowered Elliott's body to the ground. Unable to look at her dead cousin, Alanna turned away quickly, and then felt horribly disloyal.

Hunter noted her shudder, but hid his own. He broke off a leafy branch from a sugar maple and pointed back the way they had come. "I'm going to use this like a broom to scatter the leaves and hide our tracks. Sit down and rest, while I'm gone."

"You promise to come back?"

Despite her obvious terror, Hunter did not understand how she could doubt him. "Had I wanted to abandon you, I would have done it when Elliott was killed. I'd not have carried his body all this way just to please you." Thinking her daft, he left shaking his head, and sprinted back over the ground they had just covered.

Hardly reassured, Alanna sat down and leaned back against the maple. Weary, she bent her knees to provide a resting place for her cheek. She missed Elliott terribly, and she did not know how she was going to return home without him. How would she ever find the words to tell her aunt and uncle that they had lost another child? She and Elliott had allowed his parents to believe they were following their wishes and coming to New York in an effort to persuade Hunter to raise his son, when that had not been their true purpose at all. Begun with a lie, their trip had ended in tragedy, and she could not help but feel that she was to blame.

When he returned, Hunter offered no words to bolster her courage before searching briefly for a suitable branch to use for a digging stick. He sharpened one end into a point, used it to loosen the soil, and then scooped out the dirt with his hands. It was hard work, but he wanted to create a hole of sufficient depth to discourage not only Blind Snake, but predators as well from disturbing the body.

"Is there something I can do to help?"

Hunter shot her a disapproving frown. "Just stay out of my way."

Feeling very small and helpless, Alanna huddled down into herself. She was lost in the forest with an obstreperous Indian she trusted only slightly more than Blind Snake, and she was horribly uncomfortable with him. She knew she ought to be thinking of what to say when they buried Elliott, but no matter how poetic a tribute she might devise, he had been so dear to her, the moment would be heartbreaking, and she would not be able to speak. Lost in her own misery, she waited for Hunter to tell her what to do.

Remaining alert to danger, Hunter paused periodically to listen to the soft rustling sound of the gentle breeze passing through the canopy of leaves overhead. The shrill cries of birds defending their nests created a constant din, accented by the noisy chatter of squirrels. Their arrival had briefly disrupted the natural harmony of the forest, but it had soon resumed at full volume. Hearing no other break in its rhythm, Hunter continued to dig until he had excavated the hole to a depth of nearly four feet. He then climbed out and shook the loose dirt from his buckskins.

He gathered fresh pine boughs to line the bottom, and then bent down beside Elliott's body. He removed the gold signet ring from his right hand and tossed it to Alanna. "You'll want to keep that. I want you to have his knife, too. You'll need it should we become separated."

Alanna tried on the ring and found it felt secure only on her index finger. When Hunter handed her Elliott's knife, she threaded the sheath through her belt, and prayed she would never have occasion to use it. She watched him remove the handkerchief from Elliott's pocket, but the young man had had nothing else with him. When the Indian sent her a questioning glance, she shrugged slightly. "The rest of his belongings are still at your house."

"I'll use his handkerchief to cover his face."

"Wait, use my shawl instead."

Hunter stopped her before she had untied it. "You'll need it tonight for warmth. The handkerchief will have to do."

Unable to watch him lower Elliott into the ground, Alanna got up and took several steps away. Her cousin had been a fine man, and he shouldn't have died so young. "You said you'd seen Blind Snake in the Ohio Valley," she called over her shoulder.

"Yes, he might have killed Elliott then."

"Had Elliott died last summer, he would have been called a hero."

"He is one still," Hunter argued.

Hunter laid his friend's body in the hole, crossed his hands over his chest, covered his face with the handkerchief, and added another layer of pine boughs, before he refilled the hole. He packed the earth down firmly, and scattered the excess dirt so it would not be noticed. Next he sprinkled fallen leaves on the ground in a random pattern to mimic nature. He had to search for several minutes, but found a fallen branch he added to his carefully landscaped scene.

"How does this look to you?" he asked.

Not really knowing what to expect, Alanna turned around slowly, but then her eyes widened in surprise. "It looks perfect. No one will guess the ground has been disturbed, but how will you ever find this place again to retrieve the body?"

"Do you become lost on your plantation?"

"No, of course not, it's my home."

"Well, the forest is mine. I won't have trouble finding my way here again. Do you want to say a prayer before we go?"

"No, Elliott was wonderful to me, and I'll remember him in my prayers for the rest of my life."

Hunter thought it odd that she had shed no tears for her cousin, but because every second they tarried brought Blind Snake closer, he gestured toward the adjacent trees. "We dare not leave any tracks here. Watch where I step, and do not fall behind."

Feeling completely drained, Alanna doubted she could still keep up, but she nodded. Hunter turned away, again traveling north at the same steady pace he had set earlier. After a while, she saw only a blur of honey-colored buckskin up ahead, but she continued to push herself and run long after her mind had sworn her body was spent. When at last Hunter drew to a halt and turned back toward her, she collapsed in his arms.

Hunter had meant only to make certain that Alanna was still with him, but clearly she could go no farther. He was nearing exhaustion himself, but carrying her cradled against his chest, he traveled another mile before stopping for the night. The place he chose was not only on high ground, but also densely wooded. It was bordered on one side by blackberry vines heavily laden with ripe fruit, and on the other by a fast-flowing stream. There was still time to hunt, but because he dared not light a fire to roast meat, he hoped Alanna liked blackberries.

He untied her shawl, spread it out on the ground, and laid her upon it. Thinking she might sleep for hours, he washed up in the stream in an effort to refresh himself, and began to pick berries. He had eaten his fill before Alanna sat up. She rubbed her eyes, but still didn't seem to recognize her surroundings.

Hunter carried a handful of berries over to her. "We'll stay here tonight, perhaps longer. Try and eat all you can."

Alanna needed no further encouragement. She popped a berry into her mouth, and then gobbled several more. "I haven't had anything to eat all day."

"I am a poor host it seems."

"Oh, no, it's not your fault." As she reached for the next berry, she noticed Elliott's ring on her finger and drew her hand back.

"What's wrong?"

"I fainted again, didn't I?"

"You were exhausted."

Truly, Alanna could not recall ever being so tired, but she doubted exertion was her only problem. "Our trip wasn't supposed to end this way."

"You could not have foreseen the danger."

"Perhaps not, but when you mentioned wanting to search for Blind Snake last night, neither Elliott nor I took you seriously. If only we had paid attention to you, rather than force you to listen to us, he might still be alive."

Hunter nodded toward the vines, then gathered more berries for her before he sat down beside her. "The past can't be changed, and you mustn't blame yourself for Elliott's death. It was the fault of Blind Snake and his friends."

"What friends? I thought he was alone."

"We both saw him shoot Elliott, but there were shots from another direction. He may have had only one companion, or half a dozen. They would have overtaken us long before now, if they could. I think they'll go back to the trading post to wait for us. If we stay in the forest for a week or two, they'll grow bored and move on."

Alanna immediately took exception to his plan. "We can't let Blind Snake get away with killing Elliott. If you think he'll be lurking around the trading post, then we have to go back there and have him arrested!"

Insulted that she would question his judgment, Hunter's eyes narrowed to menacing slits, and his expression filled with defiance. "I do not have to do anything. If you must go back to the trading post, you'll go alone."

"You can't mean that."

"Oh, but I do. You may stay with me as long as you do what I say. If you are going to do nothing but argue, then follow the directions I gave you. Travel south until you reach the Mohawk, then follow it east to the trading post."

Alanna had seen that same intractable expression before, and knew Hunter meant what he said, but she was already so badly frightened his threat scarcely mattered. "Do you expect me to willingly be your slave?"

It was just that type of insolence to which Hunter had objected, but Alanna was clearly too tired to leave their camp, let alone return to the trading post on her own. "I have no need of a slave," he scoffed, "but Blind Snake might. The

Abenaki treat their captives very badly. If you leave me, be careful he doesn't catch you."

Alanna had not thought to ask to what tribe Blind Snake belonged, but an Abenaki was the last Indian she would ever want to meet. Her hand started to shake, and she dropped the berry she had been holding. Hunter picked it up and handed it to her. It was another thoughtful gesture which didn't match his words.

"I can't eat anymore."

"You must. Without food, you won't be able to keep up with me."

As obnoxious as Hunter was, Alanna was positive he was a far better man than Blind Snake could ever hope to be. Still, remaining with him was a choice she was forced to make out of desperation. "No, I feel sick already. If I eat anymore, I'll be ill for sure."

Hunter scooped up the berries she had left, and set them aside. "I'll save these for morning."

That morning Elliott had been alive, but he would never see another sunrise, and Alanna was overcome with sorrow. He had known her so well, and had loved her in spite of her faults. She doubted she would ever find another man who would always be so wonderfully supportive. She did not even want to look. "The Abenaki have cost me a great deal," she murmured softly.

"The authorities will never find Blind Snake to punish him, but I will. Elliott's death will be avenged."

He sounded so confident, Alanna took his remark as a promise rather than a boast. "Have you killed men before?" she asked.

"Only in the Ohio Valley, and I took no joy in it. That was war, though, not a matter of revenge."

A flurry of wings as the birds nesting in the nearby trees took flight, caused them both to jump in alarm. Hunter rose and offered Alanna his hand, but he shook his head to warn her to be silent. She stood and then reached down for her shawl. Hunter took her hand and led her around the blackberry vines and into a cluster of maple trees. The low branches of one provided a natural ladder, and he gestured for her to climb up into the tree.

When she had been small, she had scamped up trees as easily as Byron and Elliott, while Melissa had never even been tempted to mimic her brothers' boisterous antics. It was the memory of those happy, sunlit days that gave her the strength to tuck the back hem of her skirt into the front of her belt to form a billowing pair of pantaloons. With her shawl again tied around her waist, she accepted Hunter's help to reach the first branch, and from there it was easy to move on up where the thick foliage provided the perfect hiding place. It wasn't until she looked down and found him backing away, that she realized just how precarious her perch truly was.

Hunter waved to her, and then circled around to the spot where they had been resting to hurriedly restore it to its natural state. In the gathering dusk, long shadows filled the forest, and he slipped soundlessly from one to the next. He heard Blind Snake's laughter before sighting him, but his respect for his adversary grew when he saw how easily he had tracked them. Apparently tiring of their sport, the Abenaki and two of his kind were making camp for the night at a spot Hunter had considered and then bypassed. Blind Snake and another brave each had muskets, while the third was armed only with a bow.

Knowing they had to be as tired as he, Hunter considered attacking them now, but in the twilight he might easily miss his first shot, and that would bring the three men down upon him. He would have eagerly taken that risk had he been alone, but Alanna's safety also had to be guarded. Biding his time, he waited and listened. He thought he knew enough of the Abenaki tongue to follow their conversation, but the men were chewing strips of smoked venison, which slurred their speech, and often teased each other with expressions he didn't recognize.

Only gradually did he become aware that they considered pursuing him and Alanna an amusing pastime. They talked about him and his female companion as though they were deer or some other game. They argued over how they would treat them once caught, but not wanting to hear their gruesome plans, Hunter returned to the tree where he had left Alanna. He dared not call out to her, and swiftly climbed up where he could whisper and be heard.

He took a firm hold on her arm to catch her should she faint, and told her what he'd found. "The Abenaki would never have gotten this close if I could have covered our trail. There are three of them, and they'll fall asleep soon. I'd slip into their camp and slit their throats, but I don't want to leave you to face them alone, should I fail. We'll have to go. We'll walk in the stream again, but I'll leave it to create a false trail. By morning, we'll be miles from here."

"Do you think they found the grave?" Alanna asked.

"No, or they would have mentioned it. Elliott's body is safe, but we aren't. Take care climbing down."

Having never climbed trees in the dark, Alanna had considerable difficulty following him back to the ground, but finally managed it without mishap. Her knees felt weak, and she doubted she could go very far. "Couldn't we hide right here? In the morning, if they go west, we can head back to the trading post."

"And if they catch us, we'll die! Let me decide what is best. Your ideas are foolish." He reached for her hand and, jerking her along, found the stream where he moved with his usual graceful stealth, while she tripped and slipped along behind him.

The blackberries she had eaten provided so little in the way of energy, Alanna was soon gasping for breath. Hunter's stamina was apparently inexhaustible, and he turned to scold her. "Hush, you're making too much noise."

Alanna thought she was doing remarkably well, and refused to allow him to intimidate her. "Must you run? It's so dark I can't see anything but your back, and not knowing where to step makes following you extremely difficult."

"Then see how you like traveling alone for a while." Hunter stepped off the trail and stood still a moment to let his moccasins sink into the mud. "Keep following the stream. I'm going to leave a false trail before catching up with you."

Alanna dreaded the thought of picking her way over the mossy stones alone, but now knew better than to ask him if he actually planned to meet her farther up the stream. Once she had caught her breath, she started off without comment. The day had been as terrible as the one on which Melissa had died, and it did not seem that it was ever going to end. She focused her attention on the moon's fragmented reflection in the water, and tried not to slip and fall while Hunter was still close enough to ridicule her for being clumsy, but she had several close calls before she was out of sight.

Hunter stomped around to make certain Blind Snake would find his footprints, and then walked off into the woods. He continued for half an hour before finding an outcropping of rocks which made a perfect place to disappear. Now moving with far more caution, he turned north, then back west to again find the stream. Once in the water, he traveled as swiftly as the current, and in a matter of minutes caught up with Alanna, who was bent over with her hands on her knees, trying to catch her breath.

"We'll soon reach the southern foothills of the Adirondack Mountains. They won't be able to track us through the rocks, and even if they could, we'll have the advantage of having a well-protected camp and can defend ourselves. Come on, we still have a long way to go before dawn."

"Dawn?" Alanna repeated weakly. "I can't take another step."

"Do you wish to become the Abenaki's whore?"

"Of course not!"

"Then you will walk!"

Before Alanna could protest that she could not, Hunter had taken her hand and, towing her along behind him, again made good progress through the stream.

Alanna awoke as the first faint rays of sunlight appeared in the east. Hunter had removed her boots and stockings and was rubbing her feet with insistent circles, but she was so numb, she couldn't decide if the pressure of his thumbs felt pleasant or painful. All she knew was that keeping her eyes open was impossibly difficult. She didn't recall his giving her permission to take a nap, but if he had, apparently the time was up. She didn't speak until he looked up at her.

"I really mean it this time," she vowed weakly. "I can't take another step."

Hunter slapped her calf playfully. "Yes, you can. You're a strong girl, Alanna. I like that."

She was merely confused by his compliment. "I don't feel strong."

"Well, you are, or you wouldn't have made it this far. Look around. We're in the foothills. We're near Lake Sacandaga, and I'll catch us some fish for breakfast."

The mere mention of food sickened Alanna. "I think what I really need is to sleep for a week or two. Then I might feel up to eating."

"Are all white women so lazy?"

"Lazy?" Alanna sat up and jerked her bare feet from his grasp. "You kept me running all night, and you dare to call me lazy?"

For some perverse reason, Hunter was enjoying teasing her. "Would you rather that I had taken you to Blind Snake's camp, and left you with him?"

"How do I know Blind Snake was even there?"

"You think I made up that tale just to keep you moving all night?"

Hunter looked horribly insulted, but Alanna was too tired to care. "I wouldn't put it past you."

Hunter picked up her stockings and boots and tossed them into her lap. "I have no reason to be mean to you. Unlike Melissa, you and Elliott were kind to me."

At the moment, all Alanna remembered was the way he had kissed her and then told her to sleep with Elliott. That was no way to repay kindness. Had that only been the day before yesterday? she wondered. Looking at Hunter again, she could see the strain in his face; she felt that same strain clear through.

"We ought not to fight amongst ourselves," she suggested. "I'm sorry for what I said."

Choosing to ignore her conciliatory gesture, Hunter's tone was harsh. "Put on your boots and hurry, or I won't wait for you."

Alanna managed to slip on her stockings without too much difficulty, but her feet were so badly swollen, she did not think she could wear her boots. She envied Hunter the comfort of his moccasins, and kept twisting and turning her foot in an attempt to wedge it into her boot. She was certain that if she could just figure out how to get one boot on, the other could be donned with ease.

Hunter stood silently watching Alanna's pitiful efforts to make her once small feet fit into a pair of impossibly tiny boots, and knew she was never going to be able to do it. He again knelt beside her and drew his knife. "Give me that boot," he ordered. When Alanna complied, he made several length-wise slits in the vamp to give her more room. "Try that."

Alanna stared at the shredded boot. "You've ruined it!" she exclaimed.

"If you can't get your sweet, little feet into them, then they are no good anyway. Now just try it on, and if it fits, I'll cut the other one to match it."

Much to Alanna's dismay, her swollen foot slipped right into the boot; and while it certainly wasn't attractive, it was wearable. She stood up and tried taking a step. Her feet ached all the way to her knees, but at least she would not have to walk barefoot over the rocky soil.

"I suppose how my boots look is the least of my problems. Thank you." She sat down again to wait, while he made the same cuts in her other boot, and then put it on. When he offered his hand, she got to her feet.

"How far is the lake?"

"Not far," Hunter promised. "After we've eaten our fill of fish, you can bathe and wash your clothes. That will make you feel better."

Alanna could easily imagine how dreadful she looked, and she doubted a quick bath in a lake would do all that much to enhance her appearance, when what she longed to do was soak in a hot tub for hours. He was trying to be nice to her, however, and she did her best to smile. "I'll look forward to it."

It took them more than two hours to reach the lake. Hunter made no demands upon Alanna whatsoever, while he used a hook and line to provide the breakfast he had promised. He then gathered wood and built a fire to roast his catch, and gave her the first bite. "I hope you don't mind eating off leaves rather than dishes."

"Why no, unlike plates, leaves don't have to be carried or washed, and I couldn't manage either chore now."

Hunter ate the next trout himself and another, while Alanna continued to consume the first one he had roasted. She ate with dainty, ladylike bites, while he was so hungry he gave no thought to eating like a gentleman. "You should eat more," he scolded.

"Do you like fat women?"

Hunter shook his head. "You know what I like: pretty blond women like you."

Unable to believe he was flirting with her, Alanna paused in mid-bite. Hunter was smiling slightly, but it was enough to convince her there was some truth behind his jest. "I never think of myself as pretty," she admitted shyly.

"You're even prettier than Melissa."

To be compared to Melissa was the last thing Alanna wanted to hear. She rose, brushed away the particles of fish clinging to her fingers, and looked out toward the lake. "Do you really think it's safe for us to stay here long enough for me to bathe?"

Hunter could see by the abrupt change in her manner that he had hurt her, but he didn't understand how. "Yes, go on. Bathe, wash your dress. I won't bother you."

"It's not you I'm worried about."

Hunter captured her glance and held it. He thought that in many ways he was more dangerous than Blind Snake, but if she did not understand why, he was not going to explain. "Good. Now go on, hurry. I don't want to camp here all day. We need to find a more secure place before nightfall."

It was not even noon, so Alanna knew they had plenty of time. She walked down to the lake's edge and sought a spot where the surrounding foliage would provide the privacy she desired. She hung her shawl and the belt with Elliott's knife still suspended from it on a branch, then peeled off her torn and soiled dress. She waded into the lake and did her best to scrub the garment clean, then came out and spread it out over the bushes to dry. Her once snowy white cap was dirty and tattered, and after she had washed and wrung it out, there wasn't much left to dry. Too shy to slip out of her chemise and drawers, she again entered the lake still wearing them.

The water was too cold to be enjoyable, and she had to force herself to bend down to wet her hair. She wished Hunter carried a bar of soap with him, but lacking that, she rubbed her long curls between her hands and hoped that the fresh water alone would rinse them clean. She had to wash her lingerie as best she could while still wearing it, but thinking any effort toward cleanliness would be an improvement, she hurriedly completed the task and came out of the water.

She would have to wait for the sun to dry her clothes, and shook herself to fling the remaining water out of her lingerie, before sitting down on a grassy spot several feet from the water. The natural beauty of the scene, and the sun's warmth lulled her into a dreamy mood, and she soon began to yawn. She got up to turn her dress over, so the sun would dry the other side, and then returned to the comfortable patch of grass. Telling herself she had time for a brief nap, she stretched out and closed her eyes.

When Alanna didn't reappear as soon as Hunter had expected, he rose and went to look for her. When he found her sleeping soundly, he swore under his breath and reached for her dress. It was still damp, however, and thinking she could use additional rest more than a dress that wasn't dry, he let her sleep and went for a swim. He left the water clean, but no less apprehensive about their situation. He wanted to move up into the hills where no one would ever find them; impatient to go, he dressed hurriedly. He then set about erasing all trace of their campfire, thinking that when he finished, he would wake Alanna and they would move on.

Rather than Hunter's deep voice, it was a rude shout that jarred Alanna awake. She sat up with a start, her heart pounding furiously in her breast. She heard several male voices then, but they were speaking a language she didn't recognize. Praying that Hunter was talking with trappers who had happened their way, she slowly got to her feet and peered through the shrubs, which had provided such a convenient screen.

When she saw Hunter was being confronted by Blind Snake and his two companions, she felt sick, but knowing this was no time to faint, she forced herself to take deep, even breaths. Hunter's back was to the water, but Blind Snake had his musket pointed at his chest to prevent him from diving into the lake. The other Abenaki braves were standing back, laughing as their leader taunted Hunter with insults she was certain were vile.

Apparently eager to draw blood, one of the braves took a step closer. Brandishing his knife, he made a suggestion which brought forth raucous laughter from his friends. He was now standing near the bushes that shielded her from view, and Alanna was presented with the most difficult choice of her life. She could slip away unnoticed and save herself, while Hunter would undoubtedly die as hideous a death as her family at the Abenakis' hands. Or, if she found reserves of strength she had not known she possessed, both she and Hunter had a chance to survive.

Her decision made in an instant, she reached for Elliott's knife.

Nineteen

Not wanting to give away Alanna's hiding place, Hunter avoided looking in her direction, but with all the yelling Blind Snake and the other two braves were doing, he felt certain she had to be awake. He hoped she had sense enough to wade back out into the lake to cover her trail. Blind Snake kept asking him where his woman was, but he stubbornly refused to acknowledge that he understood him.

He masked the steps he had taken toward his enemy with broad gestures of confusion, but from the moment the three Abenaki had sprung from the woods to surround him, his plan had been clear. He intended to kill them all, and now regretted he hadn't made an attempt to slit their throats while they slept. He smiled and shrugged, his attention apparently focused on Blind Snake's evil smirk, but taking in the actions of his two bloodthirsty companions as well.

The man closest to Alanna's hiding place was holding a musket, but when he let out a strangled shriek and spun away from the shrubbery spraying a haze of blood from the long, deep gash in his side, Hunter didn't waste an instant. His attention diverted momentarily, Blind Snake didn't see Hunter coming, and he not only wrenched the musket from the Abenaki's hands, but drove the stock into his nose with a stunning blow. Dazed, and in excruciating pain from his crushed nose, Blind Snake staggered crazily, and Hunter's next blow caught him in the side of the head, rendering him unconscious.

Hunter turned toward the only uninjured Indian, but the man was already running for him. Before Hunter could either fire Blind Snake's musket or swing it as a club, the Abenaki dove low and hard, stabbing Hunter in the left thigh. Flinging the weapon aside, Hunter drew his own knife and, ignoring the blood running down his leg, he went for his attacker with the same wild vengeance he had gone after Blind Snake. The Abenaki was skilled with a blade, but not nearly as proficient as Hunter, and he was soon bleeding from a half-dozen cuts on his shoulders and arms.

From the corner of his eye, Hunter saw a white flash, and knew it had to be Alanna. The Indian she had stabbed had fallen to his knees, crawled a few feet, and collapsed. Mortally wounded, he was clutching his torn side and moaning pathetically. Alanna made a grab for the fallen brave's musket, but Hunter didn't need help from a woman.

"Run!" he called out to her. "Get away!"

Hunter fought on, despite the agonizing pain in his leg that made it increasingly difficult for him to maintain his balance. Through pure force of will he was relentless in his attack, striking out with a furious determination that forced his opponent to constantly back away. Then, feigning weakness, he lured the man in close, and with a swift upward thrust, drove his knife deep into his chest. His heart pierced, when Hunter withdrew his blade, the Abenaki slumped to the ground dead.

Before Hunter could catch his breath, Alanna shouted a warning, and he turned to find Blind Snake not only on his feet, but again holding his musket trained on Hunter's chest. In the next instant, the sound of gunfire echoed all around, and he looked down, expecting the front of his shirt to be awash in gore, but it was stained only by a small splattering of his foe's blood. It was Alanna who had fired, not Blind

Snake, and her aim had been as good as any of the militiamen who had battled the French in the Ohio Valley.

Shuddering with revulsion and disgust, Alanna dropped the musket and came toward Hunter. "You're losing a lot of blood. Sit down, and I'll do what I can for your leg."

Hunter glanced toward the Indian she had stabbed. He had fallen silent, and the utter stillness of his pose proved he no longer clung to life. Hit from close range, Blind Snake would never draw another breath, nor would the man Hunter had fought hand to hand. They had turned an ambush into a stunning rout, but that Alanna could take credit for two of the three kills, robbed Hunter of any sense of satisfaction.

"I told you to run and hide," he scolded, as he sat down not because she had ordered him to, but because he could no longer stand. "I didn't need you."

Alanna had had ample opportunity to observe his pride, but she believed hurting it preferable to watching him get shot or cut into little pieces, or both. "Forgive me, but I need you too badly to watch you die."

Hunter sneered. "I wouldn't have died."

Alanna knelt beside him. "You may die yet. Here, let me help you out of those pants."

"No!"

He recoiled in horror, as though her suggestion had not been the most logical way to approach his wound. "This is no time for modesty, Hunter. I don't usually parade around in my lingerie, but I truly don't think we have any time to lose. The blood pooling on the ground is yours. How much can you have left?"

Hunter was pressing down firmly on the wound in his thigh, and he was confident he could stem the flow of blood soon. "I can take care of myself."

Even with his dark complexion, he was noticeably pale, and Alanna knew that despite his stubborn courage, he was wrong.

"I might as well dig four graves," she predicted darkly. "You already know the sight of blood sickens me, and I'll not watch you bleed to death."

"I won't."

Alanna started to rise, but Hunter reached out to stop her. His hand brushed her arm lightly, and then went limp as he fell unconscious. "Hunter?" she called, hoping he was merely feeling faint, but there was no response. Now that Hunter was unable to object to her help, Alanna loosened his belt and discovered that rather than a single garment, his fringed pants consisted of a breechclout and leggings. She hurriedly removed his moccasins, peeled away the leggings, and refastened his belt to secure the breechclout. Perhaps he had worried she would think his garb strange, but she was relieved he wouldn't be half-naked while she tended him.

In order to see the stab wound more clearly, she carried several handfuls of water to wash the accumulated blood from his thigh. Then, after rinsing off Elliott's knife, she cut a strip of cloth beginning at the ruffled hem of her chemise and winding up a foot to have a sufficient length to bind his leg. She struggled to wrap the cloth tightly enough to stop the flow of blood, but not so securely as to numb his entire leg. She prayed the whole time she worked, and fought the nausea and faintness that threatened to render her unconscious as well.

When she finished, she went to the lake and repeatedly splashed her face, until the water's refreshing coolness had restored whatever calm she had had before they fought the Abenaki. She rinsed the blood from Hunter's leggings, and spread them over the bushes to dry. Then she sat down beside him and took his hand. Only a little blood had seeped through his bandage, and, cheered by that fact, she patted his hand and repeated every encouraging phrase she could remember.

Knowing Hunter had to be even more exhausted than she,

when she was convinced he was resting comfortably and in no imminent danger of bleeding to death, she did not try and wake him. Instead, she forced herself to look at the men they had killed. She lacked the strength to dig graves, but the ground had a gentle slope toward a rocky ledge and, after careful consideration, she chose to drag the corpses into the shadow of the ledge, where she could bury them beneath a heap of stones.

The man she had stabbed was lying closest to the ledge, but it took nearly as much courage to grasp his wrists as it had to plunge Elliott's knife into his side. As she toiled to pull him across the rocky soil, she looked back over her shoulder at the ledge. This fellow was the tallest and heaviest of the three, and her arms and shoulders ached with the strain of moving him. She angled his body as she neared the ledge, and then pushed it into place with her foot. She straightened up and tried to breathe deeply, but she couldn't bear to look at the dead man's face, for fear his memory would turn her dreams to nightmares for years to come.

Next came the man Hunter had stabbed. Again she took a firm hold on his wrists and averted her eyes, as she pulled him up beside his slain friend. Like the first Abenaki, he left a gruesome trail of blood, but she stepped over it as she went back for Blind Snake. When she found her revulsion made it impossible to take his hands, she grabbed his ankles and dragged him feetfirst to his last resting place.

Following Hunter's example, she gathered pine boughs to cover the bodies, and then, using another bough as a broom, swept a layer of the sandy soil over that. Next came the largest rocks she could carry; with the ledge forming the back and partial roof of their tomb, she had built a solid front that completely hid the dead men. It wasn't until she looked back toward Hunter that she noticed she had left some of the Abenakis' things scattered about. She wanted to keep the two extra muskets, and the bow and quiver full of arrows, too. She had also overlooked a decorated bag containing venison jerky, and carried it over to Hunter's side.

Her only remaining task was to erase the bloody trails which led to the mass grave, and the pine branch broom took care of those. Had it not been for the bandage on Hunter's thigh, there would have been no trace of the fight which had nearly cost them their lives. Thoroughly sickened by the work of burying their enemies, Alanna again waded out into the lake and scrubbed herself, her drawers, and her now tattered chemise. Her dress was dry, but she didn't feel like putting it on over wet lingerie. She laid her shawl on the ground next to Hunter, stretched out beside him, and was asleep before she had drawn a breath.

Hunter was pleasantly surprised merely to awaken, but to find Alanna cuddled against him was almost a delicious enough sensation to block out the pain in his leg. He sat up slightly, and while chagrined to discover his leggings and moccasins were gone, he was far more upset to find she had bound his wound with a lace-edged piece of cloth. He would have shaken her awake to complain, had he not begun to feel faint. Lying back down before he passed out again, he closed his eyes and told himself to be more patient.

He had led an active life, but until that week his injuries had been few. He reached up to trace the still healing cut through his brow, and hoped his looks hadn't been marred too badly. He also hoped the wound in his leg would heal without leaving him with a limp. He had always been strong, and expected his injuries to not only heal rapidly, but also, in the case of his leg, leave no trace of what he had suffered.

He tried to relax and get above the pain that made his whole leg ache, but such a blissful release wasn't easily achieved.

The ground beneath him was not only hard, but rocky and uneven, making it difficult to find a comfortable position. He tried wiggling around a bit, but that sent fierce jolts of pain through his leg, reducing the stones gouging his back to a minor inconvenience.

Seeking to distract himself, he began to stroke Alanna's hair lightly. Falling free, Melissa's hair had formed soft waves, but Alanna's was far more tightly curled. After a brief moment, Hunter decided he liked the golden ringlets that bounced clear to her waist. They were as innocent and dear as she was, and he crimped them through his fingers with increasing delight. When at last Alanna awoke and sat up, he dropped his hand quickly, so she would not be angry with him for fondling her.

"I'm sorry, I just meant to rest a minute, not fall asleep."

Hunter studied her worried frown with deliberate detachment. "I'll forgive you for neglecting me," he began, "if you'll tell me how a girl who was so terrified of Indians last year that she ran from me, found the courage to rush into a fight with three Abenaki braves today."

Alanna could recall the girl who had panicked at the sight of him, but only dimly, as though it were an incident she had read in a novel, rather than something out of her own past. "A great deal has happened this last year, and I'm no longer that terrified girl."

Pleased with the change, Hunter wished with all his heart that he possessed the strength to pull her into his arms and kiss her, but sadly, he did not. Frustrated by his weakness, he took his anger out on her, and gestured toward the bandage on his thigh. "I don't recall giving you permission to steal my leggings and dress me in lace."

"Are you always so ungrateful?"

"Why should I be grateful?"

"Sometimes I don't even know why I bother to talk to you.

You can be nice one moment, and so nasty the next, I'm sorry we're even acquainted. I had to sacrifice part of my lingerie, because I didn't have anything else to use as a bandage. Next time you're stabbed, try and have something suitable with you, so you won't insult the person who saves your life with ridiculous complaints!"

Infuriated with him, Alanna got up and walked off into the shady enclosure where she had left her dress. When she didn't return within a few minutes, Hunter began to worry. He called her name, but there was no response. She hadn't left him when their lives were threatened, so he doubted she would leave him now, but he did not enjoy being ignored. He propped himself up on one elbow and, expecting to see the clearing littered with bodies, he was amazed to find the natural setting unspoiled by any such grisly scenes.

"Alanna!" he shouted this time. "Where are the bodies?"

Alanna finished buttoning up her bodice, but didn't bother with her stockings and boots before she reappeared. She walked up to Hunter and, still feeling tired, sat down a few feet away. Because they had only each other for company, and she wanted to get along, she considered his change of subject an apology, and let their argument drop.

"I took care of them." When he looked astonished by that feat, she explained exactly how she had gone about it.

He was relieved the bodies were gone, and didn't comment on the way she had disposed of them, but he was nevertheless amazed that she had been calm enough to be so resourceful. He had not expected such bravery from her. "I still don't understand how you found the courage to risk death by joining my fight, rather than saving yourself. Even after the Abenaki had seen you, you could have gotten away."

Perplexed that he didn't understand her motives, Alanna tried not to insult him with her reply. "I know you and I aren't really friends, but how can you even imagine that I'd abandon you?"

Not as concerned with protecting her feelings as she was with his, Hunter responded with a rueful laugh. "Experience has taught me not to trust white women."

The Sacandaga presented a far more appealing sight than her obstinate companion's sly smirk, and Alanna glanced toward the lake, as she replied, "I didn't confuse you with Blind Snake. Why are you blaming me for Melissa's faults?"

Conceding her point, Hunter nodded. "You are nothing like your cousin, are you?"

"She's dead. Whatever quarrel you had with her is over."

Just talking had again made Hunter feel ill, or perhaps it was the distasteful subject. He closed his eyes and sighed softly.

"Hunter?"

"I'm tired."

"Rest then."

Her voice held the sweet serenity of a benediction encouraging a lengthy nap, and when Hunter next awakened, it was late afternoon. He felt stiff and tried to flex his muscles, only to be rewarded with a fresh burst of pain from his leg. Thirsty, he looked longingly toward the lake, and then called Alanna's name, but produced only a disappointing croak. Fortunately, she had been fishing only a few yards away, and came to his side.

"How do you feel?" she asked.

Hunter could not think of the precise words in English to adequately describe how wretched he felt, but that didn't stop him from trying to communicate his distress. "My leg feels like it's on fire. My whole body hurts from sleeping on this pile of rocks, and I'm thirsty."

Thinking his last complaint the easiest to remedy, Alanna brought him water in her cupped hands. He placed his hands

beneath hers as he drank, and eagerly gulped down every drop.
She made several trips to the river before he kept hold of her
hand to keep her with him.

"Enough?"

Rather than reply in words, Hunter placed a gentle kiss on
her palm. Thinking his gesture prompted by gratitude, Alanna
pulled away. "A simple thank you will do."

"I wasn't thanking you."

Too embarrassed to inquire just what had caused his affectionate display, Alanna moved back a bit, sat down, and folded
her hands in her lap. "I'm sorry to have left you lying on the
bare ground, but I didn't want to risk reopening your wound."

Refreshed, Hunter tried to sit up, but had to again settle for
propping himself on his elbow. He had so little energy he felt
as though he had been running for days and, after stopping
for rest, could not go on. "Can you gather some pine branches
to make us a bed?"

Alanna was more than willing to provide branches to form
a cushion between him and the ground, but to share such a
bed was completely out of the question. He was in no condition
to force either his cynical opinions or his handsome self on
her, so she let any further discussion of their sleeping arrangements slide for the moment, and went to fetch the pine boughs.
She had to make several trips, but in less than half an hour,
she had a fair-sized heap of tender young branches stacked
beside Hunter.

The problem then became one of finding a way to shift him
over onto them. Just talking exhausted Hunter, and she did not
want moving him to prove to be another test of her strength
and his ability to withstand pain. There didn't seem to be any
way to accomplish the task without hurting him, until she had
a sudden inspiration. "Can you roll over toward your left side
long enough for me to shove the boughs into place?"

"I can try."

He did try, and seeing how much the effort cost him, Alanna quickly slid the boughs into place, taking care to position the needles so they extended toward the ground rather than upward like a live pincushion. "Good, now can you roll back this way, while I prepare the other side?"

Hunter couldn't stand to move his injured leg, so he was much less successful this time, but Alanna hurriedly placed the pine branches beneath him. When she stood back to assess their progress, she was almost pleased. She had managed to create a thick rectangular mattress of branches, and Hunter was stretched across it diagonally. They had failed to provide enough support for his injured leg, and she thought it ought to be propped up slightly, rather than lower than the rest of his body.

"Will it hurt you too badly, if I shift your leg up onto the branches?"

Already resting far more comfortably, Hunter tried to smile. "Just do it."

Cradling his knee in one hand and ankle in the other, Alanna lifted his leg and slid it onto the pine-scented bed. Hunter didn't cry out, but she felt a wave of pain roll through him.

"I'm sorry. I wish there were more that I could do. I don't think I can find my way back to the trading post for help. Is there another settlement near here?"

Hunter managed to shake his head, but, swimming in dizziness, he passed out again. Alanna reached out to smooth his hair off his forehead, unconsciously petting him as though he were a sleeping child. She had only just begun to fish when he had awakened, and, committed to providing something for him to eat when he felt up to it, she returned to the water's edge, where she had left his line. As a child, she had fished off the dock with her cousins, and thoughts of them brought a painful tightness in her chest she had no time to assuage with tears. If she and Hunter were to survive, it was up to her.

She baited her hook with a worm and tossed it out into Lake Sacandaga with a determination born of desperation.

It was the savory aroma of Alanna's roasting catch that coaxed Hunter awake. He knew she must be rightly proud that she had not only caught half a dozen trout and built a fire to cook them, but her achievements made him feel like a helpless fool. He tried not to sulk, or at least to hide that he was.

"You're not only strong, but smart," he greeted her.

"I was hoping you'd be awake soon. I've carved a wooden cup. It isn't pretty, but it does hold water." She carried it down to the lake and returned with a drink for him.

Hunter was somewhat cheered by the crude nature of her handiwork, but he was too thirsty to tease her about it. "Thank you," he remembered to say this time.

"Do you want more?"

"Maybe later."

Alanna didn't know how to phrase her next question delicately, but tried her best not to embarrass him. "If only we had a chamber pot, you could use it. Since we don't, can I help you in some way?"

Rather than being appalled by the sensitive nature of her inquiry, Hunter was merely amused. He laughed, and then, seeing how stricken she looked, tried to behave more like a gentleman. "Find me a sturdy stick to use as a cane, and I can get up to take care of myself. Not that your offer isn't appealing, it is, but I don't feel up to returning any favors as yet."

Alanna had not been offering as intimate a service as Hunter clearly thought she had, and her face filled with a bright blush as she turned back toward the fire. He was as adept at flirting as Melissa had been, but coming from a man, she saw his teasing as a blatant request for more than she wished to give.

Recalling the kiss he had placed in her palm, she rubbed her hand lightly to rid herself of any lingering trace of his touch.

She had watched him construct a sturdy wooden rack to roast their breakfast over coals, and had done her best to create a similar structure out of good-sized sticks. Like the cup, it wasn't much to look at, but while it had grown charred, it hadn't caught fire before the fish were done, and she thought that was all that mattered. Again a handful of broad leaves served as a plate.

"I hope this is done. If it isn't, just say so."

Hunter looked at the crispy tail and fins of the roasted trout and thought it was probably overcooked rather than underdone, but he dared not criticize her cooking, when he wasn't strong enough to handle that chore himself. "This is fine," he assured her without taking a bite. "I was tired of my own cooking."

He used his knife to fillet the fish and, while the meat wasn't as tender and flaky as he had served that morning, it was still good. "I think I am lucky to be stranded here with you."

Alanna waited for him to add another thought, but he remained silent as he ate the rest of his dinner. They each had three trout, and Alanna feared she had eaten too much, while he hadn't had nearly enough. "I'm sorry, I should have given you another trout."

"Why? You're the one who's done most of the work today. It seems you've become my slave after all."

"I certainly don't feel enslaved," Alanna argued.

"Good, then you'll have no trouble being obedient."

"That isn't funny, Hunter. Our situation could scarcely be worse. What if Blind Snake and those men weren't the only Abenaki traveling this way? What if we wake to find three more, or six more, or God knows how many others storming through our camp tomorrow morning?"

"I think you better stay up tonight to make us a canoe, so we can escape them on the lake."

In no mood to appreciate teasing, Alanna lost all patience with him. "Elliott's dead, and you can't find anything better to do than make jokes?" She got to her feet and, although the light was now fading, she sent a searching glance around the camp. "I'll go find you a stick to use for a cane, but I'm warning you now, if you keep laughing at me, I may use it to beat some manners into you."

Her curls bounced across her shoulders as she stomped off, and Hunter could not hold in his laughter. She was right. Things were bad for them, but he liked her so much, he wasn't truly worried. It wasn't until she returned and handed him a sturdy branch, that he realized he was going to have to follow through on his promise and force himself to stand.

He had eaten dinner leaning on his elbow, but now sat up slowly and braced himself on his hands. He was used to being agile, and finding himself pinned down by the knife wound in his thigh was not only physically painful, but emotionally draining as well. He had thought he could stand up long enough to relieve himself, but just getting upright posed a serious problem.

Because Hunter had ridiculed her last offer of help, Alanna stood silently waiting for him to politely request her assistance, should he need it. Thinking he probably outweighed her by at least fifty pounds, she hoped she wouldn't be too weak to make a difference. She wondered if he was getting cold without his leggings, but waited to ask that question.

Hunter felt Alanna hovering over him, and knowing she did not deserve to be the target of his ill humor, he swallowed the harsh demand that she leave him be. It wasn't until he finally had to accept the fact he could not get up on his own, that he looked up at her. "I need help," he admitted grudgingly.

Not one to gloat, Alanna moved to his right side. "If I put my arms around your waist, you can lean on me to stand, and then use the cane. Shall we try it?"

Hunter nodded. Realizing clearly that it was going to hurt, he still cried out in pain, and Alanna quickly let him sink to the ground. "I can do it," he insisted.

"Of course, you can." Alanna waited until he had caught his breath. This time he managed to find the leverage with his right leg to push himself up. Afraid he might pass out again, Alanna kept her arms locked around his torso, until he seemed firmly balanced on one leg and the makeshift cane. Then she released him and took a step back.

"Can you make it?" she asked.

Hunter's head felt impossibly light, at the same time his body felt at least double its usual weight. When he swayed slightly, and came dangerously close to falling, Alanna again encircled his waist with her arms. "I'll help you walk over to the bushes. Is that where you want to go?"

To be dependent on a slender girl for a walk of no more than ten paces left Hunter feeling totally humiliated. He knew he would probably fall without her help, but he was loath to ask for it. It was only the very real possibility of bleeding to death should he hit the ground on his injured leg rather than his seat, that prompted him to nod.

"I grew up with Byron and Elliott," she reminded him. "They liked to swim in the nude, so how men are made is no mystery to me. I know you're embarrassed to have to ask for my help, but you needn't fear that I am."

Hunter was concentrating so hard on just reaching the bushes, he couldn't respond to her encouragement. He had a firm grip on her with his right hand, and an even tighter hold on the cane with his left, but the combined weakness of his limbs and dizziness of his mind made what should have been an easy few steps, close to impossible. Alanna kept guiding him gently, however, and once they had reached the shrubbery, made certain he was steady enough to take care of himself, before she stepped away and turned her back.

Hunter remained upright long enough to relieve himself, but then when he tried to reach out for Alanna again, he pitched forward into the bushes, and would have slid all the way through them to the ground, had she not been quick enough to yank him out of them before that tragedy occurred. His buckskin shirt had saved him from suffering any deep scratches, but his dignity was definitely tattered. He resorted to his native tongue to express his displeasure, but Alanna could easily tell he was swearing by his tone.

"Come on," she coaxed sweetly, "let's get you back to bed." She eased him around, and he hobbled back to the pine mattress without further mishap. Getting him back into a reclining position was almost as great an ordeal as helping him to stand, but she finally succeeded in returning him to bed. "We'll do better next time," she assured him.

"There won't be a next time," Hunter grumbled. "I'll be much better in the morning, and I'll take care of myself."

"Good. Would you like another cup of water? I wish I'd thought to look for berries, so we'd have some dessert. I'll find some tomorrow."

Missing dessert was a matter of absolutely no consequence to Hunter, and he motioned for her to lie down beside him. "You come to bed, too," he ordered in a lazy slur.

Alanna hadn't planned to sleep with him, but she had had no time to gather additional branches to make her own bed. With Hunter so weak, she easily convinced herself she ought to sleep next to him, just in case he awoke and needed her. "Are you cold? Do you want your leggings?" she asked.

The prospect of having to wiggle into them, when it would surely be a painful ordeal, convinced Hunter they were the last thing he needed. "No, come to bed."

Alanna spread out her shawl to soften the crude mattress. "I had thought yesterday was bad," she related absently. "I'm almost afraid to hope that our situation will improve tomorrow."

Hunter was too weak to reply, but when she stretched out beside him, he reached for her hand and gave it a fond squeeze. "You should have stayed at home," he mused darkly, but if she bothered to argue with him, he didn't hear it before he fell asleep.

Twenty

Alanna awakened each time Hunter stirred during the night, but he appeared to be only shifting position slightly, rather than in distress, and she quickly fell asleep again. She didn't realize he was in trouble until dawn, when he complained of feeling too warm and asked her to help him remove his shirt. The instant her fingertips brushed his skin, she drew back.

"It's no wonder you feel warm." She raised her hand to his forehead to confirm her suspicions. "You're feverish."

Hunter had fallen asleep believing he could not feel any worse, but he had been wrong. "I'll get over it," he boasted without conviction.

The Barclays had seldom been ill, and in those rare instances, they had relied on Doctor Earle or bought herbal remedies at an apothecary shop in Williamsburg, so Alanna had never gathered medicinal plants in the wild. Even if she had, she doubted the forests of New York would contain the same varieties that grew in Virginia. "Do you know which herbs to gather for a fever?" she asked.

"Among my people, medicine is women's work."

"Then it's unfortunate we don't have one of your women here with us." Alanna was deliberately parodying one of his complaints, but either he didn't notice, or didn't care. She reached for the fringed hem of his shirt, and helped him peel the garment off over his head. "Even if we can't brew any herbal teas, you should try and drink all the water you can. I'll get you some now."

Hunter watched her carry the cup she had fashioned down to the lake. She was still barefooted, and it suited her. She had to bring him three cups of water, before he had his fill. "You need to make a bigger cup," he teased weakly, "then you won't have to make so many trips."

"Rather than a larger cup, what I need is a bucket. I'll have to look for a piece of wood the right size to hollow out. Until then, we'll just have to make do with this one pitifully small cup."

"Light another fire. Use the coals to burn out the center of a block of wood. Then there will be less to carve."

"Do your women make wooden buckets?"

"No, but if you wait for me to do it, we'll no longer need it."

Alanna hoped he was referring to his recovery precluding the necessity of a bucket, rather than anything more dire. "Do you think you could eat some fish?"

The mere mention of food made Hunter's stomach lurch, and he shook his head. "I just want to sleep."

Anxious to relieve his pain, Alanna remained kneeling at his side. Believing the knife wound in his leg must have become infected, she blamed herself for not knowing how to take better care of him. He was strong and had been in obvious good health, before he had been hurt. If the infection did not worsen, then he had an excellent chance to survive, but, God forbid, if he developed blood poisoning, not even a highly skilled physician could save him.

"I'm going to get busy on the bucket," she announced. "Then I can bring plenty of water from the lake to keep you cool. I'll just rip more cloth from the bottom of my chemise to make compresses."

Hunter opened one eye. "No more lace."

Alanna rose and brushed the dust from her skirt. "If that's all you have to complain about, you're fortunate indeed."

Hunter reached out to catch her hem in a feeble grasp. "Thank you," he mumbled.

"For such an obstinate man, you have endearing ways." Alanna waited a moment, but when Hunter remained silent, she went to scour the surrounding woods for a log small enough to be made into a bucket. She found some raspberry vines first, and picked so many succulent berries, she had to carry them back to the clearing in her skirt. She hoped Hunter would feel up to eating some later, but for now, she left them piled within his reach and went back into the woods.

By the time she had found a suitable piece of wood and fashioned a bucket using Hunter's helpful tip, his temperature had risen. She used the crude wooden pail to carry water to continually remoisten the compresses she placed on his forehead, chest, and legs, but she feared she had not begun using them soon enough to be effective. She encouraged him to eat berries whenever he awoke, and he swallowed a few, but she knew it wasn't nearly enough nourishment to sustain a man of his size.

"Could you eat some of Blind Snake's jerky?" Having had no time to fish, she had sampled it herself and found its smokey flavor good. "I could cut it into tiny bites for you."

"No, I would still have to chew and then swallow."

His expression was blank, and his eyes were glazed by the fever, but Alanna nevertheless got the distinct impression that he was teasing her. She replaced the compress on his forehead and then let her fingertips graze his cheek. "You are going to get well, Hunter. You're much too stubborn not to."

Hunter was far more worried about her than he was about himself. She had used his line to fish, and had sparked a fire with the flint he carried. She still had boots, if she chose to wear them, and a woolen shawl to keep warm. She was a clever girl and would survive without him.

"If you must leave here alone—" he began.

Alanna protested instantly. "I'll not leave you."

Hunter stared at her, unable to comprehend how she had misunderstood his meaning. "If I die," he explained slowly, "go south. Follow the Mohawk to the trading post."

Alanna wanted to argue that his instructions were unnecessary, but she knew it would only tire him, and simply nodded. "I seem to bring bad luck everywhere I go," she said instead. "My family's gone, and two of my cousins. Don't you leave me, too, Indian."

Hunter reached out for her hand. While he could not be blamed for the slaughter of her family, he knew Melissa's and Elliott's deaths could more easily be blamed on his influence than hers. "I am the one who spreads death," he argued, "not you. Be careful."

"Of what? You?"

Lacking the energy for a lengthy debate, Hunter closed his eyes for a moment to gather his thoughts. When he again looked up at her, he knew precisely what to say. "Blind Snake was trying to kill me, not Elliott, and I was the one he came to kill yesterday. If death comes for me again, do not stand in the way."

Alanna surveyed the open clearing with an anxious glance. Had Blind Snake opened fire on them from the adjacent woods, they would not have had a chance. "Do you have more enemies who might be stalking us?"

"Only death," Hunter revealed.

"You don't mean a person, just the possibility?" When Hunter nodded, Alanna again removed the compress from his forehead, dipped it into the pail, squeezed it out, and laid it over his brow. "I have much better things to do than bury you," she scoffed. "There's your son to raise for one. We've not had any time to talk about him."

"Christian?"

"That's right." Alanna replaced the compress on his chest, before she continued, "He's a splendid little boy, Hunter. He looks so much like you. I know you'd be proud of him."

Hunter tried to picture the infant in his mind, but all he saw was the fierceness of Melissa's expression, when she had threatened an accusation of rape should he ever reveal they had been lovers. He didn't want that spiteful bitch's child. Surely Christian would scorn him as readily as his mother had. "I have no son," he denied.

Discouraged by the blackness of his mood, Alanna went down to the lake to refill the pail, and tarried at the water's edge. Even with the awful spectre of death on his mind, Hunter's heart was closed to Christian, and she saw that as a terrible tragedy, even if he didn't. Bitterly discouraged that her trip to New York continued to have tragic consequences, she reluctantly returned to her patient's side. He was sleeping again, and she liked him ever so much better that way.

She replaced the cool compresses on his chest and legs, before sitting back to study his color. She thought he looked less flushed, but feared it might only be wishful thinking rather than fact. She rested her hand lightly on his right knee, and decided there was no difference in his temperature. He was still much too warm. Perplexed by her inability to help him, she realized that lying directly in the sun couldn't be doing him any good. Inspired to remedy that sorry situation, she cut two long slender branches to serve as poles, then dampened her shawl, and strung it between them to form an awning.

Armed with a leafy branch from a sugar maple, she sat fanning him with lazy strokes, attempting to keep him cooled by the breeze wafting over the wet awning. Her arm soon ached with the effort, but unable to devise another way to lower his temperature, she changed hands often and tried only to think of how much she wanted him to live. He was such a handsome man, that sitting with him wasn't in the least bit disagreeable, but she wished his conversation had been more optimistic when he had last been awake. She chewed another strip of venison jerky, and vowed not to let him speak again of death. She had had far too much of the pain of loss, and craved the joy of love and life instead.

Throughout the rest of that day and well into the next, Hunter's dreams were filled with tortured images that kept him moaning softly. He was running through a dark, overgrown forest infested with evil demons. The hideous creatures leapt out at him, taunting him with vile insults uttered in strident cackles and hoarse shrieks. Their fangs dripped venom, and his buckskins were ripped to shreds by their long, pointed claws. Each time he escaped their grasp, but he had lost his knife and bow, and without a way to fight them, sought only to hide, but they were everywhere. He had to keep on running harder and harder, until he feared his heart would burst from the strain.

Looking back over his shoulder, he missed seeing the cliff until it was too late to catch himself, and he plummeted over the edge. He flung out his arms, hoping to soar like an eagle but he succeeded only in spinning head over heels, until his fall was finally broken by the icy waters of a bottomless lake. He splashed about and, finally free of the demons, awoke just as Alanna threw another pail of water on him. He sputtered and spit, then sat up and tried to wrench the bucket from her hands.

"Are you trying to drown me?"

Alanna released her hold on the bucket and sank to her knees.

"I'm sorry, but you've been delirious for more than a day, and I couldn't think of any other way to bring you out of it."

Hunter found it difficult to believe the ugly demon dreams had lasted so long. "When did you kill Blind Snake?"

"Three days ago."

Her shawl still shaded him, preventing him from seeing the angle of the sun, but he could tell by the obvious changes in her that he had indeed lost a day. Her dress was splattered with water, but seemed to hang on a figure that was rapidly becoming gaunt. There were shadows beneath her eyes, and her hair, rather than falling in attractive ringlets, was in wild disarray.

"You must rest," Hunter coaxed. "Come lie down with me."

"No, I'll bring you a drink first." Alanna struggled to rise and, weaving unsteadily, went to fetch more water. When she returned, she placed the bucket and cup within his reach, and then stretched out beside him. "I think you'll be all right now," she whispered softly, and before his hand caressed her cheek, she had given into the fatigue she had fought for so many hours.

After having slept for an equal amount of time, Hunter still felt drained, but wide-awake. He wiggled his toes, flexed his muscles, and while his leg did still ache, he attempted to convince himself that he would be strong enough to get up later. Recalling his frightful nightmares in the light of day, he wondered if death hadn't come for him again. If so, Alanna had saved him a second time, and he was extremely glad that she had. While he still felt weak, his fever had broken, and he was cheered by that small step toward recovery.

His thoughts remained focused on the exhausted young woman at his side, and he wondered if they might not have been the ones to fall in love last spring, had she not been so terrified of Indians. He tried not to dwell on how foolish his infatuation with Melissa had been, but he didn't want to fall in love with another white woman, who might soon spurn him. Even knowing that Alanna was a completely different person and undeserving of the awful doubts Melissa's memory inspired, he could not silence them.

Perhaps by the time he recovered, he would be a better judge of her feelings, as well as his own. He ought not to get well too swiftly, he vowed with a sly grin, for he wanted to savor awake the delicious attentions Alanna had obviously lavished on him, while he'd been unconscious. She would need her rest for that, however, and again winding one of her glossy curls around his finger, he began to plan how to become a much better patient. Once he had succeeded, he hoped it would not be long before they became lovers, but he would not repeat his mistakes. He would not risk his heart until he was certain Alanna's devotion would last forever.

"Would you really have married Elliott?"

They were eating a supper of trout and berries. Neither had spoken in several minutes, and Alanna recoiled slightly at the impertinence of his question. Her throat tightened painfully, and she looked away.

"Please, that's not something you should ask."

Her averted glance revealed a great deal. "It's something you should have already asked yourself."

While she had indeed pondered the question, she had not reached an answer before Elliott was killed, and it seemed disloyal to him to now discuss the matter with Hunter. Her appetite gone, Alanna rose and walked down to the river to rinse her hands. She did not return to her companion's side until her mood was again composed.

"I don't mean to be rude in leaving you, but if you'd like more berries, I'll have to pick them before it gets dark. I didn't realize you'd be so hungry."

Hunter knew she couldn't run away from herself no matter how far she went. "No, I've had enough. Stay with me."

Reluctantly, Alanna resumed her place beside their makeshift bed. Fearing he would continue asking her painful questions, she hastened to speak before he did. "I'm not comfortable here. I know you won't feel up to walking any great distance for a while, but when you can walk, if we could just move a dozen yards away, I'd be content."

Hunter readily understood her complaint about their present location. The three slain Abenaki braves were out of sight, but he was no more comfortable than she being so close to their grave. "We'll move tomorrow then."

"Tomorrow? Won't that be too difficult for you?"

Hunter had gotten up briefly to see to his body's needs, and was confident he'd not faint crossing a dozen yards. He would be no example of either speed or grace, but he could make it. "In the afternoon then."

He was teasing her again and Alanna smiled easily. Then she reached up to brush a stray curl off her forehead, and realized her hair was badly tangled. "Oh, no, I must look like—"

When she was unable to name a suitably unkempt example, Hunter supplied it. "Like a woman who's been sleeping in the woods?"

"Yes. I'm sorry. I wish I had a brush, or at least a comb."

"You look very beautiful, like a wood sprite. Is that the word?"

Flattered, Alanna nodded shyly. "Where did you hear about wood sprites?"

"They were in a book I read once."

"You like to read?"

She sounded merely curious rather than incredulous, so he chose not to take offense. "Yes, very much. Living in the forest can be lonely."

"I've asked about white settlements, but how far are we from your people?"

"Do you want to meet them?"

Alanna licked her lips slowly. "I feel safe with you, but I can't promise that an Indian village wouldn't be overwhelming. I'd not want to embarrass you."

She looked truly pained by the possibility. "How could you embarrass me?"

"By being afraid. Wouldn't that insult everyone?"

Hunter shrugged slightly. "Why shouldn't you be afraid of a pack of savages?"

"I didn't say that."

"No, but it's what you meant."

"No, it wasn't. Please don't twist my words that way."

Hunter had not meant to deliberately antagonize her, but the remark about savages had slipped out before he could censor it. "Our villages are peaceful, happy places," he finally said. "People would be curious about you. They might stare, but they wouldn't be cruel."

"You didn't answer my original question. If your village is close, I could go there and get help for you."

Hunter laughed at her offer. "If you don't think you can find Johnson's trading post, you'd never be able to find my village. If by chance you did wander into it, by the time you got back, I'd already have recovered and gone on my way. No, stay here. You'll be of no use to me, if you get lost in the woods."

Alanna couldn't argue with that, but she wished he had at least appreciated her willingness to try and bring help. Still tired, she covered a wide yawn. "I'm sorry, but I don't think I can stay awake much longer."

"Come to bed then."

His invitation was uttered in a soft, husky tone that frightened Alanna far more than their discussion of his village had.

His chest was still bare, and clad only in his breechclout, his powerfully built body took on both an appealing and a threatening quality. Torn by the desire to reach out and caress his bronze skin, as she had while he'd been delirious, and the equally compelling urge to flee, she hurriedly rose and made a great show of cleaning up the remains of their supper.

She took the bucket down to the lake to fill it, but then left it on the sandy shore and went to look for a new place to camp, while there was still light enough to see the terrain clearly. Once out of sight, however, she just sat down and hugged her knees. She knew precisely what was happening to her: she was growing much too fond of Hunter. He kept her continually off balance emotionally, and although she did not think he was deliberately trying to confuse her, he most certainly did.

She took a deep breath to clear her mind, but rather than a moment of peaceful calm, she felt Melissa's presence so strongly, she turned, expecting to see her cousin approaching. There were moments when that happened, when for a few seconds she forgot that Melissa was gone, but such forgetfulness seemed inexcusable here. Now she couldn't help but wonder what had really happened between Melissa and Hunter. Had he tortured her cousin with alternate displays of affection and scorn, the way he did her?

She supposed she could ask Hunter that question, but would he tell her the truth, or merely a lie that flattered him and his cause? Certain that he would prefer a lie to revealing a damning truth, Alanna dismissed the thought of questioning him as foolish. She would simply have to trust her instincts where he was concerned, and pray she would not be led astray.

Alanna didn't return to their camp until after dark, and although she found Hunter already asleep, she couldn't bring herself to again lie down beside him. She took apart the flimsy awning and, moving several feet away from the handsome

brave, spread out her shawl on the ground. After a little wiggling around, she found a comfortable pose and closed her
eyes, but she couldn't overcome the anxiety memories of
Melissa had brought. Hunter might be attractive and bright,
but Alanna didn't intend to repeat her cousin's mistakes with
him. Feeling lost and confused, she hoped Hunter would soon
be well enough to guide her back to the trading post, so she
could go home.

Hunter had not really been asleep, but merely dozing while
he waited for Alanna to join him. When she chose not to, his
first impulse was to get up and bring her back to his bed. He
would have gone no farther, as weak as he was all he could
hope to enjoy was her closeness, but that she had not willingly
come to him stopped him from making an issue of where she
chose to sleep. When he awakened the next morning, she was
already up, and because he knew how badly she wished to
leave, he struggled to get up, too.

"Scatter the pine branches," he suggested. "Cover the ashes,
and no one will ever know we were here."

Because Alanna had successfully purged the area of any
sign of the Abenaki braves' violent deaths, she objected to his
advice as completely unnecessary. "I could scarcely dismantle
the bed with you on it," she pointed out. "As for the ashes, I
thought we might want to cook breakfast, before we left."

Hunter had noticed how difficult it seemed to be for Alanna
to focus her gaze on his face when they talked, and had deliberately chosen not to don his shirt. He doubted that it was
his appearance that had perplexed her, though. She sounded
insulted by his advice, and he could not understand why.

"I'm used to doing everything on my own," he explained.
"I'm sorry I'm not strong enough to help you."

He sounded contrite, but the sparkle in his dark eyes belied
his words. He was hopping around with the assistance of the
branch she had found for a cane, and he already looked plenty

strong to her. "Aren't we only a day's journey from the trading post?" she asked.

"You're forgetting that you had traveled all morning before Elliott was killed. We ran the rest of that day, and into the night. We arrived here the next morning."

"So we're two days away then?"

"When people are running for their lives, they can travel much faster than when they are not threatened. It will take us longer to return to the trading post than it did to get here, but why are you in such a hurry? I can barely stand. I wish I could take you back to the trading post today, but it's impossible."

Alanna smiled nervously. "I don't know where I'll find the courage to tell my aunt and uncle about Elliott's death, but I can't avoid it by hiding in the forest indefinitely. I have to get home."

Her sudden concern for her aunt and uncle took Hunter by surprise, but he thought better of saying so aloud. "I'm not trying to keep you here. Had I not gotten hurt, we could have started back toward the trading post as soon as we'd buried the Abenaki. I know I'm a burden to you. Don't imagine that I enjoy it." He took a couple of hops toward the river; growing shaky, Hunter eased himself down to the ground. "Maybe we should have breakfast before we go."

Concerned, Alanna went to him. While he had looked fit only a few minutes earlier, he was now short of breath and pale. "It's too soon," she scolded. "You aren't going anywhere today."

Hunter leaned back on his hands. "It's already been decided. I'm going even if I have to crawl. Now hurry and catch us some fish. I'm hungry."

"I'm tired of fish."

"So am I, but you'll have to be patient until I can hunt."

"When you're well enough to hunt, we can get back to the trading post."

"We'll have to eat on the way. For now, I'll teach you how to weave a mesh basket to catch fish. It's much easier than using a hook and line."

Even though he had not been awake an hour, he looked tired, and Alanna hated to tax what little strength he had. "I'm having no trouble catching fish. You just sit here and watch."

Hunter tried not to smile too widely. "Good luck."

Alanna had discovered several places to dig worms and, once she had her hook baited, she carried Hunter's line out onto the rocks. The water was teeming with trout, and she swiftly got a bite. It took her less than half an hour to catch plenty of fish for their breakfast, and then she busied herself building a fire.

Hunter felt up to making the rack to broil her catch, then leaned back on his elbows while she saw to the cooking. Disheveled, she looked very much like the distracted waif she had been when they met. She had almost danced with excitement each time she caught a fish, and now kept circling the fire as she kept a close eye on the roasting trout. When she glanced toward him, her smile held a childlike delight he found captivating.

"I know you're anxious to go back to Williamsburg, but you look at home here in the forest."

"Really? I'd like to think it's a peaceful place, even if we haven't found it that way."

Fearing she was going to again char the trout, Hunter dragged himself to his feet and hopped over to the fire. "If you want to pick some berries, I'll watch the fish." When Alanna gave him a skeptical glance, he pointed toward the woods. "Go, watching the fire won't exhaust me." It took him a moment to convince her he was feeling better, and then she hurried off to fetch the berries. Hunter flipped the rack containing the fish, watched until they had turned a delicate golden brown, and promptly removed them from the fire.

Satisfied he had cooked their breakfast to perfection, he made no boasts about his talents when Alanna returned. She had again carried the berries in her skirt, and when she released the hem, they spilled out all around him. He gathered them up and dropped them into their bucket to rinse. "This looks very good," he enthused.

"It's all we've had to eat since we got here."

"Then we're very lucky it tastes so good." Hunter divided the fish and passed half to her. "You're getting too thin. Eat."

"You've lost weight, too."

Hunter glanced down at his torso, but he didn't think he looked any different. His belly had already been flat and his limbs lean. "We are very lucky to be here now, rather than in winter. That would have been very difficult for us."

Alanna swallowed her first bite of fish and wondered why the ones Hunter roasted tasted so much better than hers. "Elliott and I deliberately waited until spring to come see you. Of course, we had hoped that you'd answer his letters."

Hunter frowned slightly. "That was my fault," he offered grudgingly. "I wish now that I had. The next time you write to me, I'll answer."

"If only . . ." Alanna began wistfully, but her thought was too sad to put into words, and she fell silent.

"If only what? If only I had answered Elliott's letters, then you two could have stayed at home, and he would still be alive?"

"No."

"Tell me."

Alanna had difficulty finding the words. "I was just thinking, if only Melissa had married you rather than Ian. Then maybe both she and Elliott would still be alive."

"How could Melissa have married me?" Hunter scoffed. "Would she have caught my breakfast in the Sacandaga, or slept on the ground to be with me? Would she have made even the smallest sacrifice to become my wife?"

"I don't know what she might have done. Did you two talk about marriage?"

Alanna's expression mirrored the innocent sweetness of her soul, but Hunter still interpreted her question as showing far more sympathy for Melissa than it did for him. "The only conversation I can recall is our last one, and I won't repeat what she said then."

Hunter was growing adept at using his cane to get to his feet, and did so now. "I've had enough. Stay here. I'll come back."

"But I didn't mean—" Hunter had already turned away, but Alanna had seen his expression and knew that she ought never to mention Melissa's name to him again. Clearly he was the one who had been betrayed, not her cousin, and she felt desperately sorry that she had reminded him of it.

"Hunter, please wait," she called.

Intending to tell her to leave him be, Hunter turned back, but Alanna had also gotten to her feet, and as she hurried toward him, the hem of her dress swung dangerously close to the fire. "Be careful!" he shouted, but startled by the harshness of his tone Alanna drew back, sending her hem directly into the flames.

Dampened from her stay out on the rocks while fishing, rather than igniting, the fire-kissed fabric sent up a small cloud of steam and smoke that instantly caught Alanna's attention. Fearing her gown would burn as brightly as a torch, she moved back so quickly, she tripped and fell. Seeing her trapped in her still-steaming garment, Hunter rushed forward and threw himself across her feet to smother what he mistook for the first hint of flames.

Pinned to the ground, Alanna knew exactly what Hunter was doing, but she was terrified he might be the one to get burned in the process. She struggled to sit up and push him away, but, realizing the danger to her had been slight and was now over, Hunter moved forward rather than away. His momentum again forced Alanna back against the ground, and when he grabbed her hands, that's where she had to stay.

"Even a wood sprite can get burned. Why weren't you more careful?"

He was so close, Alanna had no time to reply before his lips found hers. He had shown her both passion and sweetness, but this time his kiss held more than a hint of anger, and she rebelled rather than respond. She shoved against him, but he held her too tightly for her to gain any leverage. She tried using her legs, then, fearing she would reopen his wound, she ceased to struggle. To be scolded with brutal kisses felt strange indeed, but it wasn't until she relaxed and lay perfectly still, that Hunter ended what she considered curiously inappropriate punishment.

"Answer me," he ordered.

Alanna regarded him with a blank stare. He had pressed himself against her just like this the morning she had awakened him in the barn, and now that she knew him better, the experience was even more affecting. She was fully clothed, but he wasn't, and looking up at his bare shoulders, her only thought was how much she wanted to touch him.

"I can't recall the question," she finally admitted in a breathless whisper.

Hunter would have repeated it, but distracted by his own reflection in her bright green eyes, he could not remember it either. He leaned down to kiss her again with teasing nibbles, and when he released her hands, she untied the leather thong at his nape, spilling his hair down over his shoulders. While the gesture brought a familiar ache to his heart, Alanna was the only woman on his mind.

Twenty-one

Hunter's kisses turned soft and sweet, lulling Alanna into a blissful euphoria where painful memories ceased to exist and only the rapture of the moment mattered. No longer feverish, his skin held a delicious warmth, and she ran her fingertips down his spine, then wrapped her arms around his waist to hold him close. He felt so good to her, so right. There was none of the awkwardness she felt with other men, but only a magical allure that made her cling to him with undisguised longing.

Without a pause in his ever-deepening kisses, Hunter unfastened the row of buttons that ran down her bodice, then slipped his hand inside. The top of her sheer cotton chemise was as heavily decorated with lace as the hem had been, and he pushed it aside to expose the creamy smoothness of her breasts. She was so fair her nipples remained a delicate pink, even after he had teased them into firm peaks. Hungry for the taste of her, he slid his tongue over one breast, and then its twin, before drawing the crest of the first between his lips for a more appreciative appraisal of her endearing charms.

Tender, taunting, insistent, demanding, he used his lips, tongue, and teeth to arouse her passions, until her response was as wild as his own. He wanted her out of the clothes that hampered his every move, and reached beneath her skirt to slide her drawers down over her hips. She arched her back, leaning into him to make his task easier, and the undergarment was swiftly flung aside. He ran his hand up the smoothness of her inner thigh, parting her legs with a gentle caress that left her lying totally open to him.

Considerate as well as ardent, he created superbly tantalizing sensations in a slow, deliberate assault on her senses. He could feel her desire growing with each heartbeat, and yet drew away before she reached the ecstasy he had made her crave. He sat up and yanked first her gown, and then the remnants of her chemise off over her head. Now nude, Alanna watched him with a soft, sultry glance, as he ran a fingertip slowly from her lips, down between her breasts, across the warm hollow of her belly, and through the triangle of golden curls that veiled the last of her secrets.

He had likened her to a wood sprite, but there was nothing elfin about her now. Tall and slim, her proportions were as lovely as her features, and he again stretched out beside her, eager for the thrill of her loving. Having had only a sample of her favors, he again suckled at her breasts, while his fingertips danced in a slow circling motion that dipped and slid ever deeper, testing the limits of her virginity, until she was straining against him, silently begging him to end the last separation remaining between them.

Hunter wanted her just as badly, but the ache in his thigh was now a throbbing pain, threatening to bring tears to his eyes. Fearing his injury would make him so clumsy Alanna would be revolted rather than satisfied with his talents as a lover, he chose to teach her only how good *he* could make *her* feel. There would be other days, when he was stronger, when he would make love to her until she begged him to stop, but for now, he was content with giving her pleasure with the subtle pressure of his fingertips.

Neither Rachel Barclay's halting description of romance and its consequences, nor Polly McBride's far more explicit summary of the act that insured the continuation of the human race, had adequately prepared Alanna for the splendor of Hunter's fevered kisses and adoring touch. She could scarcely breathe as an exquisite joy swelled within her to a stunning crest, then spilled forth a delectable warmth that brought her the first glimpse of true contentment that she had ever known. Lying relaxed in Hunter's arms, she felt truly loved, until she realized he hadn't spoken a single endearment, nor made any promises of love. That Melissa's first midnight encounter with the incredibly affectionate Indian had left her pregnant, made his lingering preference for Alanna's late cousin tragically clear.

Taking a practical view, she supposed she should be grateful he had not wanted to risk sending her home carrying his child. For a sensitive, introspective young woman, however, it was far easier to see his reluctance to make love to her in more personal terms. She feared she lacked Melissa's beauty, charm, and most importantly, her cousin's easy command of Hunter's heart. The glory of their affectionate interlude dissolving in a wave of self-pity, she felt too ashamed of her many shortcomings to remain in Hunter's embrace. She reached for her discarded garments as she sat up, and when she rose to her feet, her gown presented a modest barrier to Hunter's puzzled glance.

"I have to bathe and dress," she announced with forced calm. "Then we can move the camp."

Thoroughly distracted, Hunter was shocked by her sudden interest in a matter he had completely forgotten. "Whatever you like," he assured her, but she looked anything but pleased as she hurried away, and he felt that despite his best intentions, he had disappointed her. He swept his hair off his forehead and searched for the thong to secure it, then lay back down and shaded his eyes with his forearm. Alanna had such a fragile spirit, and it saddened him to think he might have frightened her with his enthusiasm for her affection. She certainly hadn't seemed terrified at the time, quite the contrary, but the sorrow in her gaze had been unmistakable.

Maybe she *had* loved Elliott. If so, then he had rushed her, and would now pay the price for that thoughtlessness. She was a sweet girl, a very dear one, and if she had loved Elliott, then Hunter feared it would take a long time for her to fall in love with him. The challenge would be to keep her with him long enough for her feelings to grow that deep.

Alanna bathed hurriedly and washed her clothes. Having nothing else to wear, she sat in the sun in her wet chemise and drawers, and waited for them to dry. She had again drenched her hair, and used her fingers to comb the tangles from her long curls. Her mood a melancholy one, she could not overcome the nagging suspicion that in Hunter's eyes, she was a very poor substitute for Melissa. Even if that assumption were incorrect, his failure to make love to her proved she was lacking in some crucial aspect. Perhaps it was merely her inexperience that had disappointed him, but he had not told her how to please him, so how could she have known what he wanted?

Despondent, Alanna stayed away from Hunter for more than two hours. When she finally gathered the courage to return to their camp, he was asleep and, relieved not to have to face him, she went on along the shore to look for another place for them to spend a few days. Partial to a small clearing bordered by raspberry vines, she sat down, leaned back against a convenient spruce, and in a few minutes began to doze. She was very grateful Hunter was going to live, but she felt far from alive herself, and her dreams reflected the loneliness which was too often her only companion.

Hunter awoke with a start, sat up, and called Alanna's name. When there was no response, he lurched to his feet and, still relying on his cane, hobbled down to the lake to look for her. He had not meant to fall asleep, and hoped she wasn't angry with him for again leaving her with all the work. When he didn't see her, he shouted her name, but it echoed unanswered over the undulating waters of the Sacandaga.

The current was swift, but he doubted she would have strayed so far from the shore that she could have been swept away by it. After all, she had grown up on the banks of the James River, so she was no stranger to the water's peril. Frustrated, he felt certain she would have gone south rather than north, and started off in that direction. Hopping along over the rocky shore he made very poor time, and was completely worn out when he finally found her. He could not imagine why she had wandered off by herself, and scowled angrily as he eased himself down beside her.

He shook her shoulder to wake her. "Do you enjoy making me worry?" he asked.

Alanna's initial smile faded when she saw how displeased he was. "I had no such intention."

"Then why did you disappear? How was I supposed to know where you'd gone?"

"It doesn't look as though you had too much difficulty finding me. If this place appeals to you, wait here, and I'll go back to get our things and erase all trace of our presence at our last camp."

That was certainly a reasonable suggestion, but Hunter shook his head. "Wait awhile. It took me so long to find you, that I don't want you running off again."

Taking that as further evidence of his disappointment in her, Alanna twisted her hands in her lap. "You were asleep, so I decided to do a bit of exploring. I didn't run off and leave you."

Hunter hadn't meant to sound so cross with her, but damn it, he was. He had made love to her, but she was behaving as though it had never happened. "Is it Elliott, is that what's wrong?"

"Elliott?"

She looked merely confused, and Hunter tried not to lose his patience with her again. He took her hand and brought it to his lips. "Elliott was a fine man and if you loved him—"

"Of course, I loved him."

"Yes, he was part of your family and you loved him, but that doesn't mean you loved him the way a woman should love a man she plans to marry."

Alanna pulled her hand from his and crossed her arms over her bosom, to prevent him from touching her. "I don't want to talk about this again. What Elliott and I might or might not have done doesn't matter anymore."

"It matters if you prefer memories of him to *me.*"

Aghast at that comment, Alanna rose and stepped out of his reach. "I'm not the one who—well, never mind. It doesn't matter now."

"Stop saying that. It does matter, or you wouldn't look so miserable!"

"Why shouldn't I be miserable?" Alanna shouted right back at him. "People are being killed. You're badly hurt. We're lost in the forest. Does that make you happy?"

"No, but—"

"I'm not leaving you," Alanna called over her shoulder. "I'll be back soon."

Eager to follow her, Hunter started to rise, but slipped; jarred by the pain that coursed through his leg, he needed a moment to catch his breath. He was trying so hard to be gentle and kind, but Alanna wasn't giving him even the slightest bit of encouragement, and he didn't know how to reach her. She was as skittish as a fawn, and he had no idea how to tame such a restless spirit. He pulled a clump of grass up by the roots and hurled it after her, but his anger wasn't nearly as easy to toss away.

As promised, Alanna returned shortly with everything they

had left behind. She handed Hunter his shirt, leggings, and moccasins, but he just laid them aside. He had picked a magnificent heap of berries, and she scooped a handful off the top. "These are very good, aren't they?"

"Delicious," Hunter agreed. He looked up at her, his expression sullen. "I'm sorry I can't hunt yet."

Alanna had brought the two muskets she had taken from the dead Abenaki, along with the one belonging to Hunter. His bow and quiver lay with them. "We have weapons aplenty," she remarked absently, "but I'd rather not fire a musket again, and I've no idea how to use a bow."

"I'll teach you when I feel better."

Worried, Alanna knelt by his side. "Are you feeling ill again?"

Surprised that she had to ask, Hunter shrugged slightly. "I'm no worse than before, but I'm far from well."

"I'm sorry."

"So am I." Hunter popped a berry into his mouth and munched it slowly. "Catch some fish, if you want them. I'm not hungry."

No more willing to chat than he, Alanna moved away and busied herself collecting fist-sized stones to ring a fire. Next she gathered firewood, but left it unlit while she went down to the lake to fish. She could feel Hunter watching her, and each time she glanced his way, she found his expression dark and brooding. Glancing up at the sky, she wondered where the day had gone. She wasn't really hungry either, but fishing gave her something to do. The trout weren't nearly as easy to catch in the afternoon as they were at dawn, but she persevered until she had six.

"I thought you might change your mind about eating," she told him.

Hunter shook his head. She had not danced over the rocks in the way that had amused him so the last time he had watched her fish. She had simply stood at the water's edge, looking as lost as he felt. She roasted her catch, and from what he could see, again overcooked it, and he was ashamed he hadn't offered to help. He knew he was being very poor company, but by the time she had finished eating supper, he was positive he knew what the problem was. He could not believe he had been so blind.

"Because I'm Indian, I know I'm the last man you could ever love, but I wish things had been different, better, so that we could stay together."

He was rolling the shaft of an arrow slowly between his fingers rather than look at her, but the sadness in his voice broke her heart. "Do you really want me to stay with you?" she whispered. When he glanced up at her, she couldn't tell if he were hurt, or insulted. "What I mean is, I'm nothing like Melissa."

Hunter swore a particularly vile oath, but wisely chose to do so in his mother tongue. "I know," he then agreed in English. "It's what I've always liked best about you."

Alanna had to swallow hard to force away the painful ache in her throat. "I didn't think you wanted me."

Hunter laid the arrow aside. "Come here."

They were seated just a few feet apart, but when Hunter extended his hand, Alanna wondered if they could ever truly bridge the wide gulf that separated them. She had so many questions. Questions she knew he and Melissa should have answered, before they had begun their brief affair. She hung back, but when Hunter began to smile, her only thought was how remarkably handsome he was, and how desperately she wanted him to make love to her. In the next instant she was in his arms, the answers she had sought, forgotten.

Afraid of scaring her off, Hunter wrapped her in a relaxed embrace. He rested his chin atop her head and patted her back lightly. "I have nothing to give you," he admitted sadly.

Alanna sat back slightly, so she could look up at him. "I have no need of things."

Hunter caressed her cheek, then slipped his fingers through her shiny curls. "Yes, you do. White women need a great many things."

"I don't need anything that you can't provide."

A slow smile played across Hunter's lips. "And what is that?"

"A home, food, whatever we'll need to survive."

Hunter wanted to give her so much more. "Is that all you want?"

His seductive whisper sent a shiver of anticipation down her spine. She reached up to trace the edge of his jaw, and he turned his head to move with her and prolong the touch. That he would lean into her caress like an affectionate cat amused her. There was an animal wildness about him that his soft-spoken manner had never fully disguised, but now she found it enormously intriguing rather than frightening.

"All I want is you," she replied in a tone as inviting as his.

"Can you wait until I'm well?"

Alanna broke into a mischievous grin and shook her head. "No, I don't think I can wait another minute." She leaned down to flick his nipple with the tip of her tongue, but when he flinched, she sat back.

"Does that bother you?" she asked.

"Oh, yes," Hunter admitted, but he sounded appreciative rather than annoyed. He wound his fingers in her hair to pull her lips to his for a fervent kiss he didn't end, until she was lying beneath him. Cradled in the soft, spring grass, her eyes glowed with the same iridescent sheen as the new spring leaves overhead, while her tawny curls caught the last of the sun's vermilion rays.

Hunter rested on his elbows and struggled to find the right words to make her understand without frightening her. "I wanted to make love to you this morning, but the pain got too bad, and I couldn't. Please be patient with me. If we have forever, a few days shouldn't make any difference."

That she had mistaken his lack of passion for disinterest, when pain had been the cause, made Alanna blush with shame. "I'm sorry. I shouldn't have been so stupid." She tried to sit up, but he blocked her way.

"The fault is mine. You couldn't have known."

"But I should have. I knew how badly you'd been hurt."

She was again blaming herself for something that wasn't her fault, and Hunter couldn't bear to see her suffer so needlessly. "I want to make you laugh until your sides ache, but neither of us is in the mood for jokes." He rolled over on his back and pulled her against him, so her head would rest comfortably in the hollow of his shoulder. Loss of blood had left him feeling tired and weak, just when he needed all his strength to impress her.

"I can't keep you with me, if I don't get well," he announced suddenly. "To take an Indian for a husband will be difficult enough. I won't tie you to an invalid."

Alanna sat up slowly. "What if *I'd* been the one who had been stabbed? Would you send me away, because I was no longer perfect?"

"It's not the same," Hunter argued.

"Yes, it is."

"No, it's the man who provides for his woman, not the other way around."

He was confusing her again and Alanna drew back. "In one breath you talk about us being together forever, and in the next of sending me away. Can't you make up your mind? I'm sure you'll recover completely, but even if you don't, I'd not leave you. It just so happens that I have some money of my own, and if it's managed properly, it will be enough to take care of all three of us."

It was now Hunter who was badly confused. He sat up so they could discuss the matter more easily. "I would rather starve to death than live off your money," he insisted. "There are only two of us," he added. "Why did you say three?"

Alanna couldn't believe he had to ask that. "Have you forgotten why Elliott and I came to see you? You have a son, Hunter, and he belongs with us."

Sickened by her mention of the boy, Hunter turned away. "His mother despised me, and her poison is in his blood. I could no more love him than he could love me. Do not speak of him again. He will never be a part of us."

The love that had filled his gaze only moments before, had been replaced by a look of such virulent hatred that Alanna couldn't bear to remain with him. She rose and walked out of the clearing without offering any apology for leaving, or promise of when she might return. Afraid of becoming lost in the woods, she wandered down by the lake until it grew too dark for her to see the way. She had forgotten to take her shawl, but hoping the night would be mild, she lay down and slept in the grass.

Hunter kept waiting for Alanna to reappear, but when he heard the howl of a wolf in the distance, he feared it might be a warning that she would never return. He thought she still had Elliott's knife at her belt and, having seen her kill two men, he knew she wouldn't hesitate to defend herself should any danger arise, but he did not want her to have to face any such challenge ever again. Frantic with both worry and despair, it took him a long time to fall asleep. When he awoke the next morning and found himself still alone, he became even more depressed.

He got up and tried putting some weight on his injured leg, but the resulting pain wrenched a groan from his throat, and he had to ease back on his cane. He knew he had to eat to grow strong, but he still had no appetite. Forcing himself to fish, he caught enough trout for two, but there was still no sign of Alanna by the time they were finished cooking. Although quiet and shy, she had been such good company, he missed her very badly and hoped she would come back before noon.

Alanna had berries for breakfast, and then, wanting to be certain Hunter was all right, she circled around their camp and approached it from the south. When she saw him leaning on his cane to fish, she crept away before he felt her presence, and returned to the spot where she had spent the night. Feeling drained of all emotion, she sat watching the lake for most of the day. She retreated into herself as she had as a child, but she no longer had her cousins' happy laughter to draw her from the sadness of her daydreams. Disconsolate, she did not even notice the sun had set, until long after it had grown dark.

Hunter had known women who pouted when they failed to get their way, but after briefly considering that possibility, he rejected it. Alanna wasn't the type to sulk. She was far too considerate a person to manipulate others. Clearly she saw herself as Christian's champion, and perhaps he had been unforgivably harsh, but didn't his feelings merit equal consideration?

Then a truly awful thought occurred to him. What if Christian was the one she loved? What if her only interest was in providing a father for the boy? With Elliott gone, he had been a convenient and logical choice, but once he had refused to raise Christian, Alanna had immediately lost interest in him. Perhaps she had not said so in words, but didn't her absence make her position clear? If it was Christian she loved, and not him, then she had made an even bigger fool of him than Melissa had.

Infuriated that he had again been duped by a white woman with beguiling ways, Hunter channeled all his energies into getting well. His leg was still sore, but he could take a few steps at least, and the next day several more. He removed the bandage and found that Alanna had wrapped his wound so cleverly, it would leave only a thin scar rather than the ugly puckered gash he had expected.

Encouraged that his leg was healing properly, he began walking a few steps each hour, making a great effort to stand tall, rather than bent over favoring his left leg. It was difficult, and painful, but by the time Alanna had been gone five days, he felt fit enough to go after her. He had rehearsed what he wanted to say, and would be brief rather than abusive. He would sign whatever statement she wanted about Christian. He would gladly give her the boy, but after taking her back to the trading post and putting her on a barge, he did not want to ever see her again.

His handsome features set in a disgusted frown, he prowled along the lake's edge, attempting to follow her last set of footprints. She had stepped across rocks here and there, but every yard or so he came across a clear print. It was no challenge to track her, but rather than return to their last camp as he had expected, she had gone on. Perplexed, he continued following the river's curving path, until at last he sighted her seated on a rocky point that jutted out into the water. She was so still, he thought she might have fallen asleep sitting up; and when he called out to her, she didn't turn, or answer.

When he got close enough, he could see that her hair was damp, but so was her dress, as though she had gone swimming fully clothed. That seemed like a very silly thing to do. Now within a few feet of her, he again spoke her name. As before, she remained oblivious to him and continued to stare out at the lake. It wasn't until he knelt by her side and touched her arm, that she noticed him.

Lacking a way to catch and cook fish, she had been living on berries, and while the juice had lent her lips a subtle rose tint, she was noticeably thinner. Perfectly calm, she sat staring at him now, her features serene, but there wasn't the slightest glimmer of recognition in her glance. Terrified that he had lost her in a way he had not even imagined, Hunter grabbed her shoulders and shook her.

"Alanna, answer me!"

Alanna cocked her head slightly. Hunter was again fully clothed in buckskins. He looked fit and strong. Compared to him, she felt very small and insignificant. He seemed insistent that she speak, but only one thought occurred to her.

"I'm cold," she told him.

As her lower lip began to tremble, Hunter's suspicions dissolved instantly, for it was painfully clear that she hadn't been avoiding him out of spite. He could see the grief that had sculpted the stillness of her pose reflected in the sorrow of her gaze, and knew that while he had worked so hard to get well, she had been silently mourning the love they had lost. He pulled her to her feet and led her to the shore, where he hurriedly helped her out of her wet dress. He tugged his shirt off over his head, and used it to pat her dry.

"You're supposed to remove your clothes before you wash them," he scolded. "Did you forget that?"

Unable to recall how she had gotten wet, Alanna just shook her head. It was very pleasant having Hunter touch her. It felt like love, even though she knew it wasn't, and she relaxed against him, unwittingly encouraging attentions of an entirely different nature.

Hunter's conscience told him that this was neither the time nor the place to make love to Alanna, but he was deaf to the voice of reason. He didn't care if they had differences which could never be reconciled, when her fragile beauty touched him so deeply. He wanted to take her for his wife, to make her feel cherished, as he knew no other man ever could. He drew her down into the grass, and covered her dear face with adoring kisses.

"I've missed you," he murmured. He removed her chemise

and drawers, and then warmed her cool skin with fevered kisses. He could count her ribs easily, and feared she might not have survived many more days without him. "You were never meant to be alone," he swore. "You were born to be mine."

Lost in a dreamlike wonder, Alanna held him in a languid embrace. She loosened his hair and pressed his face close, as he suckled at her breast. As always, his slightest touch filled her with joy, and she soon felt as though her heart might burst with happiness.

Meaning to at last thoroughly quench his desires, Hunter ran his hand over her hip and down her thigh, but when she flinched, he sat up to see what was wrong. The deep purple bruise on her knee told him. "Did you fall on the rocks? Is that how you got all wet?"

Rather than reply, Alanna ran her hand up his arm, silently encouraging him to complete what he had begun. He leaned down to kiss the bruise, and then slipped off his moccasins, so he could remove his breechclout and leggings more easily. Now nude, he again stretched out beside her and pulled her close. She was so slender, her body seemed almost to melt into his. Her skin was still cool, but gradually warmed beneath his caress.

His ebony mane fell across her breasts, and slid over her stomach as he fit the tip of his tongue into her navel. He wanted to hear her giggle, but succeeded only in drawing a small sigh of contentment from her lips. Inspired to take so much more, he again kissed her bruised knee, then licked a narrow trail up the soft incline of her inner thigh. He had pleasured her before with a delicate touch, and she did not draw away when he slid his fingers into her again.

He rubbed his cheek against her knee, deftly parting her legs, and kept up his gentle explorations. Her lithe body had an inviting perfume, and he leaned closer to savor her scent.

Nothing could stop him now; he took a firm hold of her so she could not slip away, as he dipped low to sample her taste. Rather than object, Alanna tilted her hips to encourage him to drink more deeply.

Entranced by the sweetness of her surrender, Hunter hastened to make her his own before the beauty they shared lost any of its magic. He had regained the grace to enable him to teach her what making love should be, and he hoped the inevitable pain of their initial union would be fleeting. At his first deep thrust, she clung to him rather than draw away, her anguish blurred by the ecstasy he had so tenderly nurtured.

He lost himself in that rapture now, and knowing how deeply it was shared gave him the greatest satisfaction he had ever found in a woman's arms. The bond forged between them by sorrow was now tempered by passion's flames, and for a brief instant they were truly one. It wasn't until much later that the contrast between Alanna's small white hand and his deeply bronzed chest prompted him to remember how different they truly were.

Twenty-two

Not wanting Alanna to become chilled after he had gone to such exquisite lengths to warm her, Hunter slipped his buckskin shirt over her head, before donning his breechclout and leggings. He then pulled her back into his arms and gave her an exuberant hug. "I know you want to go home, but we need time to be alone together. Let's stay here a few more days."

Alanna wasn't sure whether or not his suggestion required her approval, but she did not even want to think about standing up, let alone beginning the trip back to Virginia. She snuggled against him, enjoying both the softness of his shirt and the smoothness of his bare chest. In a thoughtful mood, she made a prediction.

"I'm afraid the forest is the only place we'll ever feel at home."

Hunter sat up slightly and combed her curls off her face with his fingertips. He leaned down to nibble her earlobe playfully, before he replied, "The forest isn't the only place we can live happily. William Johnson is married to a Mohawk woman, and given his affection for the Iroquois, no one was surprised by his choice. I can name many other trappers with Indian wives. I also know Indian braves with white wives." Hunter chose not to add that most of those women had been raised with their husband's tribe, rather than with white families as Alanna had.

"There will always be people who say we don't belong together, but as long as you and I believe that we do, we needn't listen." He kissed her eyelids and the tip of her nose before savoring her berry-flavored lips. "I know that we belong together, don't you?"

Alanna reached up to touch his hair. Warmed by the sun, the sable strands spilled through her fingers like silken threads. "I've never felt as though I belonged with another man," she revealed hesitantly.

That was scarcely the enthusiastic vow of undying love Hunter longed to hear, but considering how distracted she had been when he had found her, he thought himself lucky that she was able to provide any kind of a coherent response. "That's because you were meant for me," he assured her, and the sweetness of her smile encouraged affection that could be conveyed without words. Slow, tender, he again made certain he pleased her, so that she would always welcome his affection.

Later, when she slept in his arms, Hunter gazed up at the clouds and tried to imagine what his life would be now that he had a wife. He would no longer be alone, which he saw as an advantage. He would not be able to come and go as he pleased, but he doubted he would want to stray with Alanna waiting for him at home. The temptation would be to take her so deep into the forest that they would inhabit a private world, but he knew she needed not only him, but her own kind as well.

Recalling how she had gone out to the stable each morning, he knew she would want to own horses. The hides he had gathered were valuable, and he had saved all of his winnings from fighting. He could afford to buy her whatever she liked. Next winter, he would have a reason to work harder, and he would spend more time trapping. If Alanna did not distract him too badly. Certain that she would, he laughed to himself, as she began to stir.

"I didn't mean to wake you. Are you hungry?"

Hunter's charming smile conveyed his high spirits, and

Alanna hesitated to interject her worries, but she could no longer deny them. She sat up and took a deep breath. "Yes, I am hungry, but there's something I need to ask before we look for food. I left you because I couldn't bear to hear you say such vile things about Christian. You came to find me. Does that mean you've changed your mind about raising him?"

His shirt was much too large for her, lending her the tragic air of the orphan she had once been, but her level gaze showed a determination he had to admire. She deserved an honest reply, and he gave it. "No. I came to tell you that I would sign whatever statement you wished, so that you could raise the boy, but that I wanted nothing more to do with either of you."

Unable to reconcile that dreary confession with his abundant affection, Alanna was understandably confused. "I don't recall your saying anything of the kind before you made love to me."

Hunter's stomach twisted into a hard knot of dread, for he had known he ought not to take her innocence with such an important dispute left unsettled. He had known it, and had selfishly done it anyway. Now she had every right to feel betrayed. He had put his desires before hers, or the welfare of a child. He had had such high hopes, but he had not been a good husband to her for even one day. He squared his shoulders, and tried to undo the damage he had done the lovely young woman he wanted for his wife.

"I've lived among white men for nearly ten years, and I'm ashamed of how long it took me to learn I was more often used than respected. I admired Byron and Elliott, and was proud to call them my friends, but I think now they were merely impressed with my tracking ability. I felt out of place in your home, but I was so flattered that Melissa wanted me, I didn't realize I was no more than an attractive savage, a curiosity, to her. I think now she meant only to tease me, but Christian was the result. Had she cared anything at all for me, she would have sent for me, so I could have become her husband rather than Ian.

"It's not fair of you to ask me to raise that woman's child, when she refused to name me as the father. I can't do it, not after the way she laughed at me and threatened me."

His manner bore no trace of the strident arrogance he had shown, when she and Elliott had arrived at the trading post. Instead, he was being remarkably forthright. Alanna could see how badly he had been hurt, not merely by Melissa, but also in other apparently painful dealings with whites. It was no wonder he had grown cold and suspicious, if he frequently felt others were taking advantage of him. She reached out to touch his knee.

"You're wrong about Byron and Elliott. They both valued your friendship, and were disappointed when you left so hurriedly last summer. As for Melissa, I'll make no apologies for her behavior, when clearly it was unforgivable, but Christian ought not to be punished for her mistakes."

Hunter had been too badly hurt to view his son's situation with her logic, and refused to concede the point. "What about his grandparents? What do they say?"

"I'm ashamed to tell you how they've behaved. They've never held Christian, never gone to see him, never sent him any clothes or gifts. They want you to take him, so they can forget he exists."

"So Melissa's disgrace will die with her?"

Alanna hated to admit that he was right. "Yes, they would have been equally heartbroken regardless of the circumstances of her death, but that she wasn't the virtuous young woman they believed her to be, clouds her memory and deepens their pain."

Hunter saw things far more personally. "It's not her lack of virtue that shames them, but the fact I am Indian. When you introduce me as your husband, will they be ashamed of you as well?"

That he would continue to refer to himself as her spouse gave Alanna a burst of hope that, despite their disagreement over Christian, they might still be able to have a shared future. Her mood remained downcast, however. "They'll be so grief-stricken over Elliott's death, that whatever I do won't matter."

Hunter had forgotten they would have to impart that sad news. He did not want to become distracted by it now either. "You told me there was a woman caring for Christian. Won't she keep him?"

"Permanently, you mean?"

"Yes, until he's grown."

"She's a young widow who cares for infants to support her three children. She's very good with Christian, very attentive, but I don't know if she would agree to raise him."

"We could pay her. I earn more money than most white men."

He was a proud man, and she was touched he would take such great pains to talk with her calmly. She had seen a fair sample of how hard and ruthless he could be, and she was grateful he had not chosen to display that side of his personality with her. "What about your family? Would your parents take Christian?"

That was an option Hunter refused to consider. "My father is dead, and I wouldn't ask my mother's husband to raise a dog."

Alanna was shocked by the vehemence of his tone. "Don't you plan to take me home to meet your family?"

Hunter shrugged. "I thought about visiting them before you came, but I didn't really want to go. When my father died, everything changed. When my mother took a second husband, I left. Perhaps someday I'll take you to meet my people, but for now, you are all the family I want."

From what he had just said, Alanna gathered the impression that Hunter felt no greater sense of belonging with the Seneca, than he did in the white world. She looked out toward the lake. Her aunt, uncle, and cousins had done their best to make her feel welcome in their home, but they had never replaced the beloved family she had lost. To learn that Hunter still mourned his father, or perhaps for the life he had once had, inspired a feeling of kinship she had not known they shared. They would have each other it seemed, but she still wanted more.

"I don't want Christian to grow up unloved and bitter," she murmured softly.

"Neither do I. If he's as fine a boy as you say, someone will want him."

"I want him," Alanna reminded him.

Tortured by his earlier suspicions, Hunter's expression grew stern. "More than you want me?"

That he would even ask such a question pained Alanna deeply. "No woman should ever be asked to choose between her husband and her child."

"But Christian isn't your child," Hunter stressed, "and if you don't want him to grow up unloved and bitter, then you'll help me find him a home." Frustrated by their lack of agreement, he rose and took several steps away, but then, believing he had found a way to convince her, he turned back. "I would be the worst of fathers to the boy. Don't doom him to that, every child deserves better."

"We may have children together. If you can't love Melissa's son, will you be able to love mine?"

Hunter took her hands and drew her to her feet. The fringed hem of his shirt reached past her knees, but even dressed in buckskins, she did not resemble a Seneca maiden. He had wanted her to be the first to speak of love. Now that seemed a cowardly way to behave. He cupped her face tenderly in his hands.

"I love you and I want us to be together always. I'll adore our children, but they'll be conceived in love, as Christian should have been." He leaned down to kiss her, and she relaxed against him. Considering that a good sign, he deepened the kiss and made a silent vow to give her a child as soon as possible. He was positive that once she had a baby of her own to love, Christian would be forgotten.

Wrapped in his embrace, Alanna felt surrounded by his love, but believing him to have a far kinder heart than he allowed others to see, she prayed that once he saw Christian, he would be unable to give him away. Buoyed by that hope, she hugged him more tightly. "Nothing is ever going to be easy for us, is it?"

Hunter laughed as he contradicted her. "One thing is."

Curious as to what, Alanna looked up at him, but the sparkle in his dark eyes as he leaned down to kiss her again made his answer plain. Love flowed between them with such graceful ease, and she hoped as desperately as he that it would be enough to keep the harsh demands of the world at bay.

Hunter kept Alanna by his side all day. He showed her how to use his bow when they went hunting for pheasant, and insisted she showed promise, although in truth he had seen small boys display more skill. After her brief lesson, he shot a plump bird and kept a close eye on it while it roasted.

"You didn't help to cook the meals at home, did you?" he asked.

"No, Polly McBride and her daughters did all the cooking. Why?"

"I don't want to expect too much from you."

"I suppose Seneca women are all excellent cooks?"

"Yes, all of them."

"Good, then we can hire one to do the cooking until I learn. I do know how to sew, arrange flowers, read, and write, of course. I can do all manner of useful things, Hunter. Perhaps not as you expect to have them done, but in my own way."

Hunter doubted that he would be alive had she not had the

courage to kill two men, or the stamina to care for him while he was ill, and he did not doubt that she possessed a multitude of talents. He smiled at her and winked. "Do you expect to have servants?"

He was clearly teasing her, and she responded in kind. "Not unless you find my cooking inedible."

The pheasant was done, and Hunter removed it from the spit he had constructed over the fire. He drew his knife and began to carve the delicious bird. "The Seneca have dozens of recipes for corn, squash, soups, and stews, but none are written down. When we come back here, I'll find a woman who can teach you how to prepare the things I like."

"Are we going to live in your house near the trading post?"

Alanna was drawing the pheasant's brightly colored tail feathers through her fingers, but Hunter could see this question was a serious one. "Yes, the trapping is good here. Would you rather live in Virginia?"

"I was born in Maine. Virginia was never really my home."

"So you won't mind living in New York?"

"I'd not mind living anywhere with you."

Hunter gave her a portion of the pheasant, and sat down across from her to enjoy his own. "Thank you, but I don't think you'd like living in my village. My house is very small compared to what you would find there. We build our homes for at least a dozen families, and I think you would find them very crowded and noisy, compared to the big empty rooms of your aunt and uncle's house."

"A dozen Seneca families live together?"

Hunter found her astonishment enormously appealing. "Sometimes more. Each family has its own space, with a sleeping platform and a storage shelf above, like I have in my house. But as I said, the long houses are much larger. They can be one hundred fifty feet long, twenty-five feet wide, and nearly as tall as a two-story house."

Having seen his home, Alanna thought she could imagine such a structure. "How do you decide who lives where?"

"Each long house belongs to the oldest woman in the family, to her and her sisters, daughters, and granddaughters. They are the ones who live together. When a man marries, he goes to live in his wife's long house."

Alanna nodded thoughtfully. "Then you've made a very poor choice of wife, Hunter, because I have nowhere to take you."

"That may be true, but you have other advantages," Hunter revealed between succulent bites of superbly roasted pheasant. "There are a great many things to consider when choosing a wife. First, a man must pick a woman from a different clan. I'm from the wolf clan, and you are not, so that makes you a good choice. It's also best if the woman is not related to any of the man's female relatives. Clearly you are not related to me, so that's also in your favor."

Alanna was paying such close attention, she had difficulty remembering to eat, and paused long enough to swallow a bite. "The ideal wife then, is a complete stranger with a long house?"

Amused, Hunter chuckled. "Yes, for some men, but not for me. You are the ideal woman for me."

Alanna had donned her own clothes when they were dry, but Hunter had not bothered to reclaim his shirt. She looked at him now, seated on the ground, barechested, his ebony hair flowing free, eating pheasant with his fingers, and felt that despite the many differences between them, they were indeed the perfect pair. "To wed an Indian brave gives my life a certain symmetry," she mused.

Hunter had never heard the word. "What is that?" he asked.

"Balance, beauty of form."

Hunter nodded. "Yes, I understand. To escape the Abenaki to wed a Seneca is an unusual destiny, but it does seem right."

They had been discussing marriage all day, but Alanna still

had questions. "Do you consider us married now?" She attempted to sound nonchalant, but clearly his answer meant a great deal to her.

Hunter finished the last of a piece of breast, then wiped his mouth on the back of his hand. "We have no fancy ceremonies like whites do. When a couple wants to marry, they simply say so, and the man moves into the woman's long house. You have already pointed out that you have no house, so I have no choice but to live with you wherever I can."

"Just being together makes us husband and wife?"

"For me it does."

"I want more," Alanna confided. "I want an official marriage, one that will be recorded, so no one can call our children bastards."

Having little use for many of the white men's customs, Hunter's first impulse was to refuse, but the seriousness of Alanna's reason showed how much it meant to her, and he could not bring himself to say no. He owed her his life, but he did not want to force her to remind him of it to get her way. "It may take us awhile to find a priest who will agree to marry a white woman and an Indian, but when we do, I'll be proud to make you my wife again."

Hunter had spoken very slowly and deliberately, obviously making a concession, and while Alanna could not tell if it had been merely a small one, or a profound gesture of love, she was very grateful. "Thank you. I'll try and learn how to cook. I promise I will."

Hunter leaned over to squeeze her hand. "You're so pretty to look at, I don't even notice what I'm eating. You'll hear no complaints from me."

Alanna blushed at his effusive praise. "Are all Seneca braves as charming as you?"

"No, I learned that from white men."

Recalling the bearded frontiersmen she had seen watching

him fight, Alanna found such a boast impossible to believe. "Surely you don't mean the trappers I saw outside the trading post."

"Would that surprise you?"

"Yes, very much. Those shaggy brutes didn't look like they cared much about being attractive to women."

They had again spent the whole day together, but Hunter wasn't in the least bit bored with Alanna. She was so inquisitive and bright, he knew she would always enchant him. "No, it wasn't them," he assured her. "It was educated men with fine manners, men like Byron and Elliott, who showed me how to treat women, although they didn't realize I was watching them."

"I can't believe you really needed lessons."

"Not in some things, perhaps, but in others."

His sly smile left no question as to which skills he had mastered without tutoring, and Alanna could not help but be amused. "I didn't answer your question this morning, if it was a question. I'd like to stay here with you for as long as you like. The problems that await us in Virginia can't get any worse, so even if we are being foolish not to face them now, I think we should have whatever happiness we can."

Her words had a heartbreaking wistfulness, and Hunter feared she might well be right. For now, they had a delicious pheasant to share, and a night of passion to enjoy. He wanted it to be enough. "You must eat more," he encouraged, "or people will say I can't provide for you."

Alanna picked up a wing. "They'll say nothing of the kind, and you know it. Besides, if you're fond of plump women, why didn't you look for one to love?"

"Perhaps I did."

When he was as relaxed as he was now, Hunter had a marvelously expressive face, and emotions played across his handsome features in a subtle yet fascinating array. Watching him,

Alanna feared she had not known nearly enough about her own emotions before meeting him. Now she was ashamed that she had not understood enough about romance to send Graham Tyler away long before he had lost patience with her. Then there was Randolph O'Neil, who possessed endless patience it seemed, but she hadn't been able to share any more of herself with him than she had with Graham.

She twisted Elliott's ring on her finger, and knew that as much as she had loved him, a marriage between them would have left her feeling like a hollow shell of a woman, and he would have become badly disillusioned. Her life had been a long and painful journey up to that point, but she was certain she had arrived precisely where she ought to be. She responded easily to Hunter's jest.

"No, that can't possibly be true, because if you'd really wanted a plump wife, you'd have one."

"You see me as being that determined?"

"Yes, I do."

Hunter feared they were straying dangerously close to another discussion of his tragic affair with Melissa, and she was the last person he wanted to talk about that night. Growing cautious, he swiftly changed the subject. "The only thing I'm determined to do now is make you happy. I want to buy you some horses. I know how much you like them, and it would be good for us to own a few."

"Well, yes, I do love horses, but—"

"But what?"

Attempting to be tactful, Alanna chose her words with care. "I enjoy riding, and my uncle's horses were wonderful company when I didn't really wish to be alone, but I was never responsible for their care. The problem is, horses need shelter, especially here in New York, where the winters are more severe than Virginia, and constant care. Do you really think we ought to build a barn, and devote several hours each day to caring for horses? Won't that take too much of your time away from trapping?"

Hunter was amazed by how complicated she made owning horses sound. "I didn't realize you were such a practical girl."

"Being practical isn't generally considered a flaw."

"I thought only that having horses would please you."

Alanna could see she had insulted him, and that hadn't been her intention. "Thank you. I'd love for us to own some horses. It's just that there are so many things to consider first. Most couples, or at least the couples I've known, are engaged for several months, often a year before they wed. They have plenty of time not only for parties, but to make plans, and we've had none."

Hunter had finished eating and wiped his hands on the grass. "Is that what you want? Do you really believe if you go home and tell people we are engaged, they'll want to give us parties? Your aunt and uncle's friends won't waste their time on us, because they'll see nothing to celebrate."

His bitter sarcasm made Alanna fear she had only made matters worse. "Please, you mustn't misunderstand me. Parties have never interested me, and I don't need them now. I'll be proud to introduce you as my husband, and if people don't care to congratulate us, I shan't miss their friendship. You are the only one who matters to me, but we can't expect to always agree when we barely know each other."

"You killed two men to save me. That's all I need to know about you."

Not pleased to be reminded of that gruesome deed, Alanna could not suppress a shudder. "I'm not really the bloodthirsty sort, and I hope we'll never find ourselves in such a dangerous situation again."

"So do I, but if it does happen, I'll do a much better job of protecting you."

"You did your best."

Hunter disagreed. "I should have done better."

He looked sincerely distressed, and Alanna feared she was doing a very poor job of showing her love. Having also finished eating, she moved to his side. "It was your example that inspired me. I would never have found the courage to join in the fight, had you not been so brave."

Her smile was entrancing, but Hunter wasn't fooled by her flattery. "You are a very poor liar, Alanna. I think you would have tried to protect me, even if I had been on my knees pleading for my life like a coward."

Alanna sat back slightly. "I'm sure you never behave in a cowardly fashion."

"A Seneca warrior is taught to be brave."

"Can bravery be taught? Isn't courage a part of a man's character?"

"Perhaps." Wanting her more than to win the argument, Hunter slipped his hand into the thick curls at her nape to draw her close. "You are a part of me now, my heart, my soul."

As their lips met, Alanna had only a fleeting sense of the vast distance still separating them, before she was lost in the love Hunter was so anxious to give. His kisses were warm and deep, filled with the devotion he had just described, and Alanna wondered if every couple who fell in love shared the same delight in each other. She hoped they did, but for now, she was content to return Hunter's affection with no thought of others.

Seeking to bind her to him with invisible chains of love, Hunter treated Alanna with the same gentle sweetness he had shown earlier. She was an exquisite beauty, one he sincerely believed deserving of a slow, purposeful seduction. He circled her nipples with a lazy touch, his thumbnail barely brushing the fabric of her gown, until she was the one to reach for the buttons. He continued kissing her while she undid them, then eased her out of the gray dress he had never considered becoming.

"You're as lovely as a rose," he whispered. "You should wear more colorful clothes. Blue, green, yellow, pink, lavender, colors that are as pretty as you are."

"Thank you." Alanna hesitated a moment, as she attempted to find a similar compliment to pay him. "With your golden skin and black hair, your buckskins are already perfect for you. I can't even imagine your being more handsome."

Hunter reached for the pheasant feathers she had lain aside, and threaded them into his hair. "How do I look now?"

"Like an Indian."

"No, like *your* Indian." Hunter slipped his hand under her chemise to caress her bare breast, and nuzzled her neck with teasing nibbles. He drew her earlobe into his mouth, then traced the delicate perfection of her ear with his tongue.

"You're tickling me," she complained in a throaty giggle, but she leaned closer rather than draw away. She plucked one of the feathers from Hunter's hair, and drew it across his ribs. His deep chuckling protests simply encouraged her playfulness, and soon they were rolling over the grass, laughing, teasing, and tickling each other until the compulsion to turn their erotic game into something deeper overwhelmed them.

They cast their clothes aside, and with urgent kisses and adoring caresses, fanned passion's flames. A tall, muscular man and a lithe, graceful woman, they were a superbly matched pair, who created together a joy neither would ever have found, with another. Heightening the thrill of their loving, Hunter entered Alanna with a forceful lunge that made his possession of her, as well as hers of him, complete. He lay still as he kissed her, waiting for her body's subtle contractions to begin the ancient dance that would rock him clear to his soul.

Alanna bent her knee to caress his thigh, while her fingertips played over his back in an insistent rhythm. Hunter had expected his fair bride to be shy at first, but she had proven to be such an ardent woman, that he unleashed the strength he had held in check, and with a cadence that matched his quickening heartbeat, raced toward the ecstasy he wanted her to share. When he was certain that she had, he sought his own release deep within her.

Sated by pleasure, he believed their first day of marriage had come to a perfect end, until he glanced up and saw more than a dozen Abenaki warriors watching them from the opposite side of the lake.

Twenty-three

Pretending he hadn't seen them, Hunter ducked his head and whispered a hurried command in Alanna's ear. "On the count of three, we're going to get up and run for the trees. One, two, *three!*"

Although startled by his sudden change in mood, Alanna responded to his urgent tone; the instant he rolled aside and leapt to his feet, she grabbed his hand and joined him in sprinting for cover. It wasn't until they were safely hidden in the pines near their camp, that she dared look toward the lake. The Abenaki braves were now doubled over with laughter, but she doubted they would be amused for long.

"Could they be looking for Blind Snake and his friends?" she asked.

"They're too far from their homeland to be a hunting party, but they could be on their way to the Ohio Valley to fight again for the French. If they are, they would believe Blind Snake to be ahead of them. Let's hope they don't want to cross the lake to fight us."

"We have three muskets, two bows, and plenty of arrows," Alanna planned aloud. "If we keep moving as we fire at them, they might mistake the two of us for part of a much larger number, and flee."

Hunter's eyes widened in dismay. "You want to attack them?"

Alanna made a fast tally of the Abenaki braves. "There are

fifteen of them, and only two of us. Attacking them would be suicidal, but if they attack us, we'll have to confuse them long enough to get away. Can you reach our clothes?"

Hunter looked up to gauge the angle of the setting sun before shaking his head. Two of the Abenaki, holding their muskets aloft, had waded out into the lake. Their companions were now laughing at them, and he hoped sufficiently distracted for him to grab his weapons, if not the clothes they had left scattered about. Staying low, he left the trees only long enough to fetch his bow and quiver, along with the quiver belonging to the slain Abenaki.

When he returned to Alanna's side, he fit the nock of one of the Abenaki's arrows in his bowstring. "If they come more than halfway, I'm going to kill them," he vowed. "The others won't risk staying out in the open long enough to cross the lake."

"Perhaps not, but they can fire on us from the other side."

"That doesn't mean they'll hit us! Now hush."

Crouched beside the naked Indian, Alanna knew their lack of clothes was the least of their worries, but while she had been flattered to be described as a wood sprite, she didn't want to have to run through the forest looking like one. She too judged the angle of the sun, and feared it was not going to set soon enough to save them. "Oh, no, now another brave's coming across!"

Hunter gripped his bow more tightly. He could tell from the carelessness of the brave's actions that they did not perceive a pair of lovers as a threat. He intended to take every advantage of that mistake, and waited for them to reach the middle of the river. "When they fall," he whispered, "gather up our clothes as quickly as you can. You bring them, and I'll carry the other things, until it's safe to stop and dress."

Alanna nodded. Her chemise and drawers were within easy reach of his breechclout, leggings, and moccasins, but her dress would take another few steps to retrieve. She'd not been wearing the belt and knife, nor her stockings and boots, but the few articles she would have to pick up looked dreadfully far away. "I'll do it," she promised, but she was now shaking so badly she didn't really see how.

Hunter kept his eyes on the Abenaki wading across the lake. Their friends on the shore were shouting encouragement, but the three braves were having difficulty battling the current. One turned back, but the other two kept on coming. Their arms raised, their chests presented perfect targets, and Hunter took careful aim. A few more steps and they would either be defeated by the depth and current, or the distinctive arrows of their own tribe.

Alanna held her breath as the two braves fought their way across the southern tip of Lake Sacandaga. Swollen by melting snow, the water swirled around them, but they were strong young men who apparently relished a challenge. She felt Hunter grab for a second arrow almost in the same instant his first pierced the chest of the closest brave. The wounded man's companion was hit a split second later. From where Alanna was watching, they appeared to have merely stumbled and been caught by the current, for at one moment they were standing upright, and in the next they were swept away.

Fooled by Hunter's silent assault, the Abenaki observing from the shore believed their friends had merely lost their footing. Unaware of the braves' true peril, most again burst into laughter, while only a couple waded out into the lake to help them. Eager to get away, Alanna dashed out to fetch their clothes, while Hunter gathered up everything else. He threw her shawl on the ground, tossed on all it would hold, then grabbed the ends of the woolen square to form a bundle. With the muskets slung over his shoulder, he then led the way into the woods.

While she did not recall falling, Alanna had favored her

bruised knee all day, and she was soon not only out of breath, but limping badly. When Hunter finally stopped, she sank to the ground with the armful of clothing still in her grasp. Hunter quickly donned his clothes, and then helped her on with hers. He brushed the pine needles from her feet, before slipping on her stockings and boots.

"Here, take Elliott's knife. You know how to use it. By the time the Abenaki discover what really happened to the pair in the lake, it will be too dark for them to come after us. We're going to have to walk all night, though. Try and keep up with me. I don't want you to get lost."

When he helped her to her feet, Alanna swayed slightly, but then caught herself. "Let me carry something, the bag of jerky and my shawl at least."

"No, you'll need all your strength just to keep moving." He brushed her lips with a light kiss, turned away, and started off at an easy lope.

Alanna knew Hunter could run for hours, days perhaps, but she had an increasingly difficult time keeping up with him. She soon had to stop and grab hold of a tree trunk for support while she caught her breath, but she thought she could push off again before Hunter was lost from sight. The light was fading so rapidly, however, that before she realized what had happened, he was gone. She called to him, but still breathless, her voice echoed faintly off the trees surrounding her. The peaceful silence of the forest at twilight remained unbroken.

Bent on leading his bride to safety, Hunter did not turn back to look for Alanna until the darkness made it impossible for him to see her in a quick glance over his shoulder. He came to a halt, and waited a moment for her to catch up with him, then realized that she had fallen more than a few paces behind. He couldn't call out to her without revealing his position, and thereby also jeopardizing hers.

He had attempted to sound convincing when he had told

her they would not be followed, but he was not at all certain that the thirteen surviving Abenaki braves weren't trailing them at that very moment. In the gathering dusk, the terrain he had just crossed took on a menacing gloom, and memories of the nightmares he'd suffered while feverish came cascading back in heady waves of fear. There were no evil demons lurking in this forest, but there could easily be Abenaki braves, whose deeds would be doubly cruel. He had been eager to put as much distance between them and the Abenaki as he could, but he had not meant to run off and leave his bride to fend for herself.

Forcing himself to be calm, he retraced his steps. When he had traveled fifty feet or so, he began to call to Alanna in a hushed whisper, but there was no reply. Stealth was an important consideration, but finding her was imperative. Unable to think of a better idea, Hunter took out his flint and, after searching in the dark for dry branches, lit a small fire. Hoping that Alanna would see the glow, he waited a few minutes and then added more wood.

Once Hunter had disappeared, Alanna had been afraid to move, for fear she would stray off the path he had been following. Her knee was aching badly now and, frightened as well as hurting, she began to sob. She heard a small animal shuffling by, a raccoon perhaps, and rested her hand lightly on the hilt of Elliott's knife. Hunter had told her to travel south should they become separated, but she would be unable to set that course until dawn, when the sun would guide her way.

Feeling utterly defeated, she sank to the ground and prayed that Hunter would soon come for her. She knew she was an awful nuisance to him, but she had tried to match his pace, and simply hadn't been able to do so. Staring off into the forest, she saw a glimmer of light and, intrigued, stumbled to her feet. She doubted Hunter would have lit a fire, but praying whoever had would prove friendly, she started toward it.

Hunter heard only a soft rustling of leaves and, not daring
to again call Alanna's name, he stepped out of the circle of
light thrown by the fire, and waited to see who was approaching. Half-expecting one of the snarling demons from his nightmare, he had to suppress a loud whoop of joy when he caught
sight of his bride. He came forward to greet her. She looked
so forlorn that it broke his heart.

"I'm sorry," Alanna began. "I tried to keep up, but—"

Hunter stilled her apology with a kiss. "The fault is mine,
not yours," he assured her. "Do you need to rest awhile?"

"No, I'm afraid if I stop, I won't be able to get up again."

Hunter turned away to throw dirt on the fire and extinguished it. "This day has been too long for us both. We'll just
walk from here, and when you need to stop for the night, we
will."

"But we can't stop."

"If we can't even find each other, the Abenaki won't be
able to find us. Stop worrying, and let's go." This time Hunter
took her firmly by the hand and shortened his stride to match
hers. He had to be brave for her, but just being with her again
gave him courage.

Stretched across Hunter's lap, Alanna slept soundly until the
first rays of the morning sun grew too bright to ignore. She
stirred slightly, but because Hunter was still sleeping, she
chose to snuggle against him rather than stand up and stretch.
They had walked for hours before stopping, and she hoped
they would not have too much farther to go that day to reach
the trading post.

Easily frightened, she grew tense when she heard a whistle
that sounded too shrill to come from the birds who had begun
to sing before dawn. She hoped it was merely her own nervousness rather than imminent peril, and attempted to listen

carefully and analyze what she heard. Fully alert when the whistle came again, she was positive it was answered by a human voice speaking a language she didn't know.

"Hunter," she whispered. He opened his eyes, and she reached up to silence any response he might have made with her fingertips, then gestured toward the path which lay just a few feet away. "Someone's coming," she mouthed silently.

Hunter slid her off his lap, and then quickly surveyed the spot they had chosen to rest. He had purposely left the trail to provide them with a secluded hiding place, but now that he saw how little cover they really had, he pointed toward a cluster of blackberry vines and signaled for Alanna to follow him. Still carrying their weapons, he stayed low as he circled the vines, and when she joined him, he pulled her close.

"If it's the Abenaki searching for us, I'll let them pass and take another route back to the trading post. If they see us, I'll kill as many as I can, while you get away. Then I'll follow you."

"Don't ask me to leave you. Let's both go now."

"They're too close, they'd hear us. Don't argue with me about this, Alanna. I owe you my life, and I intend to safeguard yours."

Alanna reached for one of the muskets. "Is this loaded?" she asked.

"Yes," Hunter assured her.

Alanna swallowed hard. She had had no choice about shooting Blind Snake, but she prayed these Abenaki would not force her to kill again.

Impressed by her confidence, Hunter gave her a quick kiss and picked up his bow and an arrow. "Pray they don't see us," he whispered.

Alanna was already doing that, but she crouched even lower, desperately trying to make herself invisible. There was another whistle, this time much closer, and she was so frightened she had to remind herself to breathe. She dared not faint when the Abenaki would pass by so close she could almost reach out and touch them.

When the Abenaki at last came into view, they were traveling in a single file, spread out with several paces between them. The first man was moving slowly, scanning the trail before he took each step, but if he had been following their tracks, he missed seeing the place where they had turned east to stop for the night. He kept right on going past them. The next man in line glanced neither to the right nor left, and their hiding place remained undiscovered.

Peeking through the vines, Alanna began to count, *three, four, five,* as the Abenaki braves continued to stream by. It was the seventh man who gave a shout and started for them, but Hunter grabbed Alanna's wrist to stop her from firing. Terrified, she watched the brave bend down to peer into the vines. He was so close, she thought he could probably hear the frantic pounding of her heart, but Hunter remained motionless, and she followed his example. Her knee had begun to ache again and holding her cramped pose grew increasingly difficult, but the Abenaki brave persisted in his lazy perusal of the vines.

That his friends had kept on going rather than join the curious brave gave Alanna hope that he had not signaled a warning, but expecting to be sighted any second, she was nearly limp from anxiety by the time he straightened up and followed the others down the path. She set the musket aside and collapsed against Hunter. "I thought he would see us for sure. Was he just looking for berries?"

Equally exhausted by worry, Hunter sat down and tried to catch his breath. "Yes, that's why I let him live. Fortunately, none of these vines' berries were ripe enough to pick, or they might all have decided to join us for breakfast. Luck is still with us."

Alanna wasn't sure luck had all that much to do with it, but as composed as she was likely to get, she got to her feet. "You said you knew another way back to the trading post?"

Amazed that she had recovered so quickly from such a terrible scare, Hunter also rose. They still had some of the venison jerky left, and he handed her a strip. "Better eat this. To avoid the Abenaki, we'll have to swing farther to the north. It'll be a longer trip. Can you make it?"

Alanna bit off a piece of jerky. "I shall have to."

"Does that mean yes?"

Having spent a cold and restless night, Alanna felt anything but energetic, but she tried to smile. "Yes. Lead the way."

"You're a very brave girl."

"I certainly don't feel brave. I just want to go home."

Hunter rested his hand on her shoulder. "You're with me. You're already home."

Alanna reached up to give him a kiss, but, as she saw it, they were lost in the forest and being chased by thirteen Abenaki braves who were eager to see them dead. That wasn't her idea of being home, but she thought better of contradicting him. Instead, she slung the musket over her shoulder, and gestured for him to blaze the trail.

Despite the danger they were striving to avoid, Hunter set a leisurely pace, and they did not arrive at the trading post until the afternoon of the following day. While Alanna sat on the steps, Hunter went inside to see what he could learn about the Abenaki. All she wanted was to take a hot bath and sleep for a day or two, but she was soon surrounded by half a dozen trappers who stood regarding her with lascivious sparkles in their eyes.

Her once-stylish gown was now tattered and worn. She'd lost her frayed cap, and her long curls were a mass of tangles. None too clean, she tried to avoid their scrutiny by concentrating on the slits in her boots. Hunter had told her repeatedly that he could afford whatever she desired, and she certainly hoped the trading post stocked women's shoes.

Goaded by his friends, one of the trappers came to the bottom step. "You're an awful pretty girl to be all alone. Wouldn't you like some company?" he asked.

Had Alanna been walking along the street in Williamsburg, she knew his type would never have dared speak to her, but considering how disheveled she looked, she wasn't surprised at being approached. Deciding her best option was simply to ignore him, she looked away.

"She thinks she's too good for you, Wickert," one of the others called out, "but I'd make her pay *me* unless she took a bath."

His comment was met with hilarious laughter, and while Alanna had misinterpreted the first man's remark as friendly interest, she had no difficulty comprehending his companion's slur. Horrified to have been mistaken for a woman who sold her favors, she rose and started up the steps, but before she could enter the trading post, Hunter came through the door. Moving to his side, she silenced the trappers' laughter with a defiant glance.

"That your woman, Hunter?" Wickert asked.

Hunter had just sold the two muskets he had taken from the dead Abenaki, but he still had his own slung over his shoulder, along with two bows and two quivers. He slipped one arm around Alanna's waist and rested his other hand on the hilt of his knife. So they would not mistake his meaning, he enunciated his words clearly.

"No, she is my wife, so take care not to insult her."

"Your wife?" Obviously shocked by the unusual match, the trappers pulled their beards, whispered amongst themselves for a moment, and then, convinced none wished to argue with an Indian who had never been beaten in a fight, they shook their heads in silent dismay and shuffled away.

They had had so much trouble, Alanna wasn't even tempted to reveal she had already been insulted, and let them go without comment. "Have the Abenaki been here?" she asked instead.

"No one has seen any. I think they must have turned back and continued on their way, when they didn't overtake us yesterday. Come, let's go to my house. I can heat water to bathe, and make us something to eat."

"Do you think we'll be safe there? The dwelling is clearly an Indian's, and if I were searching for an Indian, that's the first place I'd look."

Hunter was tired and he wanted to go home. "That's where we planned to live, Alanna. Have you decided it isn't good enough for you?"

"No, of course not. What an awful thing to say. I just don't want us to be murdered in our sleep."

"I'll set traps by the doorways. Will that make you feel safe?"

To be reminded that he did not even have doors to lock didn't increase Alanna's sense of security, but she was too tired to argue the matter. "I'm sorry. I'm sure we'll be fine."

Hunter could see she had no such confidence, but he gave her a hug rather than call her a liar, and took her home. After encouraging her to lie down and rest, he borrowed a copper tub from the trading post, but by the time he had heated water over a fire, she was sound asleep, and he did not want to wake her. Making good use of the water himself, he then dressed in another set of buckskins.

He intended to cook supper, but first he wanted to make certain Alanna had a change of clothes. He sat down with the valise she had left there, and sorted through the contents. There were several sets of lingerie, toilet articles, and he was relieved to find another gown folded neatly in the bottom of the bag. She had left her petticoats lying across a storage shelf, so her change of attire was complete. He shook out the dress, and placed it atop the petticoats.

Her boots would have to be replaced, but he didn't want to even attempt that without her being there to try them on. With no shopping he could see to alone, he drew her brush through his own damp hair, and tried to imagine how his house would look when they returned with all of Alanna's possessions. Believing she would have too many pretty gowns to heap on a shelf, the house which had been perfect for him, now seemed maddeningly small. He could lengthen it, but he couldn't help but wonder if he ought not to start over, and build Alanna a brand new home of her own. It would be a great deal of work, but he wanted her to be happy.

For now, his immediate need was for a coffin and cart to fetch Elliott's body. That would surely be the saddest of chores, but there was no one else he could trust to do it. Believing he would have plenty of time to make those arrangements before Alanna stirred, he left to do so.

Not ten minutes later, Alanna awoke from her nap. Finding herself alone, she got up and hurriedly pushed aside the hides hung over the front doorway, to scan the adjacent woods for Hunter. When there was no sign of her new husband, she lowered the flap. While telling herself over and over that she was safe, Alanna filled the kettle to heat water for a bath. She first washed her hair, and had just eased herself down into the tub when Hunter returned. Startled by the sounds of his approach, she reached for the knife she had left within easy reach. After recognizing him, she dropped it quickly, but not before he had noted her fright.

"I'm going to build you a house," he decided in that instant. "Not like this one, but a sturdy structure of logs with shutters for the windows and doors you can bar. Will that make you happy?"

"I've only spent one night here," she reminded him. "I'll get used to it in time."

"You won't have to. You're a fine lady and deserve a real house." He had brought corn cakes and venison from the trading post, and set them aside before sitting down on a platform several feet away, to provide her with the privacy he thought she required. After all, she had been raised in a mansion, rather than a one-room house made of bark.

Sorry that he had misinterpreted her apprehension as criticism of his home, Alanna hastened to complete her bath. She scrubbed herself clean and used what was left of her old chemise to dry off. She donned fresh lingerie and the gown Hunter had set out for her. After spending nearly two weeks in the woods, the waistline was noticeably loose. Designed for travel, it was dark blue rather than one of the bright colors she knew he admired.

"I'm sorry this isn't a prettier dress. Does the trading post carry fabrics for women's clothes?" she asked.

"Nothing you'd wear. We'll have to buy you a new pair of boots, but you can throw them away and have others made when we get back to Williamsburg."

Alanna tousled her hair with both hands in an effort to dry it. "I don't need a lot of fancy clothes, Hunter. I used to wear very simple gowns, and that's really all I need."

Her expression and tone were sincere, but Hunter saw a fragile beauty who had already suffered through far too much to be with him. He did not want her again dressing in as humble a fashion as when they had first met. "No, you have pretty clothes now, and I want you to wear them. Earning money has always come easily to me, and I can afford to dress you in fine clothes."

"But if I don't need or want them—"

"I'm too hungry to argue about your clothes. We'll have to eat venison again. Do you mind?"

"No, it was very good." Elliott's valise was right where he had left it, and Alanna could not help but recall that the last time they had dined there, her cousin had been with them.

Hunter noted the direction of her glance and understood the sorrow that had softened her pose. "I'm going after Elliott's body tomorrow. I'm taking a wagon and several other men, so if any of the Abenaki are still lurking nearby, we'll have no trouble with them."

"How many men?"

"Three."

"Do you think four men can defeat more than a dozen Abenaki?"

"Yes, easily," Hunter boasted, "but I'm sure they're gone."

"I still think you should set the traps."

"Can you remember not to get up during the night and step into one?"

Alanna came forward and knelt at his side. She rested her hands on his knee and affected an innocent smile. "I shan't want to get up, if you give me good reason not to."

Hunter reached out to fondle her cheek. She was such a gentle creature, but also a very passionate one. The softness of her skin filled him with a longing that made it difficult to remember how worried he had been about the rustic nature of his house. He was lost in her adoring gaze, and wanted so badly for her to be happy.

"I love you," he whispered. He leaned down to kiss her, and he would have made love to her right then, had her stomach not rumbled noisily and made them both laugh. "I'm being a very poor host. Come sit outside to dry your hair, and I'll roast the venison outdoors."

Alanna followed him outside, and while attempting to be discreet, nevertheless kept a close watch on the forest bordering his home. Their home, she corrected herself, although it did not feel like home to her as yet. With nothing to do, her thoughts soon drifted to Christian. She wished she could think of a new and eloquent argument to soften Hunter's heart toward the boy, but none came to her.

The wistfulness of Alanna's expression wasn't lost on Hunter, but he assumed she was thinking of Elliott, and did not question her. One of the trappers who had shot a deer that morning had shared the meat with him, and as Hunter watched the venison roast, he decided he would have to become far more conscientious. He was now a married man and would have to provide for his family himself, rather than rely on the generosity of the men who had shared their provisions with him in the past. They had admired his skill with his fists, and had used gifts of food to gain his friendship. With the fighting over, he assumed those favors would also be at an end.

After supper, Hunter and Alanna remained seated outside to watch the stars appear. She wrapped her shawl around her shoulders and leaned against him. Neither had spoken for a long while, and yet she felt perfectly comfortable. He had laced his fingers in hers, and she brought his hand to her lips.

"I do love you, Indian," she murmured with unmistakable fervor.

As much as he was enjoying the moonlight, Hunter wanted to indulge his passion for Alanna even more. He rose and pulled her to her feet. "Let's go inside. Making love on a bearskin is far nicer than making love in the grass."

He was obviously speaking from experience, but Alanna didn't want to hear about other women, so she chose not to ask how he knew. Instead, she led him into the long house and then stepped into his arms. "As long as I'm with you, I don't care where we make love."

Hunter raised his hands to her hair, tilted her head back, and then spread hungry kisses down her throat. He needed her in a way he had never thought he would ever need a woman, and he gradually peeled away her clothing without ever once completely releasing her from his grasp. When she was at last nude, he dropped to his knees and pressed a flurry of kisses across the flatness of her stomach. In response, she slid her hands through the fringe on his shirt, silently expressing her delight before she pulled the buckskin garment over his head.

Hunter ran his hands down the back of her legs, and caressed the tender skin behind her knees with his thumbs. He had never met a woman whose skin delighted him so, but just touching Alanna was an endless thrill. He sat back and pulled her astride his lap, to bring the fullness of her breasts against the flat planes of his chest. He wrapped his arms around her waist and parted her lips with his tongue, to begin a deep kiss he planned never to end. Holding her tight, he plundered her mouth before slipping a hand between her legs. She was already wet, and when he slid his fingers up into her, she gave a small, grateful moan.

His fingertips wet with her essence, he teased her with a slow, circling touch that made her body's most sensitive bud swell with anticipation. She wrapped her legs around him, hugging him so tightly he had to suck in his stomach to release his belt, but then it was a simple matter to shove his breechclout aside and enter her with a swift, upward thrust. His shoulders against a sleeping platform, he grasped her waist to guide her motions, and eased her not only up and down, but also in a slow, grinding oval.

Riding the rapture he fueled with each stroke, every inch of Alanna's flesh was pressed against Hunter. Her hands were wound in his magnificent mane, her tongue filled his mouth, and her legs clutched his back with a strength that mirrored her desire. She wanted all he could give and, even after the ultimate joy rocked them both, she clung to him still. Several minutes passed before she felt the need to speak.

"I don't think we needed a bearskin," she whispered, before sending her tongue darting into his ear.

His passions sated for the moment, Hunter groaned, but he then vowed to prove a bearskin's value just as soon as he was able.

Twenty-four

"Of course, I remember you, Miss Barclay," Captain Henderson welcomed Alanna aboard the barge. Expecting Elliott to be with her, he looked up and down the dock for him. "Where's your cousin? Surely you're not returning home alone?"

Hunter had expected such a question, and supplied the answer to spare Alanna the painful repetition of the details of Elliott's death. "We'll need space to transport his coffin." Then he added, "And a cabin."

On one of his barge's stops at the trading post, Henderson had seen Hunter fight, and had been as awestruck as any of the other men who had had that privilege. He had never spoken with him though, and was frankly amazed to find him not only fluent in English, but supervising Miss Barclay's travel arrangements. Preferring to take on that responsibility himself, he reached out to take Alanna's hand.

"I'm so dreadfully sorry to learn of your cousin's death. While our acquaintance was brief, he impressed me as being a fine, young man. I'll find a place for his coffin, and you may have the same cabin you occupied on the way here. Will there be someone to meet you when we reach New York City?"

"I'll be with her," Hunter explained.

Taken aback for a moment, Captain Henderson nevertheless attempted to smile as though he had often seen young ladies from Virginia travel with Indian escorts. Knowing Hunter to

be an expert with his fists, he took care not to insult him.
"Will you be wanting a cabin, too, or simply passage on
deck?"

"My wife and I will share her cabin," Hunter replied.

Assuming Hunter was referring to an Indian woman, Captain Henderson hurriedly surveyed the dock, but he didn't see
any women, Indian or otherwise. "Where is your wife? We've
a schedule to keep, and must be on our way the instant Mr.
Barclay's coffin is loaded on board."

Since they had returned from the forest, Hunter had had
several opportunities to refer to Alanna as his wife, and he
had savored every one. He was proud to be her husband, but
he also took a perverse pleasure in watching how badly he
shocked people when he announced the fact. He slipped his
hand around Alanna's waist and drew her close.

"She's standing right here."

Predictably, Captain Henderson's mouth fell agape. Alanna
had impressed him as being a cultured woman, and he could
not reconcile her obvious good breeding with Hunter's announcement. In his travels, he had met a brave or two with a
white wife, but he would never describe those women as ladies.

"I don't know what to say," he blurted out.

"You needn't say anything," Alanna responded. "We shan't
delay your departure. Hunter's friends are waiting to bring the
coffin on board. If you'll just direct them where to put it, we
can get under way."

That she could provide such poised directions under what
he considered the most wretched of circumstances, sent a
shiver down the captain's spine, and preferring to concentrate
on his duties rather than the scandalous nature of her choice
of husband, he gave a slight bow and excused himself. Hunter
returned to the dock to supervise the loading of the coffin,
and Alanna moved to the far rail, where the tranquil view of
the Mohawk River was undisturbed.

She had such ghastly memories of her stay in the area, it was difficult to contemplate returning to make it her home. She tried to think only of how blissfully happy Hunter made her feel, but she had seen too many men die for that joy to be complete. When Hunter came to her side, she attempted unsuccessfully to hide her sorrow behind a brave smile.

With no hope of being accepted by her aunt and uncle, Hunter readily understood Alanna's downcast mood, and did not torture her further by commenting on it. They were together, and he hoped the prospects for a pleasant life would not elude them forever. As the barge pulled away from the dock, he drew his bride into his arms, and held her for a long moment before speaking.

"I hope the captain's lack of manners didn't embarrass you. I'm afraid his startled reaction is the best we can hope to receive."

"We shan't see him again until our next voyage up the Hudson. It doesn't matter what he thinks."

While Hunter admired her resolve, he was sorry loving him complicated her life. "If things become too difficult, we may have to pretend to be traveling separately," he suggested.

"Are you ashamed of me?"

She looked sincerely distressed by that possibility, and Hunter hastened to reassure her. "No, of course not, but I don't want people to say mean things to you, because you're with me."

He was a tall, well-built, handsome man, but he was also clearly an Indian, and Alanna understood exactly what he meant. "If tasteless gossip bothered me, I'd not have become your wife. Now let's think no more about problems, and simply enjoy the view."

Hunter leaned close to whisper in her ear. "The river isn't half as pretty as you. Which cabin is yours?"

When he winked at her, Alanna knew exactly what he wanted. Thinking that losing themselves in each other preferible to dreading the difficulties that lay ahead, she took his hand and led the way. Her cabin was small, and the bunk almost too narrow for two, but neither uttered a single word of complaint. By the time the barge finally docked in New York City, the bond affection had forged between them was deep, but Alanna had not forgotten that Christian's future still lay in doubt.

"Elliott had inquired about passage to Newport News, but we hadn't expected to remain so long with you. I'm sure we'll have to begin making the arrangements all over again."

"I know how to find a ship," Hunter assured her. "While I do, I want you to stay on board with Elliott's coffin. Not that it would get lost, but it could easily become misplaced among the barge's other cargo, if there isn't someone here to prevent it, and that mustn't happen. It will only take me an hour or two to find a ship bound for Virginia. Will you wait here for me?"

Equally concerned that the coffin reach Williamsburg safely, Alanna thought his suggestion sensible and readily agreed. They informed Captain Henderson of their plans, and Alanna found a convenient place to wait on deck until Hunter returned. The Indian hadn't been gone more than five minutes, before the captain came to her side.

"Miss Barclay, I've just learned that a ship belonging to a friend of mine is sailing for Newport News on the evening tide. I could have my men transfer your late cousin's coffin on board right now, if you like."

Disappointed his offer hadn't come a few minutes earlier, Alanna frowned as she responded. "If only you'd known that before Hunter left, it would have saved him what I'm afraid may prove to be a great deal of effort. I'll have to wait until he returns. If he hasn't completed making arrangements, then perhaps he can speak to your friend."

Believing he was doing her a favor, Captain Henderson rephrased his offer. "Miss Barclay, forgive me for what I fear

will seem to be an intrusion in your life, but I have your very
best interests at heart, and I hope you'll accept my advice in
the spirit in which it's intended. You must know that a liaison
which might be tolerated in the backwoods will be severely
criticized among Virginia's far more genteel society. Please
consider leaving now.

"When Hunter returns, I'll tell him you've already left for
home. It will spare you the embarrassment of dealing with the
brave, and no one in Virginia need ever learn of your acquaintance with him."

"You're right," Alanna informed him with an icy calm that
belied the fury of her outrage. "I do consider your advice an
unwarranted intrusion in our lives. Will you please have your
men place my cousin's coffin on the dock? I don't wish to
remain on your ship another minute."

The captain raised his hands in a plea for understanding.
"Please, Miss Barclay, just consider my suggestion. Hunter
referred to you as his wife, but did a clergyman actually conduct a ceremony, or is he following the tradition of his people
which requires no legal sanction for a marriage?"

"That's no concern of yours, Captain."

"Oh, but it is," Henderson argued. "With your cousin dead
and no other relative here, I feel it's my duty to advise you.
My interest is purely a fatherly one, I assure you. If Hunter
is not your legal husband, then leave him now, my dear, and
never admit to a soul that you knew him."

Beyond anger, Alanna spoke through clenched teeth. "Save
your advice for the people who ask for it, Captain. Now must
I summon several of your men myself? I want my cousin's
coffin removed from this vessel immediately." To emphasize
her demand, she picked up her valise and Elliott's, crossed the
deck, and marched down the gangplank. When Hunter returned
more than an hour later, he found her standing on the dock
beside Elliott's coffin.

Anger was etched so clearly on Alanna's features, that he could not mistake her mood. "What happened?" he asked. "Why didn't you stay on board?"

"I'd rather not repeat the captain's insults. Were you able to book passage for us home?"

"Yes, but the ship doesn't sail until day after tomorrow. The coffin can be loaded now, and you and I can spend the next couple of nights at an inn. Now either you tell me what the captain said, or I'll confront him myself, but I'll not allow anyone to mistreat you."

Alanna just shook her head. "The matter isn't worth pursuing."

Unable to agree, Hunter kissed her cheek, then strode up the gangplank. The captain did not see him coming in time to flee to his cabin, but as Hunter approached him, he cast an anxious glance in that direction. The man's obvious fright made it plain he regretted whatever it was he had said to Alanna, and Hunter challenged him boldly.

"You owe my wife an apology."

Assuming the defiant young woman had recounted their conversation, Captain Henderson sought to bolster his courage by taking a deep breath, and exhaling slowly. In his view, his advice had been sound and, despite the obvious danger, he felt compelled to repeat it. "I mean no offense," he insisted, "but if you two are not legally wed, it would be a kindness for you to leave her now. All you'll ever bring her is shame, and if you truly love her, that's the last thing you'd ever want."

Hunter clenched his fists at his sides. He could have killed the captain with his bare hands, but knew that was no way to prove he was a fit husband for Alanna. "I am offended," he replied, "and so was my wife. Fortunately, we have far more generous natures than you, and we'll forgive you, this time. If we should ever travel on your barge again, remember, you'll not have a second chance to show us the respect you should."

Too frightened by that veiled threat to speak, Captain Henderson simply nodded.

Thoroughly disgusted, Hunter turned his back on him and rejoined Alanna on the dock. He had already arranged for a cart to transport the coffin; when it arrived, he helped the driver to load the long, pine crate and then took Alanna's arm. "Now we need to find an inn and a preacher. I want to marry you this afternoon."

Alanna was delighted by his plan, until she noticed it was hatred rather than love that lit his gaze. "We needn't wed to satisfy Captain Henderson's notion of propriety," she informed him. "We need only please ourselves."

She glanced away as though they were discussing a matter of little consequence, but Hunter knew otherwise. She did not want their children to be called bastards, and neither did he. "This has nothing to do with Henderson. I told you when we were still in the forest that I'd be proud to marry you. This is our first opportunity to do it. Have you changed your mind about being my wife?"

Alanna had just spent a miserable hour mulling over Captain Henderson's unwanted advice. She was well aware that marrying Hunter would make her an outcast, but after her family had been killed, that was all she had ever been. She had lived on the edge of her cousins' world, basked in the reflection of their happiness, but she had never really shared it. She had never felt as though she truly belonged. Only Hunter's love made her feel complete.

Alanna looked up at him. "More than one of my aunt and uncle's friends regarded me as unbalanced. I dare say there were times when my relatives must have agreed. If you don't mind having a wife who's the subject of such unfortunate rumors, then I certainly won't mind being married to you."

Relieved, Hunter wrapped her in an enthusiastic hug. "Come on, let's find someone to marry us first. If we stop at an inn on the way, we won't want to leave our room until our ship sails."

Understanding precisely what he meant, Alanna blushed prettily. She laced her fingers in his and, with a confident stride, accompanied him gladly.

Captain Henderson watched them depart. A cautious man, he was content commanding a boat on the Hudson and Mohawk rivers, rather than aspiring to long and dangerous voyages at sea. He avoided risks of all kinds, but as he watched the unlikely pair of lovers hurry off hand in hand, he could not help but feel a small twinge of envy at their devotion.

After a second minister declined to marry them because Hunter refused to even discuss converting to Christianity, Alanna and he were wed by a magistrate at city hall. The office where the ceremony was performed was small, dusty, and filled with clutter. The prescribed exchange of vows lacked even a hint of poetry, but the marriage was legal and duly recorded, which was enough to satisfy the requirements of the bride and groom.

Hunter had given Alanna a gold wedding band, and she turned it around her finger slowly, as he inquired about lodgings at the Lamp and Oil, which appeared to be a respectable inn. Clearly astonished when the Indian referred to his demure blond companion as his wife, the clerk shook his head regretfully, and swore in an embarrassed stutter that they had no rooms available. There were keys hanging on the wall behind the desk, but rather than argue, Hunter escorted Alanna back outside. It was getting late, and they were both tired.

"I think he was lying," Alanna said.

Speaking from past experience, Hunter agreed. "I know he was. After the trouble we had arranging a wedding, it shouldn't surprise me, but it did." There was another inn a few doors down on the opposite side of Pearl Street, and he gestured toward it. "Let's try over there, but this time I want you to go up to the clerk and ask for a room. Say your husband will arrive later. When I join you, it will be too late for him to object."

"We shouldn't have to deceive anyone to rent a room."

"No, we shouldn't," Hunter assured her. "But if it's either that or sleep on the street, which would you prefer?"

Alanna needed a moment to ponder the question. "It's a matter of principle," she argued.

Hunter shrugged. "Do you want to spend our wedding night on the street? There are plenty of sailors roaming about, so we'd probably attract quite a crowd."

"You wouldn't!"

Hunter's face lit with a wicked grin. "I love you too much to promise that I wouldn't."

Alanna picked up her valise. "All right, I'll see what I can do. Wait right here."

Hunter crossed his arms over his chest and leaned back against the wall of the inn which had refused them. "I won't stray."

Alanna had never stayed at an inn, but having watched Hunter inquire about a room, she crossed the street and entered the Owl's Eye. Pretending to know exactly what she was doing, she went straight to the desk. "My husband and I will require a room for the next two nights," she announced confidently. "Do you have something nice available?"

Charmed by her soft southern accent and elegant manners, the elderly clerk positively beamed with pleasure. "I'll show you up to our best room myself. Now if you'll just sign the register, Mrs.—?"

"Hunter," Alanna replied. She picked up the pen, dipped it into the inkwell, and signed *Mr. and Mrs. Hunter, Williamsburg, Virginia*. She had the money Elliott had brought for their trip, and paid for the two nights in advance. "Is it possible to have supper served in our room?"

"Certainly, I'll see to it personally."

"Thank you. My husband will be joining me soon, and he has an enormous appetite. Please be sure you send up enough food."

"Our portions are always generous. The cook has prepared an especially delicious stew this evening. I'm sure you'll be pleased."

"I'm pleased already," Alanna assured him. She followed him up the stairs and down the hall, to a neatly furnished room which was of sufficient distance from the public tavern downstairs to be relatively quiet. The windows provided a splendid view of the harbor, and the feather bed was wide and comfortable. Best of all, it was located next to the back staircase.

"I know it's late in the day, but could I still arrange for a bath?"

"Usually I would have to say no, but for you, my dear, I'll make an exception."

"Thank you so much." Alanna closed the door behind him, counted to ten, peeked out to make certain the clerk had returned to his post, and then made her way down the back stairs. At the bottom, the passageway to the right opened onto the kitchen, while a door at the left led outside. She went through it and waved to Hunter from the side of the building. When he loped across the street to join her, she took his arm.

"Come on, there's a set of back stairs. We can come and go as often as we like, without being seen."

"And if I prefer using the front door?" Hunter asked.

"You can use it tomorrow."

"If I have the strength to leave our bed."

Knowing how much he enjoyed teasing her, Alanna just shook her head. Because they had already been together, she didn't feel as though it would really be their wedding night.

Perhaps it was because their marriage ceremony had been so terribly unromantic. Nearly a year later, she could still recall Melissa's wedding vividly. They had all worn such beautiful dresses. The flower-decked church had been filled with friends, and the reception afterward had been the lavish one Melissa had dreamed of having. Only Hunter had been missing, and he had had every right to be there.

When they reached their room, Hunter pulled Alanna into his arms, but he felt her sadness despite the gracefulness of her pose. "I'm sorry," he began.

"Don't be."

"Don't you want to know why?"

"It doesn't matter why," Alanna assured him. "You needn't be sorry about anything."

"Your life will never be what it would have been had you married a white man, and I'm sorry for that."

Alanna reached up to touch his cheek. "I'm not, although you may have been better off with a Seneca maid, who would already know how to cook your favorite dishes." She reached up on her tiptoes to kiss him, and his response was so enthusiastic that when the maid knocked at their door, it took them a long moment to break apart. Hunter stepped behind the screen in the corner and remained concealed, until the maid had finished lugging in the tub, pails of hot water, and left.

"I've never given a woman a bath. May I help you?" Hunter then asked.

Alanna had been managing her own baths for a very long time, but the prospect of having his help was so appealing, she smiled invitingly. "yes, that would be nice. I wish the tub were large enough to hold us both."

"I'm used to bathing in the river, but I can make a big wooden tub for you, when we get back home. Would you like that?"

"Yes, I would." She placed her hands over his as he unfastened the buttons on her bodice. "I'd rather not put on this dress again. They're going to send up our supper. Would you mind if I dined in my nightgown?"

"Not if it will save me time getting you into bed."

"Are you always so bold, sir?" Alanna had responded to his suggestion in the same teasing tone in which it had been given, but he looked startled rather than amused, and she realized there was no question about his boldness with Melissa. Loath to mention her cousin, she turned away and began to peel off her dress.

"I do hope there'll be time enough to bathe before supper arrives. The clerk praised the cook's talents, but I suppose that's to be expected."

Alanna opened her valise and removed her nightgown before slipping out of her dress. Hunter knew why she had changed the subject. Equally unwilling to speak Melissa's name, he walked over to the window and looked out until she was seated in the tub. He wanted only the two of them to occupy the room, and he didn't kneel down beside the tub until he had successfully banished all thoughts, save those of his bride.

He lathered up the soap and washed her shoulder. "You have freckles now from running around in your chemise. Look, they're sprinkled all the way down your arm."

"They'll soon fade."

"I hope not. I like them."

"They aren't considered ladylike."

"You've done a great many things which aren't ladylike, since meeting me," Hunter reminded her. "Having a few freckles is the least of them."

"Yes, I suppose you're right." Alanna leaned back to get more comfortable, and closed her eyes. "Do all Seneca braves spoil their wives as shamefully as you're spoiling me?"

Hunter leaned close to kiss the hollow of her shoulder.

"Why do you ask? Do you want another Seneca for a husband?"

"I can't even imagine myself being married to another man."

"Good, don't even try." Hunter slid his soapy caress down her arm and across her breasts, slowly circling the pale tips and flicking them with his thumb, until they formed pert buds. Alanna opened one eye, but his smile silenced any protests she might have been about to make, and he moved his hand down her ribs.

"You're much too thin," he lamented softly. He deliberately let the bar of soap slip through his fingers, and had to pull off his shirt to keep from wetting the sleeve, as he felt between her legs to retrieve it. In a playful mood, he did not really look for the soap until Alanna reached down to grab his wrist.

"I thought you wanted to give me a bath?"

"That's what I'm doing."

"No, it isn't." Alanna leaned forward to kiss him, and his passionate response made any further complaint about his methods too trivial to mention.

Hunter wound Alanna's long curls around his left hand to keep her mouth pressed to his, while he continued to tease her with his right. Made slippery by the soap, his fingertips slid over her inner creases and folds in an exotic dance that played upon her senses, until she shuddered beneath him in an ageless gesture of complete surrender. He sat back and waited patiently, but she didn't speak until the bathwater had grown cold.

"If we'd been in the river, I would have drowned."

"I'd not have let you drown," Hunter assured her. Pausing often to give loving hugs, he helped her to her feet, wrapped her in a towel, and then slipped the white cotton nightgown over her head.

Alanna could not help but wonder if he would respond in

the same fashion if she were to bathe him with such an intimate caress, but the maid knocked at the door before she could make that suggestion. Hunter again stepped behind the screen, but the girl saw his buckskin shirt lying on the foot of the bed.

"I see your husband's here, ma'am. I'll tell the cook to fix your tray."

Alanna followed the maid's glance, but because buckskins weren't worn exclusively by Indian braves, she felt no need to explain her husband's choice of attire. "Would you please?" She moved aside as the girl emptied and removed the tub, then closed the door behind her.

"Do you really think you still need to hide?"

Hunter crossed to the window, but while they had been playing in her bath, it had grown dark, and there was nothing to see but the glow of the street lamps in the distance. "Do you remember how you ran from me?"

"I've begged you to forgive me for that."

Hunter sat down on the windowsill. "I have, but for all we know, that maid also lost her family in an Indian raid. Let's not give her any reason to go shrieking from the room."

Alanna toyed with the lace trim on her cuffs. Hunter had told her that he had not killed anyone before fighting with the militia in the Ohio Valley, and she wanted to believe him. His expression was the honest, open one she had come to expect from him, and certain he was wholly good, she quickly forced away the gruesome images his comment had brought to mind.

"You'd be with me. I'm sure that would make the fact that you know how to behave as a gentleman plain."

"Last spring, I was with Byron and Elliott, but that failed to convince you I was worth knowing."

"Yes, I know. I was very rude."

"No, you were merely frightened. I'm being very rude now to remind you of it."

Another knock at the door announced the arrival of their supper, and while Hunter chose to stay out of sight, Alanna took the tray from the maid, rather than again invite the girl into the room. There was a small table in the corner, and she placed it there. They had been sent a huge bowl of beef stew, a loaf of bread still warm from the oven, butter, half a dozen apricot tarts, and a pitcher of ale.

"This all looks very good. I know you don't drink ale, and I should have asked for something else for you, water at least."

"The water here tastes like it came from a ship's bilge. I'm better off with nothing." Hunter came to her side and set the ale and goblets on the table. He then picked up the tray, carried it over to the bed, and placed it in the middle. "Let's eat here rather than at the table. We'll be more comfortable."

Alanna had no objection to making a picnic of their supper, and when he climbed up on the foot of the bed, she took her place opposite him. She scooped up a plate of stew for him, and then fixed one for herself while he sliced the bread. They had eaten so many meals together, that they fell into a comfortable routine, and served each other without waiting to be asked.

"Among the Seneca, we eat only one meal each day, and that's in the morning. Men and boys are served first, and when they are finished, the women and girls eat together."

"What happens if the men are so hungry, they don't leave enough for the women to eat?"

"Food is always so plentiful that doesn't happen, but if it did, the women would simply cook more. They'd not go hungry. Whatever the women leave, goes into a clay pot that's kept on the embers of the cooking fire. If anyone is hungry later, they help themselves."

"With just the two of us, I hope you don't want to dine separately."

Alanna was looking down at her plate rather than up at him,

but Hunter could sense her confusion. "You're not an Indian girl, Alanna. I'll never expect you to act like one. Besides, I would get very lonely eating all by myself. I'd much rather we shared our meals, as we always have."

"You'd tell me if there were something you'd like me to do, wouldn't you?"

"Yes, but you must ask me, too. Don't worry that because I'm Indian, I'll always say no. I'll do whatever I can to make you happy."

Alanna looked up at him, her green eyes filled with a skeptical glint. Her only wish was to raise Christian, but he already knew that. He had grown increasingly considerate, but had not once mentioned his son. Keeping to her original plan not to discuss the boy until Hunter had had the opportunity to see him, she kept quiet about him now.

"Thank you, but you're already a wonderful husband."

Not convinced of that, Hunter worried that she was merely flattering him. "Do you think a woman ought to flatter her husband?" he asked.

"Only if he deserves it," Alanna replied, "and you do."

"We've not been married even one day," Hunter reminded her. "Perhaps you should wait a week or two, before you make such a decision."

Alanna hoped that within two weeks' time, Christian would have become a part of their family. She prayed for that with every breath, but she smiled easily as though his son's welfare were not such a horribly divisive issue between them. "All right, I will, but if you continue to be as attentive as you've been today, I'll not change my opinion." Hunter responded with a smile that warmed her clear through.

"I'll try not to give you a reason to change your opinion in an entire lifetime," he vowed. "Two weeks will be no challenge at all."

Alanna reached across their plates to caress his arm. Their

experiences that day had taught her they would have to overcome not only society's stern condemnation of their union, but their own very real differences. And yet, when she touched him, all she felt was the delicious sensation of love. Wanting their wedding night to be perfect in all respects, she told herself that for the time being, it was enough.

Twenty-five

Hunter insisted that Alanna eat the last of the apricot tarts. He then removed the tray and brushed the bread crumbs off the bed. "Did you have enough to eat?" he asked.

"I'm afraid I had too much." Alanna licked the apricot filling from her fingertips. She fluffed up the pillows and leaned back against them. "That was a truly wonderful meal."

"It wasn't as fancy as what your aunt serves."

"Food doesn't have to be fancy to be good."

"That's true." Hunter stretched out across the foot of the bed. They had been having such a good time, he did not want to spoil it, but he had a concern he felt compelled to share.

"There was a lot of talk at the trading post about war with France. If it comes to that, the British will probably follow the Hudson River north, and sail through Lake Champlain to strike at Montreal and Quebec. Your aunt and uncle may tell you that living with me on the Mohawk will be too dangerous. They might try and convince you to remain with them, until all threat of war is past. That could take years. We should talk about it now, and be prepared for such a suggestion."

That he would want to discuss the possibility of war on their wedding night caught Alanna by surprise, but she already knew what she wanted to do. "I'm your wife, Hunter, and my place is with you. It won't matter what danger we face, if we're together, and I doubt anything could be worse than what we've already suffered. Not that we should admit to the killing of five Abenaki, but you and I know how to survive. My aunt and uncle are entitled to their opinions, but they'll not change my mind. I want to be with you."

Alanna looked very pretty and sweet, but Hunter would never forget how swiftly she had come to his rescue. He was embarrassed now that he had been so ungrateful. "They may cry and plead with you to stay."

"That's very unlikely."

"What do you expect then?"

"I'm trying not to think about it."

Hunter did not understand how she could avoid dwelling on her aunt and uncle's reactions. "We have to see them. We owe them an explanation about Elliott, and there's our marriage to announce."

Alanna turned to punch the pillow behind her into a more comfortable shape. "Yes, I know, but please, must we talk about them tonight?"

"I think it's good to have a plan."

"Yes, I agree. We ought to practice what we wish to say and how we'll handle their response, whatever it might be, but won't there be plenty of time for that once we're on board the ship bound for home?"

Hunter did not want to speculate on what the captain's reaction might be to their traveling together, but he was worried. "I told Captain Michaels that I was bringing my wife, but I didn't describe you. What if he believes like Henderson, that it's his duty to tell you to leave me? We may still have to travel separately."

Alanna's heart fell. She had so many fears about the difficulties they would encounter at home, that she couldn't bear to think that getting there might pose additional problems. She closed her eyes for a moment, and then came up with a plan.

"No, all we need to do is board separately. When Elliott and I sailed from Newport News, the crew was so busy making ready to depart, they just wanted the passengers to stay out of their way. If you go aboard early, and I wait until the last minute, the captain will be in too great a rush to sail to be concerned about us. Besides, Elliott's coffin will be stowed in the hold, and he won't be able to ask us to leave without taking the time to unload it."

Hunter nodded thoughtfully. "You're very bright, Alanna. Maybe you should do all of our thinking."

He sounded insulted rather than pleased, and Alanna couldn't understand why. "With the problems we're sure to have, we'll both need to have all our wits about us," she swore. "It's only that I've been away much longer than we'd planned, and I want Elliott to receive a proper burial so badly, I don't care what we have to do to get home. That's my main concern, not manipulating Captain Michaels into doing my bidding."

Hunter knew that, and he reached out to tickle her foot. "We mustn't fight tonight. It would be a very bad way to begin our marriage."

Counting Elliott, six men had died in the time they had been together, and that was already such a bad omen, Alanna feared their troubles might prove endless. "We can't let other people's uncharitable views tear us apart, but even if we have to live in the deepest, darkest part of the forest to find happiness, I'd be willing to do it."

Her fervent vow touched Hunter deeply, and he quickly shifted his position to draw her into his arms. "No, you are much too beautiful to hide." He kissed her tenderly at first, and then with increasing passion. Content to spend the whole night making love to her, he moved at a relaxed, leisurely pace. A long while passed before he slid off the bed to douse the lamp. He removed his moccasins and buckskins, then helped Alanna shed her nightgown.

"You are a fine wife," he said. "I should have told you that, when you were paying me compliments as a husband."

"Thank you, but if it's too soon for me to praise you, then it has to be too soon for you to say nice things about *me*."

Hunter rejoined her on the bed. Turning playful, he gave a low growl and began to lick her breast. "No, it isn't. This is the perfect time."

Savoring the warmth of his bare skin against the whole length of her slender body, Alanna drew him close. She loved everything about him, his tenderness as well as his strength, and it was so easy to forget all her cares the instant his lips caressed hers. She sifted his thick, black mane through her fingers, then slid her hands down his well-muscled back. She doubted a more perfect male had ever been born. His love was such a precious gift, she could scarcely believe that he had chosen her for his wife.

"I love you," she whispered.

"Not nearly as much as I love you," Hunter argued. He wrapped his arms around her and rolled over to bring her up on top of him. He then slid his hands over her hips, before gripping her waist to align their bodies so perfectly, her feminine crease caressed the length of his hardened shaft. Knowing he was also providing her with the very same exquisite thrill, he rocked her back and forth gently, creating a delicious friction, until ecstasy was only a heartbeat away.

He then pulled her astride him, and with loving gestures rather than spoken commands, urged her to mount him. Their bodies were now so finely attuned, she took the full length of him easily. After resting her palms on his broad chest, she responded to the light pressure of his hands around her waist and began a slow, rhythmic motion timed to the rapture swelling within them. When it reached its crest and seared them with a splendid heat, Hunter pulled her down into his arms and kept her locked in his embrace, until the need to possess her again overwhelmed him.

"I'll never tire of loving you," he vowed.

"Is it even possible to tire of making love?"

"Not with you, it isn't."

Completely relaxed, Alanna snuggled against him, but Hunter soon made his intentions clear with impassioned kisses and a provocative touch. Only too glad to oblige his every whim, Alanna responded with a joyous abandon that fed his desire. Ensnared in the sensuous web he spun so lovingly, her pleasure was as deep as his. With gestures as fluid as an exotic dance, the only limits to the expression of their love were the dimensions of the feather bed and, after sharing a bunk, they seemed generous indeed. When they finally fell asleep in a tangle of arms and legs, their dreams were peaceful and sweet.

Rather than intentionally shock the staff of the Owl's Eye, Hunter made his entrances and exits to the inn with such complete discretion, no one ever caught a glimpse of him. When Alanna returned their room key to the desk, the clerk was so curious about the pretty young woman and her mysterious mate, that he encouraged her to stop there again on their next visit to the city.

"Thank you, we certainly will." Alanna started to move away and then turned back. "I hope none of your other guests complained about sharing the inn with an Indian."

Confused by her comment, the clerk shrugged. "We have no Indians staying here."

"Other than my husband, you mean?" Alanna watched the clerk's complexion fade to a stark white several shades lighter than his heavily powdered wig. "Oh, dear, didn't I mention that my husband is a Seneca brave? I'll be sure to have him introduce himself, if we stay here again." She waved and left before the clerk recovered enough of his composure to respond, but she hoped he would be on duty the next time she came

to rent a room, so she could remind him that no one's sleep
had been disturbed by war whoops on their last visit.

The *Sarah René* was a brig engaged in the merchant trade
between the colonies, the West Indies, and London. While Captain Michaels eschewed the lucrative slave trade, he was not
above increasing his profits by ferrying as many passengers
as his ship could comfortably carry. Just as Alanna had predicted, when Hunter boarded the ship first, and she arrived as
the last of the visitors were going ashore, no one noticed they
were together. It wasn't until they joined the other passengers
for the noon meal that the captain realized the fetching blonde
he had glimpsed only briefly, was Hunter's wife.

Understandably shocked, in the interest of maintaining harmony on a voyage he expected to complete in a few days, he
treated the couple with good, if somewhat stilted, manners.
Following his example, the other passengers kept whatever
they thought about the striking pair to themselves. It was plain
none had ever spoken with an Indian brave, and Hunter went
out of his way to charm them, while Alanna smiled contentedly
at his side. By the time they docked in Newport News, the
travelers had become friendly, but now that a meeting with her
aunt and uncle was only a few hours away, Alanna was so
worried, she barely heard their fond farewells.

The other passengers had had only their hand luggage, but
Alanna and Hunter had to wait for Elliott's coffin, and remained on deck after the others had all departed. Fidgeting
nervously, Alanna tried to recall the explanation they had rehearsed so diligently. The news would be devastating, no matter how sympathetically it was delivered, but Alanna knew the
announcement of her marriage would also be greeted as tragic,
and she didn't think she could bear that.

"This is going to be so awful," she predicted darkly.

Hunter opened his mouth to argue, but then, fearing she was right, he remained silent. Distracted by a well-dressed gentleman waving from the dock, he touched Alanna's arm. "Do you know that man? He appears to be waving to us."

Alanna turned to find Randolph O'Neil striding up the gangplank. "Oh, no," she sighed.

"He's not a friend?"

"No, he is, and a good one." Alanna did her best to smile as Randolph reached them, but her lips still trembled slightly. "Hello, I didn't expect to see you here today."

"I came to pick up a shipment," Randolph replied. "The *Sarah René* routinely carries merchandise for me, but if only you had let me know you'd be on board, I would have come to meet you." He then cast an inquiring glance toward Hunter.

"You're very kind," Alanna said. "Mr. O'Neil, this is Hunter, my husband." She knew Randolph to be a gentleman and, despite what had to be a deeply disturbing announcement, he did not disappoint her now. There was only a very slight widening of his eyes that no one else would have noticed, before he broke into a friendly grin and extended his hand.

"Please call me Randolph. Didn't I see you in Williamsburg last spring with the Barclays?"

Few white men had ever offered their hands to him, and appreciating the gesture of friendship, Hunter shook Randolph's before replying. "Yes, I visited them before serving as a scout with the militia."

"May I offer my congratulations? I envy you having such a lovely bride." Unwilling to reveal that he had had serious intentions where Alanna was concerned, he abruptly changed the subject. "Where's Elliott? Didn't he come home with you?"

Knowing how reluctant Alanna was to supply the answer, Hunter replied. "Elliott was slain by an Abenaki brave we'd fought last summer in the Ohio Valley. He shot Elliott in cold blood, but I'm proud to say he didn't live to brag about it."

Aghast at that news, Randolph moved to Alanna's side and reached out for the rail to steady himself. "I'm so sorry. What a terribly tragedy. Do John and Rachel know? Are they coming to meet you?"

Alanna shook her head. "We thought we would be here before a letter could arrive, but I didn't want to describe Elliott's death in a letter anyway."

"Well no, of course not. In addition to a wagon to transport my goods, I also have my carriage. Won't you allow me to take you home? We can be there by nightfall."

"That's very kind of you," Alanna said, "but we've brought Elliott's coffin home with us."

"That will be no problem," Randolph assured her. "I'll have it loaded in my wagon. Where do you wish to have it delivered, to your home or to the church?"

Alanna turned to Hunter. "Where do you think? I really don't know which to choose."

"Home then," Hunter suggested. "The coffin can be taken to the church for the funeral."

Alanna looked confused for a moment, and then nodded. "Yes, that's a good plan. Let's do that."

In New York, Alanna had appeared confident, but once on board the *Sarah René*, Hunter had watched her anxiety gradually mount to the point that she now seemed no more able to cope than the day he had first met her. He wrapped his arm around her shoulders, and hugged her tightly. "No one is going to blame you for Elliott's death. You needn't be so frightened."

While Alanna appreciated Hunter's efforts to raise her spirits, she knew they would both be blamed for her cousin's murder, and she could not help but feel that whatever accusations grew out of her aunt and uncle's pain, would be justified. Elliott's death was only one of her family's tragedies though, there was also Melissa's, to say nothing of the uncertain future of the dear baby she had left behind. Feeling faint, Alanna swayed slightly, and Hunter scooped her up into his arms.

Randolph hastened to lead the way. "Poor dear, it's no wonder she's unwell. Come, let's take her to my carriage."

Hunter had seen the admiration glowing in Randolph's eyes when he looked at Alanna, but he appreciated the man's help and accepted it gladly. Randolph owned a fancy carriage with wide, leather seats, but Hunter chose to keep Alanna on his lap rather than at his side. While Randolph saw to the loading of the wagon, he attempted to restore his bride's courage.

"I won't leave you," he promised.

"Thank you, but perhaps you ought to stay outside."

"You don't want me there?"

Alanna gripped his hand tightly. "Of course, I want you there. I'm just trying to think of a way to make things easier for my aunt and uncle."

"We already know they despise me, nothing you can say or do will change their minds. I'm staying with you."

When Randolph joined them, he was shocked by the intimacy of their pose, but Hunter's forbidding gaze discouraged any mention of impropriety, and as they got under way, he focused his attention on the passing scene. "Byron's left again for the Ohio Valley with General Braddock's forces, so if you have need of someone to help with the funeral arrangements, I'll be happy to perform whatever service I can."

"Thank you," Alanna replied. "You're very kind." Worn out from worry, she rested her head on her husband's shoulder and soon fell into a troubled asleep.

Hunter, however, remained keenly alert. Randolph O'Neil struck him as a sincere individual, but he still had questions. They rode a long way in silence before he decided that if Alanna considered him a good friend, he would trust him, too. "You mentioned merchandise," he remarked. "What do you sell?"

Randolph had never spoken to an Indian, and although

Hunter was a polite and soft-spoken individual, to have to converse with him while he held Alanna draped across his lap, made concentration extremely difficult. He had to swallow hard before he answered. "I'm a silversmith by trade, but I also sell a variety of fine goods, crystal, jewelry, a few exquisite timepieces."

The elegance of the man's attire made it plain his business was a successful one, but Hunter's curiosity extended to a more personal area. "What is Alanna to you?"

Randolph had carried their luggage to the carriage, and it had not included firearms or even a bow and arrows. As far as he could tell, the brave had no weapons except for the knife at his belt, but that fact failed to still his fears. Hunter not only appeared to be strong, but fiercely protective of the young woman Randolph had hoped would one day come to love him. Again, he had to pause to clear his throat.

"I really don't know how to answer you," he began. "I've known the Barclays for many years. I would have liked to have called on Alanna, but she discouraged the idea. I hoped it was due to the considerable age difference between us, rather than because she didn't like me. Then, when she began coming into town every day to visit Melissa's son, she sometimes came by my shop as well. I suppose you could say we've become good friends. That's all, just good friends."

It was painfully obvious that Randolph had wanted more, but Hunter wasn't jealous. "Thank you for your kindness. I hope you won't shun Alanna because of me."

Relieved not to have been threatened, Randolph broke into a nervous grin. "My goodness, what a thing to say. I treasure Alanna's friendship, and I hope that she values mine. I'd not shun her for any reason."

Hunter nodded. He debated with himself the wisdom of confiding in Randolph, but since the merchant would probably hear the truth later at the Barclays, he saw no reason to hide it now. "What do you know about Melissa's babe?"

"Nothing actually. His grandparents don't allow him to have visitors, or I'd have visited him with Alanna. I can understand his father's heartbreak. I'm a widower myself, but grief doesn't give a man an excuse to abandon his child. I raised my daughter alone, and while it wasn't easy, I could never have turned my back on her the way Ian has."

"The babe isn't Ian's."

Fighting the rocking motion of the carriage, Randolph leaned forward slightly. "That can't possibly be true! Melissa was a popular young woman, but there was never a hint of scandal attached to her name."

"Believe me, it's true."

"But who?" Randolph's dismay increased the longer he stared at Hunter. The Indian's eyes were so dark he could not discern pupil from iris, but there was no trace of duplicity in his gaze. He shook his head. "My god. Who?"

"The boy is mine."

Stunned, Randolph gaped for a long moment, and then withdrew an ornately engraved silver flask from his coat pocket. He offered it first to Hunter, but when the Indian declined, he unscrewed the cap and took a long swallow of brandy. "Does Alanna know?"

"Yes."

"And the Barclays?"

Hunter nodded. "That Alanna has wed a man they all despise won't please them."

"That, sir, is a very great understatement. My god." Randolph fortified himself with another swig of brandy, before recapping the flask and slipping it back into his pocket. "You'll be lucky if John doesn't shoot you on sight."

"I was the one who was wronged, not Melissa."

"While that may be the truth, a gentleman doesn't make that kind of accusation about a dead woman."

Hunter responded with a rueful laugh. "I'm never mistaken for a gentleman."

Randolph gestured to concede that fact, but argued just the same. "That really doesn't matter. Anything you say against Melissa, will be called malicious lies."

"Alanna believes me."

Randolph glanced toward the sleeping young woman. Her youth should have made her easy to deceive, but surviving the tragic loss of her family had given her a wisdom well beyond her years. "Yes, she must, or she would not have married you. Well, that's good enough for me," Randolph insisted. "Perhaps you ought to reconsider visiting the Barclays this evening. I'd like for you to stay at my home tonight. Tomorrow I can ask the priest to go with me to tell John and Rachel about Elliott. Then, after the funeral, Alanna could tell them about her marriage. Otherwise—"

Hunter shook his head. "I won't involve you in our problems."

Randolph was far more concerned about Alanna's feelings than Hunter's, but despite nearly a half-hour of persuasive argument, he was unable to sway the Indian to his point of view. "You are either the bravest man ever born, or a damn fool. I don't know which."

"It may take years to answer that question, but I won't run from the truth and neither will my wife."

As they had talked, Randolph had been watching Alanna sleep in her husband's arms, and he knew Hunter was wrong: Alanna was already running.

Rachel and John Barclay were seated in the parlor, waiting for supper to be announced, when Randolph O'Neil's carriage drew up outside. She was working on a piece of embroidery, while he was reading aloud to her from that week's edition of the *Virginia Gazette*. Curious as to who had chosen to pay them a visit at such an inconvenient hour, John lay the paper aside and moved to the window, while Rachel remained on the settee. The light was fading, but he needed no more than a fleeting glimpse of the buckskin-clad man leaving the carriage to recognize him. Without a word to his wife, he ran from the parlor to his study to fetch his pistol.

"John?" Understandably perplexed, Rachel rose and went to the window, but she saw only Randolph and Alanna, rather than Hunter. Assuming Elliott was with them, she was delighted, and reached the front door just as her husband arrived with his pistol in hand.

"Get out of my way!" he shouted.

"Dear god, John, have you taken leave of your senses? Alanna and Elliott are home!"

"Yes, and they've brought that Indian devil with them!" Under normal circumstances the most considerate of men, John shoved his wife aside and flung open the front door. Hunter was nearing the bottom of the steps, but accurately assessing her uncle's mood, Alanna had moved in front of him, and with Randolph O'Neil at her side, John was unable to get a clear shot at the Indian.

His murderous intentions plain, he used the pistol to wave Alanna and Randolph out of his way. "How dare you bring that heathen here?" he bellowed.

All their carefully rehearsed speeches forgotten, Alanna's attention was riveted on the pistol in her uncle's hand. Since leaving home she had seen the damage a musket ball could do to human flesh, and she knew a pistol shot to be equally deadly. She could only imagine the pain it would cause, but continued to shield Hunter's body with her own.

"He's my husband," she informed John calmly.

"No!" Rachel shrieked. "We raised you as one of our own! Have you no more loyalty to us than that?"

Randolph O'Neil had feared John would greet Hunter with a gun, but to actually be a witness to such violence unnerved him completely. He wanted to get right back into his carriage and flee the unfortunate scene with all possible haste, but his love for Alanna wouldn't allow him to behave in such a cowardly fashion in front of her. He remained at her side, while Rachel continued to wail in a high-pitched whine that brought Catherine and Rosemary McBride from the dining room out into the hall. Horrified by the sight of the master waving a pistol at his niece, they ran from the house to the kitchen to beg their mother to protect them.

"Stand aside, Alanna!" John ordered. "That snake can be expected to hide behind a woman's skirts, but it won't save him." Intent upon killing the man responsible for his darling Melissa's death, he took careful aim.

Rather than brush Alanna out of the way, Hunter stepped back and moved to the side to present John with a clear target. "You are no more civilized than your daughter," he taunted.

"You don't deserve to live when she's dead!" John screamed right back at him.

John might have killed Hunter then, had Rachel not flung herself at her husband with a force that knocked him off balance and sent his shot wide. "Get away from me!" John yelled.

"Do you want to hang for murder?" Rachel cried. "Hasn't he caused us enough grief?"

His feet becoming entangled in his wife's skirts, John had to struggle to remain upright, presenting Hunter with an opportunity to wrench the pistol from his hand. The Indian hurled the now unloaded weapon toward the river. He then gestured for John to come to the bottom of the steps.

"Come," he called, "fight me here."

John was furious enough to think he could actually beat a

man half his age, and he ripped off his coat as he came toward him. "Gladly," he replied.

"No!" Alanna's voice rang out clearly. "There's been too much bloodshed already."

"Stay out of this," John hissed.

"No, this has to end," Alanna beseeched him. "Haven't you even missed Elliott? He's dead."

Stunned, John halted in midstride. He looked around, half-expecting to see his younger son standing in the shadows, but Elliott was nowhere to be found. His expression filling with horror, he turned toward his niece. "How?" he rasped.

"Abenaki braves he fought last summer ambushed us in the forest. He had no chance," Alanna explained.

Screaming out her pain, Rachel clutched at her husband's shirtsleeve, distracting his attention from Hunter. Having been summoned by Polly, Jacob McBride came running around the corner of the house, brandishing the hammer he used in his forge. Seeing him, John nodded toward Hunter. "Kill him," he ordered coolly.

Jacob did not even inquire as to why John wished the Indian dead, before he assumed a menacing pose and advanced slowly. He grasped the hammer with both hands, ready to swing it at Hunter's head. His beard hid the width of his gruesome grin, but the twinkle in his eyes readily conveyed his lust for blood.

Randolph grabbed Alanna's hand to pull her back. "You dare not rush into the middle. One blow from that hammer would surely crush your skull!"

"You're making a terrible mistake," Alanna called to Jacob. "He can kill you in a dozen different ways."

Jacob responded with a rude laugh. "He'll never touch me," he boasted.

Hunter drew his knife. The blacksmith had no idea how close they had come to fighting on his first visit to the plantation, and Hunter did not waste his breath revealing that secret now. The blacksmith was strong, but so was the Indian, and he had the further advantage of being younger and far more agile. Within five minutes he had proven to everyone watching that he could cut Jacob at will.

Bleeding from a dozen minor cuts, Jacob continued to slowly circle Hunter. His strategy was simple: to lure the Indian in close, trip him, and then with one swing of the hammer, split his head open like a melon. The Indian was fast and cunning, but Jacob was so confident he would eventually win their contest to the death, that he scarcely felt the numerous scratches Hunter had inflicted.

Polly and her daughters were huddled together at the end of the porch, a fearful trio watching a fight they assumed could have only one ghastly end. Rachel, sobbing hysterically, had slumped to her knees, while John stood with his arms crossed over his chest, silently praying that Jacob would kill Hunter as slowly and painfully as possible.

Terrified, Randolph again attempted to draw Alanna away. "You mustn't watch this," he insisted.

"I can't not watch," Alanna replied. "I've already seen too much."

Randolph kept her hand in his, but that she could be so calm in the face of what appeared to be overwhelming odds against her husband, amazed him. She had always projected a ladylike reserve, but it was totally inappropriate now, and he was positive something was very wrong. "We ought to go," he pleaded again, but Alanna gave no sign of having heard him.

His attention focused solely on his bearded opponent, Hunter ceased to be aware of the comments passing between the spectators. It was now dark, but the lamps glowing in the mansion's windows cast enough light for them to watch each other's moves. A stocky man, Jacob's rolling gait reminded

Hunter of a bear, but he cautiously kept well out of the blacksmith's reach, until he again wished to strike out with his knife.

This time, rather than a quick jab, he went for a long slash down Jacob's right forearm, and was rewarded with the first bellow of pain the man had uttered. The blood running down Jacob's arm made his grip slippery, and he had to switch the hammer to his left hand for a moment, to wipe his palm on his pant leg. Hunter tossed his knife back and forth between his hands, and catching the blacksmith off guard by using his left hand, he ripped the flesh down the entire length of Jacob's left arm.

His grip now slick with blood no matter what he did, Jacob let out a hoarse growl and raised his hammer high to strike Hunter a bone-breaking blow. Hunter, however, waited until the last second to step aside, and then brought his knife down with a savage thrust that pierced Jacob's right hand. He yanked out the blade while Jacob was still howling, and his taunting grin made it plain he would hurt him far worse on his next lunge.

"My god," Randolph whispered. "You were right. Hunter is going to kill the blacksmith, and you and I can both swear it was in self-defense."

"Stop the fight, Uncle," Alanna begged. "Or Jacob's blood will be on your hands."

Believing Jacob still had a chance to kill Hunter, John shook his head. It wasn't until a few minutes later that a freight wagon rolled into the yard, and he saw Elliott's coffin in the back. In an instant the full force of his loss finally hit him. Two of his dearly loved children were dead, and when he at last realized that Jacob could neither cripple nor kill the man he considered responsible, he raised his hand to stop the match.

He then pointed to Alanna. "Go, and take your accursed mate with you. I don't want to see either of you for as long as I live. Thank God my brother isn't here to see how badly

you've disgraced our family. It makes me sick to look at you."
He stooped to lift his weeping wife to her feet; turning his
back on his niece, he helped Rachel into the house and
slammed the door soundly behind them.

Twenty-six

Alanna had not been physically thrown out of her uncle's house, which she had feared was a very real possibility, but her feelings could not have been more hurt. "What about your loyalty to *me?*" she asked in a plaintive whisper that went unheard and unheeded. She felt Randolph reach out to pat her shoulder, but it was not his comfort she wanted.

She looked toward Hunter, whose expression mirrored her pain. He had not understood her anxiety had such just cause, and the sorrow in his glance conveyed a world of sympathy. Unfortunately, she knew he needed sympathy as well, and she couldn't summon any. Hunter wiped his knife on the grass and replaced it in its sheath. He nodded toward the river, and she let him go.

Humiliated in front of his wife and daughters, Jacob McBride's anger continued to seethe. He had hated Hunter on sight, and when the brave started for the river to clean up, Jacob could no longer contain his rage. Unable to grip his hammer, he put his head down and charged him like a bull.

Even if Alanna had not screamed a warning, Hunter would have felt Jacob running toward him, for the ground trembled beneath his feet. He took another step, then spun, and reached out to catch Jacob's arm. Using the heavy-set blacksmith's own momentum, he hurled him ten feet across the lawn, where he landed on his back and lay as helpless as an overturned turtle.

"Go home while you still can," Hunter warned. "You've no quarrel with me."

Jacob had hit the ground with a bone-jarring thud, but he was too angry to turn tail and run. He staggered to his feet and came lumbering toward Hunter, his eyes ablaze with the hatred burning in his heart. Dripping blood from his torn palm, he lunged for the brave's throat.

Hunter dodged Jacob's grasp and sent a bruising kick into the blacksmith's knee, buckling the joint and again sending Jacob sprawling. He then stood with his hands on his hips, as the blood-streaked man struggled to rise. When Jacob's knee refused to bear his weight and he slid back to the ground, Hunter drew his knife.

"This fight is over. Either you say you've had enough, or you'll die. Which is it to be?"

Jacob could hear Polly and his girls tearfully pleading with him to surrender, but he was too stubborn to speak, until his son came running into the yard. Andrew looked horrified to find his father in such a pitiful state, and Jacob knew there would be no honor in dying in front of him. "I give up," he finally murmured in an anguished whisper.

Hunter resheathed his knife and came forward to help Jacob rise, but the blacksmith waved him off and called for Andrew instead. Hunter remembered seeing the young man and, because there was nothing threatening in his manner, he again started out for the river. He wasn't sure where he and Alanna were going, but he did not want to arrive there splattered with Jacob's blood.

Randolph removed his handkerchief from his pocket and wiped his brow. "Hunter warned me that he'd not be well received, but I've never seen anything to rival this," he confided in Alanna.

He was a dear man, and Alanna now realized how placid his life must have been. "Well I have, and believe me, you'll survive." She sat down on the edge of the steps and tried to decide what she and Hunter ought to do. They should have made plans past their initial homecoming, yet neither had suggested it.

"Would you give us a ride into town?" she asked. "We can afford to stay at an inn."

"No, you'll come home with me and stay as long as you like. I've plenty of room, and Mrs. Newcombe, my housekeeper, will be delighted to have the opportunity to look after someone other than me. Please say that you'll stay with me. It hurts me to see how badly your aunt and uncle have treated you. I know I can't make up for it, but please let me try."

Alanna was touched by Randolph's thoughtful invitation, but she did not want to take advantage of his affection for her, when she could not return it. There was also the very real possibility that he might suffer for helping her, and she could not allow that to happen. "That's wonderfully generous of you, but—"

"But what? Surely you can't prefer to stay with strangers?"

"No, of course not, but I've no idea how long we'll be in Williamsburg, and if my aunt and uncle object to your helping us, they might influence their friends to stop patronizing your shop. I don't want to see that happen."

It had not even occurred to Randolph that he might suffer financially for inviting Alanna and Hunter into his home, but he had always considered himself to be a man of high principles, and he wouldn't be blackmailed. "If I have clients who are so shallow as to be swayed by your aunt and uncle's bitterness, I shan't miss them. Excuse me a moment, I want to make certain my men handle Elliott's coffin with the proper respect."

"Certainly." Alanna had not forgotten Elliott, but when she turned, she found the two men who had driven the wagon into the yard watching her with what could only be described as dark scowls. Her uncle was a man of enormous prestige in Williamsburg, and clearly the fact she and her husband had been banished from his home had impressed the pair.

Polly and her daughters had left with Jacob and Andrew, but the fact none of them had stopped to speak with her certainly wasn't a good sign. Apparently she had been disowned not only by her aunt and uncle, but by all of their employees as well. Feeling uncomfortable on their steps, she rose and followed her husband down to the river. Hunter was standing on the dock, water glistening on his hair, his shirt still in his hand.

Alanna rubbed his back lightly. "I suppose I should be heartbroken, but I just feel empty. Perhaps Byron will take our side when he comes home, then my aunt and uncle may regret being so harsh with us today."

Hunter shook his head. "With Elliott dead, that won't happen. Byron and I were never close, and he'll agree with his parents. I'm sorry. I didn't know that loving me would cost you your family's respect. Is that why Melissa turned against me?"

Alanna took his arm and rested her cheek against his shoulder. "Please don't ask me to speak for her. It's so unfair."

The question had sprung from Hunter's lips without thought, and he now realized just how cruel it had been. He turned to pull Alanna into his arms. "I never felt for her what I feel for you. I shouldn't have asked that. It's just that I keep forgetting how easy it is for people like your aunt and uncle to regard me as less than human. I am a man, the same as their sons, but they don't see it. I did nothing to harm them, and yet they blame me for all their sorrows."

Alanna licked her lips thoughtfully. "They loved Melissa too much to see her as she really was, and nothing we do or say will change that. I knew they'd take our marriage very badly, and it didn't matter to me. If there was a choice to be made, I made the right one for me. We have to live our own lives, not theirs."

Admiring the calmness of her manner as much as the logic of her words, Hunter gave her a long, loving kiss before backing away to pull his shirt on over his head. "I wouldn't have killed the blacksmith. You knew that, didn't you? I just wanted to scare him into leaving me alone."

Surprised by that confession, Alanna shrugged slightly. "The man attacked you twice, and he clearly intended to kill you. I'd not have faulted you for killing him."

Hunter rested his hands lightly on her shoulders. "Do you see me as that dangerous? Are you afraid of me?"

Alanna reached out to encircle his waist and stepped closer. "No, only of losing you."

Hunter laughed softly. "Then you have nothing to fear."

Alanna closed her eyes. She was so anxious to see Christian, but she hesitated to speak the baby's name, and knew she still had reason to be afraid.

Randolph O'Neil's home was on Nicholson Street. Faced with white weatherboards and brightened by green shutters at the windows, it was as handsome as any of the fine homes in Williamsburg. While not as large as the Barclays' brick mansion, it was as beautifully decorated and maintained. Very proud of his home, Randolph swung open the front door and welcomed his guests inside.

He called to his housekeeper, and the petite, white-haired Mrs. Newcombe rushed into view. "What do you call yourselves?" Randolph whispered to Alanna.

"Mr. and Mrs. Hunter," she replied.

"Yes, of course," Randolph agreed. "Mr. and Mrs. Hunter will be staying with us for a while. Which of the guest rooms do you have prepared?"

That her employer apparently thought nothing of sleeping in the same house with an Indian brave gave the diminutive housekeeper a moment's pause, but when Hunter smiled at her, his expression was so disarming, her initial fears began to fade. "All of them, sir. The yellow room is the nicest, though."

"The yellow room it is then," Randolph agreed. "I think what we'd all like now is some supper. Will you please tell the cook I've brought guests?"

After a gesture that hinted at a curtsy, Mrs. Newcombe hurried away. Randolph showed his guests into the parlor and urged them to make themselves at home. "I do hope you'll be comfortable here. My daughter and her family are able to visit only rarely, and I'll enjoy having your company for as long as you'd care to stay. I'll be at my shop during the week, so I won't be in your way."

With most of their conversations taking place at his shop, Alanna had not realized that Randolph was so lonely. She had been so preoccupied with Christian's future that she had not appreciated he had needs as well, and that she could not fulfill them made her feel guilty. She sat down on the settee and patted the cushion at her side, but Hunter shook his head and remained standing.

"I'm afraid I've not been nearly as good a friend to you, as you've been to me," Alanna began. "If there's anything I can do to help while we're here, I hope you'll encourage Mrs. Newcombe to let me know. I've never been waited on, and I don't expect it here."

"Mrs. Newcombe has been with me for years, and she'd be mortified if I suggested she put you to work. You're my guests. You two won't be expected to do more than enjoy yourselves, while you're here. Would either of you care to join me in a glass of sherry?"

When neither accepted his offer, Randolph poured himself

a glass and raised it in a silent toast before taking a sip. "This has been the most remarkable day I've spent in a long while."

Despite Randolph's friendliness, Hunter felt ill at ease in his home. The parlor was painted a pale creamy beige with a deeper shade of the same hue for the wooden trim and moldings. It would have been soothing, but for the rich ruby red of the damask draperies which was repeated in the upholstery of most of the furniture. Hunter had seen too much blood of late to find red an attractive color, and being surrounded by it made him restless. He circled the settee and walked over to the fireplace. Wood had been laid for a fire, but the evening was warm and it hadn't been lit. The sight of something so ordinary in the elegant home suddenly made him feel homesick for the comforting familiarity of his own long house.

"Unfortunately, our days seldom run smoothly," he mused, "but I'll do my best not to bring the continual peril of our lives into your home."

"No, please, I'd welcome it," Randolph argued.

Hunter had fought his last fight to amuse others, and he stared at the merchant with a puzzled glance. "I didn't enjoy fighting Jacob. Did you enjoy watching?"

"Not at the moment, certainly not, but now that everyone's safe, well, I'll remember the excitement rather than the fright."

"Jacob isn't safe," Hunter pointed out. "I may have crippled his hand, and his knee will trouble him for a long time. As for Alanna and me, we were hurt far worse. We've lost not only Elliott, but the rest of her family it seems. As usual, no one will think of our pain."

Randolph feared he had been very ill-mannered and hastened to apologize. "Please, I didn't mean to minimize what happened at the Barclays. I hope they'll soon soften their stance. You have my word as a gentleman that I won't repeat what I overheard to anyone."

Mrs. Newcombe announced supper then, and hungry, Hunter

was glad for an excuse to end their conversation. He escorted his wife into the dining room, and took the chair at her side. The room was painted in a deep terra cotta shade brightened with white molding, and he found the earth tone far more calming than the jarring contrasts of the parlor.

Clustered at one end of the table, the threesome shared a quiet, but tasty meal of roast chicken and vegetables. As he had at the Barclays, Hunter watched Alanna's choice before selecting a utensil, and as he always had with her, gave his best effort to displaying his finest manners. When by the close of the meal Alanna was having difficulty hiding her yawns, he was relieved to bid Randolph good night and go upstairs to their room.

Their few pieces of luggage were already there, but as Alanna pulled her nightgown from her valise, Hunter realized just how much she had left at her aunt and uncle's house. "We'll have to go back for your things. You have so many pretty gowns, and I don't want you to lose them."

"I won't need satin ball gowns at the trading post."

"Do you like to dance?"

"Following music and trying to recall the steps without trampling on my partners' toes was never one of favorite pastimes. I just wasn't any good at it."

"Maybe you didn't have the right partner."

Alanna turned toward him. His smile was enchanting. "Why, Hunter, do you like to dance?"

Had it not been for his dark complexion, she would have seen his blush. "The Seneca dance for different reasons. I've never done any of your dances with a woman."

"I'm not very good, but if you'd like to learn, I'll teach you. Another night, though. Tonight I'd just fall asleep in your arms."

"I like that."

"Yes, but not standing up."

"It might be nice." Hunter came forward to pull her into a

warm embrace and nuzzled her neck. She had replaced the combs she had lost and bought new caps while in New York, but he wanted her hair loose the way it had been in the forest, and quickly removed them. He shook out her curls and spread them over her shoulders.

"Where is Randolph's room?" he asked.

"I don't know. I've never been here before. Why do you ask?"

"I don't want to make him any more envious than he already is."

Alanna relaxed against him. "We'll have to make love very quietly then."

Hunter bent down slightly to kiss her. He wondered how many men he was going to have to fight for the right to call her his wife. The number didn't really matter. He would gladly battle anyone who objected to their being together, even if he had to fight every last man on earth.

The urgency of Hunter's kiss failed to ease Alanna's lingering sense of sorrow, but she understood his need, and shared it. She prayed they would have many other days in which their happiness would be complete, but knew they would never have a greater need for the physical reassurance each craved now. When Hunter pulled off his shirt, she spread eager kisses across his chest, and gave his nipples a playful swipe. He turned away to douse the lamp, but she caught his arm.

"No, I want to look at you," she argued. "You're so handsome." She slid her palm down the front of his breechcloth, outlining his hardened manhood, and he released his belt.

"Touch me now," he begged in a husky whisper. He pulled her hand inside his loosened buckskins, and following his lead, her caress was steady and sure. He soon kicked off his moccasins, and she helped him peel off the last of his clothes. He then pulled her down with him on the bed.

Still dressed, Alanna slid her hands up the firm muscles of

his thighs. The scar from the wound she had feared might cost
him his life would remain with him always, and she leaned
down to kiss it, memorizing the narrow ridge with the tip of
her tongue. When Hunter moaned appreciatively, she wondered
aloud if she could draw him across the threshold of ecstasy,
as he did her, with intimate kisses.

Hunter raised up slightly to look down at her. "Take off
your dress, and then do it," he urged.

Alanna reached for the buttons. Earlier that evening, she
had had to endure a frightful confrontation with her family,
but the shameful scene was forgotten as she returned Hunter's
smile. All she saw was the man she adored, and when he was
near, all other concerns faded into insignificance. She had long
since lost her shyness around him, and with but a few sly,
suggestive hints from him, she swiftly discovered what pleased
him most.

Her tawny tresses brushed across his stomach, creating a
teasing breeze that warmed him clear through. With a reflex
he couldn't subdue, Hunter tightened the already taut muscles
of his belly. He had longed to teach Alanna how to pleasure
him in this way, but he had waited, impatiently, until she chose
it of her own accord. It had been worth the wait, and the warm,
sweet wetness of her mouth lured him ever deeper into the
heart and soul of passion.

Wanting her to share in that bliss, when the rapture fueled
by her eager kisses threatened to overwhelm him, he pulled
her up into his arms and then pinned her beneath him. He
entered her with a hungry, driving thrust, but then lay still
until the urgency of his need could again be controlled. He
moved up, molding his body to hers, carefully positioning himself so that with each forward lunge, he would press against
the swollen nub that would soon shower her with pleasure.

Deliberately coaxing that rapture, his enticing moves raised
their souls aloft, and transported them both into the realm of

love's wildest dreams. Blinded by a tumultuous release, they shuddered, and at last lay still. Lost in the quest for shared joy, they had forgotten the need for discretion, and their soft cries of surrender had echoed down the hall. Their fears of the future drowned in a perfect peace, they fell asleep locked in each other's arms, while Randolph O'Neil sat on the side of his bed, alone, and ached for the affectionate young woman who would never be his.

Alanna had been too nervous to eat any breakfast, and now as she stood poised to knock on Charity Wade's door, her courage nearly deserted her. Seeing the tremor in her hand as she raised it, Hunter reached around her to rap on the door himself.

"I'm sorry," she murmured.

"No, I'm the one who's sorry. I thought you had more confidence in me."

Alanna had all the confidence in the world in her husband, when it came to any area not dealing with his son. Where Christian was concerned, however, she did not know what to expect, and was completely unnerved by dread. He hadn't spoken a word on their walk from Randolph's house, and with every step she had expected him to turn back. He had come the whole way though, but he still didn't seem to be truly with her.

"Please, let's not discuss anything in front of Charity."

"Agreed."

Charity answered the door with Christian in her arms, and her own children clustered around her. Nearly six months old, the handsome little boy had thick black hair and enormous brown eyes. He recognized Alanna and, with a gleeful whoop, reached out his chubby arms for her. Equally delighted to see her, Charity dropped him into Alanna's waiting embrace.

"He's really missed you, Miss Barclay."

Alanna hastened to introduce Hunter as her husband, before

she stepped into the small dwelling and turned to show off her cousin's child. She then couldn't decide which of them wore the most startled expression. Charity hadn't been expecting her to appear with a husband, let alone an Indian brave. That Christian bore such a striking resemblance to the man only served to increase the wet nurse's dismay. Her children, terrified by the sight of an Indian in their home, shoved and pushed as they scrambled for the best place to hide.

As for Hunter, he'd been frowning slightly as he stepped through the doorway, but his first glimpse of Christian left him staring agape at a little face that closely mirrored his own in childhood. Alanna had told him Christian favored him rather than Melissa, but he had not really believed her. Now he could see that only the boy's pale golden skin gave any hint that he might not be a full-blooded Seneca, like his father.

Despite never having been introduced to any strangers, Christian was thrilled to see a man whose coloring matched his own. Dislodging Alanna's cap, he grabbed a clump of her hair with one hand, but leaned out toward Hunter with the other. Smiling widely, he called to him in a babbling stream of syllables which held meaning only for him.

When Hunter hung back rather than take a step closer, Alanna moved nearer to him. She placed Christian's hand on his buckskin shirt, and patted it lightly. "What do you think of Hunter's shirt, Christian? Doesn't it feel good?"

With a wild swing, Christian grabbed a handful of fringe on Hunter's sleeve and gave it a fierce yank. When he tried to put the ends in his mouth, Alanna pried them from his little fist. "He seems to have your strength as well as your looks," Alanna said. "Do you want to hold him?"

Grasping each other tightly, the loving bond between Alanna and Christian was so plain, looking at them made Hunter's heart ache. They made him feel separate, apart, more lonely than he had ever felt, and he had to swallow hard before he spoke. "No. Stay and play with him as long as you like. I have to go."

"But Hunter—"

Hunter just shook his head. He nodded toward Charity, and then hurried out her door. He had no destination in mind, but he had to get away. It was not only the love which flowed so easily between Christian and Alanna that caused him pain. Seeing his son had conjured up images of Melissa that were so vivid, he couldn't stand to be with anyone else. Sickened by the memories he wanted forgotten, he strode back toward Randolph's house, bent on leaving town.

Charity closed the door and, after shooing her children into the bedroom to play, she gestured for Alanna to sit down. She had never been told the exact circumstances surrounding Christian's birth, but after Ian Scott had carried the newborn from her home, she had understood the babe's father was most definitely not his mother's husband. An apparent scandal in a fine family didn't concern her, but her charge's welfare most certainly did.

"Wasn't that Christian's father?" she asked in a tone that discouraged equivocation.

Alanna chose the chair nearest the fireplace, seated herself, brushed Christian's hair off his forehead, and gave him a kiss. "Yes, but for my cousin's sake, please don't reveal that fact to anyone."

"Your cousin's dead, Miss Barclay, or should I refer to you as Mrs. Hunter? It's you I'm concerned about. A great many men, if not all of them, are uncomfortable around small children, so you mustn't think your husband's behavior was odd. He'll warm up to the boy in time."

When she had arrived, Alanna had had no intention of confiding her troubles to Charity, but the young mother's efforts to excuse Hunter's behavior touched her deeply. She soon found herself relating how she had spent her days since she had last been in Williamsburg. The children ran in and out, but despite their interruptions, she managed to complete the harrowing tale in a breathless whisper.

"Elliott's dead, my family won't speak to us, and Hunter wants me to give Christian away. Each of those problems is heartbreaking, but when taken together . . . Oh, I'm sorry, I didn't mean to burden you." Alanna gave Christian another loving hug. "Do you really think he missed me?"

"Yes, every day. He's been, well, just plain restless without you. I may be tending the boy, but you know as well as I do that you're the one he loves. You're his mother, even if you didn't give birth to him. You can't give him away. It would break both your hearts."

Alanna sighed sadly. "I know."

"Just give your husband some time to get used to the idea of being a father. Where are you staying?"

"With Randolph O'Neil."

"The silversmith?"

"Yes, do you know him?"

Charity shook her head. "Someone pointed him out once, so I know who he is, but we've never met. I thought him a fine-looking man."

While he did not compare to Hunter, Alanna agreed. "He's not only attractive, but he's also kind and considerate as well. We can't impose on his hospitality though."

Christian was snuggled happily in her lap, but Alanna looked so dejected, Charity put the kettle on the fire to make her a cup of tea. "It's almost time for me to nurse the boy, but you're welcome to stay as long as you like."

"No, I should go." But, reluctant to leave, Alanna was easily cajoled into accepting a cup of tea. She sipped it slowly while Charity fed Christian. She had observed the same tender scene often, but now it served as a graphic reminder of how helpless the dear little boy still was. She had known all along that she wouldn't be able to give him away, but she had been hoping, foolishly it now seemed, that Hunter would love him on first sight, as she had.

When Charity put Christian into his crib for his morning nap, Alanna said goodbye and left, but she had nowhere to go. She didn't want to go back to Randolph's house, when she doubted Hunter would be there, and so she strolled aimlessly until she got too tired to keep walking and had to return to the silversmith's home. Randolph met her at the front door.

"When I came home for the noon meal, Mrs. Newcombe told me you and Hunter had left together this morning, but that he had returned alone and borrowed one of the horses. I've been so worried that he'd left you stranded somewhere."

Randolph was dressed in muted shades of charcoal gray. His watch fob and the silver buckles on his shoes were fine examples of his craft. He looked like the successful merchant he was, but she did not want him minding her business as closely as he did his own.

"I'm sure he hasn't stolen your horse. Is that what concerns you?"

Randolph looked aghast at that accusation. "Good lord, no! I was worried about you! I told Mrs. Newcombe to wait dinner for you. Now that you're here, won't you join me?"

Alanna excused herself for a moment to wash her hands, but when she found Randolph waiting for her with an eager smile, she wished Hunter were there, too. She had no more idea where her husband had gone than Randolph did, but she wasn't worried that he would not come back. Rather than allow him to pry into her life, she encouraged her host to describe the merchandise he had picked up from the *Sarah René*. It helped to pass the time while they ate.

"I'll stop by the church this afternoon, and see if Elliott's funeral has been arranged. I know you'll want to be there."

"Yes, we do, even if we have to slip in at the back after the service has begun." Alanna shivered slightly. "I'm sorry. I'm more tired than I thought. Will you please excuse me? I'd like to take a nap until Hunter gets here."

"Yes, of course. I have to get back to the shop. I'll see you this evening."

Alanna walked him to the front door, and then went up the stairs. Filled with the afternoon sunlight, the yellow room was almost too bright to permit sleep, but she was too tired to notice. She had only one dress now, and removed it before climbing into bed. When Hunter touched her shoulder to wake her for the evening meal, she sat up with a start. She had meant to take only a short nap, and the deep shadows filling the room surprised her. Where had the day gone?

"Did you just get back?" she asked, after covering a wide yawn.

Hunter sat down on the side of the bed. "No, I came in earlier, but you were asleep."

"Why didn't you wake me then?"

Hunter shrugged. "I had nothing to say."

Chilled by his icy tone, Alanna feared the worst. "And now?"

He shook his head. "I went out for a ride, and tried to decide what is best. I didn't expect Christian to look so much like me, but it doesn't make any difference. I still don't want him."

Desperately hoping to change his mind, Alanna started to argue. "But you only saw him for a few minutes. You really didn't have the time to appreciate what a charming boy he is."

"Yes, he has his mother's charm. That I could see."

"Please don't bring Melissa into this," Alanna begged. "It concerns only you, me, and Christian."

Hunter rose and lit the lamp. "Randolph told me Elliott's funeral is tomorrow morning. You needn't decide anything until he's buried. I owe you that."

"I needn't decide? This is a decision we have to make *together."*

Hunter stared down at her. "I can't change how I feel. It sickens me to look at the boy, and I won't be his father. Maybe we can convince Randolph to adopt him. He seems terribly lonely, and if he has a daughter, he might like having a son."

"You might like having a son, if you'd just try!"

Just as he had earlier in the day, Hunter shook his head and walked out on her.

Twenty-seven

Randolph had never entertained a more distracted pair, but he assumed their sullen moods were due to the forthcoming funeral, rather than a reflection on the quality of his hospitality. His cook had prepared ham with new potatoes and peas, one of his favorite meals, but neither Hunter nor Alanna had much of an appetite. He tried, completely without success, to suggest topics of conversation they might enjoy, but other than an occasional nod, they appeared not to be listening. Finally he simply gave up, finished eating, and, using the newly arrived shipment of merchandise as an excuse, returned to his shop.

Left on their own, Alanna wandered into the parlor and Hunter followed. He again chose to lean against the mantel, rather than take the seat beside her. He didn't speak until the silence between them had grown uncomfortably long.

"I'm not leaving you," he said. "Not in the way a man leaves his wife, but I've learned General Braddock has only a few scouts with him. He's going back over the same trail we cut through the wilderness last summer, which is a grave error, but with a much larger force. If I join them, I can tell Byron what's happened. I doubt that he'll welcome me into your family either, but I want a chance to win him over to our side, before his parents speak with him."

Hunter's comment was so unexpected, Alanna was quite taken aback by it. "Last night, when I suggested Byron might help us, you discouraged the idea. Have you really changed your mind, or are you just looking for an excuse to leave Williamsburg?"

She was looking down at her tightly clenched hands, but Hunter could see she was as unhappy as he. Knowing the wounded edge of her feelings was as raw as his, he was not offended by the bluntness of her question. "It's not an excuse," he denied. "It's a reason."

Reason, excuse, the words meant the very same thing to Alanna: he was leaving. "You'd rather fight the French again than stay here and fight with me? Is that closer to the truth?"

"I don't want to fight with you over this either. Just let me go."

"I'll not scream and plead and throw myself at your feet, but what is it you expect me to do?" Alanna asked pointedly. "I'm not welcome at home. I'd be lost in New York without you. Do you think you can just leave me here with Randolph, until you return? You *are* planning to come back, aren't you?"

There was always the chance he would be killed, but Hunter knew mentioning it wouldn't reassure her, so he gave the only promise she would want to hear. "Yes, of course, I'll come back for you. You're my wife."

Alanna looked up at him. She feared he was only postponing their next confrontation over Christian, but she was no more eager than he to force a decision neither could accept. "Perhaps it will be best if you're away for a while, but I'll miss you terribly."

"Not nearly as much as I'll miss you. I'll leave you all the money. Have some new gowns made. There's plenty. Buy whatever you like. Rent a room with another family, if you'd rather not live here. You must have friends. Wouldn't one of them invite you to stay with them?"

"The Frederick sisters might," Alanna suggested absently, "but we don't have the same interests, and they'd soon tire of having me around."

"I can't believe anyone would ever grow bored with your company."

Alanna was immune to his flattery that night. "It's true Sarah has always loved Byron, and Robin was just as fond of Elliott. I know my cousins liked them, but not enough to propose." Elliott had proposed to her instead, Alanna recalled sadly. "It would be very difficult for me to be around Robin knowing how much she'll miss Elliott when he—well—"

"When he wanted to marry you?"

Alanna nodded. "It would be even more awkward than staying here."

Hunter came to Alanna, took her hands, and helped her to her feet. "I've made an outcast of you, haven't I?"

"Please don't say that. We didn't have a chance to tell my aunt and uncle how you'd carried Elliott's body, or hidden it so carefully. They'd have nothing to bury tomorrow, no grave to tend, if not for you. Maybe if they understood how you had risked your life to safeguard Elliott's body, or how swiftly his murderer died, they wouldn't have been so quick to send us away."

Hunter tipped her chin, so she would have to look up at him. He had always loved her beautiful green eyes, but all too often, as it was now, her gaze was a reflecting pool of pain. "If, if, if—don't torture yourself. There are too many ifs for me to ever be a part of your family, and no amount of wishful thinking will change things. You and I have to understand each other though, and I think we do."

"Understanding isn't the same as agreeing," Alanna mused thoughtfully.

Hunter pulled her into his arms and hugged her tight. "Don't forget that I love you. Don't ever forget that."

Surrounded by his sensuous warmth, Alanna didn't doubt his love, but she couldn't understand why there wasn't enough to include Christian, too. She closed her eyes and tried to imagine how she could survive even a day without the husband she adored; his fervent vow of love didn't ease her pain. When he took her hand to lead her upstairs, she went without complaint. As unwilling as he to waste the last few precious hours they might ever spend together, she pulled off her cap and removed her combs on the way.

"We've had far too much sorrow," she said.

Luck, fate, God . . . Hunter did not know whom to blame, but he agreed. It was too soon to know if he had succeeded in giving her a child, but he did not want to miss his last opportunity to try. He was positive a babe of their own would signal the beginning of the happiness he wanted to give her, and when they reached their room, he pulled her down onto the bed eager to make the infant a reality.

Unaware of his purpose, Alanna felt only love and relaxed in his arms, but it was her sorrow she shared rather than passion, and he could not erase the taste of disappointment from her lips. He made love to her with all the tenderness he possessed, with a tantalizing caress and devouring kiss, until sated by pleasure, they were enveloped in a glorious haze where the bright sparkle of love glistened all around them. When Alanna fell asleep in his arms, Hunter lay awake, knowing the joy they shared wouldn't save them, and that if he did not return from the Ohio Valley with a solution for Christian's future that she could accept, their marriage would be over.

Melissa would be to blame if that tragedy occurred. How he hated her! She had not wanted him, but even from the grave she continued to twist his heart and cause him pain. Thinking she must have cursed him with her dying breath, he could not stop the tears that stung his eyes and rolled down his cheeks. He had never seen Alanna cry, but he could no longer hide his emotions with the courage she hid hers. He loved her so desperately, but he had to leave, before the wedge Melissa's child had driven between them, separated them forever.

* * *

The next morning, the Bruton Parish Church was filled with mourners, and Elliott was laid to rest with the same solemn dignity that had attended his sister's burial six months prior. That the Barclay family should have again suffered such an agonizing loss brought forth a wellspring of sympathy from the good citizens of Williamsburg. Taking care to remain out of sight, Alanna benefited from none of their solicitous concern. Along with Randolph O'Neil, she and her buckskin-clad husband had been the last to enter the church, and the first to depart.

The weather was warm, but despite the sunshine, Alanna felt a disquieting inner chill. She had awakened with a painful headache long before dawn, knowing the new day held no hope for the longed-for compromise she and Hunter needed so badly. Her horizons bleak, she had not been surprised when Hunter awoke in an equally depressed mood. She had clung to his arm throughout the service, buoyed by his strength, but she would always miss Elliott and the sweetness of his love.

"I'll visit his grave later," Alanna told her two escorts as they began the walk home.

Equally unwilling to create another unfortunate scene, Hunter understood why she refused to be a part of the crowd of mourners. He had not wanted her to have to attend the funeral alone, but now that it was over, he was anxious to be on his way. He knew that would seem cold, but it was an abundance of emotion rather than a lack of feeling that was prompting him to leave.

"I'd like to buy the bay gelding I borrowed yesterday," he announced abruptly. "How much do you want for him?"

Startled by Hunter's request, Randolph nevertheless recovered quickly. "Marshal? He's not for sale, but you may ride him as often as you please."

"I want to join Braddock's forces," Hunter explained, "and I'll need my own mount to catch up with them."

Appalled, Randolph stuck out his arm to compel his companions to come to a halt. "Wait a minute, are you sure that's wise?"

Unaccustomed to having to justify his decisions to others, Hunter straightened his shoulders proudly. "All I need is a horse, not advice."

Randolph noted the unspoken challenge in the shift in Hunter's posture, and quickly waved it off. "You may take Marshal. He isn't really the issue. I'd understood you to say that you'd be staying here in Williamsburg for a while. What made you change your mind?"

Hunter took Alanna's hand to encourage her to keep walking with him, and when she did, Randolph again fell in beside them. "We had no definite plans. Now I've decided to go to the Ohio Valley, and Alanna's going to wait for me here. I appreciate the loan of the horse, but I'd rather buy him."

Randolph opened his mouth to argue, for this struck him as the worst possible time for Hunter to leave his bride. As he saw it, she had just buried her favorite cousin, and the rest of her family wasn't even speaking to her. Then he realized he would be arguing against his own best interests, and swallowed his objections.

"I'm afraid I made a mistake in buying Marshal last winter," he admitted instead. "He's a handsome beast, but too headstrong for my tastes. Frankly, I'll be happy to have him gone. Consider him a gift."

Hunter shook his head. "No, name a price for the horse and a saddle, and I'll pay it."

When the silversmith hesitated, Alanna described Hunter as an extremely successful trapper and alluded vaguely to a second enterprise which added to his income. "The cost of a horse won't bankrupt us," she assured him.

Fearing that he had inadvertently insulted them, Randolph hurriedly apologized and revealed what he had paid for Marshal. "I'll sell him to you for the same price, and that includes his saddle and bridle."

Hunter knew how much the horse was worth and, satisfied Randolph's price was fair, he agreed to it. "Thank you for listening to our side and being willing to help us. I know you'll be a friend to Alanna, while I'm gone."

Randolph's only regret was that he could not be much more. He tried not to sound too eager to see him gone. "When are you leaving?" he asked.

"As soon as I can saddle Marshal. I have very little to pack."

"Now, today? You're leaving *today?*"

Hunter was beginning to find Randolph's company tiresome. "Yes, and I might be gone for several months. Do you have an opinion on that, too?"

Alanna's headache was rapidly becoming more severe. She raised her hand to her brow. "Please. This was a difficult morning. Let's just go home."

"Of course, forgive me," Randolph begged. Like most men, he preferred to carry his hat rather than wear it over his wig, and he used it to gesture down the road. He had wanted to bring his carriage, but his guests had wished to walk and he had given in to them. Randolph had planned to go on to his shop, but now that Hunter had announced his intention to depart, he remained at home to bid him a safe trip. Believing the Indian and his bride would like to be alone, he excused himself.

Alanna watched Hunter saddle Marshal. The gelding was high-spirited, but no more so than her uncle's mounts, and she decided Randolph must not be much of a horseman. His driver, Stanley Crotty, maintained the stable, but he was nowhere to be found. Rather than being annoyed by the man's absence, Alanna was relieved they didn't have to say their farewells in front of him.

She crossed her arms under her bosom; feeling that everything was wrong, Alanna couldn't stop trembling. She was positive this simply wasn't the way things were meant to be. They were good people. They deserved every happiness, rather than the endless string of tragedies that plagued them. With Hunter gone, she would have only Christian to love, but it was the fact that she loved the baby so much that was driving her husband away. It wasn't fair.

Hunter knew how to saddle a horse with a minimum of effort, but he was paying scant attention to the task, and it took him twice as long as it should have. He could feel Alanna, and not simply her presence, but her longing as well. He turned slowly to face her.

"I told you I belong to the wolf clan. Last summer I saw a magnificent young wolf, and later I heard his howl. I felt it was a sign, a warning of danger to come, but I didn't understand how bad it would be. I hope to see that same wolf again, and this time, I want him to promise me something good."

Alanna had no such faith in the wolves he might sight in the forest. "Just be certain he doesn't bite you," she cautioned. "I want you to come home to me, Indian."

"You already have my promise."

Alanna had lost too many loved ones to believe in a promise he might not be able to keep. "I know you mean to come back."

"I will," Hunter countered forcefully. He dropped Marshal's reins and, his heart breaking, he pulled her into his arms. If only she were not so loyal to Christian, they could remain together, but he also knew she showed *him* that same devotion. When she loved, she loved with her whole heart, and he could not have loved her half as much if she didn't. It took all of his strength to find the courage to step back.

"I'll come back as soon as I can."

"I know." Alanna moved out of the way. Hunter swung himself up on Marshal's back, gave her one last, sad smile, and rode away. Feeling completely lost, she remained at the stable door long after he was gone.

Randolph heard Hunter ride by, and when Alanna did not return to the house in what he considered a reasonable amount of time, he went to find her. That she was just staring off into space alarmed him. He took her arm, and when she did not pull away, he escorted her into his house.

"It's time to eat. Even if you aren't hungry, I hope you'll keep me company. I imagine Sally Lester went to Elliott's funeral, but her shop should be open this afternoon. Why don't you come into town with me and order some new gowns? You need something else to wear, and choosing new garments would lift your spirits. Out of respect for their grief, I'll wait a day or two, but then I'll go out to your aunt and uncle's place and ask to pack your belongings. They certainly don't need them, and you do."

Alanna was in no mood to share his preoccupation with her wardrobe. Clothes were the last thing she cared about that day. She recalled how Hunter had once criticized her, and thought the same comment now fit Randolph. "You're a very practical man, aren't you?"

"If by that you mean I'm being insensitive to your feelings, you're wrong," Randolph argued. "I'm just trying to help you have a normal life, and a beautiful young woman needs pretty clothes."

When they reached the dining room, Alanna slipped into her chair, but she had never felt less like eating. "I appreciate your concern, but I really don't feel up to doing any shopping today. I'd rather just take a long nap, and then visit Christian.

My marriage to Hunter will undoubtedly cause the worst sort of gossip. I won't add to it by doing something so frivolous as ordering new gowns on the day Elliott was buried."

Stung by her rebuff, Randolph nevertheless feared it was justified, and hastened to apologize. "I was only trying to suggest something you might enjoy. You will at least allow me to pick up your belongings, won't you?"

"Don't bother. They've probably been given away."

Randolph had to hold his tongue as their soup was served, but the instant they were alone, he continued. "I don't consider helping you a bother. I'll take my carriage and go out to your uncle's place tomorrow. Even if they are contemplating disposing of your things, they haven't had the opportunity yet."

Alanna had always loved potato soup, and the sight of the steaming bowl was surprisingly comforting. She hadn't been hungry, but now dipped her spoon into the thick soup and sipped it eagerly. She remained silent for a long while, but when she spoke, her thinking was clear.

"If you truly want to visit my aunt and uncle on my behalf, will you take them a letter? I want to tell them what Hunter did for Elliott, and how difficult it was for us to bring his body home. Not that it would make any difference—I don't hold that hope—but I would like for them to at least know what a good man Hunter is."

"I'll be happy to deliver anything you'd care to send."

"You're very kind. Thank you."

Encouraged, Randolph searched his mind for a lighthearted response, but Alanna's expression was still such a serious one, he thought better of it. Fearing that he had always tried too hard to impress her, he waited for her to encourage conversation, and when she didn't, he tried not to let his disappointment show.

* * *

When she was too restless to nap, Alanna left the house. It was too early to visit Christian, but, longing to see Elliott's grave, she walked out to the cemetery. An attendant pointed toward the fresh grave, but it was near Melissa's, and Alanna would have found it on her own. This was her cousin's second burial, and she knew it had to have been far more peaceful than his first. She still wore his ring, and would always cherish it.

Her first memories of Elliott were of a fair-haired, freckled-faced boy, who'd shown endless patience with a little girl who had had no one else to love. "Oh Elliott, I miss you so much. What am I going to do without you?"

Standing so close to Melissa's grave, it was impossible not to think of her, too, and now thoroughly miserable, Alanna was unaware of Robin Frederick's approach until the petite brunette called her name. Startled, she turned slowly. Robin was dressed all in black, and Alanna had to remind herself that Robin didn't know Elliott hadn't loved her.

"I'm so glad to have found you," Robin exclaimed. "Everyone was looking for you earlier, but no one seemed to know where you were." She reached out to hug Alanna, and clung to her a moment too long.

"Poor Elliott. Can you tell me how he died? I know that it was Indians, but there's got to be a great deal more to tell. I don't even know why you and he went to New York in the first place! He just rushed off without telling me goodbye."

Sarah and Robin Frederick had been Melissa's playmates. The two vivacious sisters had an elfin charm and the very same enthusiasm for life that had always made Melissa popular. Alanna had watched the three of them grow into beautiful young women, who thrived on the attention which had always embarrassed her. She knew the Frederick sisters better than she knew any of the other young women in Williamsburg, but sadly, that wasn't well at all. Robin had loved Elliott, and deserved to hear the truth, but with Melissa's memory shielded by convenient lies, it was difficult for Alanna to know where to begin.

"Do you remember Hunter, the Indian who visited Byron and Elliott last spring? You came to supper one night when he was there."

Robin's dark eyes were red-rimmed from crying, but her expression brightened slightly as she nodded. "I remember him well. He was the first, and only Indian, Sarah and I have ever met. As I recall, he was quite handsome, but very ill at ease and left before we began dancing."

"Yes, I'm glad that you remember him, because he's the reason Elliott and I went to New York." Alanna gestured toward a stone bench not too far away, and Robin walked over to it with her. Once they were seated, she refrained from mentioning the reason for their visit and simply described how Elliott had been shot from ambush. Then, giving Hunter the credit for their survival when they were again attacked, she attempted to make him sound as heroic as she truly believed him to be.

"We were able to recover Elliott's body and bring it home, but my aunt and uncle blame Hunter for his death, and have refused to have anything more to do with us."

"But that's so unfair," Robin cried. "Hunter wasn't to blame, and even if he had been, why are they angry with *you?*"

Even with him gone, Alanna found the next revelation the easiest to admit. "Hunter and I were married in New York, so whatever they wish to say or do, it will affect us both."

Robin gasped so sharply she began to cough, and then had to fight to catch her breath. "You've married an Indian?" she was finally able to ask in a hoarse whisper.

Alanna could understand Robin's flustered reaction, for wedding an Indian brave was a most unconventional thing to do. "Not just any Indian—Hunter."

"Well, of course, he saved your life and naturally you were

grateful, but couldn't you have found a less personal way to reward him?"

Alanna tried not to laugh, but couldn't suppress her giggles. "I'm so sorry. I'm not laughing at you. It's just that even though Hunter and I love each other, I doubt I could be described as a reward."

Robin stared at her wide-eyed. "I swear I've never understood you, but you've completely baffled me now. Where are you staying, if your aunt and uncle have turned you out?"

"Hunter is on his way to scout for General Braddock, and I'm staying with Randolph O'Neil."

Rather than rise gracefully as she had been carefully taught, Robin simply lurched to her feet. "You've married an Indian, but you're living with another man?" The startled young woman began to back away. "I'm sorry, but this is really too much for me. I don't want to judge you as harshly as your family has, but I've got to go."

It was Robin's horrified expression which discouraged Alanna from defending herself. Clearly the girl thought her daft, or worse—immoral. Alanna doubted anything she said now would change her opinion for the better. With Robin gone, she rose slowly and went back to Elliott's grave. "I'll never tell Robin that you didn't love her," she whispered. "It will be our secret."

She said a prayer for him and asked for his, before pausing for a moment at the foot of Melissa's grave. She hoped her two dear cousins were together, and then turned away, heartbroken to be all alone.

Striving to impress his taciturn guest, the following afternoon Randolph had Stan hitch the team to the carriage and drive him out to the Barclay plantation. Relieved to find no other callers there, he rapped on the front door and asked to see John. He was shown into the parlor, and in a moment John Barclay joined him.

"You're not welcome here," John announced gruffly, "and even if you've come to offer your sympathy, I'll thank you to leave."

"I'm sorry you feel that way, but this isn't a condolence call, although I am sincerely sorry about Elliott's death," Randolph informed him. "I've come to fetch Alanna's belongings. She needs her clothing and personal items. I thought perhaps you'd prefer to have one of your maids pack her things. If not, I'll see to the chore myself."

"Oh you will, will you?" Not impressed by the silversmith's courtly manners, John approached him with a menacing swagger. "I fail to understand why my niece's wardrobe is any concern of yours. Isn't one husband enough for her?"

John was nearly ten years Randolph's senior, but he was taller, stronger, and in robust good health. He lived a vigorous outdoor life on his plantation, while Randolph's work required him to spend long hours indoors either working with precious metals, or managing his shop. He was trim rather than muscular, and any fight between them would be disastrously one-sided, but Randolph refused to back down.

"Your niece is a fine lady, and I'm happy to help her in any way that I can." He reached into his coat pocket to extract the letter she had sent with him, and held it out. "I've a message for you from Alanna, and if you'll just have someone show me to her room, I'll pack up her things."

John snatched the envelope from Randolph's hand, tore it into half a dozen pieces, and threw it back in his face. "The only place I'll show you, sir, is *out!*"

He reached for Randolph, and while Randolph attempted to fend him off, John grabbed the back of his collar and, with a fierce yank, propelled him toward the front door. He flung it open and sent the silversmith tumbling head over heels down the steps.

"If you still want Alanna's things, wait here," he shouted.

Stanley jumped down from the carriage to come to his master's aid. A small man in his fifties, he was no match for John Barclay either, but he couldn't allow Randolph to lie unattended in the dust. "Come on, sir," he encouraged. "Let's be on our way."

The wind knocked out of him and his wig askew, Randolph needed Stanley's help to rise, but before he had reached the safety of his carriage, John began to hurl Alanna's clothing out her bedroom window. It rained down on the lawn in colorful heaps, and as soon as Randolph had caught his breath, he and Stanley scurried around gathering it up. John laughed at them and aimed Alanna's slippers to strike painful blows, but neither man was discouraged by his rudeness.

When the last bit of Alanna's apparel had been stowed away in the carriage, Randolph caught a glimpse of Rachel watching from the parlor window. He had believed her to be his friend, but she was observing him now with the same icy detachment she'd show a spider spinning his web, and he knew he had lost one of his best customers. He nodded toward her anyway, but she just turned her back on him.

Randolph flopped his battered wig on the seat beside him and spent his time on the ride home attempting to fold Alanna's garments neatly, so she wouldn't know how carelessly they had been treated. Her lingerie held a delightful hint of lavender sachet, and he held each piece up to his face to savor it. He had kept his late wife's clothing for a long time, because he had been unwilling to part with it while it still held her scent. He had absolutely no right to fondle Alanna's garments in the same loving way, but he couldn't help himself.

Ashamed of the miserable way he had carried out his errand, Randolph was hoping Alanna would be away visiting Christian, but she was waiting for him when he arrived home. Bruised and sore, he hobbled out of his carriage and tried to smile, but he knew by Alanna's worried frown that he must be a pathetic sight.

"You'll have to forgive the way I look, but I did bring your belongings."

Alanna had never seen Randolph looking anything but his best, and certainly never without his wig. She wasn't surprised to find his hair was gray, but his thick, boyish curls were far more attractive than any neatly groomed and powdered wig. He did not resemble a staid businessman nearly as much as a young man, who'd stayed out all night with his pals. It was obvious to her he had lost a fight with someone, but that only made his disheveled appearance and sheepish smile all the more appealing.

"It doesn't look as though my uncle's response to my letter was the one for which I'd hoped."

Randolph shrugged slightly, and then winced when a sharp pain shot down his back. "He tore it up without reading it. I'm sorry."

"That doesn't matter. What did he do to you?"

When Randolph brushed aside her question with an embarrassed shake of his head, Stanley provided a vivid account of John Barclay's brutality. "Damn near killed him," he swore. "That man ain't no gentleman."

Alanna took Randolph's arm. "My clothes weren't worth this. You shouldn't have had to suffer this abuse."

Enjoying her attentions, Randolph slowed his pace. "If I have to go out there again, I'll be sure to take several men with me."

"You're not going out there again, Randolph. Don't even consider it."

"May I offer you the same advice?"

"You needn't bother. I'm not even tempted to pay the plantation a visit." Alanna helped him into the parlor, where a horrified Mrs. Newcombe took over. The little woman insisted what Randolph needed was to soak in a hot bath, and hurried off to arrange it. Leaving her host in his housekeeper's hands, Alanna returned to the carriage. It wasn't until she had carried all of her things upstairs and begun to sort them out that she found a great many suspicious blades of grass.

The reason for the disorganization of her apparel was then painfully obvious. She sat down on the side of her bed, unable to imagine what her aunt and uncle must be thinking to reject her so cruelly. They had accused her of being disloyal, which she most certainly wasn't. She hadn't revealed Melissa's secret, nor would she share any of Elliott's. She had given them the loyalty they deserved, but they had treated her like trash.

Randolph was pleased to find a long, hot bath did indeed ease his discomfort. He would have to stay home for the rest of the day; clad in his dressing gown, he stopped at Alanna's open door. "I hope nothing important was left behind," he called to her.

Alanna rose from the bed and carried a handful of the grass she'd brushed from her clothes over to him. "They just threw my things out the window, didn't they?"

Randolph would have denied it to save her feelings, but because she held the proof of what had happened, he told the truth. "Your uncle was most ungracious, but I didn't lose sight of the fact he'd just lost a son."

"He needn't behave as though he had lost a niece as well." When Randolph looked pained by her remark, she reached out to touch a curl at his temple. "You have such beautiful hair. Perhaps that isn't a proper thing to say to a man, but you do. Why don't you throw away your wigs?"

"I'll throw away everything I own, if it'll please you," Randolph blurted out without thinking.

"You've already done more than enough for me," Alanna

assured him. "Now will you excuse me? I want to get everything put away."

"You'll join me for supper, won't you?"

"Yes, of course, I will." Alanna waited at the door until he
had reached the stairs. Randolph was such a sweet man, but
no matter how much she missed Hunter, she was not going to
take refuge in his arms. It was definitely going to be a temptation, but one to which she would never yield.

Twenty-eight

In less than two days' time, Robin Frederick's penchant for gossip had insured that all of Williamsburg's finest citizens had learned of Alanna Barclay's marriage to an Indian brave. Her tale was imaginatively embellished in the subsequent retellings, so that Hunter was variously described as an Iroquois chief by some, and as a bloodthirsty renegade by others. Alanna's unusual choice of marriage partner alone would have been enough to cause her to receive severe censure, but the fact that she was also living openly with Randolph O'Neil, sent many of her aunt's horrified contemporaries into a swoon. No one could recall a scandal of such delicious proportions, and it promised to keep everyone talking in hushed whispers all summer.

Randolph employed two clerks at his shop. Lena Fisher cataloged, sorted, and dusted the merchandise and kept the shop in perfect order, while Robert Platt was an apprentice silversmith who showed great promise. Randolph was fond of them both, and when their attitudes turned cool, he noticed it immediately. He was unable to recall an incident which might have upset them. It was true he had been absent from the shop on several occasions that week, but he had always thought the two liked the responsibility of handling customers on their own. Too considerate to allow what he felt had to be an unfortunate misunderstanding to continue, he asked the pair what was bothering them.

At first Lena shrugged and turned away, and Robert simply blushed, but after a few minutes' coaxing, Lena reluctantly admitted what was wrong. "I hope you'll forgive me if this seems too personal a matter for my comment, but the whole town is talking about the way you've taken up with an Indian's wife. What with you being in church every Sunday, you have to know it isn't right."

Dumbfounded, Randolph stared at Lena for a long moment. She was a mature woman, not some silly girl, and he found it difficult to believe she did not know him better. As for Robert, well, he was an inexperienced young man, and perhaps could be excused his embarrassment on that account.

"Mrs. Hunter's aunt and uncle have treated her abominably, and I have invited her to stay in my home while her husband is serving as a scout with General Braddock's forces. There is absolutely nothing improper about our relationship, and I am shocked, shocked, Mrs. Fisher, that you would repeat what can only be described as the cruelest of gossip. In the future, please refer anyone who might wish to make a comment on my guests to me."

At Alanna's suggestion, Randolph had ceased wearing a wig, and he plunked his hat atop his head and left the shop without telling his employees when, or if, he would return. He stormed down Duke of Gloucester Street, his hands clasped behind his back and an angry scowl on his face. People stepped out of his way, but he heard what they were saying behind his back.

That Alanna was staying with him was obviously common knowledge, but he could not understand why it was being viewed in such uncharitable terms. He had spent his entire life in Williamsburg, and was amazed to find people did not have a better opinion of him. He would have to write to his daughter that very day, so that she would hear the truth from him before one of her more ambitious friends sent word of her father's imagined indiscretion. Infuriated by the unfairness of the malicious gossip circulating about them, Randolph returned home in a wretched mood.

Seated at the window seat in the parlor, Alanna saw Randolph coming up the walk. He looked so upset, she laid her book aside and went to the door to greet him. "What's wrong, Randolph? Has my uncle been bothering you again?" she asked.

In the few days Alanna had been with him, Randolph had been enormously flattered by the depth of her concern. He wasn't used to being met at the door by a woman other than Mrs. Newcombe, and Alanna showed far more sensitivity to his moods than his housekeeper ever had. "No, I've not spoken with John since I picked up your clothes. There is a reason I'm home early though. Let's go into the parlor and discuss it."

Alanna understood what was the matter before Randolph had completed a halting preamble to the problem. "It's too late for me to find another place to live today, but I'll go out first thing in the morning, and look for new lodgings. Innkeepers don't have to worry about gossip the way private citizens do. In fact, a resident who's at the heart of a controversy is probably good for their business."

"No, you're not leaving here, and that's all there is to it. Neither of us is acting in a scandalous fashion, and I refuse to behave as though we were. Don't you see? If you move into an inn, people will assume we had something to be ashamed of, and we don't."

Randolph had tossed his hat aside as he had come through the door. With his boyish curls and bright blue eyes, he was such an attractive man, she wasn't surprised people were so eager to believe they were lovers. Remembering that Charity Wade had described him as fine-looking, she suddenly had an idea.

"Thank you for wanting to stand by me, but let's just wait and see what happens in the next few days. If the gossip subsides, fine, I'll stay, but if it continues to embarrass you, I'll leave regardless of how loudly you protest."

"No, you won't," Randolph argued.

"Yes, I will. You once asked to meet Christian, and I don't see any reason for us to abide by my aunt and uncle's rule forbidding him visitors any longer. Because you've come home early, would you like to see him today?"

Randolph saw through her effort to distract him from the issue at hand, but his curiosity got the better of him and he agreed. "Yes, I would." Eager to go, he rose to his feet.

"Good." Alanna kept her fingers crossed the whole way, but when they arrived at Charity's, nothing went as she had hoped. As she so often did, Charity came to the door holding Christian, but he had awakened from his nap feeling cranky and out of sorts. His face red from crying, he reached out for Alanna, but kept right on fussing.

"His gums are swollen," Charity explained. "I believe he's cutting his first tooth."

"Poor baby. He seems very unhappy about it, doesn't he?" Alanna quickly introduced Randolph, but rather than smiling prettily as she had expected her to, Charity just seemed embarrassed, gathered up her children, and disappeared into the bedroom for the entire duration of their visit. With Christian's mood so far from good, Alanna did not want to stay long anyway. Randolph's interest in the child seemed sincere, but she did not want to risk boring him. She excused herself and carried the boy into the back room.

"Why are you hiding in here?" she whispered. "I thought you and Randolph would like each other."

Charity had been scrubbing the floor before they arrived. She was wearing a faded dress, and her hair was sticking out from under her cap in long, damp wisps. "Oh, Mrs. Hunter, he's a fine gentleman, and look at me! There's nothing for him to like."

"That's not true. I'll bring him back with me on Sunday. Put on your prettiest dress, and make the effort to smile at him. He'll like you, believe me he will."

Having no inkling of Alanna's matchmaking plans, Randolph began to criticize Charity as soon they left her house. "Are you sure that woman is giving Christian enough attention?" he asked. "She seemed overwhelmed with the responsibility for her own children, and the boy deserves the best of care."

"You're mistaken. Charity is wonderful to Christian. I simply chose the wrong time for a visit, is all. Christian was fine this morning. He's really a very good little boy, even if he was unhappy just now."

Randolph nodded thoughtfully. "Even if Mrs. Wade is a capable woman, her house is awfully small for four young children. You don't plan to leave Christian with her much longer, do you?"

Randolph wasn't aware of her argument with Hunter over the boy, and Alanna saw no reason to share such a private torment with him now. "If there were a way for me to nurse Christian myself, then I'd be raising him, but because I can't, he'll have to stay with Charity a while longer."

Randolph hadn't meant to broach such a delicate subject; badly embarrassed, he remained silent until they reached home. "I need to go back to lock up the shop. I'll see you at supper."

Alanna entered the house, discouraged her plan to spark a romance between Charity and Randolph hadn't had a more auspicious beginning. She had always considered Charity attractive, but apparently all Randolph had had a chance to observe was a harried young mother with more children than hands. Well, things would be different on Sunday, and she would hold a thought for them until then.

When Randolph came home, he handed Alanna a small box. "It's something for Christian. I should have thought of it earlier."

"Thank you, how sweet of you." Alanna removed the lid to find a small sterling silver bell suspended from a mother-of-pearl hoop. Christian's name had been engraved on the bell, and it was such a beautiful gift, she was deeply touched by it. "Thank you. You're the first person other than Elliott and me to give Christian a present. It was very thoughtful of you. You made this yourself, didn't you?"

"Yes. It's not just pretty, however. I've made a great many of those over the years, and babies love to chew on them. With teeth coming in, that will be all Christian will want to do."

Alanna shook the hoop, and the bell rang with a musical tone. "You do beautiful work. I've always enjoyed visiting your shop."

Randolph sat down beside her on the settee. "Thank you. Is there anything you'd like me to make for you? It could be a wedding gift. A teapot perhaps?"

The mention of wedding gifts made Alanna's heart lurch. Melissa and Ian had received so many pretty things, and yet they had all been left for Graham and her to pack away. No one was likely to give Hunter and her such lovely presents, but rather than gifts, she would have appreciated the kind words and good wishes she doubted they would ever hear. Randolph was her only friend, it seemed; she gratefully reached out to touch his sleeve lightly.

"I'm sure it would be beautiful, but completely out of place in Hunter's home. He lives in a house he built himself out of tree limbs and bark. It's actually very cozy, but not a good place to show off silver teapots."

Stunned by the description of her future residence, Randolph placed his hand over hers. "Oh, Alanna, are you going to be happy living there?"

"Were you happy with your wife?"

Randolph nodded. "Very."

"Then you can understand how little a house matters. It's who shares it that's important, not how grand it is."

Randolph could certainly agree with that statement, because he had not realized how empty his life was until she had entered it. "Yes, and I hope you enjoy every day you spend here with me."

Alanna could not mistake the longing in his voice, but she smiled as though his comment were merely that of an attentive host. "Thank you again. I'm sure that I will."

Alanna wanted to wear the white dress adorned with violets to church on Sunday, but fearing it would be seen as disrespectful to Elliott's memory, she chose a plain blue gown instead. As they had the day of the funeral, she and Randolph arrived just as the congregation was entering the church, and took seats in the very last pew. That did not prevent curious glances from being directed their way, however. Uncomfortably aware of the constant low murmurings their presence provoked, they left before the priest pronounced the benediction.

"I don't understand why people are so quick to condemn our friendship," Randolph complained. "You're in need of a place to stay, and I've provided it. That doesn't constitute a sin."

"That people are so quick to see evil instead of good is horribly discouraging, isn't it? Hunter and I were unable to win my aunt and uncle's sympathy and understanding. I can't expect more from people who barely know me, or strangers, than I do from them. Fortunately, I don't have to remain here in Williamsburg forever, Randolph, but you do. I'm going to move out of your house next week."

"No, I won't allow it."

Astonished he apparently thought he had that right, Alanna spoke clearly. "I'm neither your daughter nor your wife, and while I appreciate your concern, I have to make my own decisions." They were walking toward Charity's, and as they reached her gate, Alanna turned toward her now sullen companion. "You were absolutely right about this house being too small for Charity and her family. I'm going to ask her if she would like to share a larger place with me."

Randolph seized upon his first inspiration to discourage the idea. "She may own this place, Alanna, and if she does, she'd be insulted by such a suggestion. After all, it's her home."

Pleased by his comment, Alanna nevertheless appeared to think about it a moment before replying. "You're right again, and I don't want to risk insulting her. Do you suppose you might make a discreet inquiry as to whether or not she owns the property, while I'm playing with Christian? You're blessed with an abundance of tact, and I know you could do it without arousing her suspicions."

"But I've just met the woman," Randolph protested.

"Yes, that's why your questions will seem the natural curiosity of a new acquaintance." Giving him no more time to ponder her plan, she attempted to hide her smile as she preceded him up the walk.

Striving to look her best, Charity was dressed in a rust-colored gown, which provided a superb complement to her auburn hair. It was far from new, but clean and pressed, and flattering to her slender figure. Her children were also carefully groomed and dressed in their finest apparel. She welcomed Alanna and Randolph to her home, offered tea and cookies, but apologized for Christian.

"I'm afraid he's still asleep. He loves the rattle you made for him, sir. It hasn't been out of his hands since Mrs. Hunter gave it to him."

Randolph had had such a quick glimpse of Charity on his initial visit to her home, that he was quite pleasantly surprised to find her far more attractive than he had first imagined.

When her children went out onto the porch to play, and Alanna went into the bedroom to see Christian, he found talking with her not nearly as disagreeable a task as he had feared.

"I was born here," he said, "but I know we hadn't met until just the other day. How long have you and your family lived in Williamsburg?"

Charity had to give her full attention to pouring his tea, and waited until after she had filled the cup and handed it to him to reply. "I was born in Philadelphia, but moved here ten years ago when Thomas and I married. He was a cooper, and worked for several of the plantations. We had hoped to buy some land and have a farm of our own one day, but he took sick and died. That was the end of our dreams."

Randolph was leaning forward slightly, wearing an expression of concerned interest, but Charity feared she was boring him, and grew even more flustered than she already was. "I'm sorry, I'm afraid I'm just rambling. I spend most of my time with the children, and talking to adults is difficult for me. I'm afraid I don't have anything more to say."

Charity's innocent sweetness reminded Randolph of Alanna, and he was charmed by her shyness. He knew Alanna was so desperately in love with her husband she scarcely noticed him, and it was immensely satisfying to meet a woman with similar qualities who appeared to be free. "I know exactly what you mean," he agreed. "When people come into my shop, they ask questions about the merchandise, or make special requests, so my conversations all tend to have a similar ring. Then I meet a lovely young woman like you, and it's difficult for me to know what to say."

It had been such a long while since anyone had referred to Charity as either young or lovely, that she could not help but blush. "Really, Mr. O'Neil, I'm not used to that kind of flattery."

"What a shame. How long has your husband been gone?"

"It will be four years come December."

"I'm a widower myself. Although my daughter is grown, I know how difficult it is to raise children alone."

Touched that he understood her plight, Charity's eyes glistened with unshed tears. "Oh my yes, it certainly is," she agreed.

Christian had awakened, but Alanna changed his diaper and kept him in the bedroom. She could overhear bits and pieces of the conversation taking place in the front room, and rejoiced that it appeared to be going so well. She liked both Charity and Randolph enormously, and hoped the gentle nudge toward friendship she was providing might develop into something more. When she finally took Christian out to join them, the subtle smiles passing between the pair convinced her it already had.

By the time Hunter caught up with General Braddock's forces, they were encamped at Will's Creek. Since he had last been there, the former Ohio Company's trading post had been fortified with a log stockade. Barracks and powder magazines had been constructed, and the site renamed Fort Cumberland. Consisting mainly of British regulars, joined by colonials and sailors, there were twenty-two hundred men under Braddock's command.

Located where the creek joined the Potomac River, the newly built fort was on a rise surrounded by thick stands of oak and chestnut. Teeming with men and crowded with pack animals and wagons, the fort presented such a disorganized maze, that it took Hunter half a day to find Byron. He knew better than to merely walk up and tap the young man on the shoulder, and so waited until an opportunity presented itself for him to approach Byron while he was alone.

Hunter started for him then, but he was still ten feet away when Byron glanced up and saw him. The look on his face was anything but welcoming, but Hunter kept right on coming. No fool, he came to a halt just beyond Byron's reach. "I have some very bad news for you," he announced so softly only Byron would hear.

Byron nodded toward the open gate of the fort; with Hunter following close behind, he skirted the wagons parked nearby and walked out into the forest. When he was certain their conversation would not be overheard by any curious strangers, he turned to face him. At first glance he hadn't noted much difference in Hunter, but now he saw the last ten months had given the brave's features the same lean, forbidding hardness he saw reflected in his own mirror.

"When we last parted, I'd no idea you'd seduced my sister. You couldn't possibly have any news worse than that."

Hunter attempted to explain how Melissa had spurned him rather than the other way around, but he could tell by the sheer meanness of Byron's sneer that he wasn't being heard. "I've married Alanna," he announced abruptly. "So you can't kill me, for her sake."

Killing him was precisely what Byron had been plotting, and he took a step forward. "You married Alanna just to keep us from killing you? I had no idea you were that great a coward."

Knowing how deeply Byron had been hurt, and would be again, Hunter refused to be insulted. "You fought with me last summer. You know I'm no coward."

Byron spit on the ground. "There are no words ugly enough to describe what you are!"

"I'm your cousin's husband, part of your family, but that isn't the bad news."

"The hell it isn't! What do my parents say about this?"

As they talked, Hunter kept a close watch on Byron's hands. He hadn't reached for his knife, but his fingers were curled inward, as though he soon might. "They won't listen to the truth, so they aren't pleased."

"Lying bastard, you don't even know what the truth is."

"And neither do you." Hunter waited a moment, and then, in as gentle a manner as he possibly could, he related how Elliott had died. He told the whole story: how he and Alanna had hidden in the forest, and later killed the braves who had murdered Elliott. He described bringing the body home, and the fine funeral his brother had had. When he finished, he waited for the questions he was certain Byron would want to ask.

Byron recalled the Abenaki who had attacked their wounded, but that they had killed Elliott was too painful a tragedy for him to accept. He listened to Hunter in dumbfounded silence; tears began to roll down his cheeks. Meaning to comfort him, Hunter took a step forward, but Byron shrank back.

"Get away from me. You spread death like the plague, and I don't want you anywhere near me! How can Alanna even stand the sight of you? She was never strong. Has she finally lost her mind? Is that what happened? She must be crazy to have married you!"

Hunter stared at the distraught young man. He could feel Byron's pain and shared it, but fearing that he was only adding to it, he started to back away. "It's a large camp. I'll stay out of your way."

He turned then and started back toward the fort. Byron hurled a rock at him, but it only glanced off his shoulder and he didn't break his stride. He had done his best, but he now felt like a fool for ever hoping Byron and he might again be friends.

General Braddock had three aides-de-camp: Capt. Robert Orme, Capt. Roger Morris, and Col. George Washington. It was to Washington that Hunter offered his services as a scout, and on the strength of his past service, he was welcomed enthusiastically. When on the tenth of June, 1755, the army began moving toward Fort Duquesne, he was out in front, combing the woods for any sign of the enemy they knew had to be aware of their approach.

Three hundred men swinging axes cleared the way, followed by packhorses, wagons, and cannon, while the red-coated British regulars and blue-coated Virginians marched through the trees on either side. The road carved out of the forest was twelve feet wide, and the line of march stretched back four miles. The men traversed steep ridges and shallow canyons, and crossed the countless streams that kept the forest floor damp even in summer. In an undulating stream they surged over the main Allegheny, Meadow Mountain, and Great Savage Mountain.

On June eighteenth, they straggled into Little Meadows. In eight days the long column had traveled only thirty miles from Fort Cumberland; plagued by fever and dysentery, the men were so disheartened and slow, they could make no more than three miles per day. After consulting with his officers, General Braddock took George Washington's advice, left the heavy gear behind, and moved on with a reduced command of twelve hundred.

Despite the fact they were bringing only the essential artillery, thirty wagons, and packhorses, the smaller force still crept along at a most unsatisfactory pace. The colonials were undismayed by the roughness of the road, while the British insisted upon leveling every bump and constructing bridges at each trickling creek. Bored with the slowness of their progress, Hunter repeatedly scouted the same terrain, but the French and their Indian allies remained unseen. Occasionally he would find an insult carved into a tree, but it struck him as a prank rather than an act of war.

On the seventh of July, Braddock's forces were within eight miles of Fort Duquesne. To avoid passing through particularly perilous country, they crossed the Monongahela River near the mouth of Turtle Creek, and traveled on the opposite side. Early the next afternoon, they began recrossing the river in preparation of their final approach to the French stronghold.

Lt. Col. Thomas Gage led the advance guard, followed by Colonel St. Clair with a work detail. Intending to intimidate the French, General Braddock himself was at the front of the remainder of the troops, creating a splendid parade marching to the accompaniment of fifes and drums. Colorful regimental standards waved in the sun-drenched air, as the light cavalry, sailors, British regulars, colonials, and artillerymen with their twelve-pound cannon and howitzers rolled by.

Hunter understood the general's purpose, for it was widely believed that when confronted by this superior force, Contrecoeur, who was still in command of Fort Duquesne, would surrender. He was known to have only eight hundred French and Canadian troops, but there was also an equal number of Indians camped nearby. In his most recent scouting expeditions, Hunter had gotten close enough to recognize their tribes. In addition to Abenakis, there were Caughnawagas, Hurons, Potawatomis, Ojibwas, Shawanoes, Mingoes, and Ottawas.

The colonials understood the Indians' love of warfare, but General Braddock discounted their abilities and considered them no match for his soldiers. The general expected the savages to flee at the first sound of cannon fire, but Hunter knew better. The entire journey he had lived in constant anticipation of an ambush. That morning he had crossed the river shortly after dawn, hoping to spring a trap and provide a warning if the place where they would ford the river had been fortified, but the natural site was undisturbed.

Now, as they crossed the river with no sign of French interference, he was positive their progress had been much too easy and still suspected a trap. He had kept an eye on Byron, without ever giving himself away; with the fort within striking distance, he looked for him again. The troops from Virginia

were at the rear; riding Marshal, Hunter cantered by them as
though he had been summoned by the artillerymen at the end
of the line. Once past them, he turned and followed close behind the blue-coated Virginians.

When Braddock's force had successfully forded the Monongahela without incident, Gage's advance guard continued to
lead the way. About a quarter of a mile from the river, they
crossed a ravine, and an engineer was mapping out the road
when a French officer was sighted coming up the path.

Capt. Hyacinth Beaujeu was stripped to the waist like an
Indian, but wearing the badge of his rank, a silver gorget
around his neck. Apparently startled by the advancing English,
the Frenchman turned to give a signal; and with shrill war
whoops, a large force of French and Indians appeared. Gage
immediately ordered his men to form a line and fire. Beaujeu
was shot dead during their third volley, and the majority of
his troops began to flee. Elated by what appeared to be a swift
victory, Gage brought up two cannon and commenced firing,
but the forest provided such excellent cover for the Indians,
none were hit.

Inspired by French officers, the Indians rallied, parted to
surround the English bunched along the path, and fired from
behind the security of the trees. In their bright red coats, the
British regulars were easy prey, while their return fire slammed
into the trees and wounded no one. Caught in a murderous
cross fire, Gage's troops attempted to fall back, only to be
engulfed by Braddock's main force rushing forward to their
aid. The result was chaos rather than the orderly form of battle
for which Braddock had been trained.

In the rear, the Virginians quickly broke ranks and adopted
the Indians' strategy, firing from behind the natural cover provided by the woods. A well-placed slap on the rear sent Marshal galloping back toward the river, while Hunter knelt down

beside Byron and began to fire the musket he had been given. "This is no time to argue," he told him. "Just stay alive."

"Watch your back," Byron warned. "If the French don't shoot you, I will!"

Hunter laughed as though Byron's taunt had been a joke, but he made his shots count and fought bravely to keep the enemy at bay. When General Braddock rode by shouting for the Virginians to form in lines on the path, the Indian thought the man daft. "Does he want us all dead?" he asked Byron.

"No, only you!"

Most of the Virginians hadn't heard the general's order, and kept firing from cover. Hunter saw George Washington ride up, and to his utter dismay, heard the general again give the order for them to form lines and fight, as though they were facing French regulars on a European battlefield. Washington, knowing the value of their present tactics, argued forcefully for the right to fight from cover like the Indians, but Braddock refused to listen.

When his fellow Virginians began to fall back to form the suicidal lines Braddock had ordered, Hunter grabbed Byron's arm. "If you want to live to fight again, come with me," he shouted above the gunfire and war whoops ringing all around them.

"I'm an officer, I can't leave my men!"

When Byron tried to pull away, Hunter slammed the butt of his musket into his chin. Byron's knees buckled and, going limp, he fell into Hunter's arms. The Indian picked up the musket and ammunition which had fallen from Byron's hands, and then half-carried, half-dragged Byron down the path. As he saw it, he wasn't deserting, just making a strategic retreat. He found cover for them both, and continued to shoot each time one of the opposing Indian allies came into view.

A model of bravery, despite his misguided view of how the battle should be fought, General Braddock continued to exhort his men to do their best. Four of his mounts were slain, but he fearlessly climbed upon a fifth. When, after three hours of senseless slaughter he finally realized all was lost and called a retreat, he received a mortal wound.

Sixty-three of his eighty-nine officers had been killed or wounded, and more than nine hundred of his troops were casualties. Thanks to Hunter's prompt interference, Capt. Byron Barclay awoke with a bad headache to find he was among the few who had been unharmed. Just as Hunter had expected, he was not in the least bit grateful.

Twenty-nine

In the rush to retreat, Byron lost sight of Hunter. Burdened with the responsibility of calming the hysteria in the able-bodied men and caring for the casualties, he had no time to deal with him. He was ashamed to have missed the last of the fighting, but the demands on his attention were so acute as to preclude the possibility of going after Hunter immediately. He intended to settle the score with the Indian at the first opportunity, however.

The French were not following the retreating army, and the Indians, bent on stealing anything of value that had been left behind, also failed to give chase. Despite the lack of vigorous pursuit, the terrified soldiers bolted across the Monongahela with a frenzy that brought honor to none. As he lay dying, General Braddock hoped to hold his position until the reinforcements they had left behind could arrive, but rather than make camp, his demoralized troops continued to flee toward Fort Cumberland, and he had to give up the plan. When he succumbed to his wounds two days later, he was buried in the road, so the passing wagons would obliterate all trace of his grave and prevent mutilation of his body.

Humiliated by a repeat of the previous summer's defeat, Byron's spirits sank lower than despair. They had all believed the addition of British troops would enable them to retake Fort Duquesne, and to have been beaten more by their general's archaic tactics than by French courage, he felt not only dis-

graced, but betrayed. They had traveled several days but were
still some distance from Fort Cumberland, when he again saw
Hunter, and his anger burst into a blinding rage. The Indian
had been helping tend the wounded, but the brave's compassion
meant nothing to the embittered Virginian. He grabbed Hunter
from behind; bent on beating him to death, he wrestled him
to the ground.

Although caught off guard, Hunter quickly recovered. He
grabbed Byron's wrists and held on, forcefully preventing him
from throwing any punches. Infuriated, Byron tried to break
free, when he pulled back, Hunter lunged forward, sending
him rolling in the dirt. Hunter sprang to his feet and assumed
a defensive stance, waiting for Byron to come at him.

Among the onlookers were several men who had seen
Hunter fight Vernon Avey; expecting another brutal spectacle,
they cheered him on. Hunter recalled Byron's warning that
each man he bettered in a contest, whether it was with his
fists or an ax, would bear him a grudge. He wasn't facing an
old enemy out for revenge now, though, but the friend who
had issued that warning. He took a step back.

"I don't want to fight you," Hunter swore.

"Not when I can fight back, you mean!" Byron crouched
low, waiting for another chance to rush Hunter.

Hunter shook his head. "Not ever."

Determined, Byron took a step closer. "Come on, I know
you know how to fight."

"I have no argument with you."

"Liar!" Byron screamed. He went for Hunter then, meaning
to blacken both his eyes, but the wily Indian blocked his
punches and withdrew without throwing any of his own.
"Damn you!" the irate Virginian swore. Reflecting his mood,
the surrounding crowd grew restless. They wanted blood, and
Byron was determined to supply it. Again attempting to knock

Hunter off his feet, he threw his whole body at him, pummeled his stomach, and tried to trip him.

Byron had adopted such a wild combination of tactics, Hunter did not know what to expect from him next, but he again concentrated on repelling Byron's blows rather than landing any of his own. Choosing only to defend himself, he disappointed the bystanders badly, and they began to boo him. Undaunted, he continued to ward off Byron's punches, and hoped the young man would soon come to his senses.

"You've no right to live when Melissa's dead!" Byron hissed.

Hunter stubbornly refused to respond to that taunt. Melissa had caused him enough sorrow, and he was far too proud a man to argue about how badly she had betrayed him in front of a crowd of strangers. He just stared at Byron, willing him to see the truth, but sadly, he did not.

Sick with a consuming rage, Byron saw only a defiant Indian who had cost him the lives of a dearly loved sister and brother, and then stolen his fragile cousin's heart. The brave had devastated his once perfect family, and Byron wanted him to pay. "I'm going to kill you," he snarled.

Hunter had survived similar threats, and wasn't intimidated. He and Byron were of nearly equal weight and stature, but he was certain he had greater stamina. All he need do was wait until Byron wore himself out with threats, and wild punches that damaged only the air. Then perhaps he could reason with him.

As Byron saw it, he was defending the honor of his entire family; confident he was in the right, he strove to prevail. Each time Hunter backed away, he came at him again. Relentless in his determination to succeed in humiliating the Indian brave in front of everyone, he fought like a demon. He landed only one punch in three, but that was sufficient to fuel his anger.

Eager to see a less one-sided fight, the crowd coalesced into a solid ring and blocked Hunter's further retreat. Forced to stand his ground, Hunter could bear only a few minutes of Byron's furious assault, before he was forced to defend himself more vigorously. With a methodical rhythm, he came back at Byron with the controlled fury that had made him a champion in New York. He knew how to hurt a man in a variety of brutal ways, but chose to incapacitate Byron with a series of rib-cracking blows that, while painful, would not cause permanent harm either to his body or his looks.

At first elated by the change in Hunter's strategy, Byron soon realized that the Indian was as tough as he appeared. His anger kept him battling Hunter long past the point another man would have fallen, but he felt only rage rather than pain, until Hunter landed a blow in his solar plexus. The wind forced out of him, he staggered backwards; and when he tried to take a deep breath, the agony that filled his chest made him cry out in pain. Bewildered, he looked at Hunter, knowing he was beaten and expecting no mercy, but rather than knocking him unconscious, Hunter came forward, slipped his arm around his waist, and began to lead him away.

Satisfied they had seen a fight worth watching, the specta-tors parted to allow Hunter to pass through their ranks. He helped Byron reach the creek where they had camped for the night. The Indian eased the battered Virginian to the ground, then unbuttoned and removed his shirt. He splashed water on Byron's face and chest, and rinsed his own blood from his opponent's hands.

"Never fight a man when you're angry," Hunter advised. "You need a clear head to win, and you can't think when you're mad."

Having expected to take a far worse beating, Byron was merely embarrassed rather than grateful for Hunter's attentions. Attempting to find a comfortable position, he laid back on the grass that flourished at the edge of the creek. He could breathe but only in shallow gasps. "I hate you," he whispered.

"Hate the French," Hunter replied, "and their Indian friends who were responsible for Elliott's death. They are your only true enemies. I've done nothing to harm you." When Byron responded with a disgusted grunt, he continued to defend himself.

"I mistook Melissa's charm for love, but it obviously wasn't love, or she would have married me last spring rather than Ian. She was the one who chose to live a lie. You may mourn her forever, but I can't.

"Your parents have turned their backs not only on me, but on Alanna, whose only crime is loving me. She expects better of you. She believes you'll take our side and defend us. What are you going to say to her when you get home? Are you going to be as mean-spirited as your parents, or will you be able to put your sorrow aside and see the truth?"

Revolted by the way Hunter twisted damning facts to protest his innocence, Byron looked away. "If for no other reason, I hate you for keeping me out of the fight. You had no right to do that."

Hunter shrugged. "Perhaps not, but I did it for your parents. You are all they have left, and I couldn't watch you throw your life away."

Puzzled, Byron turned back toward him. "My parents hate you, but you wanted to spare them additional grief? I would have thought watching me die would have been the perfect revenge for you."

Hunter pulled off his shirt and, again filling his hands from the creek, washed away the blood and dust that covered him. While not as sore as Byron, he had been hurt. One of Byron's wild kicks had struck his left thigh, and he feared it might have torn the still healing muscle.

"The Iroquois used to fight amongst themselves. One tribe would raid another, and then that tribe would have to retaliate. We would have been destroyed as much by our lust for revenge against each other as by war with the Algonquin, had Deganawidah not had a vision of the union of the five tribes, and Hiawatha not convinced each tribe of the union's worth. The League has lasted nearly two hundred years, and the Iroquois are far more powerful than our enemies. If you would put aside your need for revenge, the Barclays would be far stronger for it."

"What is left of the Barclays!"

Hunter sighed unhappily. "You have fought me and lost. That should put an end to your need for revenge."

"It doesn't." Sick to his stomach, Byron closed his eyes, effectively putting an end to their conversation, but Hunter did not leave him.

The weary Indian leaned back against a nearby oak, reviewing their conversation and attempted to find another way to make peace with Byron. There was no way to bring Melissa and Elliott back to life, and any harm Byron succeeded in doing him would only hurt Alanna. No clever arguments occurred to him, but as he pondered Byron's senseless need to avenge what Hunter considered imagined wrongs, he gradually developed the uneasy feeling that he might be equally guilty of the same blind stupidity.

Appalled, he remembered the pain reflected in Alanna's beautiful eyes, when he had repeatedly refused to raise Melissa's son. Why hadn't he realized that his contempt for Melissa had prompted him to extract revenge from the innocent child he should have welcomed with love? Hadn't Alanna been able to see what he was doing either? Shaken by his own obstinate refusal to see a truth that would have spared all three of them unspeakable anguish, he rested his elbows on his knees and tried to separate his feelings for Christian from those for Melissa.

Did he have any right to expect forgiveness from Byron, if he could not forgive Melissa? he wondered. His head ached as much from the pain of his thoughts as from the lingering affects of the fight, and he sat quietly contemplating not only the past, but the future, until his stomach began to make rumbling complaints of emptiness. He got up, went to find what he could for supper, and brought back half for Byron.

"You have to eat," he insisted. "I want us to be among the first to reach home."

"Us?" Byron scoffed. "I can't stand the sight of you."

"That's a shame, but perhaps you'll grow used to my company on the way."

Byron rose up to spit in the grass; amused by his stubbornness, Hunter moved away to eat his supper. He was too lost in his own thoughts to worry about Byron for the moment, but he did glance his way to make certain he was eating. Satisfied that he was, Hunter decided they would spend the night right where they were.

Hunter awakened in the first eerie light of dawn, when a thick mist still clung to the banks of the creek. Byron was sound asleep nearby. Suddenly fully alert, Hunter sat up and glanced around the small glade where they had taken refuge. Not ten feet away, a wolf was drinking from the stream. It was not just any thirsty wolf either, it was a young male with a thick, glossy coat and bright, curious eyes. Hunter did not doubt for an instant that it was *his* wolf. The gentle lapping sounds it made while slurping up water had been what had awakened him.

The wolf stared at Hunter with what the Indian swore was a glimmer of recognition. As if in a friendly salute, the handsome animal cocked his head to the side. He sat perfectly still for a long moment, then turned away, and vanished into the mist.

"Wait, come back!" Hunter called. He lurched to his feet and took a step toward the stream, but the wolf was gone and did not return. He had been there though, and there had been nothing menacing about his fleeting presence. Hunter had longed for a sign, a promise of something good, and he was positive the wolf had just provided it. In accepting Christian for the dear child he was, as Alanna had, he was confident he had already changed their future for the better, but sighting the wolf convinced him that he was on the right path. He turned to find Byron watching him with an incredulous gaze.

"Were you talking to a wolf?" Byron asked.

Hunter laughed out loud. "Yes. You saw him, too?"

"Biggest damn wolf I've ever seen. We're lucky he wasn't leading his whole pack."

Hunter knelt down beside Byron. "He hunts alone. Like me. That's what my Indian name means: He Who Hunts Alone. I learned something from you yesterday, and he came to congratulate me."

"You can communicate with wolves?"

"Only with that one."

Hunter got up and started to move away, but Byron called out to him. "What was it you learned?"

"That a man bent on revenge hurts himself and those he loves far more than the one he hates. I didn't realize I was trying to punish Melissa by refusing to raise our son, until I tried to reason with you. Now I want to go home and be a husband to my wife and a father to my son. I can't take Elliott's place, but I can be a brother to you, if you'll let me."

Byron shook his head. "Too much has happened for me to ever forgive you."

"For what, for loving your sister? You loved her, too."

"That was different."

"I thought Melissa and I would be together always, and you can not forgive me because she chose to wed another man? I have forgiven her."

Byron stared up at Hunter, his expression devoid of understanding. "Would Melissa have forgiven you?"

"There was nothing for her to forgive," Hunter assured him.

"I told her love was no cause for shame, but clearly she was ashamed of loving me. Alanna isn't."

This time Byron watched Hunter walk away without making any effort to stop him. He had despised him from the instant he had learned that the Indian had fathered Christian. It had been so easy to blame Hunter for seducing Melissa, and he blamed him still. It was too early to rise and he lay back, content to rest where he was for the time being.

He missed Melissa terribly, but as he thought back to the first time Hunter had visited the plantation, he was shocked by the recollection of how quickly she had sidled up to the attractive brave. She had volunteered—too rapidly it seemed now—to accompany Hunter and Elliott when they went to speak with Alanna. The next day he and Elliott had left the Raleigh Tavern after only a brief stay, when he had begun to worry about the suitability of sending Melissa riding home with Hunter.

"I should have known better!" he moaned. He could remember that outing so clearly. Melissa had flirted openly with Hunter all morning, and then her brothers had foolishly allowed her to ride home with him. She had been radiant at dinner, her cheeks aglow with color from the morning's ride, or so they had all thought. Elliott had had to go down to the dock to find Hunter, and the Indian had been as reserved during the meal as he was whenever the family was gathered together.

Byron did not want to accept Hunter's version of his affair with Melissa, but his memories of that visit were still vivid. His sister had been her usual enticing self, while Hunter had shown a shyness neither he nor Elliott had expected from the confident scout. Had he been a challenge to Melissa? Had she viewed him as an exotic pet, and gotten more than she bargained for?

The more he thought about their visit home before joining Washington's troops, the more probable Hunter's story became.

He wished he could seek Elliott's counsel, but lacking that, he had Alanna's. She had been devoted to Melissa, and her marriage to Hunter proved she harbored no ill will where he was concerned.

Byron propped himself on his elbow, and had to force back a nauseating wave of pain. It had been so easy to hate Hunter, and yet clearly Hunter did not hate him, for he was fully capable of giving him a beating that would have left him badly scarred and perhaps crippled for life. Savage or not, Hunter was a remarkable man, and when he returned with jerky and biscuits for their breakfast, Byron found it difficult to discuss what was on his mind. Instead, he ate what he could, slept a while longer, and then, with Hunter's help, managed to walk the few miles those straggling behind with the wounded made that day.

It wasn't until Hunter had bid him good night the next evening, that he finally managed to speak what was on his mind. They were again in a secluded spot where their conversation would not be overheard. "I've been thinking," he began slowly. "Remembering. I'll need more time, but I've been considering what you've told me. I'm not saying that I believe it, but only that it's possible."

Hunter eased himself down into the grass. "Thank you, but it's Alanna and my son I'm worried about. They're part of your family, but your parents have turned against them. That's an awful thing to do to someone as dear as Alanna, or to an innocent babe."

That Hunter was more concerned about his wife and child than himself is what impressed Byron most. "I'll do what I can," he promised. "My father can be very stubborn, and my mother seldom crosses him, so it may take me years to affect a reconciliation, but I'll do my best. I owe you that much for saving my life."

"You're no longer angry with me for that?"

"I heard George Washington lost two mounts and had his clothes ripped by four bullets, without receiving a scratch. I'm not nearly that lucky. Maybe I would have survived without your damned interference, but most likely I would have died. Thank God that in all the smoke and confusion no one missed me. I'd surely have been charged with desertion, if they had."

"No, I would have taken the blame for your absence," Hunter assured him, "and because I'm only a scout, not a soldier, they would have had no way to punish me. Besides, I didn't desert, I fought the whole time. It just wasn't out in the open as Braddock demanded."

"That's why he's dead and you're alive."

"Whatever the reason, I'm alive to return home, and I don't want you to hate me."

Byron was silent for such a long time, Hunter thought he might have fallen asleep, but finally the Virginian spoke. "I'll always miss Melissa, and be sorry for the agonizing way she died, but I no longer hate you. But if you ever disappoint Alanna, you can expect to have to answer to me."

Thinking that was as generous as Byron was likely to get, Hunter did not take offense at his threat. "I'm a very good husband," he assured him. "Alanna will never have any complaints."

Considering his shy cousin, and a man he thought more than a little arrogant, Byron shook his head. "Lordy, what a pair you must be."

Hunter smiled to himself. "Yes, we are."

Anxious to see his son when he reached Williamsburg, Hunter's first stop was at Charity Wade's. When he found the yard overgrown with weeds and the house vacant, he panicked. Leading Marshal, he hurried next door to ask where Charity had gone, but the residents were so alarmed by the sight of an Indian on the front porch, they refused to answer the door. Frustrated, he tried another house, and then another, until he found a soul brave enough to talk with him.

"Charity moved away a couple of months ago," the old gentleman replied. "In June I think it was, but it might have been May. No, wait a minute, it was in May, early May. I remember because—"

Hunter could not help interrupting rudely. "Please, do you know where she went?"

"Over on Francis Street," the elderly man said. "Haven't been over there myself, so I can't tell you where, but I heard it was a nice house."

"Thank you." Rather than chase up and down the length of Francis Street searching for his son, Hunter next tried Randolph's home.

Mrs. Newcombe peered out the window, recognized Hunter, and opened the door. "Good afternoon, sir. Mr. O'Neil's still at his shop. Would you like to leave a message?"

"No, I'm looking for my wife. Isn't she here?"

"Oh, no, sir, she hasn't lived here in months. She and Mrs. Wade are sharing a place over on Francis Street."

"Can you tell me where?"

Mrs. Newcombe pursed her lips thoughtfully. "No, I've never been there myself. But wait a minute, Stanley must know. He's in the stable."

Again eager for more information, Hunter rode Marshal around to the rear of the house. He called out Stanley's name, and he soon appeared.

"Well, now, I'm real glad to see you. From what the *Virginia Gazette* printed about Braddock's campaign, we didn't know if any of you were alive."

"A few of us are. Mrs. Newcombe said you could tell me where Alanna's living."

Stanley nodded. "Sure can. It's over on Francis Street."

Hunter was fast losing his patience. *"Where* on Francis Street?"

"It's right toward the end, down by the Capitol. Pretty white house with blue shutters. You'll find it easy enough."

Hunter turned Marshal toward the gate, urged the horse to a gallop, made his way to Francis Street, and raced to the end. He found a white house with blue shutters and, hoping it was the right one, he tied Marshal out front and knocked on the door. When Charity answered, Hunter put his finger to his lips.

"Is Alanna here?" he whispered.

"Yes, but there's no need to whisper," she replied. "She and Christian are out in the backyard. Here, come through the house."

Hunter had rehearsed what he wanted to say the whole way home, but the instant he saw Alanna and Christian, he doubted he could utter a word, let alone a memorized speech. His son was toddling along beside Alanna, gripping her skirt for support, but walking just the same. Alanna was showing him the garden, bending and pointing as she called out the names of the vegetables they had planted. She hadn't noticed Hunter, but he had a clear view of her. After four months, her figure was as slim as when he had left her. He would have to try again to give her a child; eager to try, he broke into a wide grin.

Taking care to avoid being seen, he approached his wife and child with a hunter's stealth, until he was close enough to scoop up the little boy and swing him high into the air. Thrilled by the unexpected ride, Christian squealed in delight, while Alanna whipped around to confront him.

"Hunter!" she gasped.

Hunter shifted Christian to the crook of his right arm, and hugged Alanna with his left. He kissed her soundly and laughed at her dismay. "I promised to come back to you. Why are you so surprised?"

Alanna reached up to caress his cheek, satisfying herself

that he was unchanged. "I'd almost forgotten how handsome you are."

"Then I have returned just in time."

"What about Byron? The *Gazette* had the most awful description of the battle, and I've been so terribly worried about you both."

"Byron is on his way out to the plantation. We're both safe," he told her, taking no credit for the excellence of Byron's health. Christian had begun to yank on his hair, and Hunter caught his tiny hand and placed a kiss in his palm. "He'll say only good things about us to your aunt and uncle, but he has scant hope that they'll ever want to see us."

Understanding Byron's skepticism had good cause, Alanna continued to sweep Hunter with a hungry gaze. She had spent every minute he had been gone loving him, and yet fearing his return. "There's been a good deal of gossip. I was even referred to as Randolph's mistress for awhile. He visits us every day, but it's Charity he comes to see, not me."

"Really? Well, he was lonely, so a pretty woman with a houseful of children ought to be perfect for him."

"She has only three children," Alanna reminded him. "That's not a houseful."

Her expression was troubled, rather than filled with the joy Hunter had expected to see, and he gestured toward the grass. "Come sit down with me." He led the way, and set Christian on his feet before he chose a place to sit. The little boy grabbed the fringe on his shirt and made his way around him. "Is he this friendly with everyone?" Hunter asked.

"Charity and her children, Randolph, you and me, we're the only people he knows, but he's not in the least bit bashful with us."

Hunter tousled Christian's hair as he toddled by, and the little boy's giggle made him laugh. "He seems like a very happy child."

"Yes, I hope so."

"And you? Have you been happy, too?"

Alanna shook her head. "Without you? No."

Hunter reached for her hand. "I've not been happy without you either. Is there room for me to live here with you?"

Perplexed by his question, Alanna didn't know how to answer. "Do you want to live here with us?"

"Only until the boy is old enough to be weaned. I won't leave here without him."

Alanna's eyes began to fill with tears. "Have you changed your mind?" she asked. "You no longer want to give him away?"

Hunter had never seen Alanna cry, not when Elliott had been killed, or they had almost died fighting the Abenaki, or even when she had told him goodbye. That she would cry now made no sense at all to him. "How I came to my decision is a long story that I'll tell you at another time, but yes, I want us to raise Christian. I want him to be our son, yours and mine."

Tears continued to well up in Alanna's eyes and began to trickle slowly down her cheeks. She caught Christian and made him a part of the hug she gave her husband. "I love you so much," she vowed.

"Then why are you crying?"

"I'm sorry. I can't help it."

With the joy of holding his wife and baby in his arms, Hunter was on the verge of tears himself. Christian began to squirm, and they let him go to continue circling them with unsteady steps. That Hunter had once hated Melissa enough to reject her son now seemed like the worst mistake of his life, and he was relieved he had come to his senses in time to make his family whole.

"Isn't Christian ready for a nap?" Hunter asked his wife.

"Soon, and the harder he plays, the longer he sleeps."

With that inspiration, Hunter saw that his little boy had a very good time indeed. Then he and his bride celebrated his home-coming with a passion flavored with warm kisses and husky laughter that lasted the whole afternoon. War with France was still on the horizon, and troubled times lay ahead, but for them, the battles were over, and all three of them had won.

NOTE TO READERS

The French and Indian War extended from 1754 to 1763. During this time France and Great Britain battled not only for possession of the Ohio Valley, but also for control of America, India, and the high seas. George Washington's skirmish at Great Meadows marked the beginning of the war. While Hunter, Byron, and Elliott Barclay are fictional characters, the conflicts described in this book were actual historical events. Like George Washington, many of the historical figures who gained prominence during the French and Indian War went on to greater fame during the American Revolution.

Gen. Edward Braddock's tragic defeat was a terrible blow to the British cause. It wasn't until William Pitt became England's Secretary of State in 1757, that the tide of the war turned in Britain's favor. When a peace treaty was agreed upon in Paris in 1763, England gained not only Canada, but also all French lands east of the Mississippi with the exception of New Orleans. France's ally, Spain, received all French territory west of the Mississippi and regained Guadeloupe, Martinique, and other islands in the West Indies from England. Britain kept Florida, but returned Havana and Manila to Spain.

I love to hear from readers. Please send your comments to me c/o Zebra Books, 850 Third Avenue, New York, NY 10022. Please include a legal-size SASE for a newsletter and auto-graphed bookmark.

WHAT'S LOVE GOT TO DO WITH IT?

Everything . . . Just ask Kathleen Drymon . . . and Zebra Books

EVERY DAY WILL FEEL LIKE FEBRUARY 14TH!

Zebra Historical Romances
by Terri Valentine